"A novel full of heart, of quiet love and the gentler side of humanity – the trials and joys we all go through, the baggage we bring with us and future we want to build – all told with the softness of a whisper."

~ Tom Lloyd

"A beautifully-written novel about the trials and triumphs and struggles and small glories of ordinary lives. It's wise about love and rock and also, in passing, about compost, and in the end it reveals itself to be a song about a time of lost innocence, a time when we thought we could achieve anything, and sometimes did."

~ Dave Hutchinson

"Now THIS is a powerful story. Richly drawn characters; gorgeous details; and a genuinely beautiful & moving ending. Kris Jamison isn't afraid to have her characters work through tough issues—and there's a courage and triumph to that."

~K.D. Edwards

love/
rock/
compost

KRIS JAMISON

SYBERTOOTH INC
SACKVILLE, NEW BRUNSWICK

Litteris Elegantibus Madefimus

Print and ebook published 2020 by Sybertooth Inc.

59 Salem Street
Sackville, NB
E4L 4J6
Canada
www.sybertooth.ca

ISBN: 978-1-927592-27-4 (paperback)

ISBN: 978-1-927592-28-1 (ebook)

Library and Archives Canada Cataloguing in Publication

Title: Love, rock, compost / Kris Jamison.
Names: Jamison, Kris, 1968- author.
Identifiers: Canadiana (print) 20200304305 | Canadiana (ebook) 20200304364 | ISBN 9781927592274
   (softcover) | ISBN 9781927592281 (ebook)
Classification: LCC PS8619.A6655 L69 2020 | DDC C813/.6—dc23

In memory of J.

/ONE/

Cold, and dark, and raining, and colder from the contrast with the kitchen, April reminding that winter might yet throw a last flurry. An earthy, clean promise of spring in the air, though. Timelag. They'd been touring in Germany all through February, and spring had been already on the door-step even in Berlin. A month of running up and down the 401 after that—felt like it had been dreary March for ever.

Emily's tail-lights disappeared up Barrie Street. She'd offered a lift, but Thomas had turned it down. Didn't mind the rain, he'd said, but what he hadn't wanted was to have to decide right then where he was going.

Water spattered the saddle of his bike the moment he took the plastic bag off it. Part of him wanted to get home by the quickest way he could, get out of his wet clothes, warm up with a shower …

There were better ways of warming up. Especially if he didn't go back to his place. Though tonight—not likely.

Was he seriously thinking of going home—such as it was— just so he didn't have to face Lindsey's need to make an effort?

It wasn't him. Lin said so. Thomas had to believe him.

Silent streets, a dreary Monday. Weaving around puddles and parked cars, keeping off the main roads. It was mostly student ghetto he passed through, Victorian houses standing shoulder to shoulder, or row houses, dark brick, tiny front gardens long abandoned to thin grass. The sort of thing Lindsey would go on about, in the right mood—what you could do with a shaded, starved little space like that, under a lovely silver maple old and massively looming as the house. How to make it into something that would draw the eye, ease the heart. An obsession with him. Imaginary gardens. Pulling beauty out of the air, making something only he could see; he played around with colour pencils and a notebook, a private game he was too shy to share lightly. It had been six months before he'd shown Thomas what he did in those expensive hardcover journals he bought—wary, fragile offering. As if even from Thomas he expected indifference, dismissal. Murky scribbles, to Thomas's vision, mostly sort of brownish, only the pure yellows and the brighter blues jumping out. But that hadn't been the point, and he'd said, tell me, make me see it, and would follow as Lindsey described what he'd set down. Texture, contrast, harmony of subtle colours that were only words to him, Scent, the way things moved, even—Lin had it all in his head. His scribbles were a memo, a key and a riff to pin the rest down. Composing gardens he couldn't plant. It was a good summer when the students in the lower flats didn't vandalize his backyard planters during some drunken barbecue.

No partying in town tonight. Students all indoors, final exams under way. The light on the bicycle wasn't much use for seeing puddles; just a warning, or maybe a plea—hey, I'm here, don't run me down. A few car headlights, blinding, rushing past.

Not west to Aberdeen and the house he rented, subletting out everything but his own locked room to students. Just a place to store his clothes, really, and the rowing machine. Didn't often keep a guitar there any longer.

Down Earl, up Wellington to William. Another tall brick Victorian. Thomas sat, one foot braced on the sidewalk, looking up. The attic flat was dark. Nearly eleven, after all. Jeans soaked through, even his heavy bomber jacket failing him, damp seeping through leather and the thick quilted lining across his shoulders.

The wind whirled another gust of rain over him.

A moment's fumbling on the veranda; the light was burnt out again, or someone had turned it off. Found the right key at last and bumped the bike in through the front door, heaved it to his shoulder and started up the dim stairs. Students on the ground and second floors. Narrower stairs up from there. He locked the bike to a staple he'd set in the wall on the upper landing, being not unjustly paranoid about that bunch down below last summer, thankfully gone in September. Crept in quiet as a truant teen, locking the door behind him by feel, waiting, blinking, to adjust to the dark. Curtains drawn, but some light seeped out from a nightlight in the bathroom, enough to stop him walking into furniture. Or plants. More plants than furniture, really.

Helmet and jacket on the unsteady wooden hat-rack, soggy shoes and socks left on the rubber-backed mat. The attic renovation was a bathroom, single bedroom and what the landlord probably called an open plan living room and kitchen. Decent floor-space, but it felt small. Even Thomas couldn't stand upright along the side walls under the eaves, except where a couple of modern dormer windows had been added to the plane of the roof. Lindsey apparently liked it. Cold in winter, hideously hot in summer. Light from all directions

He wondered if Lindsey had gone out at all.

He'd meant to call, but he got working late with Kev on something and then it was three a.m., so he'd slept at the Parks', slept the whole morning away, got dropped off at his place to change his clothes, grab his bike and get to the Seoul Kitchen because he'd told Uncle George he'd work a few shifts this week, sure … shouldn't have done that, shouldn't have left Lindsey alone. Should have dragged him along to Kev's; he could look at job postings just as easily in the Parks' basement and it didn't hurt to have a willing ear to ask, what do you think?

Lin had still been in bed when Thomas left yesterday, which was rare. Definitely one of the world's morning people.

Should have called him this afternoon, but they'd been busy at the Seoul Kitchen. Exam season. Lots of students wanting something cheap and good, fast.

No excuses. He just hadn't.

The flat felt winter-cold. Lindsey kept it cool at the best of times but now he was trying to save money by not turning on the electric heat even on this dank night. Being soaked to the skin from the waist down didn't help. Thomas shed his clothes where he was, draped them over the wooden kitchen chairs on his way to the bedroom, naked and goose-bumped. The bed was only a twin mattress. On the floor under the eaves, which at least kept you from braining yourself if you sat up unwarily. More plants. Double guitar stand in the corner. A five-foot tall Norfolk Island pine, almost as broad as it was high, overhung the foot. A wire bathroom shelf on the wall above the head held a hoya and some ivies, which trailed down almost to the pillows. Like sleeping in a forest, you'd wake and stare up into leaves. On hands and knees, Thomas felt his way in beneath the heap, two comforters and several afghans. Lin always kept the bedroom even colder than the rest of the place, seemed to like being pinned down by the weight of covers.

Warmth at last.

Probably shouldn't have run a hand up under Lindsey's T-shirt, over his chest, fingers combing into curling hair. Shouldn't have pressed a damp body up against the warm length of him. The temptation was too great to resist.

Lindsey woke with a jerk and a yell.

"Shh, just me."

"God!"

"Sexy guitar god, that's me."

"Clammy fish god, more like." Hand on his hand, stopping it crawling further and chilling new skin. "You feel like you've come out of the lake."

"It's raining."

"There are such things as towels."

"No, I'm good. Warm under here."

"It used to be."

"Hey." Nuzzled at Lindsey's jaw. "Better day?" He sounded like it, sounded more alive.

Shouldn't have said anything. Lindsey turned his face away. But spoke, at least. "Don't know. I guess. I applied for something, anyway."

"Any good?"

"Shoes. In the mall."

Which mall? Not that it mattered, but the buses weren't exactly big city frequent.

"You're not a damned retail clerk," he said.

"I am."

"You're not meant to be. Don't—undermine yourself. Anyway, do you want it?"

"No. But I can't keep drawing EI and not ever apply for anything. Same as when I ended up at Clare's—there's nothing I can do with a master's that doesn't have five doctorates lined up for it. What am I supposed to do, live off you? Go home to my mother?"

"You can live off me if you have to. Move in, plants and worms and all. At least mine's a double bed."

"It's a sofa-bed. It's lumpy. It squeaks. Loudly."

"Yes, but we don't fall out nearly so often."

That got a laugh. But silence, after. Willing just to fall asleep, maybe.

"You get out running today?"

"It was raining."

"When has that stopped you?"

"Tired."

Which he'd figured out was Lindsey-code, whether Lin knew it or not, for needing to go quiet, to shut himself up in a place where he could … recalibrate, maybe, was a way to look at it. Starting to feel overwhelmed by … whatever.

Not by him. Thomas hoped.

Had he even eaten? Left to his own devices, Lindsey would exist on toast and eggs, with maybe microwave dinners for excitement. Thomas should start something in the slow cooker before—damn, it was tomorrow he had to be in Montreal. Not the band. Sounded like it might be four or five days work for him, Kev tagging along because he owned the van and there was a second-hand digital mixer for sale that he wanted to look at. Better than what he had. Could they afford it? Well, the extent to which Kevin and his father subsidized the band didn't always bear examination, and the studio was Kev's baby.

"Lindsey—come to Montreal?"

"I can't. I have to be here 'available for work'."

"Montreal's not far. That's what the internet's for, checking the job bank from where you're not supposed to be. You could come back if the shoe store really wants to interview you."

"That would mean the bus. Expensive."

"Always an excuse."

"It's a reason."

It was an excuse, but he didn't want to argue. Probably the prospect of being a session musician's personal roadie for a week, and sleeping-bags on Anicky's ex-girlfriend's floor— their usual Montreal money-saving plan—wasn't as enticing as Thomas might hope. Especially as this ex-girlfriend came with a husband and a baby, and expected a certain amount of baby-wrangling in return for having a band, or in this case half a band, camped out in her living room.

They lay in silence. Lindsey's grip on his hand slackened. Maybe falling asleep. Thomas slid it down, caressing, asking, over his belly, hip, around to a firm runner's buttock. Hitched himself closer again. That was better. Lindsey stirred. As it were. Arm went over him, then a thigh, tucking them close.

"Someone," Thomas whispered, lips against skin, "is wearing damp pyjamas."

Almost too long a silence, but, "Possibly," said Lindsey, "that's because there's a clammy fish god plastered against me."

"Why don't you take them off, then?"

More than one way to warm up a cold night. Cheaper than

turning on the heat.

The first time that Lindsey Quinlan meets Thomas Smith Gorev he's in his third year at St. Mark's. Hallowe'en, and a Friday. The Fine Arts Department's Hallowe'en party is an annual thing, a big thing. Lindsey doesn't know why he's here. He's come with a group from his residence, but on the way back up from the basement bar to the big open foyer and the studios on the ground floor, where the DJ rules and the music is loudest, the others have all been absorbed into various happily shouting conversations, circles closing, red plastic cups of indifferent beer and God-awful mixed drinks gesturing. Even when he has sidled awkwardly near and offered a nervous smile to a glance his way, somehow he can't edge himself in. It's not that they're actively trying to close him out. He's not that much of a loser, not a creep. They're vaguely friends, some of them. People he knows. People he has classes with, whom he goes to parties like this with. "Oh, someone knock on Lindsey's door, see if he wants to come too … " It just happens. He stammers when he tries to venture an opinion, something about Krown Imperial's latest album, which he rather likes and just bought last week on CD. He likes CDs, likes liner notes and reading the lyrics, seeing the extra artwork. As with books, all his favourites brought with him from home though he never has time to reread them during term, he likes the reassurance of the row of spines on the shelf, knowing they're there even if he doesn't own a proper CD player and just rips them to play off his laptop.

Has a portable hard drive just for storing music.

Now he feels his face grow hot because he's stammering and they're all looking. Some short and bouncy girl he's seen around but doesn't know shrugs and says, "Well, I think they're overrated—I mean, half the time you can't even tell what they're going on about," and the conversation turns into a dissection of the lead singer's voice, looks, and taste in clothes and he tries to say something about the music, the lyrics—that second song in, which he listened to five times straight when he first played the album. He doesn't like arguments, even friendly ones. He can't hold his own, losing threads, losing his way in uncertainty of his own ground—everyone looking at him. That song, the way it gets inside you … obviously it doesn't. Not for them, and their looks seem to say there's something weird, something a bit wrong, about his intensity, his liking it at all. Starting to stammer again. That's the worst.

He falls silent, looking down. Worrying at the rolled lip of the cup. Cracks it. Stupid.

Anyway, look at how she dresses, the bouncy girl says of Kai Juneau, I mean, lumberjack shirts and pixie boots and look at her hair—but she's a lesbian, isn't she? Maybe she just doesn't care.

He's pretty sure that lesbians care and that Kai Juneau is married to some man, something you wouldn't expect, an accountant, maybe, and they have a couple of kids, not that it matters and why should she have to look like a manufactured pop starlet just because she's a woman singing?

And he thinks she's rather … well, sexy. Which somehow sounds weird, thinking it, not because she's almost old enough to be his mother, just the word. Do people say that any more? Anyway, sexy partly just because she is, she's an attractive person. Partly her energy. Watch clips of them live. She seems genuinely happy, having fun. Her air of simultaneously defying whatever it is people expect her to be without looking like she's doing anything other than pleasing herself. Beautiful alto voice.

The Hallowe'en costumes around him range from Dollar Store off the rack to Frenchy's drag and Salvation Army deer-hunter, plus a few amazing creations by those who are obviously seriously into cosplay and steampunk. The best he's managed is his labcoat. Mad scientist, but no Igor, no monster. He drifts away, because it's that or stand there silently looming over them all. He's six foot two and scrawny, and his thick black hair is cut too short for his liking, but if it isn't short it falls into long curls. When he was younger that, combined with his name, meant that his mother was always being told what a pretty little girl he was. He was never sure if he minded or not, back then, but she cut it short one August, his and Raleigh's both, when Raleigh had a massive meltdown about going back to school with hair like a girl. That was their cousin Makayla's fault.

It still wants to curl. There's got to be a hair product for that, one that won't set it in spikes or make it go dead-flat and sticky. Raleigh—who is sixteen months his junior and only five foot eight and whose brown hair straightens as it grows out rather than turning to ringlets—probably knows what he should be using, but will just as probably laugh at him before he offers any advice. Affectionately, of course. Condescendingly affectionate, to his weird older brother. Half-brother, Raleigh started telling people during the first week of classes, which is true, but after eighteen years why say it? Laughing. God, Lindsey, you're just so—

So *what* always goes unsaid. Fill in the blank. Hopeless? Embarrassing? Clueless? That's been the way of it since Raleigh hit grade nine and abruptly turned into one of the popular kids. Whereas Lindsey—well, he'd never been that, and there didn't seem any way out of it.

In five weeks Raleigh will die, stupidly and pointlessly, stoned and dead drunk, all too literally. Choking on his own vomit, having stumbled unnoticed out into the backyard of a party house to pass out. His body will be starting to freeze when they find it the next morning, a huddled lump beside a collapsing shed. Down to minus ten that night. He will have been dead for some time. Nobody will have thought to look for him—they'll say they thought he had gone off with a girl. An argument. She goes home. He, it will turn out, does not.

Nine months after that, their father—Raleigh's in fact and Lindsey's by courtesy, Jonas Kavanagh, will die. Parturient with grief, anti-birth of a burden grown too heavy to carry. In downtown busy Fredericton, in a rush hour thick with river fog, leaving his office, he will step out into traffic.

Why?

Distracted? Deliberate?

Ill. Insomniac. Following his one, his only real son.

Misadventure. Or suicide by dump truck?

Not yet, though. Raleigh is still alive, is here. Lindsey catches a glimpse of the familiar profile flung back in laughter, arm around the waist of a girl in tartan miniskirt and ripped T-shirt and high-heeled boots. No idea what that's supposed to be, or who she is. The girl who will go home from the last-day-of-classes party? Raleigh's got his hair slicked back and the sleeves torn off his T-shirt. Not sure what he's supposed to be, either. Greaser? Flushed, movements too wild. Probably did their drinking before they came, university party tradition. Underage, the red stamp, not the blue, on Raleigh's hand, which is disappearing up her shirt, tickling her ribs and she's laughing and squirming and then they're dancing. Raleigh's not going to welcome his company. Lindsey decides he's going to go back to the residence to read, listen to music. Krown Imperial, Queen, something with a pulse of serious drums and a voice that's a voice, not this nasal ungrammatical whoever she is they're playing now.

He heads back down the stairs to the basement bathrooms, draining the last of his beer on the way, ditching the cup in an already-overflowing bin. Even here, in the hallway, on the stairs, crowding around the makeshift bar in another empty teaching studio where speakers blast a rival music, just as trite, everyone's talking.

They find it so easy.

Rounding the corner to the stairs on his way back and there's a kid bounding down, two at a time.

Lindsey dodges right, the kid left—the kid's left—and then they go left and right, practically nose to nose, nose to throat anyway and the kid is laughing. Steps back and bows to him, grandly, doffing a ridiculous newspaper hat. Campus paper. Grabbed from the stack in the foyer on his way in? He's all in black—bulky leather bomber jacket that looks like someone's discarded dog-walking coat swinging open over a cotton sweater and tight jeans. Suede desert boots. Short—five-nineish—and ragged blond hair. He's green-eyed, gold studs in both ears, and wearing smoky eyeshadow, eyeliner, mascara. God knows what he's supposed to be. But cheekbones—

Lindsey's looking too long.

"Tango?" the kid asks.

He makes the make-up and the paper hat look … good.

And Lindsey finds he is smiling. The kid's grin is so—

"Uniform victor?" he suggests, before he can help himself, and that's the sort of thing he learnt to shut up and not say a long time ago. He can't help that his head is full of stuff no one else ever seems to know, or get—except Raleigh when he isn't in one of his Lindsey-you're-just-so moods. And sometimes it spills out.

But the kid—the kid—"Whisky," the kid says, nodding. Very serious, but he's fighting to hide that grin. He looks with theatrical sorrow at his plastic cup. "But unfortunately it was beer. Or alleged to be." He doesn't have an accent, exactly, but he's a bit old-fashioned, precise in his way of speaking, at odds with his looks. The ghost of an accent. "Apparently I drank it, which I'll probably regret." He tosses the cup over his shoulder. It bounces off a couple of girls, who yelp and then, realizing it's empty, giggle when the kid spins on his heel and claps a contrite hand to his heart, makes another hat-sweeping bow. The kind of cute that girls like. Every kind of cute. Lindsey is not into cute. But the kid turns his attention back to Lindsey once the girls pass. Not a grin, now. Not cute. Cute is for puppies. Not even smiling. Dangerous—not threatening dangerous. Wild freewheeling downhill dangerous. His eyes are bright and maybe he's drunk or something else, but maybe it's just—he's alive, like no one else here is.

He looks about sixteen. If that. Campus security was carding everyone at the door when Lindsey came in. He must be at least nineteen; he's got a blue stamp. For what that's worth. It's not like it's hard to fake an ID.

"Hey," the kid says. And now it's an entire flock coming down the stairs, girls and guys, all talking in a sort of roaring shriek and Lindsey and the kid edge out of the way together as if they're actually having a proper conversation. Now he's smiling again and Lindsey gets the feeling he's being herded, a bit, but there's plenty of room to pretend he hasn't noticed and go on his way, which is probably what normal people do when weird guys in newspaper hats start looking at them like that.

Oh God, Lindsey thinks. And he can't look away.

He knows he ought to say something.

Sorrygottogetbacktomyfriends …?

This isn't the sort of situation he gets into, except awkwardly, mostly with embarrassment, and generally, if he twigs early enough, flight before it ever reaches quite the point of—because it's never the one, girl or guy, he actually wants …

Finding his back against the wall and usually he hates that, feeling someone's got him cornered but he doesn't feel cornered at all, plenty of space if he doesn't want to be here—

—if—

—finding the kid way too close for—

—for, well, whatever it is one's supposed to think he's too close for, in such a situation.

It doesn't feel that way at all.

Seems about the right distance. Could stand to be a bit closer, but Lindsey doesn't dare move, lean towards him, put out a hand. He's wrong. He's got this all wrong. It's a joke, someone's put the kid up to it and it'll be jeering in a minute—

Breathe?

"You," the kid is saying, "are too tall for your own good."

And it's a question, isn't it? God, it's a question. And he can answer it, or he can step sideways and go lose himself in the crowd, find Steffie and say, "You won't believe the guy that was coming on to me—" except that he'd never actually say anything like that, he'd just slink off feeling embarrassed and wonder forever if the kid had been making fun of him or if he was real and wishing things done, things undone, something, everything different—

Everything's gone strange and unreal, as if he's drunk way more than a single beer himself.

"So stretch," Lindsey says, putting his hands on the kid's hips, and he can't believe he's saying that—doing this—here—in public—and people are walking by—looking, snickering—someone whistles—he's making some hideous mistake that's going to end with bruises and blood and broken ribs and the emergency room. And he doesn't stammer.

The kid puts the newspaper hat on Lindsey's head and there's a hand on the back of Lindsey's neck and—it's a good long kiss that does things to every part of him, fire under the skin. Like nothing ever has, before.

The kid tastes like beer and coconut lipbalm.

The kid's leaning into him, pressing close, a firm and eager tongue and it's Lindsey's hands sliding under his heavy coat, his sweater—he's wearing nothing at all under it, just warm skin.

Face is scratchy. Not, Lindsey thinks, the beard of sixteen. Thank God. Just very blond. And needs to shave. Is it five o'clock shadow if you're blond? And why can't his damn mind just shut up and let him enjoy this without thinking? Do normal people think while they're kissing? People in books don't. They just—dissolve.

Or the authors run out of words or something. Or get embarrassed. Except when they don't run out of words, and then it's Lindsey who gets embarrassed.

He understands the dissolving bit now, he thinks. Hasn't stopped him thinking.

Thinking mostly that it's beyond embarrassing—he's in third year and he's never asked anyone back to his room, never made the first move, never gone to anyone's room either though he's had some near escapes with a couple of really pushy girls and he doesn't know this guy, even his name, anything about him, he might be doing this every night with somebody different and it's not *safe* and anyway it's not like this kind of thing happens to Lindsey and it's never occurred to him that he should be keeping a box of condoms in the bedside drawer and he's not going to go across the hall to borrow off Steffie and he doesn't know what to do anyway …

And if they could just fall through this wall, fall into one another, invisible to everyone around … maybe they could figure it out.

"God, Thomas, you need a babysitter. Time to go."

"I'm busy," the kid says, indistinct, his mouth hot against Lindsey's neck.

Thomas. He's Thomas.

The guy speaking is older. Some stupid part of Lindsey's brain labels him 'grown-up'. As if he himself isn't a grown-up. Some stupid thought says, this is it, they've been caught, and now—

Big heavy-set guy, unshaven,

"Yeah, I can see that. Mitch found his cousin and talked her out of some gas money—we need to hit the road."

"We don't need to—"

"I'm the one who's sober and I'm the one who's driving and I say we can still make it if we go now."

He puts a hand on Thomas's shoulder and Thomas jerks away from both of them and for a moment Lindsey thinks this is going to end up in blood and bruises after all, the guy scowling like whatever's between him and Thomas, he's had more than enough of it. The set of Thomas's mouth and the way his hands clench. But then Thomas looks over to Lindsey, who's wondering what happens if someone throws a punch and should he just get the hell out of here now or pile on in, because the guy probably weighs half again what Thomas does. Whatever. He takes a deep breath, makes a fist, ready for it. But Thomas gives a smile that goes crooked, opens his hands, carefully, deliberately.

"Fine," he says. "But screw you and your schedule, Ronnie. Who's fault is it we're marooned and broke and begging anyway? Told you the starter was bad." He turns back to Lindsey, solemnly takes back his newspaper hat. "Sorry love. Better luck next time. And you're right about Krown Imperial. That's a voice with a mind behind it. Those friends of yours don't have *ears*."

Oh God, he was listening, upstairs.

Oh *God*, had the kid actually been *looking* for him?

And Thomas winks at him and slouches off, with Ronnie raising a threatening fist to move him on his way.

Threatening? Friends joking around?

He can't tell.

Ronnie lingers to shake his head at Lindsey. What's that supposed to be, warning him off? He's not getting that impression of the two of them at all, not a couple. No way that fight wouldn't have happened then. Apology? Yeah, maybe. Like, don't mind him, he's a head case, does this all the time. Ronnie turns and goes after Thomas as if he's afraid he'll lose him. People are standing in clusters on the stairs, sitting, sprawling, drinking—obstacle course they have to push through. Lindsey's left standing at the bottom, cold. Still tasting coconut.

"Hey!" Thomas, blond head leaning around Ronnie at the turn. He's lost his hat. "Hey, wait—what's your name?"

Ronnie looks back too. "You don't even know his *name?* God, Thomas, you're—" And he gives Thomas a shove and suddenly there's a bunch of other guys there, older than Thomas, younger than Ronnie, laughing and all talking at once and they engulf the pair. All shoving one another along, all obviously a bit drunk. Thomas is lost in the midst of them. Is with them. Belongs to them, whoever they are. It's not like he's fighting to get free of them.

And Lindsey hesitates. Because *that's a girl's name* and he's sick of hearing it and every damn joke and—*God, I want him, I need him*—

"What?" Thomas yells as if he's already spoken, turning back again, but one of the guys throws an arm around him and pulls and he stumbles and yet another of the crowds that has gone to the bar *en masse* chooses then to come boiling out in the same chaotic roar and they're off up the stairs climbing over and around bodies, arguing about some movie, each shouting to make their point, and Lindsey—what the hell had he been thinking—shouts, "Quinlan! Lindsey Quinlan!" and goes after Thomas, because he wants a number, an email, something—a surname, damn it.

Top of the stairs. No sign of them on the dance floor, crossing the foyer. They're gone. Into thin air, for all that Lindsey can tell. Evaporated.

Paper hat trampled on the stairs. Cinderella's slipper. He's not going back down to pick it up.

Be utterly pathetic if he did.

He wants to.

Utterly pathetic anyway. Steffie spots him. "I was looking

for you," she says. "I didn't notice where you'd gone, sorry. Do you know Ryan, over there? The guy not in costume, with freckles. He's in Fine Arts. I went to high school with him. You should meet. He's just your type. Come on. I'll introduce you."

As if there's nothing else to say of him. Hey, he likes guys, you like guys, so match made in heaven, right?

Steffie's more his type than Ryan, smart and slimly athletic, animated and interesting to listen to, when she's not complaining about her boyfriend at Dal. A bit too mothering, though, in the way that some girls seem to get if they think you're not interested. As if just plain friend can't be an option for a guy and a girl; she's got to be either girlfriend or big sister.

And, suddenly, she's not Thomas. And that matters, what he wants spiralling down to a single blond point, sparking like fireworks.

Lindsey ends up going home with Ryan. He's not sure why.

Because next time he sees Thomas he wants to know what he's doing? Because he's suddenly achingly lonely and wants to rediscover that arousal? Lousy excuses.

Not exactly a lousy evening. Not a great one. Not sure what he expected, really. He supposes people figure these things out with time. Or practice. Or something.

Ends up dating Ryan, after a fashion, off and on, for the next month. More off than on. There never is anything much to say of him. How can an artist be so boring? So passionless. So … beige. Sculpture's Ryan's thing. Cubes stuck together. Cubes in styrofoam, cubes in plaster, cubes in wood. You have to have a thing, Ryan says. A theme. Mine's cubes. People will notice you, if you have a theme.

How can cubes be a theme? Lindsey wants to argue. How

can an artist not make—beauty, anger, *something?*

You have to have a thing, a theme. Maybe Ryan really cares about cubes. Maybe they mean something to him that Lindsey can't see.

Ryan's certainly not interested in Lindsey's ferns, in riparian ecosystems and water filtration, the honours project for next year he's already starting to think about.

Are ferns a thing? A theme?

Lindsey doesn't think so.

First actual serious sort-of-out boyfriend for both of them. Because they can, right? It's the twenty-first century. You can get married.

Ryan certainly has better sense than to go kissing in public. Well, everyone was drunk, at the party. Too startled to care. And it was the Fine Arts building. There were more exciting things than that going on in the dark corners by the end of the night, or so Steffie says, afterwards.

Something foul gets scrawled on his door in lipstick. Steffie rages, tries to clean it before he sees, finds that soap and hot water leave scarlet stains in the wood that can still be read, so she tries bleach and leaves pallid blotches on the hall carpet, for which the house don threatens to dock her damage deposit, but doesn't. Lindsey erases the ghost of *faggot* with sandpaper and goes back to hardly speaking to anyone in the residence, keeping his room door closed and locked, headphones on, surrounded by his plants. Ivy, mainly. A hoya rescued from the garbage, someone's discard saved when he was in first year. A leggy lemon geranium. There's not a lot of light for it.

He and Ryan bore one another.

Ryan dumps him on the first of December, an email:

>*This isnt working met someone sorry.*

Steffie is indignant on his behalf. Don, she tells him, is the someone. Who's Don? Another Fine Arts student. Mostly Lindsey just feels relief.

He runs in to Ryan and Don more than once that week. Everywhere he goes, it seems, two or three times a day. The dining hall, the library, the student union café. Small campus, after all. Hard to avoid. They're always talking animatedly. Cubes? They go quiet whenever he passes, as if guilty. Enjoying the guilt, maybe. The illusion of drama.

"Hi," he says, looking at his feet, and carries on wherever he's going.

Nobody remembers the blond guy in the newspaper hat. It's a small campus, small town, but he can't go asking every girl in the place, hey, do you have a cousin called Mitch who went to the Fine Arts party to borrow gas money and do you know his friend Thomas … ? How much did they need that they couldn't have just pooled what they paid to get into the party? Where were they coming from, where were they going, marooned by a bad starter motor? Holmesian deduction gets him no further. Regardless, he watches, pulse quickening every time he sees a dishevelled blond head.

That kiss drifts up out of memory at the strangest times. Taste of coconut.

Then the last day of classes, Friday night, the early hours of Saturday morning, Raleigh dies. So *stupidly*. Lindsey could murder him for being so stupid, for doing this to him, to Mom, to Dad, to Carleen, who stops eating and ends up with a diagnosis of anorexia and visits with the school counsellor.

Second term of his third year is lots of worry, a house full of it every time he takes the bus home to Fredericton for the weekend, over five hours each way, which Dad seems to feel he should do for his mother's sake, Mom's face going thin and old and she's only forty-two.

What Lindsey finds is that after the first shock, a sledge-hammer-shattering, the world doesn't so much fall apart as slowly start loosening at the joints, pieces falling away … He can't scream. He can't cry. He can't run from it. It's almost—he can't find a place for his own grief. He's not allowed. Because they're all afraid of what he might do, and he has to show them he's—mature. Reliable. *Stable.*

So he proves Mom doesn't have to worry about him, at least. Dad says it, proudly, wearily, thankfully, and it's in everything they do, or don't, the relief, that Lindsey is coping so well. Carleen, on the other hand …

"Talk to your sister," they tell him. "She won't talk to us."

But Mom never asks what's wrong with Carleen, why she can't just control herself, act like a normal kid. This is different, what's going on with Carleen. This is normal, apparently.

He doesn't understand.

Lindsey and Carleen don't talk, not about anything that matters. Not about Raleigh. They sit on her bed, pillows piled against the headboard, and they listen to music. Folk metal, mostly. Her choice. Once she says she wishes she could be like him. Put all the hurt away.

"I don't—" he starts to say, but Carleen isn't listening, she's asking if he'll drive her to the drugstore; she wants to buy a flatiron, change the colour, change her hair entirely. Black. Purple. Will he help? Will Mom mind?

Does it matter? If she does she won't say so. Not if it's Carleen.

He's putting all the hurt away.

Where?

It's not a thing. There's no place for it to go. It's an ocean.

And that's before the year rolls around to September, before Dad.

… everything bending askew, and the cracks get wider. It's the start of his final year, after a summer of fieldwork, soil and water samples out in the swampy brook-margin below his supervisor's brother's sugar-bush. It's only the second week of classes when Dad is killed and he misses the rest of the month, till Mom sends him back so he doesn't lose his year, saying she and Carleen, her black and purple hair cut shorter than his own, nose pierced, five studs in each ear, will be fine, they'll look after one another.

Not a sudden falling-through. Just … drifting. Like he's something the wind has taken. Quietly. Through the cracks in the world.

Nobody notices.

He lets his hair grow.

A vegetarian goulash in the slow-cooker; Lindsey had gotten up, gone for a run before Thomas crawled out to the shower. That was good. Tempting to think a night of sweaty moaning sex was a cure-all, wasn't it? Flattering himself. *He* felt better. Scrambled eggs for breakfast, because Lindsey needed feeding up and eggs were one thing they were never short of. Lin sorted compost while Thomas cooked. Things for the worms, things to go in the outside bin.

BBC3 playing on the laptop, speakers turned up. Archived program, news from a few days ago. A lute concert; Renaissance. Nice. Resisted the temptation to go grab his guitar and make it a duet—he knew that one. Ten years of weekly classical guitar lessons from generation after generation of grad students. Half of them lutenists. Vital life-skill, reading lute tablature. His parents had just assumed that obviously, his destiny was to be a professor of music—academic guitar, because in the Atkinson-Gorev universe, what did you do but get a PhD in something, anything? But what did you do, then? Theory? Teach? Okay for some. But one of his old teachers was a priest, another a rabbi, a computer programmer, a jazz singer up north … none of them guitarists. Playing guitar, maybe. Not *guitarists*, any more.

Be fair. The jazz singer played bass in her band too.

He'd gotten in, of course, everywhere he applied. Queen's, Western, U of T. McGill would have been good except James had just taken a two-year contract in English there and James would feel little brother needed looking after, that they should live together, even, which, nothing against James, but … no. Not when you're leaving home for the first time and all the world at your feet. Went to Toronto because it held out the most exciting possibilities for, well, not being Kingston. Except Kev hadn't come with him.

Restrained parental dismay: he'd dropped out by the end of September. Other possibilities. Not all of them good ones.

Carrot peelings, crushed eggshells for the worms. Lindsey took a banana and his tea and went to the coffee table that doubled as a desk.

Thomas carried eggs and toast over, and the teapot, went back for his own breakfast. Kept meaning to find a tea-tray on his next rummage in their favourite junk shop. Proper Jeevesing, that would be. He could shimmer in with the tea-tray, Lin would be sitting up in bed all sleep-tousled and shirtless … yes, well, anyway. Returned to sit close. Lindsey was looking at the government job bank. Someone in Picton wanted a person to work in landscaping.

"That sounds better?" Maybe? It wasn't indoors. Lindsey, really, didn't belong indoors with people nattering at him all day. And a mall, all artificial light and not even a window—Thomas wasn't letting him take that. He didn't want to have to deal with Lindsey trying to make himself do that, to see this—this 'tired', this greyness—slide down into something worse.

Thomas could *shake* whatever relative it had been—relatives, the whole lot of them, one reinforcing the other in a myriad small ways, a swarm of little stings ... Shake—scream in their faces, you utter bastards don't you understand what you did—whoever had put into young Lindsey's head that belief that he was somehow abnormal, unstable ... wrong, mentally. Some weird taint from his unknown father. The fear that to admit to any trouble, any *emotion*, good or bad, proved them right. That being *good* meant doing what they—amorphous, generalized *they*, or maybe empress-grandmother—expected of him. What they thought was normal, which meant liking what they liked and sneering at what they sneered at. Dismissing what they dismissed and thinking what they thought. And then, because he couldn't do it, get it right, fit in—he read it as failure, as his being a freak, something wrong with him, over and over. He knew better. But things you learn so young could get into your bones. The way your teeth held the minerals of the water of your childhood, part of the land in you, forever.

"Experience with chainsaws and tractors required," Lindsey said. "Also it's Picton. Over an hour's drive and I can't take the car all day, every day. Anyway, it couldn't stand such heavy use, could it?" Lindsey closed the laptop.

The old Focus wagon Thomas shared with Isabel was on its

last legs, but they kept it going. The service manager at Canadian Tire knew his voice on the phone.

"Probably not, but hey, Dodger has a chainsaw."

"I'm pretty sure 'experience with chainsaws' doesn't mean 'an old lady showed me how to use one once'."

"The university has groundskeepers, if you're thinking about that kind of work."

"Nothing posted."

"Look, who shops at malls? Kids? Baby boomers? Old folks? Not people like us. Don't dress like a middle-aged shoe salesman if you get an interview. Dress like we're playing at the SandWitch and you're doing the Official Sexy Boyfriend thing."

"I don't do Official Sexy Boyfriend."

"Sure you don't." Whispered in Lin's ear, "That's why the girls all hate you." Let his tongue follow the words. Lindsey pushed him off, but laughing.

"What girls? I couldn't be fashionable if I tried. God, Thomas, are there crumbs in my ear?"

"No. Sexier when you don't try." Matter-of-fact, through a mouthful of toast. "You look at home in your body then. Borrow a scarf, something with silver threads and a fringe, lord knows Iz and I are always leaving them everywhere. Bound to be one around. Check under the cushions. You do scruffy Late Cold War European so well."

"Thomas … "

"Look, you don't want the job; it won't be good for you— don't dress for it and you won't get it. Easy."

"They're not going to interview me anyway. My resumé says I'm a florist with an MSc and no actual florists' training."

"Cunning plan. Negative attitude, but cunning plan."

"At least there'd be plants, in another flower shop."

"Scarf and hiking boots, love. Borrow some eyeshadow."

"It's not me."

"You let me do it and it could be."

"You'll be in Montreal."

"Not if I don't brush my teeth and get going. Leaving you with the dishes, sorry."

And he'd left Kev with loading the van, too.

Thomas kissed him and left to meet Kev and the van at his place. Needed to grab some clothes. He was wearing Lin's underpants.

A year ago—yes, almost exactly—Thomas is biking back from the clinic after the annual check-up and blood tests that will tell him, please, that he's fine, no thyroid problems, no heart problems, no second cancer. He's heading up a path through the arboretum below Summerhill, the neoclassical house that's the official residence of the president of the university. There's a man standing under a tree looking up. Tall. Thin. Nice shoulders, though. He glances over, steps aside for the bike.

Nice face. Black hair, longish, vaguely layered and curling, untidy, windblown. Seventies Mick Jagger in style, a bit, or someone from *The Musketeers*. Beard clipped short. What Thomas thinks of as Mediterranean-looking, with dark, dark eyes, what his sisters would probably call olive skin though apparently that doesn't mean the colour of allegedly-green olives—he knows people don't have green skin which makes that not make any sense at all—he's kind of deep gold—a battered black leather knee-length coat, which along with the hair is maybe why Thomas is thinking *Musketeers*, pale jeans, hiking boots …

He's not nice, he's bloody beautiful and … it's *him*. Oh God, it is. His labcoat bloke. Grown up and grown into …

Thomas brakes and turns the bike, putting his foot down, skidding on the paved path.

"Hey! *Hey!* Hi!"

The man—birdwatcher? squirrel-fancier?—has gone back to staring up into the tree. A bird flashes away at Thomas's shouting and he looks around again, face blank—

Thomas kicks off and coasts down to him. Oh hell, he's being an idiot. No recognition in the face at all, and anyway, labcoat bloke is hardly going to be daydreaming of some pushy drunk who kissed him once at a party, over seven years ago and a thousand kilometres away.

"We've met," Thomas says, sounding like a fool. "Hallowe'en? Years ago. St. Mark's? Nova Scotia?"

He pulls off his helmet and hangs it on the handlebars, takes off his sunglasses, runs a nervous hand through the hair flopping into his eyes—of course the man doesn't recognize him, he was just a stupid scrawny hyperactive kid and half out of his mind that evening, if he remembers right. Which he might not. "It is you! Bet you don't remember me."

But the man is smiling, like the sun coming out.

"*I* was more or less sober," he says. "You, on the other hand …"

Lovely voice. What he'd noticed first, he remembers now, the voice, soft and low and intense, defending Krown Imperial's lyrical complexity, an argument he'd have jumped into happily if Dan hadn't had him by the arm, ranting about the perfidy of mechanics and junkyards and needing quietening down before he took out his temper on some undergrad who looked at him the wrong way.

His beautiful labcoat bloke is smiling, on the edge of laughter. Yeah, he remembers.

"I never got your name," Thomas says.

"I did say. Shouted! But they were dragging you off, whoever they were."

"I didn't hear. Sorry. God, I'm sorry."

That could be apologizing for—the whole thing. It isn't. Surely labcoat bloke knows it isn't. Labcoat bloke … doesn't look like he wants an apology.

"It's Lindsey." A bit wary, then. "It is a man's name, too."

"Well, yes. Lindsey Buckingham, right? Nice. I like it. Lindsey. Lindsey what?"

"Quinlan."

"I'm Gorev. Thomas Smith Gorev. The P in the Smith is so silent it isn't even there."

Lindsey laughs. He does. He gets it. He's beautiful and he likes Krown Imperial and he reads Wodehouse. And apparently he doesn't think Thomas is an escaped lunatic, so there's that in his favour, too.

"I tried to find you, you know. I went stalking St. Mark's students on Facebook. Are you a vampire, do you not photograph?"

"Something like that."

"God, I remember there was that stupid, awful thing at St. Mark's that year, not long after. Some freshman died and there was all the usual stuff in the news, campus parties, underage drinking, binge drinking, is the administration responsible—I heard that and I had this conviction, I don't know why, this terror it was you. I was so relieved when there was a picture of the poor kid and—"

"My brother," Lindsey says, and he's looking away, looking down, hair swinging over his face, all the light gone out of him.

"Oh *fuck*, I'm sorry. God, I'm so sorry."

Wants to touch him, make him look up again. Doesn't. Keep your hands to yourself. Stop hugging people, Tank, not everybody likes it.

"I'm sorry," Thomas says again and does put out a hand, just on his arm, lightly. Doesn't say what's on the edge of his mind, I know, I know. Because he doesn't know, how can he? His *brother*.

Lindsey looks up, nods.

"Raleigh," he says. "He was—I don't know what happened. Why, I mean. Just—stupid stuff, I suppose." Adds, looking away again. "He was my half-brother, really." A breath. "I was wondering what had happened to you. I kept hoping I'd—but then Raleigh, and things got—bad, kind of, and ... " Another shrug. "I stopped looking."

"Found me now."

"That's true."

That smile again. Oh lord. He'd been such an idiot, that night, furious with Ronnie and Dan and the lot of them, such bloody amateurs in so many ways. A bit out of his head, yeah, he'd admit that now. Reckless. Stupid.

Better to be finding Lindsey now, meeting him now. He didn't much like himself at nineteen, looking back. Hadn't at the time, even, if he was honest. Doesn't expect Lindsey would have liked that boy much either, really, not in the long run.

"So what are you doing in Kingston, anyway?" Himself, Lindsey—Thomas doesn't remember who asks it first. The obvious.

They end up sitting on the curving steps of the Summerhill veranda looking down over the park towards the hospital. Talking. Knees just touch, nothing obvious, but he's acutely aware of it, that light pressure, that slight warmth. His breast pocket's going crazy, vibration of his phone. Texts. Irate, Thomas where the hell are you texts, probably. He ignores them. It'll be Emily, on behalf of Uncle George. But they knew he had an appointment. Might not be irate, just asking, how behind are they at the clinic, how long are you going to be.

They can wait. He's busy. He and Lindsey are filling in all the years they've missed.

But God, finally, the time, he can't put it off forever, not fair to Uncle George, who is Kev's uncle, not his, but adopted extended family since Thomas first sent Kev to the hospital with an accidental—it *was*—shovelful of sand in the eye the day they met, a Saturday playdate at the park with the new little boy next door, their immigrant mothers, his from England, Kev's from Holland, geology professor and piano teacher, bonding over *My God wasn't that a long winter …* And whatever he's feeling, whatever he thinks, hopes, that Lindsey is feeling—the man's hardly going to be looking for a date, is he? Those dark, dark, thick-lashed eyes, the line of his jaw accented by his beard, not hidden by it, his throat … those long fingers. He wants to touch. To explore. To be explored.

Labcoat bloke hasn't been some great unrequited love, but Thomas hasn't exactly forgotten him, either. He's been there, a what-if enduring in memory. A fantasy he can't shake off. Something glimpsed and lost that comes to life, to regret, whenever other things are going wrong, as they so often had in the Toronto years, in the mess that life had become then.

Stupid. Desperate? This feeling that it's—just right. The puzzle pieces, clicking together. This is how it goes. Ah.

Obvious.

Like coming home to Kev, after Toronto, except—well, obviously, not exactly.

He's setting himself up for heartbreak and embarrassment. Get it over with.

"Look, I've got to get to work. About an hour ago, actually. I don't suppose you'd be free to go out sometime … ?"

Lindsey's cheeks darken. He looks down, up again.

"I … sure." And then, "*Yes*." Fervently. As if he's afraid the word, or Thomas, might disappear on him.

Really? Unattached? What's wrong with the people in this town?

"Tonight?" Because he's not getting away again, he's not.

"Sure. Sure! Yes."

"Ah, it'll have to be late, though. I'm working. Ten o'clock. Seoul Kitchen. It's not a regular gig, just, they call me in when I'm in town and Emily or Laura or Uncle George wants a day off. Go around and bang on the back door. We'll still be cleaning up. Come collect me? We can … " He waves a vague hand. "Coffee or something?"

Or something, right.

"Corner of Barrie and Earl? I know it, okay. At ten."

"Right, then." Thomas stands up, grinning down at him. Passers-by. A gang of engineering students, yellow jackets permanently stained from their conformity-cult initiation. They give the pair of them a look, and it's probably not because they're worth looking at. Weirdos, the pair of them, to the mundane world. He knows it. And clearly both suffering a cruel addiction to unfashionable thrift store leather coats.

Another sign it's meant to be. Obviously.

Maybe they're clones, the wannabe engineers. They all have

the same haircut.

Darlings, give me a guitar and I'll make you scream. And your girlfriends, too.

"You know, you have the most seductive eyes, Lindsey Quinlan. See you, love."

Thomas bounds down the steps, cramming on his helmet—yellow he can see, so presumably even a bike-blind motorist can—sunglasses. Grabs his bicycle and kicks off, bumping across the grass, then onto a path, veering towards Arch Street.

Get out of here before he's saying, to hell with my secret identity as an emergency backup Korean cook, come over to my place and let me play you some music.

As it were.

Thomas was gone. Lindsey sat in his living room. The squashy old armchair swivelled, could turn to be social with the couch, or away, to face a choice of windows, of islands of plants perched on clementine boxes, spilling from second-hand fernstands. He had closed the curtains. Didn't want to see roofs, to see wires, to see city. Didn't want to hear the cars going by below. Didn't want music, either. Didn't want anything, really. Just sat, with the tallest camphor reaching for him, the lemon geranium spilling scent where the chair had brushed it in turning its back on the room. He hadn't found anything to submit his resume for except another retail job, some mall clothing store he'd never even heard of. Sent in an application for the landscaping thing in Picton anyway. They wouldn't interview him—no need to worry about chainsaws and lack of transport. Didn't want to do any of it. Wanted just—he didn't know. To be outside somewhere, with space around him. No one telling him what to do. No people at all.

Lighthouse keeper. Hermit. Except there was Thomas.

A year ago. Lindsey means to go to the laundromat. He's had a three and a half kilometre run before breakfast, but laundry seems a miserable waste of his day off when the breeze is warm and the air smelling of spring, so he goes for a walk to listen to the birds and see what's coming up in people's gardens.

Oh God, what if he'd gone to do laundry, been sitting there in the steamy tedium, some book held as a barrier against other people's noise …

He was real.

He's real.

Thomas.

Guitarist. Singer. Used to be with Exit 369, which, he says, went down in flames. Slowly and sordidly. Well, the real story's more complicated than that, when Lindsey learns it, and the band in fact is still around, but right then all Thomas says is 'pretty derivative stuff really, but the guitars were good when we let loose.' A couple of albums, even.

Now, though. Now, Strange Pilgrim Road. The Kingston band, after he came back to his hometown, a few years of post-Exit session work under his belt. The Pilgrim Road is his baby, he says, his and Kev's. "Don't be jealous of Kev, it's not like that. Pretend he's my twin or something. Just remember he's the good twin and I'm the evil one, and you'll be fine." Kevin Park the bass, who seems to be in charge of a lot of the production of things as well, if Lindsey's understood Thomas on that point, which he's not sure he has. And Anicky Bell the drummer and her sister Frankie, who's rhythm guitar and also keyboards when they want that. Friends Thomas talked into shifting their base away from Toronto.

Lindsey has heard of Strange Pilgrim Road. That's a bit unreal. Seen flyers up, posters, playing around town and not just in bars, never stopped to study faces. What would he have done if he recognized Thomas, anyway? Gone to hang out in the front row trying to catch his eye? Yeah, right.

Doesn't go out much these days. Or at all.

They're on the road intermittently, all up and down the Quebec City-Windsor corridor, especially the golden horseshoe, but Montreal, into Detroit and northern New York State a bit. Two albums so far. Recorded, produced themselves. They have their own studio, which Thomas seems to think is important. Rising indie stars. Maybe? Thomas shrugs, using that phrase, grins, making a joke of it. Enthuses about his personal trinity: Knopfler, May, and Eric Johnson.

Lindsey likes even the sound of the name. Strange Pilgrim Road. It promises—he's not sure what. They're a band driving hard under the influence of Queen, Zeppelin, Iron Maiden, Jethro Tull … Genesis, Dire Straits, Rush … "You get the idea," Thomas says. "The old guys. But not trying to be them. We want to say hey, you can still have this be the foundation under your feet and go someplace new." Lots of guitar, drums. Not disdaining solos. Lyrics that need footnotes, Thomas says his sister Isabel complains. Some of them. Hard rock with a bit of prog. A bit experimental, some of it.

Sounds like maybe Lindsey's kind of thing. Right now he'd be willing to think so if it was … almost anything. Country … ? He can't imagine Thomas singing through his nose, he's safe there.

Looks at their website. Links to a few videos, the sort of that are mostly just the band in the studio or messing about somewhere, not actors and script because who has that kind of money? No one without a big company behind them. Buys the albums, downloads them. The first is self-titled, the second called *Ways and Means*. He still doesn't like streaming services, wants to own the music, not rent it. Wants quality sound. Hard rock, electronic, true-voiced thoughtful pop— all deserve that richness of sound. Still buys physical discs whenever he can, if they're not a fortune and needing to be imported from Europe.

Then he's sitting in the squashy velour armchair, pacing around the apartment. Restless.

The cover of the first is a black and white photo, very arty, chiaroscuro. Kev—yes, he's curious about Kevin, the way Thomas talks about him. Important person. Straight, good. Thomas did make a point of mentioning that and Lindsey pretended he didn't need to feel relieved. A bit taller than Thomas, wavy black hair to his shoulders, parted in the centre. Asian, maybe, but not his nose, which is large and crooked and keeps him from being handsome, a sort of awkward charm to him, somehow, even in a photo. A short beard, contrast, deliberate? to Thomas's clean-shaven face and finger-length fluffy blond tousled-ness that's—yeah, he wants to touch.

Wants to touch, and know, *mine.*

He's terrified of this.

He'll screw it up. He's never got it right. He can't get it right, ever.

Thomas and Kev lean together, close as brothers. One of the women has long light hair, a sceptical quirk to her eyebrows, the corner of her mouth. Thomas's height. Drummer, he thinks. Just the robust look of her, jeans and tank top and tattooed bands of Celtic knotwork around biceps that make him think he should be doing more push-ups. The other girl—startlingly young, looks like a teenager—has short dark hair, jeans and jean jacket. Sharp, pretty face. If he's guessed right, it's Anicky at Kev's shoulder, Frankie sitting in front of them, leaning back against Thomas's legs, barefoot, ankles crossed, arms folded. The photo's down on the waterfront under the stark angles of the sculpture called "Time," two square prisms that thrust towards one another, never meeting, angled to pass one another by even if they could launch themselves clear of the earth. The lettering's a startling, brilliant light blue, a scrawl that looks like it was done with peacock ink and a calligraphy brush.

That middle bit of the fifth track ... Turns it up louder. It's ... one of the "a bit experimental" ones, like Thomas said. Warned? "Black Mirror", it's called. Words like half a dream, suggesting ... he's not certain what. A journey. Darkness, not without hope. Like fragments of a story lost in time. Two voices, Thomas a baritone, Kev a tenor, trading off. The guitar goes off on its own. Is it a dialogue, even? A woman's voice joins in.

He wants more.

The second album, the cover black and white again, the band—he knows that place too, he'd swear, it's out at Gould Lake, the conservation area, the steep trail that goes down the ridge covered in beech trees, autumn-pale leaves. The four musicians walking away, up the ridge, strung out. Thomas has an electric guitar slung over his back, the only one with an instrument. The same style of lettering, and bright blues again, different shades for the band name and album title.

It's just as good. It's better? Well, it's just as good but there are couple of songs that he can tell are more—likely to have more people liking them, put it that way. The cryptic and beautiful's not given up, but it's balanced by more of the stuff you'll turn up the volume for and sing along with in the car. Something that catches you and doesn't let go.

He's got decent speakers for his computer, an indulgence, but when both albums have played through once he converts and burns them to CD and plays them again on Dad's stereo. Carleen brought it up to him a couple of months back, she and two friends on a reading-week roadtrip to Kingston, everything jumbled in the back of someone's SUV: Luxman turntable, 5-CD changer, double cassette deck, Dad's LPs in their old bright plastic milkcrates: blue, yellow, red, proclaiming property of Baxter, Scotsburn, Northumberland. Rock, new wave, some synthpop. The few CDs Lindsey hadn't already pinched. Plus miles of speaker wire, the lot. Serious KEF speakers. Mom was having another fit of clearing out. She's gone digital.

Thank God Carleen remembered to lock down the tone-arm.

He's feeling the bass in his ribs now, the windows rattling. Damn.

That kid he's—admit it—held close and intimate in his mind so many lonely nights. Thomas is not that kid, that bright sparking longing. He's these guitars, this voice, this poetry and the sound that's hauling out something deep inside—

And Lindsey's got a date with him. Oh God.

What on earth is Thomas going to see in someone like him?

The apartment's a mess. He should have done laundry. There's a litter of dry geranium petals, red and white and pink, on the floor by the south-west window, and he knows the ruffled Boston ferns have been shedding all over in the bathroom, despite the humidity from the shower. Fragments of fern get tracked all over the apartment.

Does the place look too cluttered, too filled with plants? Ivies growing all over. His camphor trees. A terrarium, miniature ferns and mosses, interesting stones, in an aquarium salvaged from someone's end of term clear-out. It's not quite … normal.

There's a blue plastic tub under the kitchen table. He's been vermicomposting for a couple of years now.

He's a biologist. Does that make it seem less weird, to have all these living things around? Explain it? What the hell is normal, anyway?

What if he and Thomas end up back here? Does he even have anything to eat? There's popcorn. Too childish?

"There's nothing wrong with popcorn," Raleigh says. "Stop making yourself crazy. Anyway, he said you're going out for coffee."

At ten o'clock at night?

Maybe he should get a bottle of wine …

Lindsey goes out, gets the wine, a baguette—more grown-up than popcorn—some humus, humus is good. Other things that, well, one might decide one wanted.

If it turned out they weren't just going out for coffee.

Lindsey's vacuuming. The vacuum cleaner, like the round oak coffee-table which was such a beast to lug home on his own, came from the junk store on Queen. A favourite haunt. He's proud of the coffee-table, a warm natural amber now that he's stripped the patchy dark brown varnish and refinished it. It looks nice. He does have a few nice things. Maybe? The vacuum wasn't quite such a find; it smells of burning rubber.

Maybe he should move some of the plants out of the bedroom, at least. Hide them—where? The bed—such as it is—is a bit overhung.

    "Getting serious, vacuuming the bedroom."

    "Raleigh, go away."

    "You don't mean that."

    "Tell me you're not going to hang around tonight."

    "Do I ever?"

    "I don't know. Yes."

    "I don't. That's disgusting. I don't want to know what you get up to in bed, really I don't."

The plants stay where they are. Lindsey needs them.

Lindsey shuts off the vacuum, opens the window to try to get the burning rubber stink out. Can't afford a new vacuum. Broom isn't any good on the patchwork of carpet-tiles with which all the floor except the kitchen-corner and the bathroom is covered. Maybe one of those old-fashioned carpet-sweeper things …

Drops down on his knees by the window's island of green, leaning on the sill.

Idiot, idiot, idiot. What made him think they were coming back here anyway? Or going anywhere, beyond some awkward, embarrassed sitting in a café until they could decently say goodnight and Thomas could be rid of him. Stupid.

    "Hey." Raleigh's there, kneeling down beside him, arms, chin on folded arms on the windowsill as well. His shadow. *"Thomas. You found him again. Seriously, what are the chances?"*

    "It's not going to—it's stupid. This isn't going to work. It never does. I'm too … " Messy. Messed up. Whatever. Not quite right. Somehow. Somewhere inside. He'll find out. He'll be able to tell.

    "Lindsey. Lindsey, he remembered you for seven years. Seven years! You want weird, that's weird. Good-weird. Your kind of

weird."

Thomas reads Wodehouse. Reads fantasy, science fiction, too—he can tell by the songs. Someone in the band does, anyway. Maybe Kev writes the words, maybe it's one of the girls. Maybe all of them. He wants a proper CD, liner notes. He wants—he wants to stop thinking.

"Just—go with it. Get on with it. Get it on with him! Anyway, there's nothing wrong with you that isn't your own stupid mind trying to mess you up because you think that's how things should be."

"Yeah. Right. What about you?"

"I'm not messing you up."

"Why the hell are you here, then?"

"You tell me." Almost he sees Raleigh's grin. *"Driving you crazy? That's what brothers are for, right?"*

Lindsey's blinking back tears, angry. At himself. At Raleigh, for being there.

For not being there.

"Hey."

There's not a hand on his back. No warmth, no touch. Because there can be no one there.

"You came crashing in here all incandescent and look what you've done to yourself. You're so ... Go do the dishes, Lindsey. You don't want to spoil the mood with yesterday's dirty dishes. Get on with it. Shove the anti-Lindsey back in his box and lock it. Think about whatever you were thinking about when you came in that door. But don't tell me about it, because, ugh, if it's dirty and involves a guy, I really don't want to know."

Coconut lip balm.

He can just about see Raleigh making that *Lindsey, you're just so ...* face.

And the feel of the skin over the kid's ribs, his back … No one's felt like that to his touch, ever again. Which is weird, because you'd think the feel of one person's skin, another, is pretty much the same, objectively considered. And the heat of them, bodies pressed together, for all the frustration of jeans in between.

"I said I don't want to hear about you groping some guy. I really don't want to know what's going on in your jeans. Or his. Really, really not his."

"I didn't say anything."

But he's smiling to himself, because it's what Raleigh would say and Raleigh's right, the kitchen smells of yesterday's canned ravioli and the dishes need done. He starts an album on the laptop, something he knows by heart, not Strange Pilgrim Road because that needs serious listening to again, that's for after, while he's waiting for nine-thirty to happen, for it to be time to leave, to meet. Pet Shop Boys. *Yes.* Loves the song "Pandemonium". Puts the album on shuffle and that's the first track to play.

Thomas will say, sometimes it's important to listen to an album in order. There's thought in how the songs fit, a plan, a plot, even. Something the artist is trying to say.

Sometimes you just stir it up and see what happens.

Like bibliomancy.

They'll be dancing to it before the night's over, because it turns out Thomas loves the Pet Shop Boys too, the greatest contemporary poets, he says, subtle and complex and then the way they make stuff that's always dancing in the shadow of death and depression. But happy. They can do happy, too. Aren't afraid of silly. Orchestral complexity. And Raleigh's gone wherever it is he goes. Back into Lindsey's dreams. Because he isn't real. Sometimes Lindsey remembers that.

Dancing. Not very drunk, just a little bit set free—one bottle of wine between them—but that's the effect Thomas has on him anyway. Liberation. Singing along. "Did you see me coming?" "More than a dream." "Pandemonium"—loud, no thought for the students in the apartment below.

And Thomas can *sing*.

You fall in love in pieces. A voice that wraps around you. A freedom that says, hell yes, dance, because we're happy and why not dance? Eyes, eyes laughing and inviting—so much. Wanting whatever it is he thinks you are. Wanting what you are, you can believe that, now, in this moment. The scent of his soap, of a kitchen, savoury in his hair. Taste of sweat. The hot hungry urgency of a mouth. Tangle of legs, weight of a body on you, filled out with muscle yet still that compact, warm, life-sparking kid, whose hands run over you, making a song of his touch. The way you breathe together in the end, slow, clutched close on one pillow, and the wind cold through the open window, and you hold tighter because you're not getting up to close it. Pull the covers up, two bodies locked resting in one S-curve.

You pretty much have to lie like that. Lindsey had been thinking he was never getting involved in a relationship again, never, ever, with anyone, when he bought a twin mattress.

/Two/

Mood:
Bruce Dickinson, "Jerusalem" & "Trumpets of Jericho"
Dim stillness beneath spruce

"*Let's run away,*" Raleigh said.

Mocking. Maybe he's quoting a song. Maybe not.

Lindsey tucked his feet up, pulled an afghan over himself. Mom had gone through a crocheting phase while he was at Queen's. Afghan for Christmas, blue granny squares. Afghan arriving in the mail in February, burgundy and cream stripes, heavy Briggs and Little wool rather than practical cheap acrylic, in case he was cold. Lacy afghan in quiet greys, in July, with no explanation and another in a huge, expensive parcel for his birthday, patchwork greens, wool again, and matching cushions, because someone who liked green had given her all their odds and ends from a lifetime of yarn-hoarding. But after the second Christmas, hexagons of green and pink and burgundy, she had turned her attention to wallpapering the inn. Just as well, Carleen had said. You can't sit down here now without moving an orgy of cushions first.

Why an orgy?

Because it's obscene, the way they huddle up on one another, all fat and hairy.

51

Hairy?

"You should see some of the fancy yarn she was buying last fall. Wait a sec." And Carleen had disappeared from the screen, leaving a view out her bedroom window, the river, chunks of ice floating down to Saint John, all vague blurs to the web-cam. Skype. Checking up on him, he sometimes thought. Fair enough. He liked seeing her. Changing hair colours. Always wary that there might be more piercings, but she never did the gruesome stuff: lips, tongue, even the time she shaved her head to a short fuzz. "Hairy!" she said in triumph, shaking a fat cushion in front of the camera. "And beads. Like shiny eyes peering out of the fur at you." She was right. Where did anyone find yarn like that? And why? Some kind of fake-fur thing? Maybe there was a bag of it at a yardsale Mom couldn't resist. "It's like the living room's full of stuffed dead monsters," Carleen had said, hurling the offensive cushion out of view. "Giant hairy spiders with no legs. Trust me, wallpapering's a better use of her time."

A big box with three hairy, bead-studded cushions arrived later, from Carleen, not Mom, with a scrawled note: *Sharing the horror. She'll never miss them.*

Run away. He and Raleigh did once, when they were nine and ten. Ran away for a whole July afternoon.

Their summer world, the Quinlan cottage near Pugwash. Gamma, the queen bee of the hive, around whom the rest must swarm, obedient. His grandfather dies the year Carleen is born, when Lindsey is five; all he remembers later is the way the old man—not really all that old, in his fifties, a school principal with long years to go until retirement—sings along to The Kingston Trio, The Henchmen, The Clancy Brothers and Tommy Makem, Pete Seeger … the big Crown Vic packed with grandchildren: him and Raleigh, Aunt Tanya's Makayla, Aunt Michelle's Julie and toddler Piper, before Aunt Sandra's hockey-mad Darren and Zack, or Carleen, are ever born. Going out for ice-cream, inevitably. Mostly Lindsey remembers the heavy cigarette smell of him, which will linger forever in the furniture, the curtains, the very walls of the cottage's four tiny rooms. Gamma moves to a smaller house in Dartmouth soon after, so there's no memory there when they go for Christmas, beyond the photos on the wall, but in the cottage, Grandad Quinlan's ghost persists in the smell. Stale cigarette smoke always makes Lindsey think of licorice ice cream—his favourite in those days—and "We come on the sloop *John B* … " Why that in particular? Probably because of the next line " … my grandfather and me … " There's a cluster of camping trailers permanently moored around the cottage as the next generation marries, one for each of the four sisters.

Lindsey loves it. Hates it.

Loves the ocean. Hates the summers.

Running away in Pugwash means him and Raleigh and Mika their dog in some farmer's woodlot across the road, well supplied with gingersnaps and apples and a blanket, planning to camp under the spruces by the spring forever or until everyone and especially Gamma stops taking Makayla's side. She's stolen their treefort, filled it with her own toys, is always there with Julie and some girls from other cottages, giggling and whispering. 'No boys' she says standing at the base of the ladder, barring the way, "especially Spiderlegs." And so Raleigh hits her, but she starts it; before she comes down the ladder and gets hit she throws a stick at Lindsey and tells him he isn't allowed double, because even if he has a girl-name he's a boy and nobody knows who his father is, you're just an accident, Spiderlegs, Spiderfingers, you don't count, nobody wants you, you can *get rid* of babies you don't want, Aunt Trish should have *got rid* of you.

Horrible emphasis. She savours it, though neither of them's quite certain what it means then.

She scrambles back up the ladder when Raleigh hits her and clings there kicking at them as they both try to pull her down, but she cries like always as soon as an aunt comes to investigate the yelling. Gamma takes her side and says they have to share the fort, boys shouldn't bully girls, even though Lindsey and Raleigh were the ones that built it all by themselves and it's their own private place and the only bully around is Makayla.

Far back in the woods, they've almost finished making a hut of broken branches and are trying to decide whether they have to go back to the trailer because they forgot dog biscuits and if they do, will Carleen and Piper come tagging after them, when Mika barks and Dad is there. It's past suppertime. "They're only out in the woods, they'll come back," is Mom's attitude, unperturbed by this sort of thing, but Dad, who has just arrived from Fredericton for a few days, is frantic, thinking of kids wading, slipping off rocks, kids swimming unsupervised, messing about in forbidden boats, falling out of trees ... At that point he's still working shifts in the emergency room. He sees stuff.

Not allowed to play out of sight of the cottage whether Dad's there or not. No more exploring.

Dad buys them both Nintendo Game Boys. Pokemon will keep them out of trouble for the rest of that summer.

❀

Let's run away ... Thomas didn't run.

Thomas pretended otherwise, pretended it was because extra cash never hurt and he enjoyed cooking, but he still had to work as a cook sometimes, couldn't afford to hang around just exploring all the music in his head between gigs. You could be brilliant and still not make enough to live on, in a world of piracy and legal streaming services that paid next to nothing and expected you to be grateful for that—you could make more going online and just begging, if you could present the right personality, the right brand of neediness. And he was happy, and he'd had bad things behind him, he had that shadow, still, that fear, that someday ... something was going to catch up with him.

Thomas woke up out of nightmares that he was in hospital, still. Crying with an old loneliness and terror that made him start laughing at himself, holding on to Lindsey.

It never stopped him. It never made him fear the night.

Queen. "Breakthru." That moment in the video, after the long intro that was really a fragment of a different piece, when the song gathered to *"Now!"*

That was Thomas. That image, that moment.

Never Lindsey.

Lindsey made himself eat lunch, a couple of slices of toast, anyway, and some tea. Had to dunk the toast in the tea to swallow it. Toast and margarine, not butter. One of Thomas's things. No dairy, except really good quality cheese on special occasions. No meat. It had begun with an irrational childhood terror that things going wrong in your body had to come from somewhere, eating some sick animal and you ended up sick— it had made mealtimes a tantrum-fraught minefield, so Gorev family lore had it. Thomas denied the tantrums. But he'd never gone back to eating meat, and extended that to dairy in an attempt to cut back yet further on saturated fats when he was in Toronto.

At least they still had fish. And eggs, animal fats or not. No shortage of eggs. Dodger kept hens.

Not that Thomas imposed his diet—it was just easier. Lindsey didn't mind finding himself mostly vegetarian, if he could eat a hamburger or japchae when they went out or got what Thomas persisted in calling takeaway. The SandWitch and Brew did a real ham and extra-old Wilton cheddar on rye with alfalfa sprouts he'd happily eat a couple times a week if he could afford it, which he couldn't.

He'd gone out running to stop Thomas asking him why he didn't. Maybe he'd felt better, a little. That hadn't lasted past trying again to find a job to apply for.

Put some music on. Adam Lambert. Suited his mood. Angry and lonely.

Which was … wrong. All he had to do was call. Thomas and Kev would hardly be to Montreal yet. He opened the curtains. Raining, again or still. He hadn't set up his rain barrel yet. Should do that, splice in his diversion of the downspout again. Unpack the bags of leaves from around the planter of Japanese maple seedlings he'd weeded—scrumped, Dodger said, like stealing apples—from a university flower bed under a magnificent big specimen. What he was going to do with a half dozen Japanese maples he didn't know. Bonsai them. Pack them in leaves every winter, hope for the best … He needed trees and was starting to think he'd never have them. He should clean the worm bin, take the castings down to his planters, start getting them ready for spring. Might be able to sow lettuce already. Maybe he'd try peas in one, with some twine up the board fence for a trellis. Snow peas for stir-fries? Thomas would like that. This year's students in the apartments below seemed okay; it was probably safe. The three girls on the second floor had even been using the compost bin Thomas had got him for his birthday, though he'd had to nerve himself up to talk to them about the chicken bones, scare them with warnings of rats.

Tomatoes already started in a row of cans in the south window, Scotia and Basket Vee and some new cherry tomato. Purple basil.

"I gave my love a composter, without any muck," Thomas had sung, playing his Takamine twelve-string, his busker's guitar, he called it, sitting in a pile of leaves, not-very-helpfully watching Lindsey study the assembly instructions for the bin last September. "I gave my love—"

"You are not going to rhyme with that," Lindsey had said, and Thomas had wandered off into "Scarborough Fair," laughing.

Who got you a composter for your birthday?

Someone who saw you, and liked what they saw.

He changed the music to Jethro Tull. *Rock Island.* Hauled the worm bin out from beneath the table, rolled up his sleeves and spread out a garbage bag on the floor. Do something. Anything. Don't sit thinking.

Problem was, sorting out worms and worm-cocoons and rotten banana peels and whatnot from worm castings wasn't exactly intellectually demanding, and the mind just kept gnawing away at itself.

And he should have gone out and got newspaper first. Nothing for new bedding. Too much thinking, and not enough.

The worms would have to make do with the week's fliers.

"What's wrong with you, anyway?"

Wasn't sure if that was Raleigh's voice or his own.

"Nothing." Answering them both. "I'm just … "

Tired. But that was a falsehood he never believed himself, even when he said it. Even when he could lie, at least half asleep, on the couch all afternoon. Napping. Because there was a stillness there, at least, that shut out … everything.

"You're not tired."

That was Raleigh. Almost, if he looked … there. Leaning against the counter, hands in pockets. Hair hanging in his eyes, the long bangs he'd grown when he was in high school. That was how he looked always. Fifteen, sixteen. Raleigh, grade ten. When they weren't kids any more, but … he wasn't that freshman, either, that guy at the party pretending he didn't even see his brother.

"I did see you. You were with those artsy types."

He hated it when Raleigh answered like that. Thoughts that seemed—what Lindsey couldn't know.

It worried him.

"You could stop talking to me."

"I can't."

"So what's wrong with you?"

Aside from talking to his dead brother … ?

"Shut your eyes and pick a word."

"What?"

"Do it. Tell me. Say it."

"No," he said. *He was just … he felt lost.*

"Lost," he said.

Raleigh was silent. Satisfied.

Like somewhere, he'd taken the wrong path, unknowing. Trees, endless spruces, circling, and this path wasn't the one he'd thought his feet were on and he'd lost Raleigh and Mika and couldn't find his way back to the road, the cottage, the shore—Dad's fear, the kids lost in the woods …

Lost. It wasn't even a turn he'd taken. The world falling away around him, to be replaced by this … wilderness. Bewildered. And sometimes there was a clearing, a little space, where he could be safe if only he didn't look up to see that he was still in the darkness, no way ahead—if he just kept his gaze fixed on the ground, didn't look for horizons, just swept the floor and rang in the sales and made the arrangements, each identical to the last, to match the pictures in the catalogue, *congratulations, happy birthday, get well, love, father.*

He'd thought he could do it. Carry on like this. People did. Worked jobs they didn't care about, lived for their evenings, their days off. There was Thomas.

It wasn't even losing his job, or wasn't only that. He'd felt things slipping away all this year; the light, even that cast by Thomas, narrowing. The darkness beyond thickening. Like his last year at St. Mark's, like his years at Queen's all over again. Couldn't tell himself, pretend the way he had the past few years, that this was normal. And what was pushing him down into that place again … it wasn't what had happened with Clare; it wasn't being on EI, the money, the uncertainty, not in itself.

Facing it: this was where he was. Not temporary.

He couldn't do it. Defeated.

Give up. Quit.

Quit what?

Everything.

"*Go to the doctor,*" *Raleigh said.*

"*No!*"

Gamma's voice in memory. "For God's sake, Tricia, if Jonas won't admit there's anything wrong, take that child to another doctor, someone with more experience. It's not normal, the way he carries on over every little thing. What's wrong with him?"

"Nothing. He's just highly strung. He'll outgrow it. You always said I was a difficult child."

"Not like that, you weren't. He must get it from his father. No knowing what kind of problems he had."

Did adults not think children heard? Did they not think they would remember?

Unstable. That was a word. He didn't know where it had come from. It was there, attached to him, from when he was small. Makayla used it. Something her mother said.

"*If you're depressed—*" *Raleigh began.*

"*I'm not.*"

He goes to a doctor, his last year at Queen's. A day he finds himself sitting down on the boulders of the breakwater, watching the waves, thinking how like the ocean the lake is here, grey and rolling, an inland sea. And just wishing …

He doesn't know what.

To be nothing. To be over.

Scares himself, there watching the water. Raleigh gone silent. No voice in his head, whisper in his ear. Nerves himself to it. Student health clinic. Roll of the dice, what doctor you get. One of the honours students from his lab went after a bad fall in a basketball game. "Homesick, pregnant, or do you want to go on the pill?" the doctor asked her. "Um, I'm pretty sure I have a broken collarbone … ?"

Lindsey wonders if he has the same doctor. Isn't sure what all the questions about his sexuality have to do with anything. He hasn't said anything to start that off, only, stammering, nervous, that he's kind of feeling, well, really tired, really grey all the time, he's … Not looking at the doctor. Of course. He can't, not when he's confessing this. Or when he's trying to, and having the wrong conversation altogether. Is it his looks that are against him, or what? He doesn't look particularly—anything. Does he? Does she ask everyone these things when they came in about something else altogether? Hands between his knees, because they're shaking.

He can't find a way to say, no, I'm fine, I'm not here to talk about sex, it's only that I'm afraid. I'm tired. I want to go home and there's no place to go. Home's not home and I'm trapped here. There's this girl thinks I'm the love of her life and I only ever agreed to go to a movie, it wasn't anything more, ever, she just assumed and kept telling everyone and now I'm sleeping with her so I don't hurt her feelings and I hate it, I hate her, I hate myself and I don't even care. I'm too tired to think how to get out of it and that's not the problem—if I wasn't so tired I could deal with that, and I'm doing what I've always wanted to do, university, a PhD in front of me, science, and I can't care about it any more. I could just walk away without finishing and I wouldn't care, only I can't, they'll all say, Lindsey couldn't deal with it, he can't deal with things, he goes all to pieces—and I don't, I haven't since I was little, I don't have panic attack tantrums when there's something new I didn't have time to think about, when something scares me. I don't get angry, I don't hit, I don't cry where anyone can see me, and

I still can't be normal.

I keep locking myself in the bathroom to cry and I'm a grown man …

The doctor seems suspicious that he's trying to get himself medicated. Why? Why would anyone, if they didn't have to, if they weren't at the point where they couldn't cope otherwise?

He's not there. He's sure he's not. Yet. Not quite there yet. That's the point. He doesn't want to be.

At cross purposes. He's trying to say, I just want to talk to someone about this, I just need to find a way to understand, to figure out whether that's even what I need or not … She doesn't want to hear it, this doctor, for all she manages to make him understand that he's manipulating her, she's merely humouring him, his desire for antidepressants. He can't seem to fumble through an explanation that makes sense. Words running down into silence. *I feel like crying all the time. I pretend I talk to my dead brother.*

I think I pretend.

I'm afraid I'm crazy.

Maybe … he had wanted a map, he thought now. Not a set of instructions—go here, turn left, twenty paces. A map, look, you can go this way, or that, or take that road, and understand where you are. If you can understand where you are, see ways you can go, you won't be trapped, be lost … the darkness will lighten some. Won't it?

But OHIP didn't cover counselling, the sort of therapy Lindsey vaguely knew was out there, someone to talk to, to help people learn to find a way through … whatever they were trying to find a way through, whatever they needed to figure out. A better way of facing the world. He'd looked it up back in December, warily, as if even typing in the search terms labelled him. Committed him. And if the university insurance had covered it, back then, he didn't know it and the doctor certainly hadn't mention it.

No money for that sort of thing now, for certain. No supplementary insurance.

After seeing that doctor four, almost five years ago, he had ended up with a prescription for antidepressants and so much guilt for supposedly asking for it that he had never opened the bottle.

But he supposed that was on his medical records now, another reason not to go back, that he had some kind of sexual hang-up. One problem he'd never had, really, which was—he couldn't even be a messed up teenager in the ordinary way. He'd always known what he wanted and not been bothered by that.

Just by the tricky interfacing-with-real-people part to get it, right.

Until there was Thomas, a great flare sent up over no-man's-land …

Mountain of compost. Worms wriggling in a plastic dish, unhappily corralled in the light. An adventurous one already out on the floor. He returned it. There were always two or three that went adventuring when the bin got too wet, too cold, escaped from under the screen and lid and ended up dead, dried and glued to the floor in some dark corner.

Lost.

Maybe not so much that he was lost, as that he'd lost himself along the way, somewhere, hadn't he?

Couldn't see himself, except—

"*Thomas sees you,*" Raleigh said.

Thomas shed light, and in it he could see himself.

"So what do you see, then?"

Nails black with worm castings. He liked it. The feel of it. Life. Growth, waiting to happen. He couldn't pick out the tiny amber cocoons, each holding two or three infant worms, wearing kitchen gloves.

He started shaping the sticky mound of castings, flattening a path, fingerprint-wide, winding up the side.

They used to make mountains like that, mounds of beach sand, of garden soil, whatever. Hills, mountains, rivers. Too old to be making sandcastles, Makayla jeered. You guys are so weird. She and Julie would get the younger ones, Carleen and Piper, Darren and Zack, playing tag around them and then someone would inevitably trample what they'd built.

At home in Douglas there are forests of club moss and bracken from the woods that he never succeeds in getting to grow, transplanted under the white pine by the fence, slowly dying there. Landscapes for adventuring, ever yellowing autumn.

Carleen, torn between sibling loyalty and desire to win the approval of the big girls, is an enemy in the summer, and goes back to being an ordinary pest once they're home again. She wants her farm animals to play, little cows and sheep and horses.

"Go make a village, over there by the roses," Raleigh says. "Our guys can stop for the night and fight the raiders."

"Who are the raiders?"

"Bad guys."

"What bad guys?"

"If our guys stop for the night, there'll be bad guys. They're going to come steal your sheep, but it's okay, we'll defend them."

But Lindsey is always bothered by the farm animals. They aren't to the same scale, in the same style. They're wrong. The red barn Dad built for her last Christmas dwarfs his forest. They don't fit together. One makes the other not-real.

"It doesn't matter," Raleigh says. "Just pretend. And if we don't let her play she'll cry."

Lindsey lends her some of his guys, elves and dwarves and his second-best warrior girl, tells her she can play adventure too. But she's too young, she wants her cows to go on the quest and fight monsters too, heroic characters, and gets upset and cries when one of them dies in the battle that invariably happens, the die coming up a one.

It's never proper D&D, their adventuring. Not even Dad's old D&D Battlesystem game, for which they find the rulebook at some point. Just something of their own, making a story, but using dice, a simple high score. It gets more complex, more influenced by the proper rules later, to figure the outcome of fights between characters. But it isn't about the battles; they just happen along the way. It's the maps, and the stories Raleigh makes to go with what Lindsey draws. Adventuring, they call it. Adventuring with the guys, which are Dad's old metal D&D miniatures from his student days, divided between them, and some of their own they started collecting too, metal and plastic both.

In the winter Lindsey makes maps on pieces of paper laid edge to edge, spending more time designing the landscapes than paying attention to the adventures Raleigh is narrating.

Dad buys a cottage on Grand Lake, close to Fredericton. No more summers in Pugwash with the Quinlan clan. Dad doesn't like Makayla's influence over Carleen. They hear Mom and Dad arguing about that, one night, raised voices in the living room. Sneak to the stairs, he and Raleigh, to listen, as afraid as if every squabble that autumn of after-bedtime squabbles means that grim word, divorce. Aunt Tanya is divorced. Mom says that's why Makayla is so mean; she's just "acting out." But Makayla has always been like that. Lindsey hears his own name, Dad going even more serious than when he said that about Carleen, but his voice lowers and Lindsey and Raleigh can't catch the words.

Lindsey is pretty certain what Dad's saying.

Dad found him sitting in the Pugwash woods crying, back in August. Someone new in one of the neighbouring cottages, watching the herd of grandchildren on the beach. Lindsey and Raleigh had been trying to make something that looked like Krak des Chevaliers, an old encyclopedia from the cottage open beside them. Within earshot. But people thought kids were deaf.

"Such a nice family. You must be so proud of them all," the gossipy new old woman said. "Who's that dark boy with them?"

"Oh, he's adopted," Gamma said.

Not one of the real grandchildren. And he was. He was the only one who was even a Quinlan.

Until then, Lindsey pretended sometimes that he had been adopted, because if he had, it would have been because they had wanted him, Mom and Dad. *We're having a baby and he needs an older brother …*

He was too old to be crying like a baby, he knew it. Dad didn't say it. He hadn't told Dad why. Probably he'd known. Dad just said, "Let's go for a walk," and they had, and they'd talked about stuff, like when Dad was a boy and he got lost doing orienteering when he was in Scouts and how scared he'd been, and … nothing to do with Gamma or anything, but Lindsey had felt better. And then out of the blue, Dad said, "Your biological father—don't pay any attention to what Tanya or Makayla say or your grandmother either. He was just someone your Mom knew, a nice guy, she said. She liked him but she wasn't in love with him. Can you understand that? I don't know who he was, but I do know there wasn't anything bad happened between them. Do you understand, Lindsey? Nothing bad. Don't think that, ever."

Dad knows the kinds of things Makayla says. Things that make Lindsey ashamed. As if they are about him. As if he must be that kind of person too. Bad.

"She didn't plan to have you," Dad said carefully, "but once she knew you were happening, she wanted you. She chose you. And I did, when I met her. I loved her, and I wanted the baby she was going to have. I wanted you before you were ever born, okay?"

Was that true, or was it lies you told children? Because when he's older, Lindsey will wonder—if they were already engaged when he was born, why didn't they just put Kavanagh on the birth certificate and make Dad his real father that way?

Did Mom think that somehow, it might matter someday, that Lindsey didn't have another man's last name? That it might matter to him? Or to whoever that man was, that nice guy she didn't even tell that she was pregnant? How could it matter, if Lindsey never knew the man's name, and the man never even knew Lindsey had happened?

Dad wanted him to answer.

"Okay," he had said.

Is it his fault they aren't going to Pugwash any more? Mom

is quietly mad about it.

Dad is quietly mad about other things. Gamma, mostly.

Anyhow, Lindsey is glad. And after a while Mom starts making quilts for the new cottage, telling them each to pick what colour they want, sewing patchwork while they're at school, using flower-sprigged flannelette sheets for the backing, holding the layers together with little tufts of bright yarn, and there aren't any more raised voices downstairs in the night, so they must have made up, Mom and Dad.

They read *The Lord of the Rings* that first summer at Grand Lake, him and Raleigh, out loud to one another. Mom and Dad read them all *The Hobbit* the previous Christmas, taking turns. Now, having discovered there's more, ravenous for it, they read on rainy days and at night, Carleen creeping in from the cot in the smaller of the two tiny rooms over the ground-floor main bedroom, Lindsey coming down to Raleigh's bottom bunk, the three of them sardined there with a flashlight, feeling they're being bad, staying up late—as if their parents can't hear the voices and don't find it amusing, a secret Mom betrays later, how she and Dad chuckled over that, them down in the cottage's main big room with a bottle of wine and her favourite jazz, their kids being so sneaky up the narrow stairs, reading past their bedtime, past their school-dictated supposed reading levels. Carleen misses a lot of it, falling asleep, needs a quick summary each time they start again. They roll her down to the foot of the bed, cover her with her yellow-flowered quilt off the cot and leave her to sleep there.

Their heroes and monsters spend that summer adventuring through a world full of borrowed names. Carleen's favourite cows still get to go along, victorious over orcs in battle. Elf-cows. Magical. Heroic.

Mom sells the cottage when she moves down the river to Gagetown. Lindsey would have liked to have his cottage quilt, and Raleigh's, the burgundy and the green, but she gives all the bedding, the towels, the dishes, even the furniture, to the Salvation Army before he realizes.

Up the mountain and down the other side. No tunnels. Raleigh had especially wanted tunnels, caves, underground adventures in their games. Lindsey made an experimental burrow in the compost. It collapsed. No dragons, only worms. A joke. Raleigh would have gotten it.

Idiot, and his eyes were all tight, hot.

He'd thrown out the pills, finding that even having them around made him—worry about them. About taking them, not taking them. Sneaked them into biohazard waste at the department.

Retrieved wandering worms, went back to strip-mining, scraping castings carefully off the upper layers of his mountain, checking each handful for cocoons and the worms, who were supposed to all head for the dark heart of the mound, leave the outer layers free of themselves, but worms didn't read vermicomposting websites.

"Sometimes—" To give it breath was to make it real. Even if it was only Raleigh he told. More secret than a Catholic confessional, wasn't it? But he spoke it. Heard it said. His voice. Aloud. "Sometimes I wish everything would stop."

"Tell someone. Tell Thomas."

"No. He'd be upset."

"Of course he would. That's the point. He'd make you see a doctor."

And the doctor would get his medical records from the

clinic and they'd say he was neurotic and unstable and—

> *"For God's sake, do you want to die?"*

"No!" Aloud, again.

> *"Okay, good starting point."*

Sometimes he thought it would be easier to be dead.

He didn't say that, even to Raleigh.

Raleigh didn't react.

Raleigh wasn't real. Raleigh was—

He'd scared himself. Scared Raleigh into silence.

Worms. Deal with the worms. Stop thinking.

He couldn't. That was part of the problem, wasn't it?

What did Thomas see in him, anyway?

> *"That sounds like something Makayla would say."*

Raleigh never shut up for long, once he started.

Thomas called Lindsey beautiful, which was unnerving and also not true, but Thomas was weird, everyone admitted that. Good weird. But what else? Why would anyone want him?

What was Thomas? Music. Heat. Life.

What was Lindsey?

Something hidden so well even he couldn't find it.

> *"Maybe you should just ask Thomas."*

Worms all back in new bedding of damp, torn-up flyers, presumably as contented as worms could be, their assorted half-rotten banana peels and whatnot all put back as well; pail of worm castings to be mixed into the planters. Kitchen floor cleaned, nails scrubbed. Tea. CD of Brian May's *Back to the Light* playing, one of his absolute favourite albums, the stereo just on the edge of too loud for the size of the room.

He felt exhausted, like the aftermath of a crying jag.

"Okay," Lindsey said aloud. "You listening?"

"*Maybe.*" *There, maybe, in the corner of his eye, corner of the couch. Feet on the coffee table, just because he knew it would bug Lindsey to do that.*

"*My birthday,*" Lindsey said. *Not out loud. It was seeming—too easy, hearing his own voice really in his ears. Wondering if he heard Raleigh's.*

"*What about it?*" Raleigh asked. "*You'll be twenty-eight.*"

Raleigh had been eighteen. Raleigh would never be more than eighteen, eighteen and almost eleven months, forever.

Twenty-eight was ten years older than Raleigh would ever be.

"*If I haven't found a way to … to do better, to work things out, to stop feeling like this all the time, by my birthday, I'll see a doctor.*"

Because medication might take the weight off, a bit. It wasn't going to fix the truth, change anything. That, he needed to do himself. Somehow. And if he could—maybe he wouldn't need the doctor.

This time.

"*September. That's months.*"

"*Yes.*"

"*Too long. You should make an appointment now.*"

"*No.*"

"*But you promise.*"

"*Yes.*"

"*Word of honour, as a gentleman.*"

He hesitated. The most solemn vow, between them. He didn't remember what Raleigh had been reading, what he had, where that had come from, along grade six, seven, eight. Word of a gentlemen. Inviolable.

"*Yes.*"

"*Okay. But you have to tell Thomas,*" Raleigh said. "*You have to make it real.*"

And that wouldn't be a weird text to send, no, not at all. What could he even say? Lindsey took out his phone. Didn't do it. Put the phone away. But on his birthday, on the Emily Carr calendar hanging on the wall, on September the 3rd, a Saturday, he wrote, very small *?call doctor?*

It was telling Thomas, in a way. He might see it. He might ask. When the page turned to September, anyway.

Lindsey would have to have found a job by then. Would have to have taken whatever he could find.

It wasn't an encouraging thought. It only made the greyness seem heavier.

Lindsey does his master's at Queen's, up in Ontario. But as it nears its end, he doesn't apply for any NSERC grants, any funding at all. Doesn't even apply to a PhD program. His supervisor hasn't pushed, made any suggestions—hasn't even noticed, that he's failed to do so. Hasn't spoken of it at all. And yet his marks are among the best, and there's nothing but praise for his work, his ideas, when he nerves himself up to speak them. He's drifted, more and more, into not joining the discussions in the lab, heading off on his own at the field station. As if conversation has become a weight and lifting that weight wears him out. He'll sit, and listen, and find he lacks any urge to join in. It isn't even the fear of nervous stammering, of everyone looking at him like he's some kind of performing ape, all arms and legs and hunched, averted gaze. Just … everything grown too heavy. And as it grows heavier, he grows … thinner. Harder to see.

Invisible, in the end.

He doesn't see it that way at the time. That's later, looking back. He's just tired. Burnt out. Can't find the energy to care any more. To be interested. And Raleigh's being really annoying, persistent, telling him, talk to his supervisor, tell her he's having trouble. Or if he thinks her indifference is just going to brush him off, talk to one of the other profs, someone he likes, he trusts.

He doesn't.

And there's Megan, of course. Shooting him looks he can't interpret, or doesn't want to.

Burnt out. Uses up all he has left, disentangling himself from her. A couple of dates and she devoured him, her need, her holding fast and he hadn't even thought they were going out in any official high school going-steady way, he'd just been lonely and she'd been there, a housemate, someone he'd thought he could just hang around with to stop hearing the distant lonely whimper in his own head, but she was telling everyone they were a couple, telling everyone that it was so wonderful that he felt the way she did; she was talking, within a couple of weeks of that first movie together, of what they'd do in the future, how easy would it be to find jobs together in their field, maybe they could do some kind of job-sharing, that way someone would always be home with the kids—

Calling his mother, "Just to chat, girl-talk, it's good to be friends with your Mom-in-law … "

What?

Months, possessed by her.

He's just a stick man she can hang her fantasy on. Such desperate clinging, making him into something that she thinks is missing in herself …

Kris Jamison

He didn't do that with Thomas, did he?

He finds the attic apartment on William Street. Moves his belongings, what little he has, mostly plants and books and CDs, a kitchen chair and a battered green drop-leaf table he uses as a desk, a pine dresser, in a frantic, furtive afternoon. He has a bed, just the cheapest mattress and box spring on one of those metal frames, but Megan moved into his room at Christmas and a friend of hers moved into the room that had been hers in that biologist-filled house on Bagot and now has her bed. He can't leave her sleeping on the floor and the mattress won't fit on the roof of the car he's borrowed from a post-doc to ferry his things away—the dresser, the table barely did, strapped on in turn with all the comforters and afghans underneath because there's no roof-rack and—it's several hundred dollars he can't afford to spend again but he doesn't want to be sleeping in that bed, anyway. He'll sleep on the floor, he doesn't care. And, with apologies to memory of Ryan, wherever he and his cubes have got to, he sends Megan an email, once he's sitting safe in his new place, everything heaped all anyhow. Salvage from a wreck. Robinson Crusoe on the shore.

>*This isn't working. I'm really sorry. I can't be what you want. I can't do this. I've moved out. I'm sorry.*

He doesn't even have any dishes.

Megan keeps calling and texting, until he blocks her number. He prowls the various thrift stores for curtains, cutlery, dishes—a complete set. Cobalt blue with bright sunflowers. Buys a microwave, more essential than a bed. Finds pots and pans, gets a cast-iron frying pan new when the thrift stores don't oblige, seasons it properly but can't find the energy to cook. Fills the freezer with supposedly healthy frozen dinners.

Canned baked beans are good, too—proper Maritime ones, molasses or maple syrup, no tomato. Kraft Dinner, even. He eats a lot of Kraft Dinner. Former housemates take sides. He's a jerk. He's had a lucky escape. Then Megan announces she's forgiven him. He was confused, he hadn't meant to hurt her, she understands. He was just having trouble finding himself, he needs a little time to come to terms with who he really is …

She appoints herself his big sister, tries to set him up with some guy in biochem.

He doesn't remember his thesis defence. It goes well, apparently. Doesn't stammer, once he gets into it. It isn't even forgetting to be afraid. There just isn't any fear. It's work he knows. Things he understands and can't be rattled on. Just an interesting conversation, a chance to talk about what he's done. He doesn't care enough for fear, that's the truth.

Everyone else who started their degree with him looks on theirs with terror. Gets drunk to recover. It's traditional. Amber and Justin, who are doing their PhDs, and Rob—and Megan, of course—want to take him out. He doesn't join them, though they're waiting at the grad club. Goes home to his too-expensive attic, where he sleeps folded up into a zigzag on a hairy tweed couch one of the departmental secretaries was selling for eighty dollars. Not even a sofa-bed.

"Taking a year off?" Mom says. "Well, people do. You've been working hard. Are you coming home?"

"I don't know," Lindsey says. Home, New Brunswick, does she mean? Gagetown isn't home. He's never lived there.

He hasn't said he's taking a year off. Just, that he's not going on.

"Well, you have to do something, but probably getting out of Kingston's a good idea. Come help me with the Vic.

There's always a lot to do. And UNB's so close, you could talk to someone there, start part-time in January, maybe. Live at home. People commute from Gagetown, even in winter."

"Oh."

"I've been wanting to redo the ceilings, put up that stuff that looks like the old tin panels. That'll give you something to work on, keep your mind off it."

Off what?

"I'm sorry things didn't work out with Megan."

He wasn't.

"She seemed like such a nice girl. But these things happen. You can have the bedroom over the kitchen. It has its own stairs. That's one of the ceilings that needs work. Actually, the plaster's come down. We can start with that. When do you think, next week? End of the month?"

"I don't know, Mom. I need to rent a van."

Books—far too many—plants—likewise—to get back. The table, which turned out to be rather nice when he stripped and varnished it one weekend in a fit of energy, trying to make himself do something, anything. An antique, and maple under the green paint. His tweedy couch? He's only owned it a couple of months, is he fond of it?

"Let me know when you're coming. I'll clear the plaster off your bed." She laughs.

"Okay."

And the call ends. He sits looking at nothing.

"You don't want to go back," Raleigh says.

"No."

"What are your other choices?"

He doesn't see any. He doesn't want to go home. It isn't home. It's a bed and breakfast, a long white house on the river, the Victoria Inn, named not for the queen during whose reign it was built but for a paddlewheel steamer that churned her way up and down the St. John. He's stayed there, but only weekends, Christmases. She moved in the summer after his fourth year, sold the house in Douglas north of the river, went as if she were fleeing something, taking Carleen with her.

Go home. It won't mean only being a general handyman— that wouldn't be so bad. But to be receptionist, server of breakfast coffee and muffins, chambermaid, tourism greeter, one of the attractions, spilling stories of the river, Loyalists and Acadian gold, the ghost of Madame La Tour with a rope around her neck, paddlewheel steamers … he's heard all about it from Carleen, whose speciality, when Mom's not around, is lurid ghost stories of tragic river deaths and sightings of burning steamers, the cries of the passengers still drifting over the water … She's waiting for one to turn up on some website as Authentic NB Folklore.

"Choices," Raleigh says. "Write it down. Think about it. Good and bad. Stay or go. And if you stay, you have to pay your rent."

Lindsey starts making a chart. Reasons to stay in Kingston, reasons to go home. Crumples it up, throws it away. He doesn't need to see his failure set down.

What can he do? Any work as a lab technician is going to grad students. He spends an hour, then two, a day, two, three, searching—there should be jobs for biologists, botanists, ecologists, even without a PhD. Maybe. Ottawa. St. Andrew's. Montreal. Morden, Vineland … government things—but no, there aren't. The Harper government's busy destroying federal science. Research libraries thrown in dumpsters. Environmental organizations. Other organizations aren't getting the fund-

ing they need. Few jobs going, and demanding in their qualifications. There'll be fresh new PhD's competing for the least
of them, desperate; they'll want an interview, an interrogation;
they mean moving; they mean getting there, even for an interview, and he doesn't have money, no debts, which is rare, he
knows, something he should be grateful for, he had scholar-
ships, grants, and there was Dad's insurance, Dad being well-
off in the first place, a doctor, and prudent, and saving for
kids' education from when they were babies, even Lindsey,
who wasn't his ... But he can't expect Mom to make him an
allowance now and just paying the rent is hard enough, living
alone in a city geared up to prey off students.

Reasons, or excuses?

He just feels so ... like he's run all through with cracks, and
any more weight ... he's going to shatter.

And he doesn't want to go home.

Was this how Raleigh felt?

What made someone drink like that? Undergraduate stu-
pidity didn't seem—a sufficient answer.

Raleigh's silent. Not there, when he looks up.

Of course not. Raleigh's dead.

Clare's Flowers is looking for help. Full-time, too. Minimum
wage. Lindsey feels queasy, thinking about it. Facing people.
But—feels sick, tired, weepy, thinking about crawling back
home, too. All the aunts and their husbands, the cousins,
his grandmother. They'll accept it, and smile, confirmed. It's
Lindsey, what did we expect? Because he's not quite right, he
can't handle things, he can't cope ...

At least it's not a call centre.

He makes a CV. A resumé, he should say, applying to be

a shop clerk. Delivers it by hand, goes home and throws up. Nerves. But there's this, at least—the warm green smell of the place when he walked in.

He's called for an interview. He stammers his way through the initial questions, though there's nothing about Clare, the plump, white-haired owner, to make anyone normal nervous. He has no business experience, no retail experience, which she finds very hard to believe. Everyone has retail experience. It's what people do, work in shops and sell things to other people. But she asks something—he doesn't remember, later, what, but they're talking about plants and he's not looking down at his hands ...

"It's mostly sweeping the floor," she says. "Leaves, cut ends—they get tracked everywhere from the workroom. Sweeping, preparing the cut flowers for the arrangements, alone in the back room."

"I like working alone," he says.

"And working the cash, of course."

Lindsey nods. He can do that. He can. He has to. People coming into a flower shop—they're just going to buy something and leave. They're not going to try to talk to him. They're not going to decide he's weird, look at him because he's said something strange.

He doesn't know about lonely old ladies, then, but he gets along all right with the lonely old ladies, it will turn out, because they want to talk about plants; they won't mind that he knows things that they don't, and—Clare will say—they get a little thrill out of a handsome young man taking an interest.

Teasing. They're just lonely, happy to have someone listening.

His girlfriends, she will call them.

Her chief concern in the interview seems to be that she'll get him nicely trained to use a broom properly and he'll be off to do something better paying and more in his line.

"No," he protests. "I'm taking a year off. At least a year. I—needed a break from studying."

That sounds normal, doesn't it? People say that, and it doesn't mean, I think I'm having a nervous breakdown in slow motion. Just, having a break. Normal people do.

"Deciding what I really want to do," he says. "What direction I want to take this in."

"Choices," she says. "Not many young people do take the time to stop and think about them."

Is that good, or bad?

He gets the job.

"Are you staying?" Clare asks, when it's been almost a year, and he does.

The part-timers, undergrads mostly, come and go. He likes the back room, preparing the flowers, stripping the thorns off the roses with the thick rubber-coated gloves, trimming the ends of the cut flowers, standing them in pails of water to open. Sweeping, watering, misting, polishing leaves, pinching off faded blooms … mindless work, but quiet. There's the cash, of course, but it's not as bad, after a while, and he starts being able to look into faces without an effort, doesn't have to remember and jerk his gaze up like some nervous and disobedient thing from his hands and the cash drawer. Meet their eyes. It's okay. They don't bite. The phone is the worst, taking orders, dealing with complaints. He goes home at the end of the day tired, not from the work. Restless and wound up and exhausted at once, all the voices echoing. Even the nice old ladies who come just to buy a packet of fertilizer spikes and chat have that effect on him.

He makes excuses when someone calls, Rob or Justin or Amber, they're going out, does he want to meet up, they can sign him in to the grad club … It's just … too much. Too much more. Talking. Voices. Answering questions. After a while they stop calling. Then Justin's gone to Waterloo, Amber's at Dal. Rob's working out west and there's no one to call. Megan—still in Kingston. Working for some environmental group, doing publicity, not science.

The other reason for not going out.

He looks at their posts on Facebook once in a while. All busy, happy, doing things. Rob's engaged. Lindsey doesn't post anything himself. What is there to say? That he's taken up flower-arranging?

He's a cliché.

Clare teaches him more florist's work and leaves him to deal with wholesalers, sometimes. Then there's Thomas. The world changes. The shop stays the same. Clare leaves him in charge, as his fourth year there begins to pass, when she goes out west after Valentine's Day to stay with her newly-divorced daughter. Assistant manager, in effect, but he's still paid as a clerk. He needs to talk to her about that. Feels sickish, thinking about it. She'll tell him she can't afford it, any one of the part-timers could be taught to do what he does, really … The business isn't doing too well. From what he sees of the accounts—breaking even? Not even that? Clare tells him no, when he offers to make a website, just something on some free hosting service. Not for online sales, just a place to post about plants, new stock, what sorts of services they offer, pictures of flower arrangements. Something to help people find them when they're looking up local places to buy a houseplant or order a bouquet. Not worth the bother, she says. But people don't look in the yellow pages any more when they want flowers. The shop can't keep going on old people who buy a few fertilizer spikes or a cachepot or their Christmas poinsettia there because that's where they bought flowers twenty years ago.

Not long after Clare's vacation, one day in March, almost three and a half years after he began working for her, he arrives at the shop and Clare isn't there. The door's locked, which is normal, since it's not opening time yet, but he knocks and she doesn't come. He has a key, knows the codes for the alarm.

Lindsey lets himself in. Calls a hello, gets no answer. The alarm … isn't set. That's odd, if she's not here.

And all at once he's sweating, cold, all his joints feeling strange, hot and loose though he's starting to shiver and this is stupid, getting worked up over nothing, she forgot to set the alarm last night, she overslept, she's just popped out to pick up something, she's in the bathroom …

His heart is racing, blood pounding in his ears.

Clare's in the workroom, by the back door. On the floor.

She's breathing. Her eyes open when he touches her. Mouth moves, noises. She's wet herself, he can smell it, but she's soaked, too, lying in spilt water. Her clothes have wicked it up. Her skin feels clammy. Okay to move her? Her face is strange. Drooping, sagging. Drooling. Turns her to her side, head cradled on her arm, covers her with his coat, telling her, it's okay, he's here, help is coming, she's going to be okay. It all takes seconds, and he's calling 911.

The shop's mere blocks from the hospital. It seems hours

before the ambulance is at the door. They ask a few questions while they work. He doesn't know when she fell, but she's wearing yesterday's clothes and she doesn't normally do that, he says. Same baby-blue sweater, same frilly little scarf. She hasn't just arrived—she's been here all night. She was the one closing up, always the last to leave, if the two of them don't leave together and yesterday he went first. He doesn't know her medical history. He doesn't know her family doctor. Finds her purse under the counter, her wallet, her OHIP card.

Her cellphone. Locked, of course. Family in town? He doesn't think so. But the daughter—Melissa, he says. In Edmonton. Melissa—he doesn't know her surname. Maybe Aldridge like Clare, but maybe not. It'll be in the records, won't it? Next of kin?

He locks up, after they leave. Not even opening time yet. Cleans up the workroom, the pails of water and carnations knocked over when she fell.

He doesn't know where she lives, if there's a cat, a dog, a canary … Her husband is six years dead, he knows. The paramedics took her OHIP card but everything else is still where he left it on the counter. He finds her driver's licence. Car keys. The part-timers all use her minivan, making deliveries.

Calls Kelly, one of the kids—they're only a few years younger than him but he and Clare call them the kids—gets her to come in right away, not at eleven as she's scheduled.

"I can do the arrangements we've already taken," he says. "Go ahead and take new orders for anything small. If it's a big thing like a wedding, get their number and tell them we'll call them back. Clare's already done our ordering for the week, so deliveries are going to keep coming. Keep an ear out for the back doorbell and sign for anything that comes. Call Ruthie to come in to help you, if she can, or Patrick. I'll be back to do any flowers that need to go out today." There are a couple of things still in the glass-fronted refrigerator, people who hadn't been home yesterday. They'll have to call.

He has the van keys in his hand. "Where are you going?" Kelly asks.

"I need to call her daughter and I can't get into her phone. There's no address book in her purse, nothing on the list in the office. And what if she has a dog? There'll be something at her house, or a neighbour who might know how to find Melissa." He doesn't have the daughter's number; it had been Clare's own cell he was supposed to call for emergencies while she was out west.

He sounds so certain. Kelly's crying, unawares, but now she realizes it and wipes her face on her sleeve and nods. Hugs him.

"Right," she says. "I'm so glad you're here."

He pats her on the back, awkward.

The address on the driver's licence is out in Portsmouth. A tiny post-war house, very neat. A row of square-pruned alpine currant to hide the foundation, nothing else but a square of lawn and a mature Norway maple dwarfing the house, a big sphere on a stick. Boring, he thinks, and sad. Come summer it'll shade everything, suck all the moisture out of the upper layer of the soil. Periwinkle might work, though, for a bit of colour and texture.

The front door opens easily to the second key he tries. He feels like a trespasser, a burglar.

"Hello?" he calls, but he can tell there's no one there. It has that feel.

He thinks he's going to be sick. Same as when he went

into the shop, hardly more than an hour ago, a lifetime. The silence. The emptiness.

Cat, a wide-eyed stare, a vanishing flash of white tail. He shuts the door, goes past the little living room—all very nicely done, white carpet, pale cream upholstery and curtains and the sorts of plants he recommends to people who just want something green they can't kill—into the kitchen. Also very neat. A slow cooker, a smell of overcooked food. He turns it off. The cat reappears, rubs around his ankles, arching its back. In what seems to be a combined broom closet and pantry he finds a container of dry catfood and a scoop. Feeds it, gives it fresh water. The smell of the food, something, is still making him feel sick.

The knowledge she's never going to eat her stew. That she's never going to walk in here and the cat rub around her ankles. You don't bounce back if you have a stroke and lie on a cold rubber mat in a pool of water and carnations all night.

Puts the hot slow cooker crock straight into the fridge, to be rid of it, and there's a page of handwritten notes stuck to the freezer door with a magnet.

Snowy, says the first. Half a scoop twice a day. Treats at night. Kitty litter in basement under stairs.

Something left for the neighbours when she went out west. The shop's number.

Then, "Lindsey Q, shop" and both his cell and his landline. That's an odd feeling, seeing himself as a thing in her life.

And "Melissa". Cell, home, work.

There's a phone on the kitchen table. It's … just past ten-thirty. So it's, what, eight-thirty in Edmonton? He calls the home number.

A child picks up, not speaking to him but shouting, "Moooom, it's grandma." Thank you, caller ID. "Hi, grandma."

"I'm a friend of your grandmother's," he says carefully. "I need to speak to your mother, okay?"

But there's a woman's voice now, saying, "Mom?"

"Melissa?" he says. "I'm sorry. Clare's in the hospital. I think—it's not good. I'm sorry," he says again, because she's gone silent.

"Who is this?" she asks then.

He explains. She's still silent. Yells suddenly, get your coat on, you're going to miss the bus, at the child in the background, pestering, "Can I talk to grandma, I want to talk to grandma."

Starts crying, saying, Oh my God, oh my God. Stops, as suddenly. No, she says. No, thank you. All right. All right. No, the hospital hasn't called, I'll call them, which is it, and he doesn't know where they'll have taken her, Hotel Dieu or KGH but he looks up numbers for both in the phone book that's there and asks about the cat—who had been looking after it before? Someone has to take thought for it. Next door, she says, a young couple, the Limas, and they have a key for emergencies. Which next door? Number 28, she thinks it is. Thanks him again. She'll call him, she says, once she finds out how soon she can get to Kingston.

He'll take the van back to the shop, Lindsey says. They need to make deliveries, keep things running, is that okay?

Yes, but he thinks she hardly understands what he's saying.

There's nobody home at 28, so he leaves a note in the front door, saying that Mrs. Aldridge is in hospital and can they look after Snowy? Puts his phone number on it. Adds, he's called Melissa.

Locks the door. Sits in the car, eyes shut. Not crying, just—needing some quiet. Calls Thomas, who's just back from Europe. Drives back to the shop. Thomas is there before he is, which has sent Kelly and Ruthie into a subdued flutter, grim though they all feel. Thomas has that effect. He's brought hot chocolate all round from Tim Hortons, and box of doughnuts, and he puts his arms around Lindsey there at the back door and rocks him. Lindsey holds him tight. It's for Thomas's comfort as much as his own. Thomas knows all about going into locked places and finding ... what you're afraid is going to be a body.

Thomas can't stay long, and what could he do if he did? The band's off to Toronto tomorrow and they're rehearsing some new stuff today. He's needed. He'll come over in the evening? Yes, Lindsey says. Yes. He doesn't want to sleep alone. Probably Thomas doesn't either.

He can feel Clare's weight when he moved her, weirdly inert mass.

Thomas leaves with a kiss, though there are customers in.

"You didn't say he was gorgeous," Kelly says, and fans herself.

"Well, what did you expect," Ruthie says, with a sidelong look at Lindsey. God knows what that means.

He takes the stack of orders and starts on the day's arrangements. Keep busy. Keep everyone busy, keep the ship afloat, till someone else with better right can take charge.

Get well. Birthday. A funeral wreath.

Melissa arrives the next day. Comes from the hospital to the shop just before closing, weary, pale face blotchy. It's not good. But can he carry on for the rest of the week? Don't place any orders with suppliers, though. Don't take any calls for arrangements beyond that. Can he cancel any standing orders with the wholesalers? She doesn't know how it all works, can she see the books?

They go through the filing cabinet together, and the safe.

Melissa goes back to the hospital.

Clare lives. After a fashion. Lindsey goes to see her. She doesn't know him. Thinks he's another doctor. Melissa makes arrangements, finds a nursing home in Edmonton. Starts wrapping the business up. Clare had left instructions, giving her daughter such powers in the event of her incapacity. They could keep it going and try to find a buyer, but it was going down. Melissa doesn't want the bother, trying to sell it as an active concern. Or the worse hassle of dealing with it all after Clare's death. Sell the assets now to pay for her care, wind it up.

Lindsey's left with only Ruthie, the longest-serving of the part-timers, to oversee the going-out-of-business sale. Half price. Everything must go.

And in the end, Melissa comes back and they clear out all the oddments, the kettle, the coffee cups, the broken umbrella they used for running to the bank. Lock the doors for the last time.

It's three weeks severance pay, for three years and six months worked, and thank you, and an apple-blossom pink azalea in a marbled blue cachepot he's long admired.

And then EI.

Johnny Marr's *Playland* on the stereo; the tentative pencilled list Lindsey had been making in a notebook had turned into planning a view of rhododendrons under birches, a path winding through them. A challenge, trying to make it for zone 4, things that might have survived in Douglas. Just a bit colder than Gagetown's 5a, where he had offered to put in flowerbeds along the foundation and the front walk across the narrow lawn between the inn and the sidewalk, things that wouldn't take much looking after, if Mom would buy the plants. He'd sent her a list … He'd been planning to take a week off to go and do it next month, if only she had put the plant order in. A legitimate business expense. She hadn't gotten around to it. Next year, she said. Dwarf rhododendrons would be good there, and daylilies for later colour, ornamental grasses, a few hostas … Something simple. A climbing rose—he'd decided against that; she wouldn't find time to look after it.

His rhododendron walk was not something anyone could do around here, Frontenac County, Lennox and Addington, mostly alkaline clay over limestone. He added some native deciduous holly interspersed. Colours. In winter it would be white bark, green rhododendron leaves folded close against dry air, red berries on bare holly twigs. A distraction. The coffee-table was scattered with books, most of the browser tabs on the computer open on lists of rhododendron varieties.

The doorbell startled him out of it. Students looking for other students and hitting the wrong bell; it usually was. Rang again when he ignored it. Couldn't think who'd be wanting him.

Not students. Blonde head, bobbing green to blue to amber in the stained-glass sidelight window. Isabel. She waved.

"Hey," she said as he opened the door. "Is Tank here?"

"He and Kev went to Montreal."

"Oh, right. I knew that, I guess. Are you busy? Can I come in?" But she already was in, shaking water off her umbrella, grinning when he had to jump back from the spray. She was halfway up the stairs before he'd shut the door. He locked it and went two at a time up after her.

"It was you I really wanted to talk to, anyway," she said. Boots on the mat, coat on the stand, umbrella dripping a puddle. He took that away to stand in the shower, found her in the kitchen when he came out.

"Smells good. What's for supper?" Isabel filled the kettle and plugged it in, dumped the dregs of old tea into the steel compost pail, reached for tea-tins. "Earl Grey, Irish Breakfast, or plain old Red Rose, is that's what in the cookie tin?"

"It's oolong in the Earl Grey tin and keemun in the Irish Breakfast. Just use the teabags." He wasn't sure Isabel invading his apartment warranted special tea, especially when he was counting non-existent pennies. Of course, it was Thomas who kept the ever-changing tins and canisters of loose tea filled. "Or keemun or whatever you like. There's Russian caravan in the thing with rabbits on it. You choose."

"Red Rose. There's something reassuring about orange pekoe, don't you think?"

"Really strong with lots of milk, yeah."

"Do you have milk?"

"Well, soy milk."

"How do you put up with him? Seriously, he'd drive me crazy. He drives me crazy and I don't even live with him. I guess you don't live with him either, really, not that anyone could tell. You guys should just move in together and get it over with. But you'd probably end up murdering him, if you couldn't boot him out and send him home when he gets annoying."

"I don't find him annoying. The whole Tank thing—I don't see it."

"Yes, you're infatuated. And he's improved with age. Not so much of the plucky little steam engine rolling over people thing as there used to be. When I was little I thought his name *was* Tank. I was quite shocked to find out it wasn't, like everyone had been lying to me. Did you say what's for supper?"

"I didn't, and I don't know. Why do you want to know?" Teasing. As if it weren't a foregone conclusion.

"Aren't you going to ask me to stay? You'll be eating leftover whatsit for the rest of the week if you don't."

"That was probably Thomas's idea. He thinks I don't eat properly if he doesn't feed me."

"Well, you don't."

"I don't have time to cook."

"Lindsey, you're unemployed. You have lots of time." Isabel was at the slow cooker now, steam wreathing her head as she poked at its contents. She looked around, lid in one hand, wooden spoon in the other. "Sorry, did that sound rude?"

"Yes."

"Sorry. It's something thick with a lot of paprika and chickpeas and specky bits. Caraway seeds, maybe? Do you have caraway?

"I have no idea what I have."

"Let's call it goulash. It's not quite done, though. Carrots are still a little hard. How about I make scones or something—you've got baking stuff, right?"

"Probably. That's Thomas's department. Almost everything in the kitchen is his."

"See? Tank. He just takes over. Okay, scones. And look, you have rolled oats. And a cookie sheet, yay. Oatmeal scones. They're good for you, too."

"Did Thomas tell you to come over here and harass me?"

"No!"

"Really?"

"Honestly, Lindsey, I'm here to harass you all on my own."

"What about?"

"Oh. Nothing, really. You wouldn't want to work at the SandWitch, would you?"

"Why, are they looking for someone?" He couldn't be a bartender. He couldn't. Cooking fries and making sandwiches on their famous homemade breads, everything hurry, hurry, now now now … no, that'd be not much better. He liked Stefan and Michael as friends; as his bosses—it wouldn't work. Baker's assistant? That's all he needed, to be Isabel's underling. But—maybe. Yeah.

"No, I was just wondering, in case something came up."

"I wouldn't be very good at it."

"You wouldn't be very happy at it," she said, rummaging in his cupboards. "You should be outdoors. What are outdoor jobs? Farmer? Lumberjack?" She snickered. "No, seriously. Forest ranger—how do you get to be a forest ranger? Like Mike in Tank's precious *Psmith* books."

"Mike wasn't a forest ranger. He was an estate manager and a farmer, eventually. Mostly he just played cricket." Carleen's degree was in forestry—not something that had been an option at St. Mark's. She'd spent last summer, after graduation, planting trees for Irving, which he didn't think you even needed high school to get hired for. Pulp plantations. The kind of thing she railed against. But that's what passed for a managed forest in NB. She'd had to go all the way to South America to get something that let her deal with ecosystems, she claimed.

"Or what's-his-name. The guy Lord Emsworth was always talking to about his pig. The gardener."

"That wasn't the gardener, that was the pigman. Or the pig-girl, later. With a degree from an agricultural college, I think. I don't want to be a pig-girl. Or a pigman. I don't know anything about pigs."

"Well, you could do a certificate in pig-care, I bet, if you could find a pig-loving earl these days. Or you could find an earl anyway and be his gardener. Hey, the bish has a gardener."

"Really? Do they pay bishops that well in the UK?"

"Not like earls. No, but there's someone who comes around and does stuff sometimes."

"Lawn-mowing."

"No, real garden stuff. Prunes roses. Just like in Wodehouse. Of course they're not really his roses, they're diocesan roses, and it's the diocese that hires the gardener, I suppose. But there's still a gardener. Where's the baking powder?"

"I think all that kind of thing's on the second shelf and to the left."

"Lindsey ... Lindsey, I knew Tank wasn't here. I wanted to talk to you. Alone."

That sounded ominous. "You're talking to me."

Back to him, head bent over the mixing bowl into which she was throwing this and that, using a sunflower teacup to scoop flour, tipping the baking powder straight from the jar.

"Lindsey—I'm pregnant."

"What? Isabel!"

"Don't shout at me."

"I'm not."

"No, you weren't. Sorry. I just—sorry."

"Oh, Iz. How? I mean—"

"In the usual way. You had a girlfriend—you should know how it works."

"I meant who. I meant—"

"You meant, did I mean to. You meant, who is he and what does he think about it. You meant, what am I going to do."

"Yeah. Sorry."

"We should stop apologizing to one another."

"Okay."

She didn't say anything more, went back to mixing eggs and canola oil and milk together in the cup, just sloshing the amounts any old how. Dumped it in on the flour and rolled oats and whatnot, splashed more milk after it. The bread at the SandWitch and Brew was always great. Maybe she used recipes, there. Maybe she was just some kind of baking genius.

The kettle boiled. Lindsey made the tea. What did you say? Congratulations, or God, I'm so sorry?

"What do you want the oven at?"

"350, thanks."

He poured milk into a couple of big poppy-splashed pottery mugs, present from Carleen, took them and the teapot to the table. Watched as Isabel kneaded the dough together, greased a cookie sheet with a little margarine, slapped the dough on it, patting it down into a couple of thick, misshapen discs. Scored a cross in the top of each and put the sheet in the oven, washed her hands. All without looking at him.

She didn't look pregnant. Just … ordinary Isabel, kid barely out of high school. No mysterious aura of motherhood radiating from her. She'd been working in the SandWitch's kitchen when she was still in school, too young to tend bar. When the SandWitch's baker left them she simply took over that side of kitchen. She'd only turned twenty last month.

Too young to be anyone's mother, surely.

Older than Thomas had been, that first time they met.

Older than Raleigh.

Poured the tea. Good and strong. As if that could help.

Sitting down, Isabel wrapped both hands around her mug, took a long drink, eyes shut. "That's good," she said. Opened her eyes again. Startling, sometimes, how much she looked like Thomas, the fluffy blonde hair—girls weren't wearing their hair short much these days, but she did, weird how saying a boyish cut and a mannish cut made such a difference to how you thought about a woman, some kind of misogyny there—the green eyes, the same bones in the face made feminine. Thomas wouldn't go for purple eyeshadow. But Thomas avoided colours altogether, because he couldn't tell when he got them wrong. Why eyeshadow, purple or otherwise, on a Monday afternoon?

Because she'd been crying before she came over and meant to hide it.

Dutch courage, his mother would say. Girl's version.

"Izzie … "

"Maddie says I should have an abortion."

"Oh." He drank some tea.

"Would you?" she asked.

"Would I ..?"

"Have the baby? If you were me?"

"There's adoption, too. If you don't want—There are lots of people desperate for a child. There's even, what do they call it, open adoption. You could visit, be involved. Like an aunt, maybe."

"Answer the question."

"I don't know. I've never thought about it."

"Liar."

He looked away.

"Of all the men I know, you're the one who would think about. You're the one who has to have thought. How old was your mother?"

"Older than you."

"By how much? A year, two?"

"She was in fourth year."

"So two or three years older than me. Not much. Anyway, she kept you."

Harder to get an abortion back then. The year he was born, that was the year Morgentaler went to the Supreme Court over abortion. Too late for his mother.

Yes. He'd looked it up, in a dark mood. She hadn't had that choice.

"It was a stupid accident," Isabel said. "I forgot a pill, once, I guess a couple of times. That's all. Stupid excuse, but it's what happened. I just forgot. An accident. But at least—if I do have it—I'd be having it for its own sake. I think I'd make a good mother, really. Someday. I just … You know they only had me for Tank."

"For Thomas?"

"He hasn't told you that?"

"No. What do you mean?"

"He'll walk all over you if you give him half a chance and charm you so you don't notice, but you can trust him," Isabel said with satisfaction. "He doesn't tell other people's secrets. They had me for my stem cells. Rolling the dice." Isabel made a dice-throwing gesture, knocked over her mug. Already emptied. "Sorry. Is there more tea?"

"Are you supposed to drink a lot of tea when you're pregnant?"

"How should I know? I've never done this before. Sorry."

Lindsey poured more tea for them both.

"They really had you for your stem cells?"

Thomas never really talked about details much, only, apologizing for nightmares, what it was like being a little kid in the hospital, alone in the night in all the endless thrumming, whispering noise, and thinking how some time you just wouldn't wake up. A recurring nightmare that he died and they took him away with the dirty laundry in one of those hampers on wheels. And Aunt Dodger Smith, who was really his godmother, his mother's favourite teacher from her schooldays but also some kind of cousin of the bishop's, taking early retirement, coming from England to sit reading to him in the hospital or at home, when he couldn't do much but lie around on the couch. Hour after hour, at least in his memory. Tolkien and Lewis, Ransome and Sutcliff, Jansson and Nesbit and Jones and Buckeridge—with oddments of Wodehouse, though he was only seven. Maybe why he had that ghost of an accent, more so than Maddie and James, who had been born in the UK. Things he lent to Lindsey now. *What do you mean you've never read Jennings, it's the funniest thing ever, the fish in the chimney; how can you not know what a Moomin is? You have to read Jones, how'd you ever miss her? Ransome, Ransome was written for kids like you*—and he'd bring them over and read them aloud, bits and pieces, until all Lindsey's reading last fall and winter had been Thomas's most precious books, and yeah, he liked them, and he saw what Dodger had been doing, too, not just classics, but escape, and quiet heroism, and friends, sunlight and forests and lakes, solitary weird children in inexplicable worlds—and adult suffering and endurance. Sutcliff wasn't what he expected in books meant for children or even teens at all. There were at least two of her books ended with the hero's suicide, and one with their being sacrificed. But maybe those were ones Thomas had read later, on his own. Or maybe not. You never knew, with Dodger.

"Yeah. Really. He was going to die and the chances were better with a relative than with anyone else and none of them matched whatever it is they needed to match for a bone-marrow donor. Sometimes people do IVF. They do tests, figure out which—is it a blasto-whatsit?—to implant, which one's going to be right. For umbilical stem cells, I mean, not ones from bone marrow. From the blood in the umbilical cord. Mum and Dad didn't do that, the IVF thing and checking the genes to get the right one. I don't know if people didn't do that back in the nineties or if it was just they didn't like the idea. Mum's a bit quietly religious, you know, Grandad being a bishop and all. But they did decide to get pregnant, to see if they could get lucky, while the doctors went on looking for an unrelated donor. And before that happened I was born and they did get lucky. Yay, me. I'm in Tank's bones. It's weird. I mean, think about it. He's full of my blood. That makes us kind of twins. Or maybe clones."

"Not really."

"A little. But anyway, they wouldn't have had me otherwise. I wasn't supposed to know, but I found out. Well, Maddie told me when she was being a snotty teenager one day. Probably I was being a snotty four-year-old or something."

"They love you."

"Of course they do. I'm not being all bitter. Once I was here, they wanted me, of course they did. They would have wanted me and loved me even if I hadn't been the right baby and even if nobody had ever found the right donor and Thomas had died. That'd be weird. I mean, having a brother I never knew, only existing because of him but never knowing him. But the thing is, they didn't have me because they decided, gosh, what this family really needs is baby number four. It wasn't even, gosh, I feel happy tonight let's go to bed darling whoops hah-hah guess what we forgot, which I bet is how they ended up with Thomas. I mean, I'm pretty sure they meant to stop at two, after Maddie and James. Nice and tidy, one of each. They're very tidy, the old folks. That's why Tank and I worry them so much. We're not. And why they like you so much, Lindsey. You're very tidy, life-wise. They think you're good for him."

Once he figured out precisely what Isabel meant by tidy, he'd decide whether he felt complimented or insulted.

"Do you—what about the baby's father?" What was his name? Tyler? Ricky? They both always seemed to be around, sponging off her, even though they dressed like they had money and one of them drove an Audi. Losers. User losers.

Isabel swirled the tea in her mug, looking down at the table. Just shook her head.

"Does he know?"

Somewhere out there was a man who had a son and didn't know it. Because, "It was my problem, not his," Mom had said. "Not yours either. Jonas is your father in every way that matters."

Which he was. Had been.

But it still meant there was a man out there who didn't know he had a son. And maybe he might like to know.

Lindsey was pretty sure he would, if it were him.

"So," Isabel said. "Would you?"

The original question. He couldn't answer that. He didn't know.

If he'd been a girl, if he and Thomas had had a few hours more, if Thomas had vanished, off with Exit 369 in their disintegrating van, disintegrating lives, and he'd been alone, and pregnant, and not even knowing where to find Thomas again or what he would say if he did … would he have had the baby?

He didn't know. He … thought not. He … did not know.

The rest of his life to be shaped by and for some—thing—growing in him that he hadn't wanted, hadn't planned for. Before he'd ever even found his own life.

Distracting sidethought. What had Mom been expecting to do with her life, before he happened to derail it? Get married to a medical student she met at her cousin's wedding, just like that? He doubted it. B.A. in PolySci, honours. She must have had plans, once. She was a planning kind of person.

Second distracting sidethought. Thomas as a father. Suited him not badly at all.

Take Thomas out of the equation. If it had been Ryan, if …

That was an easier *he thought not.*

Cubes, that imaginary child said. *There's something profound about cubes.*

Why had she kept him? He had never asked his mother that one. Never dared. Suspected, only. In defiance of Gamma. Keeping him to spite her own mother, because she was told outright not to.

The deciding factor? A claim of autonomy over the self? *This at least is mine, my action, my mistake, my choice, and you can't take it from me.*

It was my problem. Not even "the baby". Certainly not "you." It. The problem.

Isabel was nodding her head. Saw the answer he wasn't giving. *No.*

"Well, that's you. This is me." A deep sigh. "It's easier to think what I want, when I hear someone else say it."

"I didn't—"

"You didn't have to."

"It's not something someone else can decide for you, Iz."

"I know."

"In the end. In the end it has to be you. But—what about the father?"

"The father—it was Ricky."

"The guy in commerce?"

"Yeah, him. Tyler—I kind of liked him, but he's gone out west to find work. And Ricky was around and I was lonely and the one you want never sees you, and I didn't want to go hang out at the SandWitch on my own because that's just so pathetic, and all my friends from school have gone off to Toronto or Waterloo or wherever, and you guys were all off in the studio that night doing something, and you know, nobody says men are sluts when they sleep with someone just because. Or forget a pill."

"I'm not—I wouldn't ever think that, Iz."

"Yeah, I know. Sorry. Ricky, he's not a father. He's just … a sperm. He said it was my fault for not being careful and I'd better deal with it and not to expect any help from him. Which is—I can almost see his point. I guess. But—"

"He's still got to share some responsibility, whether he wants to or not. He could have taken precautions too. Should have. For lots of reasons."

"He didn't even say, what are we going to do? He didn't even say, are you okay? Just, you stupid—"

"Don't say it."

"Yeah, the bish wouldn't approve of that sort of language.

You can imagine. It was all accusing me. Like I'd done it on purpose. Like this was 1916 and I was trying to trap him into marrying me, of all the stupid things. Getting knocked up for his money, he said. If he has money, why does he owe me two hundred because he didn't have enough for his rent?"

"Iz—"

"I know, I was stupid."

"You're not stupid. Stop saying that.'

"Gullible."

Couldn't quite contradict that. Must have shown something in his face.

Isabel made a face back at him. "Yeah. So good luck making him help. He'd probably demand a DNA test or something to prove it was his. And I don't want him involved. A guy like that—if that's his attitude, he'll just mess up the child's life anyway."

"Don't make a big mystery out of him, for the child. If you decide you do want ... I mean, when they get the age they start asking, just say, his name was Ricky whoever and he was kind of immature back then, he wasn't ready to be a father, so he went his way and I went mine ... but don't make it some big mystery that they can think all sorts of bad stuff about. I know, right? That, I do know."

"I don't feel like being that fair right now. It wasn't all nice and friendly. He said—a lot more things. About me. I said if he felt that way he could just fuck off, whatever I did I'd do on my own."

And then she was crying. Tears just quietly spilling.

"Hey." Lindsey went around the table. "Isabel ... "

She clutched him, face against his ribs. He put his arms around her, rubbed her back. She sobbed like a child, then, noisy and gulping.

"I'm scared, Lindsey. I thought I was sorting things out, I'd decided what I wanted to do. I was going to start school again in the fall, history, like Dad, but modern, and then law school and now ... "

"It's okay. Whatever you do, it's okay. We're going to be here, whatever you decide. You're not on your own in this. You know that."

Eventually it seemed she was cried out, just holding there, until she sniffled, sniffed, and pushed him away.

"Scones!"

Not burnt at all. Isabel went to wash her face while he served up the goulash. Smelt—amazing. That and the hot scones. He was suddenly ravenous.

"Who else have you told?" he asked.

"Just Maddie. I mean, you're supposed to lean on your big sister for things like that, right? But she was—just, right, this is what you should do, so go do it. No discussion. And it's more complicated. It's not like, help, I don't understand my math homework."

"What about your parents?"

"No. I can't. Not yet. Them, James too. I mean, I think in the end they'd say it's up to me, they wouldn't ever say I made the wrong choice, either way. Whatever they feel they'd choose themselves, if it was them. Even Mum. And Maddie won't, once I do decide. It's just she thinks it'll be easier if she decides for me. Even the bish wouldn't say it was anyone's decision but mine, if he knew. Well, I'm pretty sure he wouldn't, though he'd prefer ... But ... no. I can't tell them, not till I'm certain, and then—maybe not. Depending. I mean, it's a pretty private thing, you know?"

"Thomas?"

"Will you tell him, if I ask you not to?"

"No!"

"Would it be hard not to?"

"Yes," he admitted.

She nodded. "I'll tell him, at least. Once I know what I'm doing, either way, I'll tell him. But not yet."

"Iz, are you sure—about being pregnant, I mean. Really sure? Not just, you know, a false alarm?"

"Oh yes. Six weeks. Morning sickness and everything, which is really fun when you start work as early as I do, in a place full of food smells, I can tell you. I went to the doctor."

"Okay. Look, if you ever need—if you ever want to call me, you can. Anytime. I mean, three in the morning, whenever. You know that. If you need—anything. Someone to hold your hand. Whatever."

"I know that. You're an awfully good brother, Lindsey. Carleen's lucky. So am I. I'm really glad Tank found you."

Washed the dishes, more scone with jam for dessert. Thomas called. It felt weird, saying, yeah, Isabel was over, they'd had supper, maybe they'd watch a movie, no, he wasn't a shoe salesman yet, and not mentioning anything serious at all. Started watching something on Netflix—he shared Isabel's account, luxury he didn't have to give up, not till he had to give up his internet, which was going to happen unless something changed.

Isabel chose; he was never that into superheroes himself, but Lindsey found himself enjoying it, while she fell asleep halfway through, slumped over on his shoulder. Got her to curl up with her head on a pillow, so she didn't get a crick in her neck. Watched the rest of the movie on his own, Isabel's head and her pillow on his lap, because now he needed to see how it ended. Didn't want to walk her back to her Barrack Street apartment so late and in the rain, so he woke her up enough to get her to lie down properly, found her a blanket and a heap of afghans, and took his computer back to his own room.

Wasn't sure he slept that much himself.

Isabel was up and away early, even by his standards, to start the day's bread at the SandWitch and Brew, leaving coffee made and the afghans neatly folded, a purple scarf down the back of the couch, her phone on the kitchen counter, and an umbrella on the hatstand. If she'd been sick, he hadn't heard.

Lindsey took the computer to the kitchen, ate Weetabix in his housecoat, staring at the screen. Streaming BBC3, catching the hourly news so he'd at least hear if the world had blown up. Apparently it hadn't.

Hadn't shut the computer down overnight.

Certificate in pig-care, right.

Hadn't been able to quiet his mind, soothe himself with the rhododendron walk, or Mom's front beds, either, though he'd sketched the latter again, about three in the morning. Crocuses, for the spring. Thinking about other things. Then he had closed all the tabs about rhododendrons.

What remained ...

Results of a search he'd done at about four, just before he fell asleep again at last. An idea, a seed, unfurling.

Outdoors. Not a forest ranger or an earl's pigman, no.

Horticulture certification ... distance education ... landscape design.

"What does that even mean?" Raleigh wanted to know.

"I think ... in real life? Probably being overqualified to

mow other people's lawns," said Lindsey, "and probably ending up mowing other people's lawns."

Making gardens.

Papers everywhere. Notes. So many browser tabs open he kept accidentally closing the ones he wanted, having to retrace his steps.

Lists.

He hadn't gone out for a run. Hadn't even showered.

The lists were ominous. Places. Options. Guelph. St. Lawrence. Ryerson. Course fees. And the Employment Insurance program was not interested in supporting training, something to help you get a better job. Commendable to take a course, federal information said, but if your course interfered with your being able to take some dead-end job, then tough, quit the course. Shouldn't be so much of a problem with a distance-education thing, though.

He could see … maybe. Something.

There were people out there who wanted gardens planned and planted, there had to be. Landscape design? There was always landscape maintenance—his search turned that up too, a lot more small businesses, one-person things, offering that—but surely even that could mean something more than mowing lawns and tidying up driveways with an appallingly noisy, polluting leaf-blower, like the crew Kev's neighbours in the Gorevs' old house had come around every week. That was just "lawn care" and not a lot of care taken in it.

It would be like Thomas's session work—you found out what the client wanted, and maybe you'd make suggestions if it really wasn't going to go well, but basically you'd just get on with it, figure out how to do what they wanted and do it, do it well, put the best of yourself into doing it well and not mind that it wasn't really your style, your thing. You weren't doing it for yourself, except in that satisfaction of competence, of skill. Whatever you thought of the piece, of the design, of the desired end.

And you made your own art, your own name, your own thing aside from what was paying the bills and hoped it would grow, that you'd be able to shift, more and more, over to that.

There'd be people hard to deal with. There'd be bad days, frustrating days. There always would be. But there'd be knowing he was the one who knew what he was doing, too. Being, if not entirely what you wanted to be, on the road to what you knew you could be. That, at least.

Your own master. Old-fashioned phrase. Work that he could just get on and be left alone to do, not constantly having to interact with people.

Maybe?

A hope of that, anyway.

Working for someone else's company—face it, that was the likely start. But only a step along the way, skills to acquire, not a missed dividing of the ways, a dead end swamp. Not a plateau to settle on, unless he let it become one. Not a gravity well to slide down into, trapped. Not if he kept his focus on where he wanted to go.

Believe that. He had to, because if he didn't even work to believe it, he would certainly never be able to find the road before him.

So ...

He wasn't afraid. Wasn't feeling sick.

Excited. As if he needed to begin at once, before the moment could turn grey and crumble around him.

Which was—

He couldn't give it a chance to die.

He texted Thomas.

>*Got an idea. Know what I'm doing. Not how.*

>*Find out how on the way, Thomas sent back almost at once. >What is it?*

>*Tell you when you get home.*

Because he wanted to talk, to show the university and college websites, to have Thomas there beside him looking and saying, yes, yes, yes, of course it makes sense to do that. And he needed to pull everything together, to write more stuff down, to think it through, before it all began to feel impossible: too much, too hard, too burgeoning with defeat, with failure …

No. He could do this.

One huge hurdle to overcome. Except—it wasn't, really.

Email. To his mother.

>*Hi. I think I might need to borrow some tuition money …*

No answer from Mom, but he'd sent it to her personal email, not the inn's, so she might not be checking it more than once a day. Wanted an answer, though, now, now, now. Wanted decision, certainty. If she said no—but she wouldn't. She might drive him crazy, she might think he was crazy, she made him feel like an alien, but she was always there for things like this, because that was the sort of thing she understood. That kind of support for your kids was what you did. Even if they were nearly thirty.

It meant buying textbooks. A computer program for 3-D modelling … Might be included in the course materials … yes. Actual qualifications, not just reading everything he found and thinking he could do this, for himself, if only he had a hundred acres and freedom … Why hadn't he looked this up earlier, years ago, found this was a choice, something people did? An art, a skill, a career.

Maybe he hadn't been ready to find it, then.

Still not dressed and it was almost noon. The doorbell. Isabel, grabbing a break and come back for her phone; the SandWitch was only a few blocks away, on Clarence. He went down barefoot. Couldn't see anyone in the coloured glass side-lights, had to open the door.

"Oh," he said. "Hi."

Not Isabel, and it made no difference that he had on pyjama pants and his housecoat was securely tied—he'd been sleeping without a T-shirt and he was all exposed and mock-able arms and legs, cranefly.

"Hey, Lindsey."

Megan. With a puppy on a leash. He cinched his house-coat tighter, tried to pull the collar together. Hiding all the skin he could. "What's wrong?" Because she wouldn't show up unless she wanted something.

"Can I come in?"

"I'm not dressed yet."

"That's okay, I won't stay long." And she was walking in, and what could he do, physically bar the way? The puppy wove back and forth, nose down, white-tipped tail straight up like a little flag. Megan lifted it and clamped it under her arm without looking at it, stumping up the stairs. She always walked like that, as if each leg were an effort, trudge trudge trudge.

Gamma walked like that and always had, even before she was old and arthritic. Like she had a grudge against the earth under the feet.

"*Like a troll,*" Raleigh whispered. "*Bones of stone.*"

"*Shut up.*"

He followed, impatient, pushed by and opened the door for her, before she could just walk in like she had a right. The puppy squirmed, trying to reach its nose to him. A little hound, black and white and a bit of rusty brown. Cute. Pink tongue swiped at the hand he offered.

Megan waited in the way on the doormat, as if she expected him to offer to take her coat. He didn't.

"Oh," she said then. "You're living with someone? That's new. Anyone I know?" She flicked a finger at Isabel's scarf, draped on the hat-stand. Smirking. Was she smirking?

"It's Thomas's," he said. Could be. The scarf collection, like the car and the Netflix account, was a shared resource. Which was how Thomas had played one notable evening wearing bright lipstick pink silk around his neck, to Frankie's great amusement. Well, whatever, he'd said. He'd thought it was maybe orange.

"You really shouldn't have taken it then," Anicky had said. "There's no excuse for looking like you're hunting deer."

Megan had met Thomas, run into them at the SandWitch not long after they found one another. It'd been late; Lindsey'd been a bit drunk. Enough to not feel awkward seeing her, only leaning back into Thomas's arm and, they must have been more than a bit drunk, cuddled up, a leg around him too, chin against his shoulder, both of them crammed into the corner of a booth, the band and hangers-on all there, noisy and cheerful—Jon the sound guy's birthday and Isabel had made a caramel and apple cheesecake—and he'd introduced Megan as "She was in my lab," nothing more, but she'd said, "We used to be engaged," and Frankie had snorted, choking on her ginger ale, needing to be thumped on the back, going red.

And Megan had looked hurt. She had retreated to the girls she had come in with, whispering together. And he'd protested frantically, they'd *never* been engaged.

"You upgraded, anyway," Thomas had said. But Thomas knew all about her by then.

"Thomas? Oh, that weird guy you were making out with in the bar that time. The actor or whatever. He's still around?"

"He's not an actor."

"He looks like one. Very … " She shrugged. "I wouldn't have thought you were his type. And going on like that— you'll really get yourself in trouble. You need to be careful in public."

"It wasn't public, it was the SandWitch." And anyone who started that sort of trouble would find themselves out on their ear, when all two hundred pounds and six foot four of Stefan came surging out of the kitchen. "What do you want, Megan?"

"I need a favour."

"Of course she does. If it involves being her date so she can go to a wedding, lock yourself in the bathroom till she leaves. And go put a shirt on."

Lock Raleigh in the bathroom, till he'd done with this. He wasn't leaving Megan unsupervised in his living room. She nosed into things.

Screensaver hadn't kicked in yet. Lindsey closed the laptop. "What sort of a favour?"

She plunked the puppy down. It wandered off, trailing its leash. Disappearing into the plants by the gable window.

Oh. No.

"I'm going back to Winnipeg and—"

"Is this about your dog?"

"I can't take her with me."

"Why not?"

"Well, I'm flying."

"People do fly dogs."

"And our apartment's really small."

"And mine's not? Who's we?"

"You've lost already," Raleigh said. *"Don't argue. You don't care about 'we'. Just tell her you can't."*

"I'm engaged. I've got a job with the city. Mosquito mitigation awareness."

"Good, congratulations."

"Poor guy. I wonder if he knows about it. I wonder if he even knows she's coming."

"Raleigh, shut up."

"And Logan works long days; he's a teacher."

"Most people work long days, even people with dogs."

"Yes, but—"

"I just need someone to look after her a bit."

"I can't, Megan. My lease says no pets." He had no idea whether it did or not. No parrots and no storing coal on the balcony he didn't have, he did remember seeing that, finding it a bit perplexing.

"Well, you've got worms, don't you? I remember Amber said you had worms."

"I bet the puppy does."

"Raleigh!"

"Compost worms aren't pets," he protested.

"Please, Lindsey. You're the only one I haven't tried, and if you can't, she's going to have to go to the shelter."

"If you can't look after her and don't want to keep her, then you should take her to them, so someone who does want a dog can adopt her. They probably don't have any trouble finding homes for puppies."

"Well, yes, but they'll try to make me feel guilty."

"She should feel guilty. Poor little thing."

"That's not helpful."

"And I think there's a fee. I could try some kind of online ad, but there's no time. I'm leaving tomorrow."

"I notice she's not pretending any more that she's coming back for it. Are you paying attention?"

"Where did you get it, anyway? The shelter?"

"Oh no! She's a purebred."

"What's that got to do with it?" Raleigh muttered. Over by the plants, following the puppy. There were boxes of books over there too that it would be good she didn't either chew on or pee beside.

"One of the secretaries at work, her sister's dog had puppies. She's a purebred beagle, only not registered of course. This was the last one and they were going to—well, nobody wanted her and they couldn't keep her. I only paid fifty dollars. They were selling them for a hundred."

"I'm not paying you for her."

"Well, no. The crate wasn't cheap, though."

What crate? "What have you done with my bed? If you're flying—"

"That old thing? I threw it out."

"You threw out my bed? It was my bed!"

"Well, you left it behind."

"I was being nice! I didn't want to leave you sleeping on the floor!"

"I know, you're such a nice person, Lindsey. That's why I

thought of you right away." She reached up and straightened the collar of his housecoat, folding it back. Brushing it off as if he had crumbs, which was possible. Hand over his chest. He flinched back.

"Don't." Disarrayed the collar, wrapping the neck tighter again.

"Silly. It's not like I haven't seen you naked, Lindsey." Her smile was more of a smirk. Enjoying that she'd made him flinch.

Cranefly, she called him. All arms and legs. It had some-how never sounded affectionate.

"Troll," Raleigh said. "Vampire troll. And I bet the boy-friend said no to the dog. Awfully last-minute, if she's leaving tomorrow. Better come make sure it's not eating anything poison-ous, Lindsey."

Lindsey went after the puppy. Feeling shaky. Angry. Scared. Which was ridiculous.

Makayala has him backed up into the corner of the stairs at Gamma's house. Easter in Dartmouth. Pinching, hard, over his ribs, through his shirt. The torture game, she calls it. It happened a lot over that last summer in Pugwash, and again at Christmas, but this time it goes on and on.

"Let me go," he whispers, frantic, trying to push her off, wanting to escape without drawing the attention of anyone else, and she says, he has to take it, if he can stand it for thirty pinches she'll let him go.

"If you cry, Spiderlegs, you're a crybaby," she says. "A girly crybaby, and if you yell I'll cry and tell Mom you were doing *things* to me, things like your real Dad did to your Mom."

"He didn't." That makes him mad, mad enough to hit and

he's going to, but she keeps whispering.

"And they'll take you away. They take boys like that away and lock them, they'll say you have something wrong in your head, everybody knows it and they'll lock you up."

He doesn't hit her. He stands there and lets her pinch him. Up to fifty, his eyes tearing despite himself, and finally she gets bored. "Crybaby," she says, "Little girl. Spiderlegs. Spiderfingers." And she goes away. He has red welts that turn to black bruises, sore all up and down his ribs. He has to get undressed for bed in the living room, where the boys are sleeping in sleeping bags, Aunt Sandra's family with Darren and Zack there from Cape Breton, his back turned so they don't see.

Raleigh sees. The next morning, Easter Sunday when they've all been sent out into the backyard, sunny but cold, barely spring. Lindsey's sitting on the deck trying to read, nose running from the cold, fingers chill and stiff but Gamma wants everyone out from underfoot. The younger ones are playing soccer. Makayla and Julie stand under the apple tree sniggering over something Makayla is whispering. Raleigh walks up to Makayla, punches her in the stomach. Hard. Saying nothing.

She runs inside, wailing, and then throws up on the kitchen floor where Gamma and Mom and all the aunts are cooking dinner.

Lindsey is hotly glad. Would hug Raleigh, if they were a hugging kind of family, which they're not.

Gives him, later, his best one of the adventuring guys, a curly-haired warrior girl on horseback. Doesn't say why. Doesn't need to.

At Gamma's it's Mom and Aunt Tanya raising their voices at one another, Gamma saying *someone's* having a very bad influence on Raleigh while looking at Lindsey, and Dad asking sternly, why would he do something so bad, he knows better than that and it isn't like him. Raleigh looking sullen, looking at his feet, but still not answering, and Lindsey saying nothing, because if he says anything against Makayla she'll tell lies and he's terrified and as ashamed as if he's really done the kinds of things she says she'll say, and he knows Gamma and Aunt Tanya will believe her over him because they think he's bad anyway, bad with something wrong with him. But finally he mutters, wretchedly, feeling like he might throw up too, "Dad—" and Raleigh jerks his head up then and says, "Don't you dare." So Lindsey looks at the floor in silence, too.

Raleigh has to eat his Easter dinner alone, sitting in the spare room at a wobbly old tray on legs thing. No dessert, which is a chocolate pie with whipped cream that Aunt Sandra makes for special occasions. Nobody's allowed to talk to him. Lindsey picks at some turkey, slowly destroying everything on his plate without eating it, until he's allowed to leave the table. Dad's watching him. Stay downstairs, he's told by Mom. Leave Raleigh to think about how horribly he's behaved.

Makayla seems to have a pretty good appetite.

He sneaks upstairs, goes to sit against the closed spare-room door. Scratching at it, watching down the stairs in case anyone comes. Raleigh comes to sit against the other side. Fingers searching through the gap beneath, in the pile of the carpet. They just touch.

"Thanks," Lindsey says.

Raleigh says, "I wish I'd killed her."

Dad comes then, and Lindsey isn't keeping a good lookout; Dad walks softly and they don't hear, they're still whispering, fingers still together under the door. Boys, he says, and he opens the door, carefully, not to mash Raleigh, who is scuttling back. He doesn't sound mad any more. They sit on the floor, backs against the spare-room bed, the three of them in a row, Dad in the middle.

"Is there anything you want to tell me, in private?"

Silence. Then, "No," Raleigh says.

Dad sighs. "Alright," Dad says. "But there will be no more fighting with Makayla. Whatever she does, whatever she says, you turn your backs and walk away, and you come to me."

"Okay," Raleigh says, and "Okay," Lindsey whispers. But they know they won't.

They're supposed to stay overnight again, spend Monday driving back to New Brunswick, stopping at the Kavanagh grandparents' outside Hampton for a second Easter dinner, but Dad loads them all up into the car once the adults have had their after-dinner coffee, Carleen crying because it isn't fair, she wasn't the one who was hitting and she and Zack and Darren and Piper were having a soccer tournament. They drive across two provinces home.

They spend a lot more Thanksgivings and Christmases and Easters with the Kavanagh grandparents after that. It's pretty quiet. Dad's only got the one brother. Maybe Mom's upset, because the Quinlans make a much bigger thing of get-togethers like that, Lindsey can't tell. Maybe she's secretly relieved, some pressure removed. The Kavanagh cousins are alright, all three older than him, friendly the way you are to younger kids who aren't pests, even though the boys, Roger and Jack, are teens and the girl, Sam, is pretty much grown-up, already in university. She gives him and Raleigh her old portable stereo, because she's got a better one for her birthday.

They start listening to Dad's music in their room. It's the

beginning of something important.

It's kind of embarrassing, though, at that age, for your younger brother to be your hero, the one who avenges you. Who would have saved you, if only he'd come sooner.

If only he, someone, anyone, had been there, had come sooner …

As if Megan could be any physical threat. He was a foot taller than her, and if she was heavier than she'd been—a fair bit—so was he, in a healthier way. Because it was embarrassing being so scrawny when Thomas was so fit and Anicky could beat him arm-wrestling without breaking a sweat. He'd gotten serious about the push-ups, bought some dumbbells, exercise that wasn't just running, which had always been just—running, nothing to do with keeping in shape.

Of course, Anicky could still beat him arm-wrestling.

Life advice: don't arm-wrestle the drummer.

The puppy was chewing up a fallen camphor leaf. Not really poisonous, not one leaf, but not something meant to be taken internally by small puppies, either. And the baby amp Thomas had brought over when they'd been—not so much dating, but just, together, a thing irrevocable, opposite poles of a magnet, for only a month—that sat over here too, and a cable, all too chewable, that. He scooped the critter up. She writhed around happily in his hands, snuggled up, cradled against his side. Plunged her nose into the plush folds of his housecoat and sneezed. He sighed. Megan wasn't a threat, some schoolyard bully. Just a pest, needy and self-deluding, and only as much of a vampire as he gave her power to be.

"Didn't I used to tell you that?" Raleigh asked.

Female meant more expensive; spaying cost more than neutering, some part of him thought. And beagle—really? Those were pretty big paws for such a small puppy.

"How long have you had her?" he asked.

"Oh, only a couple of weeks. I don't think she'll pine for me or anything."

"You knew you were going out west and you went and bought a puppy from some—"

"Don't make her mad, Lindsey."

"Are you okay, Lindsey? You're not usually like this."

"Like what?"

"She means, you aren't just shutting up and going along with whatever she says. I miss having a dog around."

"We take Scooter and Scout for walks every Sunday."

Dinner with the Parks and Gorevs, alternating between suburban Bayridge and wooded Nicholson's Point on the lake on the way to Bath. Both families' dogs included as a matter of course. Ancient tradition. Also a chance for them and Iz to do their laundry for free, whichever household they gathered at.

"I don't think that actor guy is good for you."

"It's nothing to do with him."

"Have you ever tried meditation?"

"Megan, the point is—" He forgot what the point was. The puppy seemed to have fallen asleep. "Look, do you even want this dog?"

"She is rather sweet," Raleigh said, sounding like Thomas.

Megan looked away. "Her brother-in-law was going to shoot her. She said. The secretary. Because she was the last one and nobody wanted her. What else could I do? She's an awful lot of work and like I said, we've only got an apartment and we're both going to be working, and—" She shrugged. "I'm more of a cat person, honestly. And I paid fifty dollars to save her already. And bought a crate, because I couldn't have her running around making a mess everywhere. Dogs are so needy."

"How old is she?"

"That's just playing for time, Lindsey. Do you think your common sense is going to kick in?"

"Eight—no, I guess ten weeks old."

"Has she had her shots? Has she been wormed?"

"Well, I've been pretty busy getting ready to move. And she doesn't have worms."

"Puppies always have worms."

"What's Thomas going to say?"

"He likes dogs."

"He likes Scooter and Scout, and neither of them are tiny little chewing machines that're going to pick the Paul Reed Smith to teethe on."

"Oh God no."

Had he said that aloud?

"Lindsey? Lindsey, please?"

And Megan was going all teary. She did that at will, he remembered. Whenever he tried to resist anything, her eyes would water up and she'd do this weird little pouting thing with her lips and full cheeks that she must think made her look childlike and vulnerable and wounded, but only gave her a goldfish-face, and what followed was always some quaver-voiced explanation of how unfair and unreasonable he was being about whatever it was, whatever assertion of self he was daring, how much he was hurting her, how selfish he was, how thoughtless, how much he had embarrassed her in front of the others …

"This is not a good idea. Though a dog might be good for you."

"No," Lindsey said. "Don't, Megan. That won't work any more. But fine, I'll take her off your hands. I need that crate you're talking about and anything else you've got for her, and you don't get to show up in a month saying you've changed your mind. And I'm not paying you for any of it. You threw out my bed!"

"Don't keep going on about the bed. You're so obsessive. That's why I knew it was never going to work out, you and me." But all trace of tears and trembling lip had vanished. "And don't be such a bully. Is your actor-guy into being pushed around or something? Come get the crate. It's in the car."

"You go down. I'll put some clothes on."

"Are you sure you're okay? I mean, it's kind of a self-care thing, you know, taking the time to get showered and dressed."

"I was working on something."

Lindsey herded her out the door, locked it as soon her footsteps were stamping down the stairs. Unclipped the puppy's leash—the collar had heart-shaped rhinestones and was too tight. Looked like a cat collar. He took that off too, rubbed her neck. She wriggled happily, mouthed his fingers. He shut her in the bathroom with a towel to snuggle in, the place she could do least harm unsupervised, pulled on hasty clothes and went down, bare feet in duckboots. Megan had parked across the street, had her car's back door open but was waiting for him to wrestle the tightly-wedged crate out. Not what he'd been expecting, one of those plastic kennels, but a big folded-up wire cage with a thin tray of galvanized steel to go inside as a floor. Well, that would be good, given how the apartment was all carpet and he'd better go scrounge some newspapers right off—Stefan and Michael had a subscription and lived over their pub. Take Isabel's phone back, too.

The tray smelt of floor-cleaner.

"How's her housebreaking coming?"

"She's pretty young."

"Well, you have to start." Before ten weeks, he was pretty certain.

"There hasn't been time."

"So she's just—she thinks the cage is the right place? Megan, do you know anything about dogs?"

"You've gone awfully misogynistic since you took up with that actor."

"He's not an actor and I'm not. What did I even say?"

"You've been doing nothing but criticize me since I got here. As if I don't know anything."

"What's that got to do with misogyny? I'd hate to hear what Frankie would say about her."

"I—okay, fine, I'm sorry. Are you coming up?"

"No! Don't invite her. She'll be wanting coffee next."

"No," Megan said, leaning out, holding a reusable shopping bag. She already had her seatbelt on. "I've got to take the car to the woman who's buying it. Here. Food to get started with. She's very sweet, really."

"Yes, we've established that," Raleigh said.

"You said it, too."

"Shut up, Lindsey."

"Thanks." Lindsey slung the bag from his wrist. "Um, yeah. I hope things work out, out west."

"We're very happy," Megan said. Too much defiance? "Thanks. Give me a call if you're ever in Winnipeg."

"Right." He shoved the rear door closed with his hip, clutching the cage. Megan drove off without waiting for him to cross the street.

Afraid he was going to change his mind?

"Oh great," Raleigh said. "We have a dog. Do you know what dogfood costs? Good dogfood, because you can't feed her that supermarket junk."

"I can guess what vets cost."

"Going to call Thomas and break the gladsome tidings?"

"Gladsome tidings? Don't talk like Thomas."

"You hang around with weirdos, you have to expect it be catching. Are you going to call?"

"Tonight. He'll probably be in the studio. Right now I need to—"

Assemble the wire box. Big enough for a medium-large adult dog, which would be good if she she grew to fit her feet. Beagle—no. Surely her ears weren't the right shape? More like Scooter's. Maybe she was actually more of a Lab?

No. He wasn't doing that, pick her looks to bits to figure out what she was. Shades of Gamma. "What about Lebanese? Maybe he's Lebanese."

Of course with dogs it was different.

Make another list. Newspapers. Proper dogfood; it was all yellow-label canned stuff clinking in the bag, no dog of his was going to be that desperate, and bad for her teeth, too, Dad had always said. A proper collar—dog-licence, that meant city hall?—martingale collar for walking, a leash that a puppy couldn't bite through with one chomp. Some kind of chew-toy. Biscuits for training. Dog pick-up bags. Maybe an old towel or two for a blanket for now, he must have some that were getting thin. They'd have to be washed a lot at first. A thrift-store bedsheet to make that cage into more of a den, so she could feel safe and quiet …

Find a vet. Make an appointment, Megan was such a—

Let her go. Don't give her headspace. She wasn't his problem any more and she was leaving town and he'd never have to see her again.

"I think her name is Bunny," Raleigh said.

"What? Why?"

"She looks like her name is Bunny."

"Seriously? I was thinking—I don't know, Lucy or something."

"Bunny."

"Hey, Bunny," Lindsey said, opening the bathroom door, squatting down there, wiggling his fingers. "Bunny, come! Good Bunny! Let's go look at the backyard and then you can sleep in your nice box while I go do some shopping."

"Don't forget to put socks on," Raleigh said.

/THREE/

Mood:
Adam Lambert, "Better Than I Know Myself"
Honeysuckle and hot earth

Hot June evening, and Bowie was singing "Rock 'n' Roll Suicide." A pedestal fan going at either end of the flat, windows open after having them shut and curtained all day in a futile effort to keep the heat out. Bunny had temporarily given up trying to eat the furniture. She was sprawled on the floor, stretched out, offering her spotted belly to the moving air. Thomas had pretty much done the same, wearing nothing but cut-offs. Even Lindsey, who seemed to have a thing about exposing his legs, had resorted to cargo shorts when he got back from the garden centre. He was draped sideways and shirtless over the armchair, eyes closed, a sheen of sweat on his skin, dark-tanned arm hanging down, empty bottle of Heineken by his hand. Decorative, but Thomas wasn't going to tell him so, spoil it with some self-conscious coiling-up. Claimed the couch for himself. Settling in for the evening, now. Isabel had been around for supper; they'd walked her back to her place even though it was perfectly safe daylight. Lin had gone very protective, which was sort of sweet. At least he hadn't taken up knitting.

125

Mum had. And Maddie. And Jessie, James's fiancée. Mysterious female urges, apparently. Hadn't stricken Dodger yet, thank goodness. Even Lindsey's mum down in NB was crocheting some little baby afghan or something.

Late November, early December baby. He'd be an uncle. He felt too young to be an uncle. Lindsey seemed to be really getting into it, though. Well, he'd been the first one Iz told, after Maddie. Weeks before the rest of them. They'd been on the road, New York, Pennsylvania, Ohio, last half of April, all through May, but still … there were phones, there was fast-food parking lot wifi and email …

He'd wondered if he felt hurt by that, himself, when he found out. That she'd turned to Lindsey and not him. Decided that he didn't. Of course she'd felt that Lindsey might have—well, an understanding of the thing that none of the rest of them did. He could see that. It was actually—it felt good, didn't it? That Lindsey had become that, to Isabel. Family. Someone to have your back when the hard decisions had to be made. Weirdly, it was Kev who'd been most upset. That Iz was pregnant. That she'd told Lindsey and not him. Well, he'd known her all her life, of course. The baby sister he'd never had. And he and Jon and Frankie had been all for going to find that jerk Ricky and—No, Thomas had said. Because violence wasn't Kev, shouldn't be, not at all, and himself, he'd been too long hanging around with people who really did haul off and get physical when they were angry and it didn't fix a damn thing and would just make trouble for Isabel, for the band.

Lindsey put at least twenty dollars he couldn't spare into a Twinings Prince of Wales tea-tin on the counter every Saturday night. Meant for one of those expensive baby necessities in the end: stroller, car-seat, something.

"Another beer?" Thomas asked.

"Is there any?"

"I stocked up." He'd had to. Lindsey had stopped buying things like that, which was fair enough, but the weather demanded it.

"'Kay."

Bunny only opened her eyes, thumped her tail and shut them again, didn't pop up to trot after him to the kitchen in case food was happening. That's how hot it was. Cooler outside now, but the students from both flats below had claimed the backyard, some kind of lethargic party going on.

Lindsey was watching, when he came back. Sat up cross-legged in the chair to take the opened beer.

"What's wrong?"

"Nothing."

"Thomas ... "

"Nothing's wrong. Not—wrong."

"But?"

"How can you tell?"

"You're not babbling."

"Unfair. It's too hot to talk." Set his own bottle on the floor by the couch, went to the bedroom—door always closed now, puppies forbidden, and another fan on the floor pointed at the bed—to grab a guitar. Spruce-top Yamaha classical from the seventies, a generation older than he was, his first good guitar. A sound like warm sunlight. The other one over here right now was the Telecaster, not something he used much with the Pilgrim Road—his Strats and the PRS Custom 24 were his main babies—but he was fond of it. They'd been places together. Well, had times together. Big investment for a kid in grade nine, a Squier Tele had been. But Bunny wasn't keen on live music and hated anything involving an amp worse. She'd prefer Dowland.

Headed back to the couch.

Security blanket? Not really. He just needed something to do with his hands.

"So—what?"

"Not you, Lin. Don't always think that, okay?" A-major scale running up and down the neck, into "The King of Denmark's Galliard," memorized long ago. Stuck near the end and faked it, made a face at Lindsey, who heard what he'd done, made a sceptical face back. Drove Lin crazy, that he would, that he even could, sit and play something to himself while listening with half an ear to something else. Went back to scales. Helped him think. Clunk and whirr from the stereo, disc changing, and Krown Imperial began singing "Never forever."

"Sorry. I know, I—." Lindsey ducked his head. Took a drink, not looking at him. "Sorry. But is there—is there something bothering you?"

"Not anything wrong, exactly. Just … Heavy thinking."

"Don't sprain something."

"There's … a decision I need to make."

"Oh."

"It's not about you. It's not about us, alright? Don't—" Thomas shook his head. Just tell him. See what he thought. "Tasha Meyer wants me to tour the States with her. Six months. A few weeks off here and there but pretty much six months."

"Seriously?"

"Yeah."

She'd had him for most of the tracks on her new album, which had gotten hung up in production a while, nothing to do with him. He'd almost forgotten over the winter. Written two of the songs with her, even, and one of those was coming out as the lead single. Early August. Driving, dancey summer song, bittersweet teen love, the whole shebang. "Sweetest Summer Lie." Meyer and Gorev. Which sounded like a firm of lawyers, actually. He was—

Cautiously optimistic. This time, this time, this time. If the radio, if the CBC, could get itself interested in anything but The Tragically Hip.

"That's ... big. Isn't it? When's that album coming out, anyway?"

"September. Not your thing, I know, but ... "

"Too pop. No bones."

"Music with bones in. Lindsey's picks ... You could do a blog. Reviews."

"I was thinking of that. Plants, though. Things about gardens. Or, I don't know, urban composting. Something like that for now. Kind of, advance advertising, for when I get the business going."

The litter of books around the azalea on the coffee table wasn't all the usual garden magazines and novels: things on starting a small business, on bookkeeping ... Sue Park's recommendations, mostly. Uncle George's eldest, no interest in cooking. She'd done accounting, while Laura mixed computer science and business courses and Emily went off to Niagara to do Culinary Arts. Closest thing Strange Pilgrim Road had to management, Sue and Laura, between them. Keeping it all in the family, as it were. He should put Laura onto his session work, yeah, she could handle it; she'd been growing with them, quit her kitchen-store manager job, returning to kitchen work for her father in order to have the freedom to wrangle Strange Pilgrim Road, back when that hardly gave her pocket money. He'd give her all the contacts he had and throw her in to sink or swim.

Blog. Lindsey, behind that safe shield, talking to the world? Next thing you knew he'd be on Twitter.

"Do it. Ask Laura if you want design advice—she's the website genius. Kev can probably lend you a decent camera if you need one." A few ringing plucked chords. Bunny got up, martyred, and retreated into her box.

"I'm going to. Tasha Meyer. When did you find that out?"

"Few days ago."

"You didn't say."

"No."

"It would be—good, wouldn't it? Decent money?"

"More than decent."

"And—she's getting pretty big, isn't she?"

"Juno last year, not that that means anything. Especially in the States. But yeah."

"That sounds good, then."

"But?" he prompted. Push. "Come on, Lin. Tell me."

"Teen—teen pop's not quite your thing, either. I mean, for the long term."

Thomas wrapped himself around the guitar, cheek to the neck. "I know."

"What happens to the band?"

"Yeah."

"Oh."

Thomas remembered he had a beer. Bottle sweating, warming.

"You're playing that Mud Festival out in Glenburnie, end of August."

"And isn't that going to bomb. The only music thing any-one can talk about for August is The Hip's concert. But no, we can do the festival either way, Tasha's tour doesn't start till October."

"Were you guys going to Germany again?"

"Looking that way. Kev's been talking to those guys we toured with last year. Cult Snakes. Germany, France. The Netherlands, too. Crash on all Kev's Dutch cousins … That's the plan, anyway. Tentatively."

"So if you're off with Tasha Meyer … "

"And we need to get another album out. We do. Kev'll pro-duce it again. Take a month or two, shut ourselves up in the cellar … Anicky wants to try recording a drum track in my folks' boathouse, which'll be—interesting. There will be mut-tering, I expect. Kev will resist, his precious electronics near all that water."

"They can't go to Europe without you."

"They can't—do anything, without me. We're a business. I mean, a band doesn't look like one but it has to be if it's going to survive. And it's mine and Kev's. The Bells are … we're all the band, but without me and Kev, it's not Strange Pilgrim Road. They could be something else without me. Not Pilgrim Road."

"So if you go with Tasha … everyone's kind of left strand-ed. The band's on hiatus."

"If I go with Tasha, it's over. We can't keep Anicky and Frankie tied up like that. They're good. Anicky's getting no-ticed. She could go back to Toronto, go it on her own. Start another band, she and Frankie—they could. They don't need to hang out in Kingston. They're here for me. I dragged them here, talked them into my band, my dream. Anicky had a good job she quit to do this. I can't ask them to put their careers on hold while I go off and chase money. I've no right. And Kev … "

"Kevin needs you," Lindsey said.

It's three a.m. on a February night when Thomas's phone chimes. Wrong number or something bad. Ronnie wanting him to deal with Dan. But it's a 613 number and he had it memorized in childhood before ever his own. God, not—the thought's not even there in any coherent form, just the sick fear—something, someone—even as he's answering.

"Tank … "

Kevin's voice. So is it Uncle Henry, his parents—it would be James, Maddie calling if it was his parents, except they're far away, Kevin might have bad news first, Kevin would—

"What's happened?"

Not an email, a text, between them since Christmas. Seems they've nothing to say, any more. Nothing that they're willing to, anyway.

Two years since Kev's mum died, three since she first fell ill, just when they were leaving high school, about to head off into the bright expanding world. They'd been going places, he and Kev. Three years, he's been in Toronto with Exit 369.

Cancer. Of course. Isn't it always? He was in Toronto for most of it, but back off and on, as Elke van der Meer was being eaten away, by the disease, by the treatments. Kevin gave up everything they had planned, the moment she came home with that news. Did an electronics course at St. Lawrence instead, living at home, helping look after her, working at Park Electronics, helping keep things going. He's been looking after his father, too, though nobody realizes it at the time. Nobody sees what's beneath the surface. Henry Park has always been a shy, self-contained man. Quiet. Always there at Elke's side through it all. Strong. Coping. Underneath he's going quietly down as his wife sinks, never crying out for help, never a hand groping above the dark water swallowing him. And then she's gone.

For Thomas, she was Aunt Elke. She taught him piano; she taught him theory.

But she was Kevin's *mum,* and there's no way Thomas can understand the depths of that loss, that rent in the fabric of the world.

Mum and Dad, Uncle George and his wife Jung-ah keep an eye on the bereaved father and son but nobody understands just how bad it is because you simply don't talk about those things in the Park family. Even the younger generation doesn't.

Even to your brother, your best friend.

When they talk, this past couple of years, it's been … trivialities. Like strangers. His fault? Kevin's? He doesn't know.

Three a.m.

"Kevin," he says, into the phone's silence. "Kev, are you okay?"

And Kev says, voice cracking, "No."

And then a rush. He can't, he's saying. He can't do this any more, he's so tired, he's so afraid, come home, just come home, I need help. I can't do this any more.

Thomas is used to late night incoherence, Dan when the kick's wearing off, Dan when he's mixing vodka and who knows what, Dan gone weepy and apologizing again, promising he'll sort himself out, promising who knows what, doesn't matter because it won't happen and Thomas has given up caring anyhow. Equally incoherent, Ronnie bawling him out, why can't he keep Dan out of trouble. And after the last shouting match and Dan taking a swing at him with Mitch's bass—which being sober he'd ducked and André had caught or there'd have been murder done, of him by Dan if that blow had connected with his head, of Dan by Mitch if the bass had been damaged—nobody should be thinking that anything to do with Dan was Thomas's job any more …

Incoherent. But not drunk, not anything else, not Kev.

Breaking.

Exit 369 has a gig that coming night but Thomas is on the first bus east in the morning, before the sun's even up. Brandon will have to play lead whether he wants it or not; Ronnie will freak but that's what he gets the hah, big bucks for, herding cats, wrangling his brothers and the rest of them, his dreams of managing the next Toronto breakout.

Aunt Dodger picks him up at the bus station. Dodger's not going to fuss like Mum and Dad before he's figured things out. If you need to call someone at 5 a.m. to say, bus station at nine, it's an emergency I think, and be met with a thermos of tea and a homemade muffin and only the practical questions asked, like, 'Where are we going?' Dodger's the one. She doesn't wait out in her truck, though, at the Parks', where he has his own key and doesn't bother knocking, afraid of—of no one answering. Wanders in after him, in her felt-lined rubber boots and patched jeans and grubby barn coat, because she'd had to feed the hens before she met the bus, and the donkeys, and hadn't bothered to change.

Uncle Henry's still in bed. Kev's curled up on the couch in yesterday's clothes, unshaven, dark hollows under his eyes, Scout coiled up on the floor nearby. She doesn't run to greet them. Thumps her tail and makes a little squeaking noise.

Like she's on guard, on duty, and doesn't think she should leave Kev's side.

Has Kevin moved since he called Thomas? Did he look that bad at Christmas?

To the latter, yes. Almost.

Running the business more or less single-handed, trying to keep it afloat, pay the bills, keep track of all the adult things you're supposed to grow into, mortgage, banking, bills, accounts, bookkeeping, payroll, taxes ... making his father shower and eat. Zombied with exhaustion, with grief and worry and overwork. Henry just seems to want to fade away, passively follow Elke into some place where there's no pain, no feeling.

Kev's all but broken.

And Thomas didn't ask. He didn't say a damned thing, because he had problems too. Blind and selfish git.

"Right, then," Dodger says, as Kevin sits up and Thomas slides down beside him, arms around him. More than a day since he's showered. Smells, not dirty-bad, but stale. Not fastidious Kev, not at all. "Tea." She heads for the kitchen. Scout, holding herself relieved of duty, licks Thomas's hand—good, you outrank me, you take over now—and trots after her.

Dad hasn't spoken in days, Kev says. He won't even go in to the shop any more, he won't go for a walk, he won't take Scout out, he won't go to the doctor, and "I can't—I can't do everything any more, Tank, I can't do anything, I can't, I'm so tired, I want Mamma." And he's crying, sobbing, on Thomas's shoulder.

They all end up in the kitchen. Scout is out in the fenced back yard, dirty snow, no-one's been picking up after her.

Dirty dishes piled in the sink, the dishwasher full. Drifts of fluffy black dog-fur rolling in the corners. The bread's mouldy. Dodger's making porridge instead. The garbage smells.

"I can't," Kev says again. "There's too much, I can't, and he won't even get up half the time and just stares at the TV when he does, it doesn't matter what's on, he'll watch the Weather Network for hours—" Head buried in his arms on the kitchen table, shaking. "I just can't, any more."

"It's okay, Kev. It's okay." It manifestly isn't. "We're here now. And dishes I can do. That's a start. You go brush your teeth, take a shower, and then get your dad up, okay? Everything'll be a bit easier on a full stomach. Call and say you can't make it in today. Or just close. Tell what's his name to put up a closed due to illness apology. We'll sort things out."

Turns out both employees are gone. One Kevin fired for too often not bothering to turn up, someone who'd decided he wasn't going to treat a kid of twenty-two as his boss. The other just left for something better and anyhow there didn't seem enough work for two any more.

But too much for one, though whether they can pay the rent on the store next month …

"You and young Kevin get Henry to a doctor," Dodger says, once Kevin's dragged himself upstairs. "Today. Tell them it's an emergency. Trust me, twenty years a head teacher, you learn an emergency doesn't always mean bleeding on the floor. I'll make a start on things here."

But it's Dodger does some calling. Mum and Dad, Uncle George and Jung-ah, Susannah and Laura and Emily, even teenage Isabel, missing school, unwontedly quiet, scared by it all, sticking close to Mum—they all end up at the house on Danbury as the day goes on. No more secrets. Cleaning.

Cooking. Talking.

Especially talking. Uncle Henry seems—like a someone in a dream. Passive, doing what he's told. But then Thomas, vacuuming, walks in on him in the living room, crying, Dad kneeling by him, patting his knee. Leaves again. That's good, surely that's good. If you end up crying, you end up talking. Right? No one's called the doctor yet. Thomas dials. Kevin, stumbling in his words, persuades the receptionist. Maybe it's the shattered sound of him that does it. The doctor will see Henry that afternoon. Dad's going to go with him.

So. Leave Henry to the elders. Sue the newly-fledged accountant is looking at the shop's books, catching everything Kev's started missing, juggling too long, dropping eggs. Thomas, Laura, and Emily take Kevin downtown. They walk along the waterfront, bundled up against the cold. End up at some new pub the Park girls are disloyally keen on, the SandWitch and Brew, where they get a pint of stout and a roast beef sandwich and plate of sweet-potato chips into him. Take him home, put him to bed in clean sheets, a clean house, clean yard, clean fridge, freezer freshly filled with homemade meals. Thomas sleeps in the spare room that night, and several that follow.

After a week Thomas goes back to Toronto and Exit 369 and Dan and the lot. Ronnie's fury at his desertion. Do that again and you're out …

Uncle Henry's on anti-depressants for a while, and seeing a therapist—Kevin maybe should be too, but he's got Thomas and his cousins Susannah and Laura and Emily close around him now, knowing, watching, *talking,* so he's doing okay— and it's a slow climb but Henry makes it back up into daylight. Park Electronics moves into a smaller place, but easier to get to, a strip mall rather than an industrial park. Nearby, walking distance. Business picks up. Laura's just got a job as an assistant manager for an upscale kitchenware store but she comes in, moonlighting, and then they hire a young technician full time again. Come summer, Henry makes Kevin his partner in the business and puts him on the deeds of the house just as it's paid off, which panics him as if it's some preparation for suicide, though it's only saying, partner, son, not a child. Respect, it's saying, and pride. An old-world kind of thing. Generations staying together. That's all.

Thomas tries to get back to Kingston more often, and they call a couple of times a week, and talk, lost brothers found. Kev drives up from time to time or takes the train, once his dad is doing better, though he doesn't much like Dan, but be fair, neither does Thomas quite a lot of the time and he breaks up with Dan yet again. He's seeing someone else. Nice guy. Grad student in Classics of all things. Nothing serious. Ends amicably at the end of the year, when Sandor—his name's Sandor—goes off to Oxford to start his PhD, the academic big time. He's still got half an eye out for that sultry-eyed lab-coat bloke from St. Mark's, every crowd. Just a chance. You never know. Everyone ends up in Toronto sometime or other. Kev starts playing again, so they have that, whenever they get together. Remembering what music's supposed to be about. Kev finds a girlfriend. Breaks up. Doesn't get more than ordinarily down and cranky about it.

By the time Strange Pilgrim Road is born, Park Electronics is employing two technicians, one full and one part-time, which will let Kevin devote himself to the band more. Kev doesn't worry about his father when they're on the road.

Not more than his general background worry, which never

quite goes away. But Kev worries about everybody, looking after everybody. He always has.

There isn't anyone to look after him but Thomas, not since the last girlfriend didn't work out. Her or the band, that last one said.

Apparently there wasn't any real choice to make.

They're tied together, he and Kevin. In this thing, on this road.

If Thomas leaves him behind … he'll go quiet; he'll stop playing again; he'll just … die away. Because he'll never move far from his father, head off with Anicky to someplace bigger, write with someone else, find another guitarist.

Kevin needs him.

Lindsey sees that. Understands it. Accepts it.

Thomas doesn't deserve either of them. Needs to be the person they deserve. Both of them.

This second life's a gift, his grandfather says. Every life lived is, first or second. We need to make them matter, lives. Gifts.

Yes, but …

"We can't make a living," Thomas said. "We can't go on at this level. It's fine, now. We've got our fans, we've got a following. But that's not enough. We're going to get older. We're going to get old, be sick, maybe want to have families, have a real house, a proper grown-up life—some security, stability, want to be not on welfare when we're old and sick and arthritic and deaf." If he lived so long … He never could shut down that voice. Live to be old and sick and arthritic and deaf and be grateful for every day of it. "Why the hell should we have to stop doing what we do best, making the music we make that nobody else can make, music people want to hear, so that we can afford to grow old, so that we can afford to have a family—?" Not that he wanted kids, himself, didn't think Lin did, but he knew Kev did, and who knows, Anicky might, and Frankie, someday, and that wasn't the point. And he was going to start ranting about piracy and streaming and Lin had heard it all before. He took a breath.

"We've hit a plateau. We need to climb higher and I can't see how. That miracle, lucky break—and I don't see it. Not enough people recognize: *great* drums, *great* guitar. Good enough is—good enough for them and they don't notice if you're better than good enough. Some do, some care, but not enough of them. It's as though—they can't tell the difference, and I don't understand how they can't, but, I don't know, I look at someone's garden and think it's nice, and you say it's okay but it's boring and just like all the others on the street. And there's lots of good enough, the world's saturated in it. So we work and work and work, we're way better than good enough—I'm not arrogant—"

"No, never."

"—and it's not there, that one chance, we can't find it. We need to be bigger, we need to be not just getting by, not being bailed out by my parents or Uncle Henry, not me and Kev throwing whatever we can earn from our other work into the band so we can keep it going. We need—God, we need to have been born in the fifties. Mid sixties. No later. We would have been big. We would have made it, before it all fell apart."

He would have died by the time he was eight.

Lindsey didn't say that, if he even thought it. He said, "You'd be old enough to be my father."

Thomas waved his beer. "Obviously, you'd have arranged to have been born then too." Put the bottle aside, settled the guitar properly again. Picking out the melody, building it up like some Renaissance lute theme and variations. They were on to Krown Imperial's "Electric in the Night," Kai Juneau's vocals soaring, aching.

"Thomas."

"Hm?"

"Have—have you ever thought about—getting someone else? Into the band, I mean. To sing."

"Why?"

"Nothing. Just wondering."

"Lindsey." What had he ever done that Lin should go like that, act like he was afraid to look at him? For God's sake … He grabbed one of the hairy cushions. "Lin!"

Lindsey's head jerked up. Thomas hurled the cushion. Lin swatted it aside. Ricochet off the dog-box. The puppy leapt up, yapping at the treacherous bombardment from on high. Stuck her head out. Carefully took the cushion by a corner and dragged it out of sight. Forbidden, not a toy, but if the humans were going to throw it at her—

"Bunny, no!" Lindsey scrambled to rescue it. She'd disembowelled one of the others, quietly and methodically—they'd even been there, cooking supper. Thinking the dog was being so good and quiet. They never did find the beads, but presumably they'd passed on through.

Some scurrying flamenco. Lindsey on his hands and knees, crawled half into Bunny's box after her. Growling, not real growling but more the puppy saying, "Grrr, grrr," and from the sound of it, clang clang on the wire bars, thrashing her tail madly in joy at having enticed a human to play. Lindsey emerged triumphant, abomination in hand. Bunny got a biscuit for surrendering her prize. Thomas went to put the guitar away, fetch another couple of bottles, and that was three and probably enough for one evening, given how early Lin had to get up if he was going running before it got hot; he had to be at the grocery store garden centre for eight-thirty, too.

Lindsey was folded back into the chair. Thomas climbed up over the arm, wrapped himself in around him. Leech, Maddie would say. Or James: Anglo-Saxon gripping beast. "Okay. Here, have more beer and stop looking at me as if I'm going to start raging like the Duke of Dunstable. When have I ever? Just say what you were saying, alright? I know you don't mean you think I shouldn't sing. I mean, you're not saying I can't sing?"

"Of course not. I was in love with your voice before the rest of you."

"Which other bits of me in particular?"

"Thomas ... "

"I thought it was my general air of *je ne sais quois*."

That worked. Lindsey's voice was steadier when he said, "No, actually it was the newspaper hat."

"And Kev."

"I've never been in love with any bits of Kev."

"Me neither. Honestly. No-one believes it but I swear it's true. I do love him, mind you."

"That's okay. You're allowed."

"I meant, you aren't saying Kev can't sing."

"No, of course not.

"Or Anicky."

"You can all sing. That's not—"

"Even Frankie, actually. She just won't."

"Thomas, do you want to hear or not?"

"Yes."

"Okay, then stop doing that and listen."

"Doing what? This?"

"Thomas!"

"Sorry."

"Kai Juneau only plays guitar at all on few pieces. Kendra Robinson plays lead and she doesn't sing anything but backing vocals."

"Yes?"

"Electric in the Night" was one of those God I wish I'd done that ones. He'd seen Krown Imperial live, twice now, and next chance he got, he was going to make damn sure he and Lin went together. Kev had actually run into their bassist in Montreal a few weeks ago, on a solo expedition in pursuit of used equipment for the studio. The man had been chasing the same whatever-it-was and if Krown Imperial wanted it and thought it good enough second-hand ... it had probably been way out of their price range, whatever it was. Kev hadn't come home with anything that time, except some nice cheese that had temped even him and a carefully cool, Oh yeah, and I ran into Romeo ... Romeo who, Thomas had asked, like an idiot. Oh, Romeo Kennedy, you know. Nice guy. We had coffee.

Bonding over bass amps or effects or something. Kev had had CDs in the van, *Strange Pilgrim Road* and *Ways and Means* both, the genius, and yeah, probably anyone with that status got hopeful kids thrusting flash-drives of demos at them every time they stuck their nose out of doors, but still ...

Not that anything had come of it.

Pay attention. Lin had a point to make and if he'd nerved himself up to say anything he thought Thomas wouldn't like ... it was bloody important he listen.

That soaring voice …

End of the song and and the album, clunk and whirr again and they were on to Queen. "Radio Ga-Ga."

On the subject of soaring voices …

"You need a singer," Lindsey said.

"We've got—"

"No. A … a lead singer who's only that. That's what you're missing."

"We don't need one. It's not a rule. Even for the old days. Rush. Police."

"Bassists. They're not—I'm not saying it's easy, you know I'm not, but it's not so demanding—as a performance—as what you do. But Kev's not a lead singer type. You try to be but you can't do—what you do and—"

"May. Knopfler."

"May makes my point. He's good. So's Taylor. Their solo albums and the songs they did sing the lead vocals on prove it. Him, Taylor, both. They could have been the singer, in some other band. Well, they did that, they had their own bands. The Cross had some really good stuff and I wish May had done more like *Back to the Light*. But Queen still needed Mercury to be—that extra thing. Because you can't—can't concentrate on everything at once. Live, you can't. I mean—I mean, Queen started bringing in someone else to play piano live, even, didn't they? And Mercury was a first-rate pianist. You need someone to engage with the audience. Someone out front, holding them. Maybe. I—I don't know. It's just an idea. Knopfler, he's—he's—the thing about Dire Straits—I don't know, they always lean more towards the folk blues thing, a bit different in performance, isn't it? Watch an old concert online and—there's nothing to hold you if you're not watching his hands. Better just to listen. People went to the concert because it was them, because they already knew the music. To see him play. He's not a *performing* singer. And Johnny Marr, his albums are great but live he's just—just—he's still great to listen to, he's a good singer, I'd rather listen to him than Morrisey, but he doesn't have that extra thing you want to *see*. His live performances—I think—I think today mostly you—you've got to get them live, if you're going to get them to buy your music, come to your next show. Live or a video, which almost comes to the same thing. You're so—you can be so flamboyant, you're a good frontman off stage, you can talk to people but not when you're playing, you change so much then. When you're playing, your face goes all still. You smile sometimes or you look at the others, you interact with them a lot, but the audience, not so much. You're playing for them, singing for them but you don't—you don't play *with* them, the way a really good live singer can. It's just you and the others and the music. And it's beautiful. But it isn't what—it's not what the majority of people, the kind who'll really like a song and get it on their iTunes or whatever but they won't buy the CD and read the liner notes, that sort of person, it's not what they'll go on about the next day. It's kind of the reverse of the usual sort of frontman singer type, isn't it, all extrovert and ego on stage and then shy and nervous and bashful in interviews off. Sor—sorry, I don't know what I'm talking about, really, it's—I was just thinking—I—I mean, I love to watch you play, I can just watch your hands and love it, I love to listen to you sing, I sit and watch a drummer and enjoy that like it's someone dancing but I think a lot of people can't. They—they want some kind of personality they can connect with, that single focus—because they can't—they can't tell what you're

Kris Jamison

doing, they can't see what they're hearing, only they'd miss it if it was gone. That didn't make sense. I mean—I mean—"

"I know what you mean. Stop. It's okay, Lin." Because he was stammering and stressing out, his voice going all tight. "Sh." Pulled his head to him, down on his shoulder, wrapped around him, sitting over him, chest to chest. "You're not hurting my feelings, if that's what you're afraid of."

Well, not exactly.

"I love your voice," Lindsey said, muffled. "I do."

"Yes, well, I love the sound of my own voice, too, just ask anyone."

"Funny."

"I try."

"You've got a good voice, Thomas."

"But we need a great voice, to get off this plateau I've metaphored into existence, is what you're saying. A great voice and a stage presence to carry it."

Lindsey shrugged, still not looking at him.

"Okay." Kissed his hair, his ear, his jaw. "It's a fair point."

Lindsey pushed back from him. "What are you going to tell Tasha Meyer? Have you decided?"

Changing the subject. Almost. Not quite. Tangled together. Two roads diverged and all that.

"I don't know, love. I just don't know."

Bunny came nosing at them then. Time for her bedtime walk, probably. She'd gotten the hang of the critical "let the humans know you want out" thing.

Sandals. Shirts. Far cooler outside. Wanted to hold on to Lindsey, reassure him, because Lin being Lin, he was still all knotted up, feeling he'd done wrong. Didn't. Forty-nine dead in Florida. Maybe a good reason to hold hands and damn scaring the horses. All students along here, for what that was worth. Let the back of a hand brush against Lindsey's, at least, smiled when he glanced over. Down to Ontario, along four blocks to West and up the edge of the park, back on Wellington. Tree-lined streets, not much traffic. A bit of a breeze off the lake. Golden light, the sun hanging low. Students out roaming, sitting on steps, music playing. A couple of other dogs being walked. The usual, "Oooh, isn't she sweet, what is she, is it okay if I pat her?" Bunny accepted the attention as her due.

They didn't talk. Just went home as the sun was setting, shut Bunny into her box with her bedtime biscuit. Showered, went to bed. Left all the fans going.

Thomas always slept close enough they were touching. Even on the rare occasions they ended up over at his place, where the sofa-bed, creaking and so thin you felt every spring, was at least a double. Insecure child, Thomas said cheerfully, mocking himself. Chronically starved for cuddling from the whole no-immune-system episode. So physical, and it wasn't about sex, even. Just contact. He'd stand close, sit close, touching. It had felt awkward at first, sharing the narrow mattress. Lindsey had been afraid to turn over, worried about waking Thomas, but he didn't seem to mind, even if he did half-wake. Just rearranged himself and slumbered on. Like a cat. Lindsey had gotten used to it himself, someone lying so near, rolling over, shifting around in the night.

Too hot.

He shouldn't have said that.

"He wasn't angry," Raleigh said. *"He doesn't get angry about things like that."*

"*He said he wasn't. Doesn't mean he wasn't. I just about said they weren't good enough and that wasn't what I meant at all—*"

"*He heard what you said. He understood what you meant.*"

"*I shouldn't have said it. And anyone would say he should go with Tasha Meyer. He should. Choose his own career.*"

"*He won't. And that isn't the life he wants, being someone else's guitarist.*"

"*I know. I don't want him to do it. I just think—anyone would say he should. It's the smart thing to do. Not holding out for that big break that'll maybe never come, no matter how hard they work and how good they are. It's luck. Too much of it is luck.*"

"*He'd be somebody else, if he did.*"

"*He and Kevin—nobody else could make what they make, together.*"

Yeah. "Locked Doors," "Over to you," "Machine Line," "Dead Inside," "Night and River," "Hearts of Brass and Iron," "Black Mirror" …

"'*Black Mirror', that's so—It's one of my favourite songs ever. And 'Runaway', why isn't that—that's just—that's one of the great songs too. By anyone.*"

"Yeah." Raleigh, agreeing? "*Go to sleep. Someone needs to get up by six, and it isn't me.*"

But he didn't. Dozed, maybe, fitful, beneath the fan's low thrum.

Restless. Lindsey had taken Bunny out, then gone for his run—she was still too young for more than a walk herself—showered and eaten and headed off to work on the bus. He'd be laid off again come Canada Day, the first of July, when the seasonal garden centre closed.

Thomas had dragged himself out of bed only when Bunny, shut in her box again, began squeaking and then yapping, annoyed. There was still a human in the flat so being locked up was Not Fair.

Had that groggy, too-much-thinking hangover feeling. Head full of sludge. Lying awake stewing too long, trying not to toss around, disturb Lindsey.

"Alright, alright." But he didn't let the puppy out till he'd showered. Didn't matter how many chew-toys she had, it was the furniture she liked best.

Breakfast. Guitar, the Tele, with headphones to stop both the dog and the students below complaining. Something half-formed in his head that couldn't find its way out. Needed his PRS, maybe, the right sound. Couldn't settle down. Dog bringing him her hard rubber chew-toy and dropping it on his toes repeatedly so he'd throw it and she could chase it didn't help. Wanted to get on his bike and go, but that meant locking Bunny up again. Isabel had said, get a basket, take her with you like Kev says they do in the Netherlands, but the way she was growing, by the time she learnt to sit still and enjoy it she'd be the size of a small Lab, so that wasn't going to work. Settled for fast walking, down along the lake. Bunny barked at gulls, at waves. They played tug with sticks. She wouldn't go into the water after them, though. Out at Nicholson's Point, at the park by the lighthouse, she always ran up and down the rocks yapping in what seemed excited like horror while Scooter swam out to fetch, his favourite game. Up tree-lined streets to his own place, narrow, dark house, aligned so it got little sun. Heap of shoes in the hall, and a couple of bicycles. Nobody around. The kitchen was a mess, a loaf of bread on the counter, bag open, drying out, unwashed pots and pans, the dishwasher full of dirty plates and mugs. He found the bag of cheap detergent pods, filled the dispenser and started it up. What did their parents teach them?

Ugly modern—if the seventies were modern—light fixture like a wagon-wheel. Flicked the switch, the better to see the squalor—no, just checking. There'd been a problem. The light dimmed and flared. Turned it off again. Still a problem, right. The landlord was supposed to have done something about that, which Thomas had been hoping would turn out to mean replacing it with something less repulsive. It wasn't bad bulbs—in one socket the bulb would burn out within a week of being replaced, every time, so he only put bulbs in the other two and even those were a bit suspicious, that flare and dimming. Buy compact fluorescents, the landlord said, that'll fix it. Yeah, sure. The upstairs hallway light buzzed and crackled. That wasn't right, either. He went to check, since he was apparently going into Annoyed at Landlord mode. Still doing it. Sticky note still over the switch. *Don't use.* So. Time for an email, something that laid out in writing the fact that he'd phoned three times over the past couple of months and been assured two weeks ago that an electrician had been called, which was clearly not the case. He was a bit fed up with this and the kids who actually lived here had a right to be, too. Maybe they'd keep the kitchen cleaner if they could actually see how awful it was.

Maybe not.

Went back to check the whiteboard on the fridge. *Thomas,* it said. *Mice chewing up soap in bathroom!*

Stop leaving food out in kitchen! he wrote.

Went down into the cellar, which was stone walls and flagstone floor, dry and earthy, wires running along the beams and bare bulbs dangling, casting light that was swallowed before it ever reached the corners, old rubbish of past tenants stored and long abandoned, unclaimed. Dusty bicycle, a stack of ugly abstracts in oils, thick textured brush-strokes and heavy daubs, almost lumps—he could see why whatever student it was, one who graduated the first year he rented the place, left them behind, though he was pretty sure she'd said she was coming back to get them—mysterious shapes in black garbage bags, some storage totes with the name Theresa written on them, a couple of battered suitcases ... mousetraps he'd bought last fall. The students had felt sorry for the mice and hadn't set them when he wasn't around.

There'd been rats in that wretched house in Toronto. They'd chewed through a guitar cable and his computer's speaker wires, too. Just for the hell of it, as far as he could tell. Mice weren't so evil but they shat everywhere.

He baited the traps with someone's peanut butter, set one in each bathroom by the soap, two on the kitchen counter.

Traps set, he added to the whiteboard. *Dispose of mice in organic waste or bury them in yard, with prayers and flowers if you must, wash traps, bait with peanut butter and set them again. Wash all mousy surfaces, numbskulls, or you'll get horrid diseases.* And a little scowly face, so they didn't take the numbskulls too seriously. *P.S. Am informing landlord of problems with light fixtures in writing so maybe we'll get that fixed, let me know if electrician actually comes. Bex, I need last and this month's rent NOW or you're out, I mean it. I will call your parents if this goes on.*

"Really," he said to Bunny, who'd watched all this with great interest, especially the parts involving peanut butter, "Was I like this when I was twenty? I feel like they still want their mummy to think for them."

He found a clean mug, made green tea in the microwave while Bunny had a drink from a cereal bowl. Unlocked the door to his room, which had been the living room when this was a proper house. Dark. Venetian blinds angled for privacy, but the two windows faced east, where there was a tree and a house across the street, and north, where there was a house with only a narrow gap between, so not much light at the best of times.

No plants. No life.

Something in him always unkinked a little, a kind of relieved stretching of the soul, when he opened the door to Lindsey's flat. Living light, the smell of a garden.

Nice and cool, though, this gloomy cave. He let Bunny loose to explore, flung himself down on the bed. Sofa-bed. Eyed the rowing machine, which he made a discipline of coming over to work out on once a week in summer when he was biking around town and twice in winter. When he wasn't on tour, anyway. Too easy to start thinking that eating well was virtue enough, to let your body start getting away with things, and he couldn't, he couldn't trust it, he didn't dare. Though he'd push himself and then think, had he just overdone it or was he too tired, was that normal … It's normal, Lin would say. If you go crazy, rowing for twenty minutes longer than you usually do, of course you're tired. Idiot. And kiss his hair. Shh. You're fine.

And he knew that healthiness wasn't any kind of magic talisman; against some things, yes, but not the random other, the one that he couldn't shake the shadow of, the stalking monster in the dark that he could never lose, that was going to reach out after him and kill him before he was done—

No. It was not. Statistically … he'd got this far, his chances were pretty good and don't think about it, don't, think about Lin and music, the beautiful curves of guitars and they had a dog, an actual dog, they were a couple with a dog, like real grown-ups and they were going to grow old together and yesterday in Cooke's when he was buying coffee-beans, because Lin liked a cup of coffee first thing in the morning and he deserved nicer than instant even if he couldn't afford it, that new cashier had blushed and said, "Um, sorry, but—you're Tank Gorev, aren't you? From Strange Pilgrim Road?" and asked for his autograph, on her T-shirt, no less, and when were they getting another album out … So he'd sold her on going to the Mud Festival then and there, though she'd never been to a festival in her life … Bring your friends, he'd said. Bring a gang to hang out with.

Too hot for vigorous exercise today. No rowing, even in this dungeon. He wasn't being slack; he didn't want heat-stroke. So there.

He liked the thought of going running with Lindsey, actually, but that was Lin's thing, a quiet place, a meditation, almost, he could see that. Some aloneness that Lindsey needed. So he didn't ask. Because Lin would say yes, even if he didn't mean it.

Maybe he should get a stationary bike. Keep an eye on Kijiji; he might be able to afford a secondhand one, people sold off exercise equipment they'd hardly used.

Didn't have much other furniture. The old coffee table he'd had since Toronto, a spare amp from back in the days when he'd actually lived here with a guitar or two. Notebooks, just scribblers, ballpoint pens, not the fancy stationary Lin liked. He did come over here to work on stuff still, lugging a guitar and his computer. No distractions. But furniture, no. He'd never bothered with more. Kept his clothes in plastic laundry baskets, one each for jeans, T-shirts, sweaters, and socks-and-undies, a few shirts and coats hung in a plywood wardrobe. It worked for him. Drove Lin crazy, which was why the clothes were mostly still here and he collected what he needed every couple of days and dropped his clean laundry off on Sundays. Books and discs, right back to childhood, were still in the bedroom he and James had shared at Mum and Dad's, expanded to James's shelves now that he'd got a tenure-track position and a real live mortgage with bookshelves of his very own. Guitars and all his other gear in the studio, with strays at Lindsey's. Didn't feel comfortable leaving them here when he wasn't really in residence, locked door or not. Too often the front door wasn't locked, and they were mostly music students and maybe one guy in art history, with other wannabe musicians hanging around, and ... nice kids but just, no.

There was beginning to be a bit of that ... you know Tank Gorev? He lives here. That's his room. That thing. Which was kind of flattering but ... time he got out.

More flattering if they actually bought albums and made their friends buy albums and got all excited on some useful social media, of course. Preferably just before a biggish gig.

Why was he even paying rent on this? A expensive clothes-closet was all it was now. Inertia.

Two Men and a Dog in an Attic? And nine guitars ... No, those'd go on mostly staying in the studio, which had climate control, and alarms. Be nice to have his books with him, like a real grown-up. Lin already had a lot of books ...

Maybe they could find a bigger attic. No way the rowing machine was going to fit in, even if he got rid of his coffee table and couch. And if he added the stationary bike … Maybe set up a decent rig, enough to record more than just a raw sketch of an idea, keep one of the good Strats there, if he was living properly with Lindsey. Do some writing there, he liked that idea, working on something while Lindsey drew gardens … But Lin didn't like change. It stressed him out, badly. He'd need some time to get used to the idea.

Bunny was into the socks. He snagged her leash as she pranced by, play-growling and shaking her victim. Hauled her up with him, took the doubled-up pair of socks away and hurled them back towards the basket.

"No," he said. "Thomas's socks."

Tea still too hot to drink. Collapsed again, hands behind his head. The puppy bounced around a bit, finally circling herself down into a sleeping knot.

Bare walls. Lindsey put old calendar pictures into cheap frames and hung them around his place, mostly forest landscapes or Japanese gardens. Just the one picture here, something Iz had done for him in her art class when she was in grade nine. A sort of joke. Christmas present. Poster sized rectangle of old wall-panelling, painted black. Outlined in white and pale blue, which he could recognize as blue, an also-recognizable caricature of a thin man all arms and legs and long, wild-corkscrewing white hair, half painted, half coated wire that had been wound around a pencil or something. The pasted-on arms of the man were cut from wrapping paper printed with stars. The body of the guitar was shiny foil paper. Red she said. Different black against the black, anyway. Strings waggled loosely across it, snipped from his discards, ends stapled down. *Brian May is God,* it proclaimed, in drippy splashes of white.

Anicky kept threatening to do some editing. Add some stick-figures in chalk, a little blond behind some drums, those other two guys whoever they were, make it a pantheon.

Queen's pantheon had worked.

A more or less stable balance. Strange Pilgrim Road had that now. He didn't want to throw everything off.

Didn't want to risk what was good, chasing what might be great?

Was that even him, any more?

Going somewhere, he'd always thought he was. Losing what, along the way?

You could hold on to the wrong things.

Friends weren't one of them, never a wrong thing to hold to. Neither were a few guitars and your collection of Anthony Buckeridge books. A plateau of safe stability might be, when the mountain still rose above.

Old-fashioned way to do it. Might have been the seventies. Ad stuck up on the bulletin board in the lobby of one of the music buildings. Band looking for a guitarist.

Thomas is a guitarist looking for something. He's not sure what. This'll do to be going on with.

Ronnie's brainchild. Thinks he's got something in Dan: a voice, a look. Herding cats, he calls it, trying to make something of his brothers, Dan and Brandon, Brandon's friends André and Mitch, but their previous lead guitar defected to a jazz band and Brandon knows his limits, doesn't think he can carry it on his own. So they get Thomas, and Exit 369 takes flight.

Wallowing into the air. Barely. Sometimes it works. Sometimes they fly. But Dan's the golden boy, and it's fun, and it's flattering, yes, and if they say, Christ, no one wants a friggin' epic, Tom, what does that even mean, and refuse most of what he comes up with on his own, he's still getting some music out and Mitch can write what Dan can sing, which is love and anger and hey girl lyrics, and that's all most punters want anyway. And Dan's—more fun than he expects when they first meet. But Dan's a problem, too, and the ego's only part of it.

Fun is what Dan's after, he says. Living. Stop being so uptight, Tom—stop calling me Tom but other than Ronnie they never do—and live while we're young and beautiful. Going off into giggles, helpless. Staggering helpless drunk, high—Thomas takes him home from too many parties in that state, deals with the hangovers, deals with the moods, the crashes, the tempers, the sound-check tantrums, the fights with Brandon, whenever Ronnie washes his hands of his brothers, which starts to seem like it's at least once a week, and it's Thomas who's supposed to be responsible for Dan—Dan's curious enough to sleep with him and stupid enough to boast of it to his girlfriend, and then decides to be open about it, Ronnie saying he doesn't care whose screwing who but it's not the band image he wants so keep it out of sight ... Too many nights, too many rehearsals that end up everyone placating Dan, trying to sober him up, soothe the temper, flatter him back to the mic ... He's the star and the rest of them are expendable, as Ronnie tells Thomas and André when mutiny stirs, and there is something there, between them, on stage at least, something worth making, but off—Thomas has had it with the lot of them.

He says that about as often as Ronnie tells him he's expendable, guitarists a dime a dozen, every acne-oozing basement-lurking teen who can't get a date.

Yeah, but they're not me, he says, and walks out and slams the door. Not for good. Sulks up in his room a day, that's all.

"Get out," Kevin tells him on the phone that night, as he's told him before, often, in these days after Uncle Henry's recovery and Kev's with it has begun. "They're a mess. You're too good for them, Tank." And he should, he will, but they've got three songs already with all the tracks laid down for the new album, they've got a tour half-planned through Michigan and New York State …

So where the hell's Dan, Ronnie demands of him a few days later, as if he should know, and they've rented studio time and the clock is ticking …

Not in the claustrophobic rooms of the grimy house they rent, all jammed in, instruments and several ever-changing girlfriends and André's pet rabbits, reek of pot and stale deep-fryer grease … Dan went out last night, maybe, Brandon thinks. Dan's got a girlfriend again. So go drag him out of her bed, Ronnie says, and it's Thomas he means to go, because Brandon and Dan, they can come to blows over just about anything these days.

Dan's girlfriend *du jour* has a basement flat, one of those that's probably not even a legal conversion. A narrow passage that squeezes back from the driveway between an old garage and the wall of the house. Dan's Kawasaki bike's parked there, mostly blocking it. Thomas edges by, goes to the back door. Seems to be shared with the rest of the house, two bells. Nobody comes when he presses either, so he pounds on it. A student-type girl comes to open it. Not the girlfriend, much healthier looking than the aspiring fashion designer, retro-goth, who's been hanging around lately.

Student-at-the-door saw goth-girl, who's apparently named

Bethany, go out an hour or more ago, heading to class, probably.

"Dan's bike's still here," Thomas points out.

So they stand crowded together in the closet of a retrofitted entryway and both bang on the locked door that goes down to the basement. No answer.

Thomas goes out, gets down in the unweeded flowerbeds and peers into grimy basement windows never meant to light a proper flat. Nothing to see. Dark towels tacked up as curtains all round.

They hammer on the door some more. He shouts. The girl bites hangnails. Another couple of girls from the main house join them.

No, they don't have a key. They don't really know Bethany that well. They dither. The landlord would have a key, but … she's out in Scarborough. They're going to be late for class. They look to him. The man? The tough guy in black leather? They look older than he is, for God's sake.

"Okay," Thomas says. "You're not seeing this. If it turns out—if the stupid git's just forgotten he rode his bike and taken the bus, you didn't see this, you just came home and found it this way, right?"

"You can't break down the door!"

Worried. Thrilled. Uncertain.

"No," he says. He probably could. It's just one of those hollow cheap plywood types. A bit harder to pass off as an accident when it turns out there's nothing wrong, though. He goes out, picks the window in the side passage, where the bike and someone's car in the driveway will screen him from the street. Puts his foot through it, which is cool and stupid, should have found a stick or something, but it's done and he knocks shards of glass away with a leather sleeve and—are they going to check for fingerprints, is this going to be a burglary or—screw it. Pulls the towel-curtain down to cover the edge of the sill for what protection that will be and squeezes through feet-first into the dark room beyond. Glass crunches.

Low ceiling. Even he wants to cringe down. Dark and dreary. Kitchen, apparently. Empty vodka bottle on the counter, couple of glasses, bowl with a few chips still in it, ashtray, over-filled and stinking. Uses his elbow to flick the light switch on. More than the remnants of vodka on the counter. Zip-lock bag, a couple of pills left. God knows what, he gave up keeping track of what Dan's playing with months ago and it keeps changing anyway.

It's gone beyond playing around. Can't face the stage without something to give him an edge, he says. Can't cope with the dull days in between. Can't, won't, find some better way of—of screaming, of filling up whatever's missing inside him. Nagging old maid, he'd said, and, fuck off out of my life.

Coffee-maker, on, light shining, half a pot of coffee stewing. A used mug. Bottle of extra-strength Tylenol. Bottle of Gravol. Breakfast of fools.

The walls have been painted black. Seriously? Or who knows, maybe it's red or dark purple or something but surely that's just as weird.

"Dan?" he shouts, and goes through the flat, elbowing on lights, touching nothing, because with the lights on it's harder to believe it's anything but Dan being stupid and he's probably already at the studio complaining about his hangover and Ronnie's about to call and if the landlord decides to get the police about the broken window he doesn't want fingerprints left …

"Are you okay?" a girl calls through the window. "Are you going to open the door?"

"Just a minute."

Living room. Sewing machine, dressmaker's dummy, a couple bolts of pale cloth half unrolled over the couch. Bathroom. Someone's been sick and not quite aimed well, not quite cleaned it up thoroughly, either. Dedication, going to class at all. Or maybe it wasn't her.

Bedroom. Bedclothes heaped, half on the floor. The idiot's there.

"Dan, you stupid—" Thomas goes to shake him. It stinks. He's been sick here too. Someone has. She can't have left him here like this, can she? He was well enough to be sick recently, then. That's good, maybe? Out of his system, whatever it is? Is that even how it works?

"Dan?" Puts a hand on him. Dan's shivering, skin clammy. Thomas is bloody furious.

In a few years, he'll be thinking—he could have been Raleigh. Raleigh could have been Dan. Someone should have come, anyone, why didn't anyone look, why didn't anyone go out, even just to be sick, look in that dark corner of the yard, save him. Spare Lindsey so much … Raleigh so much a ghost in his mind, caught from the scars in Lindsey's …

Now he goes up the dark stairs, unlocks the door to the back entry, because the students are banging on it, impatient. Goes back down to try to get Dan up, mobile. Get something into him, ginger-ale, even cola, that's sensible, isn't it? It's helped before. Stupid fool. Are any of them medical students, do they have better ideas of what they should do with him? No, of course not.

Dan mumbles, sitting, swaying on the edge of the bed, eyes

dilated black, not tracking him. Falls back, convulsing. That hasn't happened before. Not good. Thomas drags him down to the floor, puts him on his side, shouts at the students to call an ambulance.

Nothing to do but keep him from hitting his head on the leg of the bed, and wait.

One of the girls wants to flush the pills, to stop trouble for Bethany.

"Don't," he says.

The paramedics will need to know what he's taken. What he might have taken, anyway. God knows what else might be in his system.

So nothing gets recorded that week, and their studio booking's gone by the time Dan's back, recovered, more or less, subdued, repentant, though likely it won't last; it never has before. Maybe going to be charged with something, maybe not, it's all a bit confused, or he is, whether he even knew what he was taking, whether Bethany did. Minor, apparently, whatever it was. Possession, not dealing, not enough to count.

Thomas doesn't stick around for the aftermath. Because it's all happened before, without the seizures and the ambulance, and it's all going to happen again, and Brandon blames him, messing Dan up in the first place, dumping him—he's packing up his things, not even sure where he's going, if he's really going, when Brandon comes in, drunk enough to be belligerent, sober enough to hit straight and hard and oh God, it's some back alley fight, in his room and the guitars are still in their rack, and Brandon slams his head against the wall while he's trying to reason with him, shouting, knocks him down and kicks him in the ribs and that's it, Thomas grabs his ankles and brings him down in turn, shoves Brandon out the door as he struggles to get up and they're fighting in the dark because the bulb's burnt out and it's always someone else's job to do these things—

They crash against the banister and it creaks but doesn't give and even that doesn't shock Brandon into sense—

So Thomas gives up fending him off and puts him down, instead. He doesn't fight fair. Never has. Grade nine wasn't good. Because he's a stuck-up little city kid defying them all. Hick school, Ernestown, is his arrogant feeling and he wants to be at Bayridge with Kev but his parents have moved out to Nicholson's Point that year and he's mad at the world and wears his sister's eyeshadow to school to make sure someone notices—

One of the tough guys obliges. Thomas doesn't exactly beat the crap out of him, but it's not him who's on the ground when the principal shows up and calls time. In-school suspensions all round, and parental—concern.

There are a few bad weeks when he's watching his back all the time, and his locker gets trashed, and a scuffle in a hallway turns into black eyes and another round of suspensions. There are discussions.

He transfers to Bayridge Secondary. Better music program, is the official justification, though not an entirely plausible one. It's Frontenac has the rep for music, or did, back before he was born. Whatever. Gets dropped off as the old folks drive to work, a detour for them, walks home to the Parks' with Kev.

These are the kids he's been in school with since Kindergarten. Not friends. They never have been, really. He's always been the weird guy, too intense, too—not like them. Not interested in the normal things and because he doesn't fake it, doesn't pretend, they say he's too stuck-up, too out of it. Too much the outsider, always. But at least he's their known, predictable, familiar weird guy. Kevin's friend, and if they can't figure out why Kevin still hangs around with him now he's old enough to know better, they're used to tolerating him. The fighting here's mostly more—token. And off school grounds. And the one time it's not just some half-joking hassling, the only time it goes bad, on the way home—freaks Kevin out, he didn't know Thomas could be that—vicious, Kev says.

Kev's so upset Thomas actually goes and apologizes to the guy the next day. The guy's still walking a bit funny. Weirdly, it's okay after that. Not Sunday school stuff, I have seen the error of my ways and now we are friends. Just, that Gorev kid's a psycho freak, stay away from him.

He'll take it.

Plus everyone likes Kevin and Jon, and they're a bit of a shield.

Brandon's not okay, gasping on the floor and a nosebleed that's not doing anything good for the crusty carpet. Thomas gives him a hand up, helps him stagger to the bathroom, wash his face. All in silence. It's Thomas holding the cold washcloth to his nose, steadying arm around him.

"Fucker," Brandon says. Exhausted. No malice in it now.

"Yeah."

It's not worth it. He's out. André and Mitch help him load the van, his couch hanging out the open back doors; André dumps him and his junk on this other drummer he knows. Just for a few days.

Gets a room, what Dodger might call a bedsit. It's a bad, lonely six weeks, and he's seriously thinking of just crawling home. She shows up unexpectedly one day, allegedly driving all the way to Toronto to bring him a mere two dozen eggs. One room with a tiny bathroom in the corner, no kitchen. Five guitars in a rack, cases, couple of amps, pedalboard … a path between cables. Surviving with a microwave and a kettle and the old sofa-bed from home, cheaper than them buying him a bed, he'd told Mum and Dad when they first delivered him to Toronto, and they'd been planning to get rid of it anyway. Dodger goes out for an hour and comes back with a shiny new bar fridge, a slow-cooker, an electric steamer, and an electric frying pan. Also some wooden spoons and a proper knife and a cutting board. Between those, he can cook just about anything, is her thinking.

"All the time and tears and prayers and modern science people have put into getting you this far," she says, "you need to start looking after yourself properly, my young idiot. Or you'll end up getting into a state, same as Kevin."

He doesn't even have a table to put them on; the microwave's on the floor. She drives him to the nearest junkshop when he says no, his big amp is not going to double as a some kind of kitchen work-surface, absolutely not. They come back with an extra-long coffee table he can use as a sort of kneeling-height counter to array all the new appliances on. No cooking in the rooms, he was told, but the building manager never turns up even when the guy in the end room floods the hallway with a blocked shower drain, so he's probably safe.

Possibly the parents were worried and carefully not saying so, Dodger their of-course-we're-not-interfering compromise. You'll tell us if you need money, Dad says every time he goes home. You know we'll help. Yes, he says, of course, and doesn't ask, because he can do this, he can. Mum slips him a cheque tucked into a new vegetarian cookbook every now and then.

"Just a little something for extras," she says.

Through with bands. He's gone freelance.

He's *that guy, used to be with Exit 369,* for a while. The blond one, the guitarist. *Oh, them.* Wariness. Suspicion. But he can work, and he's good, and he's reliable, sober, not the problem they think he's going to be and he proves it over and over again, until people forget, until they believe in him and he's Tank, Thomas Smith Gorev, and yeah, you want him, and hey, he's got a band these days, Strange Pilgrim Road—you should take a listen.

Didn't want to be touring with Tasha Meyer, this year, next year, someone else the year after, forever and ever amen.

Wanted Strange Pilgrim Road up there. A name.

Didn't want to be wrangling some hyped-up diva who thought himself the frontman, God's gift to rock 'n' roll, not again.

Control freak, he was. Yes? Maybe?

Injustice to singers. Wasn't it? Tasha was fine. They weren't all Dans.

Lindsey had no faith in himself, but Thomas—Lindsey believed in Thomas.

Lindsey thought he could be that. What he wanted. That it was okay not to settle for what he was being offered, to chase instead what he needed to be. Lindsey wouldn't say, ever, when—if—it all faded away, you should have taken that gig with Meyer after all. Not ever. Even if the garden thing didn't take off either and they lived in a trailer on some back road and ran a lawncare company with a beat-up old pickup … he and Kev would play weekends in bars and Iz's kid would come round to make sure the weird old uncles were eating properly

and remembering to take their codger-vitamins or whatever
…

Or what? *I had a band once, back in the day. Used to write. You wouldn't have heard of us. We weren't around long.*

Sat up abruptly. Bunny twitched awake, gave a bark of alarm, looking around. No monsters. Wagged her tail when her eyes fell on Thomas, yawned, tongue curling, went back to sleep.

Thomas texted the lot of them. *Council of war tonight. Studio. I'll make supper. Curry?*

And to Iz, *I'm taking the car.* Which meant walking all the way over to Barrack Street in the mounting heat. And to Lindsey's first, because that's where he'd left the keys. Going to be a well-exercised puppy today.

Remembered to drink the tea, nicely lukewarm now.

Called Kev while he walked. Bunny had rebelled, flopped down on the sidewalk and refused to move. He slung her up against his chest like a baby. Chin on his shoulder, looking back. Smug, probably. Silly dog. What did she think she had legs for?

"Tasha Meyer," Kev said. "Oh. When do you leave?"

"I don't. I'm saying I can't."

Silence. Then, "Tank—you won't get another chance like that this year. Turn down work like that too often and you'll stop getting offered it, period."

"I know. I know. But—I've been thinking—it's Lindsey who's been thinking, actually. He's smart, you know. He sees things."

"Odd but smart. Inexplicable taste in boyfriends." Kev still sounded a bit wary. "Thinking what?"

"We were talking last night, Lindsey and I, about Pilgrim

Road. Where we are, where we're going. What we might change, to get there ... "

"Tasha Meyer?" said Frankie. Twirling in the middle of the living room floor, dancing alone to a playlist she'd started on Kev's tablet. New electronic stuff. Eyes shut. She'd had work at the university all week; still in her office clothes, which always made her look like she was in disguise. "And you said no?"

"I haven't yet, but yes, I'm going to. Say no."

She paused in mid-twirl, arms raised, eyes wide open now. Frowning. "And this brought on an urge to make curry?"

"Kev and I want you—"

"You're not going to say 'you girls', are you?"

"Frankie, sit down. You're making me dizzy." Anicky was stretched out on a couch.

Frankie stuck out her tongue and folded up where she stood, hitching her skirt, short and tight, up high enough to go cross-legged, inelegant and—okay, maybe a pair of men's Batman boxers wasn't exactly indecent, but seriously ...

She saw he'd seen. Winked at him. He shook his head.

"You two," Kevin said. "You Bells. Tank and I want you Bells to think about this idea."

"What idea?"

"A singer."

"Who?" Anicky asked. "You've got a song in mind for someone else?"

"A lead vocalist," Kev said. "Someone who can focus on that, free up Tank to just be Tank."

Anicky sat up. "Seriously?"

"Yeah."

"Small pie gets smaller," said Frankie.

"Whole pie gets bigger, is the idea," said Thomas.

"No," said Frankie. "Why? We're good."

"We're stalled," said Anicky. Looked at Thomas. Shrugged. "Sorry, Tank. Cult following—it's not enough."

"No, I know."

She looked away. "We had to borrow to get groceries last month."

"Stupid student loan," Frankie muttered.

"At least one of has a good degree to fall back on," Anicky said sharply. Put her hands to her face. "No, sorry. Frankie, I'm sorry."

Silence. But Frankie only shrugged. "Whatever."

Frankie'd ended up missing half of grade twelve, touring—and the paperwork, if you had an underage musician, permits and permissions and at least her guardian wasn't a problem, but the rules differed province to province and over the border it was worse, but they'd found if she did her face up a bit nobody ever asked, down in the States where they wouldn't run into anyone who knew them personally. She'd done her GED while they worked on their first album. Price of her Gibson. Was having no truck with further education. Then did a short office assistant certificate after they badgered her into it, which was getting her temping jobs now. Meant they had to keep two cars running, so neither had to turn down work when it was offered in the band's down time—Anicky was doing supply teaching.

Thomas breathed again. "You should have said. I could have—"

"It's all right. Don't—I shouldn't have said anything." Anicky shrugged. "We're fine for now."

Which meant they'd borrowed from someone, Dodger or

Mum and Dad, probably.

Another few years in Toronto, full-time teaching, and she'd probably have paid off her student loan, got Frankie into some program, community college at least, something practical, been saving for a down payment on a modest condo … Instead they were renting a shabby mini-home out back of Yarker, cheaper than a flat in town and they could make all the noise they wanted, though Anicky's main kit and Frankie's Gibson Les Paul and best Epiphones lived in the studio.

Not a trailer, though Frankie called it one. It had probably been a decent place when it was built, those narrow pre-fab bungalows usually were, two or three bedrooms and as much floorspace as any other small house aside from having no basement. But this one hadn't been kept up. The front porch was rotting and the back steps consisted of a board laid over milk crates. The roof leaked over the bathroom and in the corner of Frankie's bedroom. Their landlord had slapped some tar around, which hadn't done much. It needed reshingled before it got mould growing in the walls.

Could have been a teacher, burning out. Growing tired and bitter, losing the wild sister, the one running directionless, and her own music dying … Because—Anicky was quiet, clichés about drummers notwithstanding—when not safely within the fortress of her kit, she was the most restrained and socially-inhibited drummer he'd ever met. But deep down, she was like him. The weekend amateurs weren't ever have going to have been enough to keep her soul intact.

"When you said Tasha Meyer wanted you, I thought, that's it, we're done."

"Noooo," said Frankie. Mock-wailing. She curled up on the floor, arms over her head. "We don't want anyone new."

Anicky poked her sister with a bare toe. "Just be quiet a minute."

Bunny trotted over to investigate, nuzzling into Frankie's face, which got her up again. She gathered the puppy to her lap.

"Do you want us to be done?" He was startled to hear he'd said it. "Anicky? Do you want to go on?"

"Yes," said Frankie. "Don't be stupid, Tank. Of course she does."

Anicky didn't answer.

"Anicky!" Frankie pushed herself around scowled at her over Bunny's head. "What else can we do? What else can I do?"

"You could get a proper job. Secretarial. Go back to school. Or do what Thomas does."

"Tasha Meyer's not asking me to tour."

"No. You're barely nineteen. Tank's put in the time and the work, getting to that point."

"You can't go back full time. You hate teaching."

"I don't hate it."

"Hah. And I've never done anything else but this, Anicky! I can't—"

"Frankie, you're smart and you're good and you've got no idea how lucky you are, everything Thomas has done for you."

"Anicky, no," Thomas said.

"No, she doesn't have a clue. She's just walked into this—this teenage fantasy, in a serious band while she was still in high school, and yes, she's good enough, she's got the talent and she's worked hard and earned the place she has, I'm not saying she hasn't. But she's never had to fight for it—she's never had to believe in it when she couldn't see it. It's always been there for her if she worked hard enough, ever since we met you. And she's young and—but you and Kev and I are getting older, we're getting to where we have to choose, we have to look further ahead. There's no pension plan for the band."

"Are we voting on whether we break up or not?" Frankie demanded.

"No! I'm just saying—I'm just saying I have to choose for myself what I do now. Not for you. This time, not for you." Anicky's voice was shaking. Bolted to her feet. "I'm taking a walk. Save me a beer."

"I'll come—"

"You'll stay," said Kev.

"Let her be, kiddo," Thomas said.

A few nights live, a short-term project the singer's pulled together, though she said it might turn into more. It's not really gelling, not as a long-term thing. Nothing dramatic; they're just not the right people, together. Suits Thomas, he's not looking to belong to anyone anyway. The drummer, though—they've got something, he and she. Anika Bell, she says. Anicky. We blonds have to stick together, he says at some point about something, the rest of the project being dark, and she laughs at him. Apparently she's a redhead. Walks with a long, free stride, impatient with city streets. Usually has a book to hand when she takes a break. His kind of person. A few years older than him, a teacher in her day-job. High-school French. Had to do something, she says. A bit envious of his impoverished freedom, he thinks. Most nights there's a slight, dark-haired girl hanging around, waiting for her. She watches Thomas the whole time and it's his hands, not his looks. Girlfriend? he wonders, the first time, though she's kind of young.

But too old to be a daughter. "My little sister," the drummer says. Francine. She looks like she's barely out of high school. Turns out she's not, but she's living with Anicky, a cramped flat not far from the convenience store over which he has his room. Decent salary, her job, by his standards, but she's paying off big student loans, saving up for Frankie's future.

Religion, Anicky says.

"What?"

"You're wondering why she lives with me. Religion. As in, the parents have it. I escaped. Took up percussion in high school and the pastor of our church got some of us teens into a little Christian rock group of awfulness, but it meant it was an allowed hobby and I got to actually save up for my own kit. And defected to atheism at the first available opportunity, i.e. first year university, when I went home for Thanksgiving and mentioned I was in a band again, very definitely not mentioning other things, and was told to put away childish things and also if I wasn't playing for Christ I was doing Satan's work and don't come down to dinner unless you put on a skirt. And they'd thrown out all my CDs and books while I was away. But meanwhile Frankie had caught a bad case of guitar and there was a new pastor by then, the whole church getting more extreme and my parents with it. No acceptable outlet for music, not what she wanted to play. She kind of—"

"Ran away," Frankie says. "I saved my allowance and bought a guitar from this guy at school and hid it under the bed. Our brother snooped and found it and ratted me out. They broke it and threw it in the garbage. It was a piece of junk, but it was mine."

"Ran away twice," Anicky says.

Frankie shrugs. "So I was so wicked they washed their

hands of me and gave me to Anicky."

That's the short version. The long one he hears later. It involves shouting and hitting and a girl locked in her room until she asks forgiveness on her knees, school suspensions, missing persons reports and the police and a month on the streets of Montreal.

It could have been even worse.

"I'm not religious, myself," he offers, feeling nonetheless a weird need to apologize on behalf of religion. "But my grandfather's a bishop. Plays mandolin. Big Jethro Tull fan. And Led Zeppelin."

"That's practically Satanism, you realize."

"Mandolin?"

"Catholicism. Though you're right, there's something pretty Satanic about mandolins, too."

"Church of England bishop—Anglican. Roman Catholic bishops don't have grandsons."

"That's what they want you to think."

Frankie's torn between an obsession with Rush and a love for the latest electronic. Dances to anything. Starts turning up at his place when school's out; half lessons, half jam sessions. She's got a decent Epiphone and is taking piano. That's the bargain Anicky struck with her. Stay away from drugs, yes, that means pot too, do you *want* to stunt your brain, no drinking except maybe a beer or a glass of wine with Anicky on a weekend evening, stay safe, stay—within reason—home, and she can put everything she's got in her into music. Do all that, get decent grades, and Anicky will buy her a genuine Gibson Les Paul when she graduates. Some of his gear drifts over to their place. A better amp than what she's got, something he buys cheap from a fellow he knows solely in order to make her a permanent loan of it. He helps her put together a proper rig, effects pedals, the lot. She tags along when he's working. Not his girlfriend, he has to say, more than once, cross. She's a child, for God's sake. Fifteen, she says indignantly. I'm his tech.

My young apprentice ... A few arguments with Anicky. Too many late nights. Frankie's letting her homework slide. School matters, he says. You've got to earn that Gibson. Compromises are reached.

Takes the Bells home at Christmas, when he realizes they have nowhere else to go. Do *I* have to pretend to be your girlfriend, Anicky wants to know.

Good lord no. They'd think the end days had come if he brought home a girl in an official girl capacity. It's just an excuse to have her drive him, he says, so he doesn't have to take the bus. Since she's a proper grown-up and owns a car and everything.

Ah, that's all right then, Anicky says. Exploit me.

Would have been nice if Kevin and Anicky could have hit it off romantically, a kind of present he could have given each of them, but that wasn't in the cards. As people, though, things seem good between the four of them. That's a relief, when your friends find they can be friends too.

Kev has done a lot of work on the studio. It's expanding out of the original workshop space, taking over all the basement. He's bought a good synthesizer. Is he planning some sort of solo recording project? Not really, he says. Let's try that thing we were working on at Thanksgiving and see how it sounds. Get Anicky to program some drums ...

Maddie and James are home, with boyfriend and girlfriend in tow, and one of Mum's brothers has come from England with a couple of cousins along, so the house is full of Gorevs and Atkinsons. Dodger shows up to spend the night and they go off in a convoy to the midnight candlelight carol service on Christmas Eve at little St. Peter's, and pretty much drown out the rest of the congregation. There's something about "O Holy Night." He's not religious but he doesn't much care for commercial secular Christmas. There's no awe in it. *Fall on your knees ...* Or maybe just the key it's in, with the darkness and the candles and the scent of the pine and cedar boughs on the altar, crazy fire hazard. They end with guitars and piano at home, and everyone singing Jethro Tull's "Ring Out, Solstice Bells" and "Another Christmas Song," to guitar and piano, Atkinson family tradition, with eggnog and fruitcake. Christmas Day, Kev and his father show up for brunch.

He chances on Frankie scrubbing tears on her sleeve. "Don't look like that," she says. "It's just, I'm going to adopt your mom. Okay?"

"Adopt away," he says, and hugs her. "Like solar power. Enough Mum for everyone." Goes to find Mum and hugs her, too.

All a revelation to Anicky and Frankie. He hadn't really thought about family before—about not having one. About having nowhere you could go home to, when you needed a place that was home to go to. Or just to have at your back.

A revelation, Kev and Anicky as a rhythm section, even if they don't have a proper drum kit along.

Strange Pilgrim Road isn't quite born then, that first Christmas they're together. But there's that feeling—they're together, the four of them, and it's gestating.

A good cook always cleans up after himself, Uncle George

always said. A decent motto for life. Frankie left the rounding up of plates to him and Kev, disappeared. Maybe to join Uncle Henry and a British mystery in what they called the front room, the grown-ups' space, it had been, when he and Kev and the Park cousins were teens and claimed the lower-level family room for their own.

"You better go talk to her, Tank."

"Why me?"

"You remember being nineteen?"

"I try not to."

Sound of the front door opening, dog barking—dogs, Bunny getting in on the action. Lindsey and Isabel, come on the bus in search of curry. Kev was already dishing out the leftovers for them.

"How was your day?"

"Survived," Lindsey said. Leaned on him a moment. Sweat and potting soil. "How's the band meeting going? Where is everyone?"

"Anicky went for a walk. Frankie's—"

"Downstairs, I think," Kev said.

"Oh," Lindsey said.

"You had nothing to do with it other than giving me a shove at what I've been working very hard at not seeing."

"It's okay, Lindsey," Kevin said. "It's good."

"Too bad Lindsey doesn't sing," Isabel said. "Thanks, Kev. Kev, I might be eating for two but the other one's not that big. Seriously, put some of that back. Actually, does Lindsey sing?"

"No!"

"He's okay if the music's really loud, but not really—"

"I absolutely do not sing."

"Too bad I don't."

"I've heard you sing, Iz," Kevin said. "Sorry."

"What's wrong with my singing?" Isabel demanded.

"You fling yourself enthusiastically after notes you can't reach."

"She flings herself enthusiastically after notes that are in another song entirely," Thomas murmured at the ceiling.

"Oh, thank you, Tank."

"Well, you do."

Kev turned him, pointed him at the basement door. "Go talk to Frankie and don't fight with your sister."

Right.

Ran her to ground in the studio, headphones on, feet braced against the cabinet of the mixing board, his Fender baritone, thank you very much for asking, plugged in, amp to mixer. Recording something.

"Hey, Frankie-mouse."

She didn't look round till he tapped her shoulder. Stopped what she was doing, which looked like nothing much, just a hypnotic march of chords.

"Sorry," he said, as she pulled the headphones down.

"It wasn't going anywhere."

"You want to borrow that?"

"Not really."

He went to get his baby, the Paul Reed Smith that he practically handcuffed himself to if he took it out of the studio, plugged in. Frankie uncoupled things from the board. Started again, or anew.

"I do like the baritone, though. Maybe I'll buy one when we're rich and famous. Can't think what I'd use it for, really."

"To mess about with." He turned their volume down, started chasing what she was doing, weaving through her. "Look, we're not talking about breaking up the band, not as such."

"If you leave—"

"I'm telling Tasha Meyer I can't do it. That I've got commitments with my own band."

"If Anicky quits—"

"Then we'll have to find another drummer. People do that, Frankie. They leave for all sorts of reasons. They don't get along, they don't like the direction the music's going, their partner's ill and needs someone to look after them, they want a solo career, they're tired of chasing tomorrow and just want to stop being ground down and down in debt."

"Anicky's too young to give up yet."

"Anicky's been bringing you up since she was ... how old? Twenty-two, twenty-three, something like that? Since she was just out of university, anyway. The point where maybe, maybe most people would only be thinking about starting a family, your first baby, or more likely you're just sorting out who you are and what you want, just starting to really figure out being grown up. Finding a partner. A career. Saving for a down payment. And suddenly she has to be a mother to a teenager and not an easy teenager at that. And then I talk her into quitting her job, and it was a good job. A safe job. A pension, like she said. Summers off. She could have paid her loans, put you through university—"

"I didn't want that."

"She's getting to the age where if she's going to have children, she needs to be thinking about doing it. And she's had a couple of people in her life who didn't want a girlfriend who's always on the road, didn't want to be 'her indoors' who keeps the home fires burning while the other half's touring or in the studio till midnight, didn't want a live-in teenager and didn't want—"

"Her. If they don't like who she is, they don't deserve her."

"True. But I think she's tired."

Scowling. And momentarily losing track in the baritone's alternate tuning. "Shit. Swap?"

"Language."

"You're the most Victorian maiden aunt of a rock star wannabe I've ever met. Despite your habit of draping yourself all over Lindsey like he's some sort of coat-rack."

"I was nicely brought up in the shadow of a bishop." What you don't know, kiddo … And maybe it was partly being trailed by Frankie, looking up to him as a real grown-up and everything she wanted to be, had made him stop and really think about the bouts of—provoking people to pick fights with him, admit it, that'd been him, in high school. And after. Not all the Exit's problems had been Dan's doing. "And Lindsey's not a coat-rack. I was born to be a cat. Obviously. That's all." They swapped guitars.

"I could move out."

"Then you'd both have a harder time paying your bills."

"I know. And I do my share—I mean, I'm not living off her."

"Nobody thinks you are."

"If we had a proper house instead of a trailer I could move into the basement bedroom like a real teenager. Though the bedrooms are at opposite ends—it's not like baby sister's on the other side of the wall, if she found someone she wanted to bring home." Wicked grin. "Or if I did."

"Who are you seeing?"

"Nobody. That was a what-if. The guys my age are all kids who want to tell me how to play guitar because they know three chords and that other tricky one they can't quite remember, and the older ones who try to pick me up always turn out to be creeps who get off on the fact I'm a teenager still. I'm waiting for someone to grow up."

"Wise."

"Boring. Do I look like a nun? What happens? If Anicky decides to go back to teaching, what happens to me?"

"Nothing. It's not like you're joined at the hip or anything. What, do you think we keep you around like some kind of mascot?"

"I don't know. Maybe."

"No! Sure, when you were tagging after me in Toronto, when you were a kid and I was telling people you were my apprentice—but not when we started talking about expanding Strange Pilgrim Road into a band. It was just going to be a one-off, two-man studio project, you know. But we had the drummer we wanted right there for the asking, we hoped, and we were listening to you that night, remember, we were all down here fooling around with Queen and Maiden and then some of the stuff Kev and I were working on and we just said, yeah, that's it, that's us."

"But now you want someone else."

"Yes. I do." They'd circled back to where they began. The music, too. "Lindsey said it. That missing extra thing. I know how good we are."

"We're great."

"And humble. We're very humble."

"And not arrogant at all."

"Never. But the lead singer's merely quite good, just not up to the greatness of the rest of the outfit. And Strange Pilgrim Road doesn't settle for less than great."

"Yeah but—"

"We don't."

"Me, too?"

"Keep at it."

"Oh, thanks."

"You're not a favour to Anicky. Don't let it go to your head."

"You're not very good at compliments."

"Come on back upstairs, Frankie-mouse. There's probably ice-cream."

"I'd rather have a beer. I am nineteen, you know."

"One. We're all on our last round unless we're crashing here overnight."

"Ever had a beer float?"

"Sounds disgusting."

"Seriously. Porter and french vanilla."

"That's an abomination. Get upstairs. I'm going to pretend the last part of this conversation never happened."

Anicky was back on the couch in the living room.

"I'll give it another year," she said. "Then we'll see."

/Four/

Mood:
Brian May, "Resurrection"
Blueweed and heat-shimmer, shoulder of the road
Maple leaves float on the river

Thomas had been all day down in the studio; coming up was like leaving the climate-controlled habitat for the surface of a hostile alien planet. Instant sweat. Another sweltering day. July was turning out to be as hot and dry as June. Lindsey's rain barrel was empty and he was having to carry pails of water down to his planters every evening. People like Dodger, who was out between Camden East and Centreville, and Anicky back of Yarker were starting to worry about their wells, and even the lake was looking low for this time of year, shoreline exposed, stone with a dry crust of algae. Lawns crunched, though that was normal. The air conditioning in the Focus hadn't worked in years and even though he was travelling downtown against the suburb-bound rush-hour traffic he still ended sitting on Bath Road going nowhere, some delay ahead. His shirt was soaking, plastered to him, by the time he parked the car at Isabel's, and half a kilometre to walk from there. He made a detour to pick up some bottles of restorative stout. He'd need it by the time he got home.

A bark announced him while he was still on the stairs, and then, startling and new, a sort of *whoo-whooo-whoo* siren wail. Lindsey let Bunny out to come galumphing down at him, tail whipping in excited circles.

"She's learnt to howl," he said. "Or whatever you call that. This may not be a good thing."

"But she's so pleased with herself!" Thomas handed over the beer, picked Bunny up. "Silly dog." She was getting too big for that. Beagle, hah.

They shut themselves in, hushed Bunny when she ran in circles, *whoo-whoo*ing again, showing off. The stereo was playing Pet Shop Boys. Lindsey's happy music. Or for a safe place, when he needed to remember happy. *Release*. One of their best albums, whatever people said.

"Supper? It was so hot I skipped lunch, but I made devilled eggs, potato salad."

"Sounds great. How's the job hunting?"

"Nothing today." But Lindsey didn't seem too down about it. Getting used the rhythm of it, the ritual of checking, of keeping his EI claim active. Looking forward to the courses in the fall. His mum had told him that for goodness' sake, just concentrate on his work, come September she'd make him an allowance while he was studying, so he could not worry about getting stuck in some retail job again, not worry about EI, concentrate on what he needed to do. She could manage it. He had a bit of that stressed look around the eyes, though ... Tired. Or maybe it was only the heat.

Books, scattered across the floor. Not like Lin, that disorder. "You okay?"

"That? Only Bunny, when she heard you. Crashed into every stack leaping around. I was sorting."

"Sorting … oh." Raleigh's boxes, which had sat nearly forgotten in the corner by the bookshelves, mostly hidden behind plants, for months.

"Things to keep, things for a used bookstore." He shrugged. "Mostly those. A few I might read, though, or that look like you might. Some mysteries for Iz and Kev." He started stacking books again, fending off Bunny, nuddling them, excited all over again by foreign smells. "It's—not what I expected."

"The books?"

"Yeah. He was heading for med school. I mean, he always wanted to be a doctor, like Dad. But, well, there was that biology text but—no chemistry. I know he took chemistry, too, because he was saying he didn't like his lab instructor, the second week of classes. We had coffee. I remember it because—we didn't, much. Meet up, I mean. That's—the only time, really. I mean, we ran into one another on campus but we weren't in the same residence and … anyway, it was coffee in the Student Union Centre. Coffee and danishes. Stupid thing to remember. Those danishes. Blueberry. But no chemistry text. Just—those."

Those, indicated a heap of mostly thin paperbacks.

"Pirandello? Sounds like an opera I haven't heard of."

"It's plays. They're all plays. Modern, I guess. Not that I'd know. Not stuff from high school English, anyway. There's a huge Shakespeare, too. Everything, in one volume, with footnotes."

"Ah!" Thomas pounced on that. "I know this edition. James has it, full of sticky notes from some course. That's for your keep pile. I like Shakespeare."

"Do you? I guess I do. I'd rather watch it than read it, though."

"If you're reading it you've got to taste the words. Read it aloud. How about I read you sonnets this evening?" Hopefully. Reading, beer, all the fans going. Reading in bed after Bunny was tucked up in her box for the night …

Lindsey did smile. "Alright, put it in the keep pile, there."

It was a small stack, mostly paperback novels. Lindsey really had been sorting, not just clinging to everything that had been his brother's, which was—a bit of a relief, to be honest. Healthier. He could be so intense about Raleigh, sometimes.

"Stanisklavski," Lindsey said, beginning to pick up the scattered books. "Growtowski?"

"He was—studying Polish? No, there's a Euripedes. Brecht, I recognize that, too. *Goodnight Desdemona (Good Morning Juliette)* with brackets, no less, that'd make a great song. Hey, Donald Jack, Dad has all his *Bandy Papers*—great novels, but I've never heard of *The Canvas Barricade*. Maybe he'd like this." It went into the keep pile. "What's a Barba? *Dictionary of Theatre Anthropology* … Dictionary of one or the other but both together?"

"It's all plays. Plays and I don't know, drama theory, I guess you'd say." Lindsey opened up something called *On Directing and Dramaturgy*. Showed him a page. "Mostly used textbooks from the university bookstore, but they don't seem like first year things. I think he was maybe—reading on his own. Intensely. Devouring, if he was getting through all this stuff. There's underlining, especially in the Barba."

"Used texts, though—"

"I know, but a lot of the underlining's in green fountain pen, which was a thing of his. I used to tell him to use pencil if he was going to write in books, especially if they were mine—but … anyway, it's him. There's notes sometimes. Just saying things like, 'This!' and 'No' or 'But see so and so page X.' Serious stuff. Not like just underlining a line you like in a poem or something. I think he dropped his chem, maybe other things, and was taking at least the first year drama course, and—there's this, too." He offered something. Sheaf of papers, stapled. Marked up with ink so pale Thomas could hardly see it. No excuse for writing in presumably-green, there just wasn't. Dates circled, fees …

Thomas leafed through them. "National Theatre School," he said. "That's Montreal? Someone James knew in high school got in there. She's at Stratford, now. Huh. Professional program registration. Admissions and auditions … Lin."

"He didn't want to be at St. Mark's at all. He didn't want to be taking pre-med. And he didn't say."

"The poor kid. But would your parents really have been upset, if he'd got an audition, gotten in, gone to do this instead? Your mum doesn't seem the sort to say, you must follow in your father's footsteps and uphold the family honour and all that."

"But she just decides things," Lindsey said unhappily, picking up the Shakespeare again. Opening it as if it might say something more. Lots of almost-invisible underlining. "Decides, that's how they should be and that's how they are and—he was the one who was good, he was the one who was doing all the right things. And—it was always, Raleigh's going to be a doctor, like his daddy, he'd—she'd, tell people. From when he was little. Really little. At the age when, you know, I was going to be a cowboy."

"Seriously?"

"Yeah, we had this old picture book from when Dad was little. About cowboys. Not shoot 'em up westerns. Real cowboys. Out under the sky, you and a horse." He shrugged. "Or an engineer. Driving trains, obviously, not building bridges. And an archaeologist. I was pretty serious about that one, that was from when I was ten or twelve right into high school, but they didn't have even an intro to archaeology at St. Mark's and we had to go to St. Mark's, that was just how the world was. And by grade eleven or so it was definitely botany, ecology, so that was okay."

"Carleen didn't go to St. Mark's."

"Things were different, after."

"Yeah, I suppose. Oh, Lin."

"But no, they wouldn't have freaked out. They wouldn't have gotten angry. They'd have said, yes, if you're really sure that's what you want to do, we'll help. I know they would. They always backed us up, things like that. Maybe Dad might have been disappointed but not disappointed in Raleigh, just, you know, thinking it would have been nice if someone had done what he did, but he'd never have shown it. Mom—she'd probably have said something about spur of the moment decisions and are you sure and stuff like that, acted like it was something amusing and inexplicable, maybe, but not, no you can't, or you're making a big mistake, this is the rest of your life, never that sort of thing. Gamma and them—but Raleigh was always better at just tuning them out."

Now he was holding the Shakespeare like it was Bunny, a child, close to his chest.

"When I was in second year, he was in grade twelve, he was in the drama club play at school. They always did Shakespeare. *The Tempest*, that year. He was Prospero. I didn't get to see it; it was in April. Exams." Very quietly. "Carleen said he was really good." Blinking too hard. "This looks like—I mean, it's really looking like—What else can it be? He was going to go home at Christmas and tell them he wanted to try for this, that he didn't want to be at St. Mark's, he didn't want to go into medicine. And he was scared, and stressing out about it, and he didn't talk to me because I was always like Mom, Raleigh's going to be a doctor like Dad, isn't that great—and underneath it, Raleigh's going to be the proper son, do all the right things, the things I can't do, and that's good, that fixes everything that's wrong with me, that he can be the right kind of son, the real one. So he *couldn't* talk to me, because I couldn't see him. And you get so tired, and—carrying that, when nobody sees you, and you want to get drunk or something and just leave it all behind and I never could, it scared me too much to do that, but he—that's what he was doing. Because he needed someone who mattered to see he was real and there wasn't anyone. That's how he killed himself. Because he was alone. And he shouldn't have been."

He folded down on his knees, as if he was falling. Shaking. Crying. Thomas went down beside him, held him.

You couldn't say anything. What could you? All just guessing, psychology, what-ifs, but it seemed all too plausible. Ordinary stupid overdrinking, bad luck, happened anyway, but saying, no it was only that, you're just guessing at all this—that was no consolation, and drinking too much on a night you were, what? Angry, maybe. Tired, exhausted, if he'd been doing all this extra studying, trying to prepare. Scared you were going to fail, exposing yourself by even trying to seize that chance and they'd all know, and if you failed to get in … they'd know. And they'd be sorry and tell you, well, you can still do it, there's still the drama club or whatever, because they didn't understand that that wasn't enough, it wasn't real …

And you'd been fighting with your girlfriend, you were alone, you were carrying something you thought you couldn't talk to your best friend, your brother about, because—Lindsey never could see himself, he was shy and awkward and weird, maybe, but brilliant, and intense, a scientist, and of course you admired him, and you had this one thing *he* admired, this going-to-be-a-doctor thing, and yet you hated it and wanted to throw it away, go off to be, what, an actor, write plays ... and you had to tell your parents, stand up under the weight of everyone thinking—you thought they'd be thinking—what a huge mistake you were making, how foolish, how reckless ... he knew that one, actually. Drinking to run away, just one night, that's all you wanted. Running away, not caring, just that one night and you'd be sick in the morning probably but right now it felt good. And tomorrow, the day after, next week, after exams, you'd go home and you'd tell them you were applying to audition for theatre school and—and deal with it. But not tonight.

He'd been there. Not that he'd even gotten as far along as his midterms.

Been there. Just not that drunk. Or not that unlucky.

"Not your fault," he said into Lindsey's hair. "It isn't. It never was. People never see each other fully, they never understand everything, they can't. He'd have told you at Christmas, told them. You'd have been proud of him, you'd have told him he'd do great, you'd have talked. You know that's how it would have gone. You'd have figured things out between you, you'd have been talking again. Like me and Kev. It was just bad luck, it was an accident took him, and Lin, you know this isn't meaning he deserved it, you know I'd never mean that, but you know it was his own doing. We've all been there, done some stupid thing and by some good luck survived it. Everyone. Me, for certain. Probably you. Not always alcohol, drugs. Just—running across a busy road, diving and you miss that rock by two inches, taking the boat out when there's wind coming and you've been told not to—Everyone does something stupid that could have been deadly, and they survive so it doesn't become the tragedy. And then sometimes someone doesn't, but it doesn't make it your fault any more than if he'd just ended up in emergency."

All the wrong things to say. Not helping. But Lindsey was quiet now, just holding on to him, and his shirt was wet again, tears, not sweat now, kneeling together on the floor, and Bunny nosing into them, concerned, trying to lick Lindsey's face.

"Oh, Lindsey," Mom says, pausing, one foot in the car, hand on the door. Carleen's already in, fiddling with her phone. Probably giving Piper the play-by-play.

>*And we're off—nope, she's thought of something else she's forgotten to tell Lindsey …*

Everything from warning them not to take their eyes off the toaster-oven if they used it, "It goes from this bagel's not toasting to this bagel's on fire in about two seconds," to "Oh, and if you let the budgies out and they won't come down from the curtain rods, try a banana."

"I knew there was something else. Up in the attic—books of your brother's that I boxed up when we moved. I thought I'd finally get around to clearing them out, make some space. Take them over to the used book place in Jemseg. I know you took most of your books and whatnot when you went up to Ontario but you'd better have a look, see if anything of yours is mixed in. I was going to do that next week, before the book people close up for the winter."

"Okay," Lindsey says. Another of her fits of clearing out. He wonders if she'd have thought to mention it if he hadn't turned up. Carleen had rescued the stereo and records from being given to the county historical society's yard sale at the last minute, stacked all its components and the albums in the over-the-kitchen bedroom with big notices taped all over saying, *Take to Lindsey don't give away!!!* until she'd had a chance to deliver them.

There's plenty of space in the inn. He wonders if it's more the space in Mom's mind she's trying to reclaim in these fits of getting rid of things. Notices how she doesn't say Raleigh's name. Keeping that distance.

"Have a safe trip," he says. And to Carleen, "Let me know when you get there."

"Sure. I'll bring Thomas back a present. Exotic eastern delicacies."

"From Dartmouth?"

She shrugs. "We could feed him dulse." Gives an evil grin.

"What's dulse?" Thomas asks.

"Purple seaweed," Carleen says, but Mom is in the car now. Door slams and she gives them a little honk on the horn, backing out, waving.

"What's it for? Sushi?"

"Just eating. A snack"

"What's it taste like?"

"Hm. Sort of like—the seashore."

"I'll try it. But salmon, that's is what we need. Lovely fresh Atlantic salmon. Or mackerel. Or both. Let's go shopping. Do you go to Oromocto or what?"

"Yes. And we can probably get dulse there, too, if you want.

The best dulse comes from Grand Manan, anyway, not Nova Scotia. After the attic, though?"

Thanksgiving weekend down east. Their first Thanksgiving together. It had seemed important somehow to bring Thomas to meet Mom and Carleen, the Kavanaghs. It's Monday they'll be going to Hampton, though, Grandad and Grandma Kavanagh and everyone. He just—couldn't face Gamma's. Aunt Tanya would be there, with what Carleen called *l'homme du jour* in tow, and Makayla likewise … And he's feeling all peopled out just from wandering around the village with Carleen, since she seems to know everyone and they all want to chat. A relief: they're on their own, he and Thomas and the budgies, for the rest of the day and much of Sunday, too.

The attic is huge. The ceiling of the second storey's been insulated, bats of pink fibreglass laid between the joists, a floor of boards put in over that in the central space but out under the eaves it's just fibreglass with here and there some sheets of plywood. There's not that much junk stored, really.

"The bouncy horses!" Amazing they haven't gone. Horses hung in a frame on springs—Dad had had to find two of them to stop the squabbling over whose turn it was. Because they had to be riding together, racing, being knights, cowboys, something. That was when they still lived in the apartment in a house on Charlotte Street, before school, before Carleen. The bunkbed that had later gone to the cottage, the horses in the living room, the weird loud pattern of blue and purple flowers on the upholstery of the saggy couch and armchair that he'd always found so distressing, so wrong, not like proper flowers, two different shapes on one sort of vine-thing, and the foliage all blue and brown. Almost the first thing he remembered, that living room, him and Raleigh riding those horses. Or maybe that was a photo he was remembering, something that had been framed on Dad's desk in his office.

He pats each nose, going past. Doesn't care if Thomas sees. The Fisher-Price castle that had been Dad's when he was a boy is there too, and all the little people that go with it in a clear storage bin.

"Ooh, the Park girls had one of these," Thomas says, crouching down to poke at the trap-door in the tower floor, raise and lower the drawbridge. "Do you still have the dragon?"

They spot it in another bin, this one full of Carleen's farm animals. And a cloth Christmas gift-bag he recognizes.

"I don't know, mixing dragons and cows seems a bad idea," Thomas says. "Didn't your mum ever read *Farmer Giles?*"

Lindsey goes after the bag, rattling, heavy.

"Treasure?" Thomas asks.

"The adventuring guys." He tips them out on the floor.

"Oh, minis! I didn't know you were into D&D."

"We weren't, not properly. Dad was, when he was young. We just used them for adventures." He stands them up, one by one, elves and dwarves and humans and halflings and monsters. They'd been divided between him and Raleigh. All back together again. He picks out the mounted warrior he'd given to Raleigh that time, one of the unpainted, pewter-grey ones he'd always liked best, the unfinished monochrome somehow leaving more room for imagining. Puts her in his pocket. There's one of his own he remembers. Laughs. Another favourite, she was. Bard, with a harp and a sword.

"Here. This one's you. Take it."

Thomas takes it, turns it through his fingers. "To keep?"

He nods. Can't say what he means. It's a piece of where I've been. I want to give it to you.

Thomas picks up another one. An elf-ranger with cloak and sword, one they'd always debated over, not able to decide if it was male or female. "She needs a friend," he says. "If that's me, this one's you, alright?"

"Yes."

Thomas puts them both in his pocket. Lindsey gathers the rest of the figurines, puts them back in their bag, back in the tub.

There's Carleen's red barn. A full-page note tied to it with yarn, written in black marker: *Do not give this away. Do not give away any of the toys or my Nancy Drew and Artemis Fowl and Harry Potter—I mean it. Someday your grandkids will want them.*

"I detect a certain anxiety regarding your mum's cleaning binges."

"It's because it's not cleaning, I think," Lindsey says. "It's more like, she has fits of feeling she can get rid of something that hurts. So she doesn't think about it, she just does it."

"After so long—no, sorry, it's not that long at all, is it, that was stupid."

Almost a third of his life, though, and getting further distant every year.

Does a time come when that not-thereness stops being an everyday thing?

"Do you want it to?" Raleigh asks.

"Thought you'd stayed home with the worms."

"I was going to. But here I am." Raleigh wanders off around Thomas to crouch down by the bouncy horses, eye to eye, solemn. Remembering. Remembering their names. Blaze. Thunder. Out of a story?

No. The attic's all weird light, small slanting patch of sun, weak bulbs switched on, harsh shadows.

Lindsey looks away. "I guess—everyone hurts in their own way, too."

"Yeah. It's a good thing my folks don't have an attic. We're all keepers of stuff we think is important, or might be important. Mostly books. Or in my case, guitars *and* books, and in Mum's, rocks. It's supposed to be kids who come home with their pockets full of rocks. At least without an attic they can force us all to take things away like proper grown-ups should. Leaves more room for rocks and their own books, of course. Oh hey, a real live trunk."

"That was Mom's. Her parents sent her off to university with it, like someone going to boarding school in one of your Jennings books. Weird, when she was only a few hours away and could go home on weekends if she'd forgotten something. She keeps her wedding dress and stuff like that in it."

"Can we look? Would she mind?"

"I don't suppose she'd care. That used to be a treat, when we were little. Her taking things out of the trunk to show us. Little knitted and crocheted baby things, and you'd be all of eight or nine and thinking, how was I ever that tiny?"

"Ooo, I want to see your sweet little booties."

"Seriously, Thomas … "

But Lindsey has seen the boxes he's looking for, down at the far end under the gable window, beyond other boxes of no interest, "X-mas" they say, and "curtains", beyond more, bigger clear plastic tubs: yarn, hats and mittens put away for winter, and then fluffy animals and dolls, soccer balls and Lego. Do soccer balls even keep, in the freeze and roast of an attic? He's glad the stuffed animals haven't gone out in the garbage, though, glad Carleen's claimed them, a few memories to share with the next generation. He's got the one essential one, a grubby—though he had washed it—teal dragon, sitting at home, guardian on a bookshelf. Saw Raleigh's beloved polar bear in Carleen's room yesterday, with her tiger, whose tail she'd sucked all the plush off as a baby, side by side on her bookshelf. Glad she has Bear, still something special, still remembered.

Five liquor-store boxes. "R - books" on them in blue marker, Mom's writing. Not even his name. There's no Raleigh's room, the way there's a Lindsey's room even though he's never lived here either. Strange and outright creepy if there were, and yet ...

Photos on the wall in the upstairs hall, on the side of the house that's private, a door between them and the guests. All that's left of Raleigh here.

No shadow by the bouncy horses, either.

Lindsey gets down on his knees by the boxes. They're not taped shut, just folded. He opens the top one. First-year biology text. He has the same one, still on his shelf in case it comes in useful, which it probably won't. Time to get rid of that, probably. Underneath, it's like a snapshot of what Raleigh was reading around the time Lindsey went off to St. Mark's: Kate Elliott, Steven Erikson, Tom Lloyd, a textbook on statistics, a French dictionary, hardcover Cherryh, something that looks like a mystery by someone he's never heard of, Ian Rankin, Terry Pratchett—that's his copy of *Wintersmith*, he'd had to buy another when he couldn't find it a few years back ...

He can't do this. He shoves the books back in, closes the box up again. Just breathes, for a few moments, because he's—

Eyes are stinging.

"Lindsey," Thomas says. "Hey, Lin?"

"What?" He makes himself get up. Thomas has the trunk open.

"Come look at this."

"Baby knitwear. I've seen it."

"No, these."

Thomas hasn't lifted out the inner tray. From what he remembers, the wedding dress, the lacy little booties and bonnets and jackets and, what are they called, receiving blankets, are all folded up in tissue underneath. An embroidered tablecloth made by Mom's grandmother is all that's ever been in the tray, too fine, too venerable, to actually use. But what use is it folded up, only even looked at once a decade?

What Thomas has is a yearbook. Four yearbooks. He recognizes the colours, the red and faded amber. There'll be a winged lion with a book in its paw stamped on the cover. The St. Mark's *Leonine*. He has four quite like them, shinier, brighter, lying on top of his tallest bookshelf back home. Dad's from UNB and Dal will be around somewhere, he supposes, but—

"Have you ever looked through them?" Thomas asks. Gone all serious.

Oh.

"No. I've never seen them before." He must have. The cover had looked familiar when he got his first yearbook, the 2006-2007 ... They'd probably been there under the tablecloth all along, glimpsed but never handed out, when Mom was showing them the dress, with its wide princessy skirt that in the photos made her look a bit like a wedding cake, and the tiny knit things, all pink and blue and yellow.

"Do you want to look?" Still serious.

Yes. No.

"Yes," Raleigh says.

He ignores that voice.

Shakes his head.

"Lindsey," Thomas says, very gentle. "Lin, love—that question's there in you, all the time. Maybe you should. Just—there's probably nothing to find, but—you won't know till you look."

"No," he says, with something like panic rising, clawing at him from inside. "I-I-I can't. Not-not right now, not-not here. I—"

"Sh, okay. It's fine." Thomas hesitates. "Are you going to check those boxes for any books of yours, like she said?"

"I can't." Not that, either. "I—" He turns away.

"Hey." Thomas, a careful hand on his shoulder. "Leave it, then. If you haven't missed them before now, you won't, and anyway, it's not like she's throwing them out. A used bookstore, someone else will enjoy them. Yours or his."

"No. No, Thomas, can we—it's only five boxes, I want to look at them, I need to look at them, not in case they're mine—because they're his, but I can't, not right now, I can't. I—will they fit? In the car, in the back, it's only five boxes and they're not big, could we—?"

Thomas is silent, looking at the boxes. Then, "Sure. We can put the bags on the back seat, and my guitar, I guess. Everything'll fit. We'll make it fit."

"I'll look at them later."

"When you're ready, yes. It's alright."

He hates breaking down like this. Betraying himself. It isn't the first time. A day of panic and misery in June, over nothing, just that he's so—so not what Thomas should have. A mistake, Thomas's mistake, even wanting him, he's going to leave him, of course he is. A night in August when suddenly he couldn't face going out, the band, the pub—everything. Anything.

And Thomas just gets like this. Quiet. Calm. *There.* Not arguing. Not getting angry, going off. And in that he finds something solid under his feet, inside himself. Can breathe long enough to make that clawing thing inside go quiet. Can say, give me a little time, I'll be okay, I'm sorry.

"I will look through them," he says. He's not going to hoard them away unopened forever, some kind of fetish.

"Creepy," Raleigh says.

"I just need some time to sort of—to sidle up to the idea. Slowly. To get used to it. That's all." He wants to see. Books tell you things. He wants to understand—whatever there is to understand. To hunt for that unhappiness he hadn't seen, hadn't guessed, as if there might have been some clue unrecognized in plain sight all along on Raleigh's bookshelves. Or something.

"What good will that do?" Raleigh asks.

"At least I'll know."

"It won't fix anything."

"But I'll know."

There's nothing to know. Stupid, tragic accident. No deep meaning underlying it.

But sometimes he wonders if he can see Raleigh any more at all, as if there's this missing person, not the last years since he died, but the ones before, those years in high school where in the vast crowd Raleigh was going more and more his own way, the years Lindsey was at St. Mark's, the two school-years that Raleigh's January birthday put between their sixteen months age difference become a shadow into which his brother had already begun to dissolve.

"Sure. Makes sense, I guess," Thomas says.

For a Lindsey sort of sense, maybe Thomas thinks, but if so he doesn't say it.

"For a Lindsey sort of sense," Raleigh says.

Thomas has picked up one of the yearbooks again, has opened it, leafing through. A glimpse of the usual sorts of things: club photos, montages of events, beer-gardens, residence groups, rows of formal graduation portraits.

"Don't," Lindsey says. "Not now. Please."

It's being in this place, in this house that isn't home, it's … he doesn't know what. But he just can't look right now. As if all sorts of old anxieties are in the air, threading into his lungs.

"Okay," Thomas says, and then, "Who ever goes back and looks at their yearbooks anyway? Do you?"

"God, no."

"Yeah." And Thomas goes over to the boxes labelled "R - books", and opens them all up.

"Thomas, don't … "

Thomas takes out the thick biology text. Two yearbooks fit in that space. The other two squeeze down the side of what looks like a box of paperbacks. The biology text—"Do you or does anyone want this?"

"No. There'll be a new edition by now."

"I notice you're not protesting," Raleigh says.

The biology text goes into a box labelled "Crochet mags."

"So. There. For someday, okay? Let's take these down now, so you're not worrying we'll forget them when we leave. And you can deal with it all when you're ready."

"I will. Just not now."

"I know. I believe you. It's okay. Give yourself time."

Lindsey closes up the the trunk while Thomas starts down the narrow stairs with the first of the boxes.

Cute little booties. Thomas is such a—they have to go down to the ground floor and back up to the over-the-kitchen bedroom. It doesn't connect to the rest of the house. Hugs Thomas, then. Just holding fast, saying nothing, before they go back for the next boxes.

"Go take a shower," Thomas had said, after supper. A quiet supper. He couldn't talk, really. Empty, drained. They'd packed up the books, putting the ones he was keeping, most of the fantasy and science fiction, the big Riverside Shakespeare with Raleigh's green underlining in it and the couple of his own Pratchetts and Cherryhs Raleigh had pinched, on his shelves, setting aside the Donald Jack play for Dr. Gorev and the mysteries, all modern settings, British police things, not the historicals and fantasy-mysteries he liked, for Iz and/or Kev. The rest, bookstore. "Destress, cool off. I'll do the dishes, take Bunny out to visit the yard. Join you after? Don't lock the door, eh?"

"Yeah."

They kept them there in the bathroom, on the glass shelf with the ferns under their grow-light. The three little lead, or pewter, or whatever they were, adventurers, warrior and ranger and bard, together in their fern-forest.

"He's right, you know," Raleigh said, while he was brushing his teeth. "Not your fault. We should have talked. Both of us. About lots of things."

"Yeah."

"It's okay. You're okay, you know. You're strong."

"That's a weird thing to say." Especially to someone who'd

been sitting on the floor crying all over his boyfriend.

That grin, Raleigh when he knew he was being annoying, teasing. "Yeah, so. It's still true."

"Am I right? I am, aren't I?"

Silence, then.

"You'd have done well, Raleigh. You always made the best stories. Made the little guys real, on all the adventures. Even the cows."

Silence, but it wasn't absence.

"Okay, go haunt the living room or something, I'm taking a shower."

"Yeah, bashful. I've seen you naked. And there's a picture of us in the tub together on Mom's wall."

"Sorry, we're babies in that. Go. Thomas is coming to take a shower."

"Is that what you call it?"

Raleigh was gone. Not for good, never for good, just away, leaving him to the lukewarm water in peace. Eyes shut, just listening to it, letting it fall over him. Waiting. Not many dishes to do. Thomas tapped at the door, let himself in.

Watched hands wave up in the air, peeling off his T-shirt, all sweat and tears.

"Hey, you. Okay?"

"Yeah, I'm okay. Thomas?" Hand out past the curtain, catching his hand.

"I'm here."

"Thanks."

He didn't really sleep, that night. Exhausted, hazy. Maybe it was the heat. Naked, and the fan blowing over them, but he kept the sheet pulled up to his chest anyway, always felt too exposed without some kind of cover.

Neither of them had mentioned the yearbooks, left on the coffeetable by the computers and the azalea.

Maybe he should just tidy them away again, out of sight, out of mind.

He was happy, just lying here. Being here. Lying with an arm up over Thomas. The warmth of him, the scent. He moved closer, carefully, not to wake him. Wrapped himself around him. Thomas mumbled, dreaming. Sighed. Settled into the embrace.

That trip home. He'd thought it was going to be a mistake, and yet had known he had to do it. Get it over with, maybe. Carleen had been excited, wanting to meet Thomas before she headed for South America. Mom—he hadn't told. Not the important thing. Because it had seemed too difficult, and not for the usual reasons, she wasn't like that. Just—somehow, some huge, reluctant inertial mass, sitting there. See, this is me, and you haven't seen me properly, you never did. This is me.

Too easy in the dark to go astray passing Fredericton, to end up on an unlit road through nowhere, heading for Saint John down the wrong side of the base. He'd done it, that first summer Mom had been in Gagetown.

"Oromocto," he says to Thomas, whose turn it is to drive, but Lindsey would rather be driving himself; at least he sort of knows where he's going. Thomas looks on every missed turn or wrong exit as an adventure. "Just keep heading for Oromocto and we'll be okay, at least—go right in to Oromocto and we can reorient there. If we get on the wrong road before then, there's no way to cut through the military base to the

love/rock/compost

road we actually want and I've driven down the wrong side for half an hour in the dark before I even realized where I was."

"No exit for Pohénégamook?" Thomas says, and they both go off into helpless giggling like a couple of six-year-olds. "Pohénégamook, Pohénégamook, Pohénégamook," Thomas sings, with rising operatic grandeur. " Pohénégahénégahéné-gamook!" They've been driving for something like fourteen, fifteen hours. That's including the carwash. Possibly they should have done something sensible, like stop for the night at a motel in Rivière-du-Loup, but time, money ... you can do it all in a long day, Kingston to Gagetown, but night has fallen and their breath is rank with coffee, minds gone giddy, the body saying, that's it, enough, time to sleep.

"Pohénégamook," Thomas says, like a curse, an invocation, and brakes too suddenly, flipping the turn signal on. Luckily there's no one behind them. "Oromocto. Tea. Green tea. I can't take any more coffee."

"We're nearly there."

"Tea and doughnut. Or ditch."

"I think it's probably my turn to drive again."

"I think you're right."

Somewhere in Quebec, after Rivière-du-Loup and before the border, there's a sign on the Trans-Canada. "Nouveau-Brunswick" it says, and an arrow, an exit.

"Um, I don't think—" Lindsey says, even as Thomas, singing along to the thunderous strains of Taylor's "No More Fun", abandons the highway.

"No?" Thomas asks, breaking off mid-line, but he's already turned again, missing his chance at crossing to the on-ramp. They're heading away down some secondary road, no hesitation, and somewhat over the speed limit. Lindsey turns the music down. Maybe they need something calmer. Thomas put together what he called the road-trip-staying-awake playlist on his phone. It starts off with Empathy Test, Loreena McKennitt, and Eric Johnson in the early morning and gets heavier, pulsing through the day. Calmer isn't on it at this point.

"No," Lindsey says firmly.

"But it said New Brunswick. Nouveau-Brunswick. It did."

"I think it was lying. The Trans-Canada just goes on. And on and on. No turn-offs."

"Well, that army convoy is following us. They must know where they're going."

"What?" Lindsey looks back. There's been a string of army trucks behind, some towing jeeps or guns, for the last half hour. The convoy had been at the last rest stop, pulling out after them and staying there. He'd speculated they were heading for the base at Oromocto, just upriver from Gagetown. Thomas had proposed seeing if they could hitch the Focus on behind one of the trucks when everyone had their next coffee-and-bathroom stop. Wouldn't work, Lindsey had said. They were the wrong colour. Someone would notice.

"I think the army's been led astray, too."

"Maybe it's a shortcut?" Thomas suggests. "Surely the army knows where it's going."

"Um." It's possible, he supposes. Some old back road that crosses the provincial border, ends up—somewhere or other. They should be able to pick up the Trans-Canada again below Edmundston, in that case … ? He doesn't know the west of the province that well. It's just a lot of spruce forest and potato fields to drive through, above Woodstock.

They bump along. The army confidently follows. Tailgating, in fact, which he assumes is why Thomas isn't looking for a chance to turn around. Probably in the cab of the leading truck a couple of soldiers are saying to one another, "Aren't we supposed to stay on the Trans-Canada?" and "Maybe it's a shortcut?"

The army's route is marked with little symbols on the roadside signage, just for them, spades or clubs like a deck of cards; right now he can't remember which. Anyway, he's not seeing any here.

"Yeah," Thomas agrees, when he points that out, evidence this isn't some shortcut known to the military. "But now they're saying, 'Look, those guys up ahead obviously know where they're going … '"

"You see, this is why normal people use GPS."

"GPS is why people drive into quarries and wedge trucks under overpasses."

"Pohénégamook," Lindsey reads off a sign. "Okay, we're now heading for Pohénégamook."

"Where the heck is Pohénégamook?"

"Never heard of it." Lindsey's digging out the map. He likes maps. Deciding to take his holidays this week and go to Mom's for Thanksgiving provided a good excuse to get a new map of Quebec. "Pohénégamook … is on the US border and we're heading due south."

"Did you bring your passport?"

"No! I don't even have a passport. I've never been out of the country in my life."

"Seriously? You'd better get one. What if I want to drag you down to New York with us some day?"

He's not too sure he wants to go to the US, even with the band. Not too sure about American paranoia, and looking, well, not Irish, anyway, while having an Irish surname. Then he wonders if it's racist, to protest that he's not all the various things people have asked him if he is, over the years. But how can he be those things? Being darker than his sister doesn't give him any claim on some other culture.

"We'd better turn around before we end up in an international incident," Thomas says.

"Why an international incident?"

"Well, look what's behind us."

Lindsey snickers. "'No, really, I know it looks like an invasion but honestly, we just got lost. Can you at least let us through until we can find a place to turn around—the guns aren't even loaded … ?'"

"Time to lose our tail." Thomas accelerates, putting a little distance between them and the leading truck. Zips into the first visible driveway.

Except it isn't.

A rutted wood-road.

Possibly a mistake. Water fountains. They lurch and jar to a stop.

"Whoa," Lindsey says.

"Okay, what just happened?"

"We fell into a pit?"

"Don't exaggerate," Thomas says severely. "This is not a pit. It's a puddle."

The windows and windshield are brown with mud. Thomas tries the wipers. They rearrange the dirt a bit.

"Right," Lindsey says. "A puddle."

"A deep puddle." Thomas puts the car in reverse. Steps on the gas.

Wheels whine. Mud sprays. He shifts back to park. "Well,

that was impressive. I think I just dug us in deeper."

"It's a logging road," Lindsey says.

"Now he tells me."

"If you'd slowed down long enough for me to yelp in alarm—"

"Yes?"

"I'd have yelped in alarm." Lindsey turns the music off—it's on to Malmsteen and that's really not helping. Opens the door and scrambles out to higher ground. They're well and truly mired, just about up to their axles in muddy water, and lucky, maybe, it is all one puddle and not two ruts, or they'd have torn away the exhaust system and such. The Focus isn't exactly a high-riding car.

Thomas waves him off and Lindsey realizes his intent and runs for shelter behind a spruce.

If Thomas is trying to paint the woods in mud, he's doing a good job. Rocking the car free, not so much.

Lindsey waves him to stop, before he wrecks something.

Thomas scrambles over to dry land and joins him, considering. "Time to bat our eyes at the nice soldiers with their big trucks and winches, I think," he says, and heads for the road, waving at the truck that roars by, towing a jeep. The driver waves back.

And that's the last of the convoy. No stragglers appear.

"I wonder how far we have to hike to find a tractor?"

Lindsey is cautiously probing the puddle with a stick. There's solid ground down there.

"Brush," he says. "We need to cut some brush, even some of this bracken and stuff, and get it under the wheels. I think we can back out, then."

"I don't think Iz keeps a machete in the glove compartment."

"Jackknife. Doesn't have to be big stuff. Just something for the tires to grip."

"You have a jackknife?"

"I always have a jackknife."

"The things one learns in moments of crisis. Okay, you cut, and I'll sacrifice my shoes—no, I'm doing this barefoot, I like these shoes and the suede will never survive. It's hard to find good desert boots these days. Anyway, I'll do the muddy stuff. My fault we're in this hole. Literally."

"Barefoot's not a good idea."

"My feet will wash."

"Just put your hiking boots on. They'll wash."

"They'll never be the same."

"Neither will your foot if you walk on something sharp in that mud. There could be anything down there. Broken bottles. We're probably a long way from the nearest emergency room. Don't be an idiot, Thomas."

"Okay, okay."

It's muddy work, even safely on shore, as it were, and the jackknife isn't the greatest tool for stripping small branches, still holding onto their autumn-browning leaves, off the alders. Works better on bracken. The spruce proves too tough. He should have brought pruning shears, but somehow, he just didn't think of such things as necessary equipment for a Thanksgiving road trip. Thomas has crawled back into the car to change his boots, tucking the legs of his jeans into his socks, for what good that will do. Grimaces, wading out, beginning to pack the armfuls of brush under the front and rear wheels both.

"It's cold," he announces.

"Wading in October, yes."

"Doctor Foster went to Gloucester ... " Thomas sings.

"What?"

"It's a nursery rhyme. Don't you know it?"

"No. What brought on a nursery rhyme?"

"In a shower of rain. He stepped in a puddle right up to his muddle and never went there again."

"Ah. Why muddle?"

"Other than the rhyme, I don't know. Maybe it works better in some eighteenth-century accent? We can ask James, if we ever get out of here. Probably too modern for him, though. He stepped in a piddle right up to his middle?"

Lindsey snickers. "Are we done?"

"You tell me—you're the one masterminding the great escape. Oh lord, I'm going to have to get out front and push, aren't I?"

"We could try without," Lindsey says doubtfully.

Thomas shakes his head. "I'll push. It's going to take that extra rocking to get it to bite on the branches, you know it is. But root around for Scooter's blanket and put that on the passenger seat for me afterwards, because I'm going to look like some kind of disintegrating golem before this is done." He strips off his bomber jacket and sweater with the air of a man readying himself to step into the ring, throws them into the back. "Make damn sure you get it into reverse, will you?"

"God, Thomas!"

"Sorry."

Lindsey makes the scramble back into the car, starts the engine again. Realizes he can't actually see out, tries the windshield washer and is rewarded with the sight of Thomas slogging around to the front, then leaning, braced into it. Doesn't dare roll down a window. "Ready?" he shouts.

Thomas nods.

Reverse. Horrible image, why did Thomas have to say that? God, he could drown in this if he gets knocked down under the car. Keeps his foot hard on the brake, reverse, yes, triple-checking. Okay. Gives it a little gas.

Mud flies. The car rocks a little. Thomas, head down, heaving at it.

Thomas gives up, looking up, shouting something. Lindsey shifts back to park, lowers the window a crack. Doesn't want the mud on it getting into the gears, or whatever it is actually makes it work. "What?"

"You're going to have to gun it. Going gently's just going to dig it in deeper."

"Okay."

"On three. One—"

Two, and reverse, definitely reverse, with his foot on the brake. And three.

Thomas putting his whole weight into it, muscles standing out on his arms while Lindsey floors it and the engine roars. They lurch backwards, mud spraying up in great rooster-tails before him, and flying sticks and Thomas has vanished but he keeps going till he's on the hard shoulder. There's a mud-man scrambling after him.

He kills the engine again and opens the door.

Thomas falls more than leans on the fender, laughing hysterically, trying to wipe his face. "Oh God, Lin, I went straight down. If this doesn't teach me to look before I leap—Hold me, Lin."

"God, no." He swings his legs back in, shuts the door. Thomas wipes a clean patch on the window, presses his face to it, making pathetic eyes. Lindsey motions him off and gets out.

"Sitting on the dog-blanket's not going to save the seat. You've got to change."

"Grab that water-bottle and see if you can get my face clean, at least."

"Strip your T-shirt off first or it'll be a wasted effort. In fact—you'd better strip altogether."

"What, here?"

"Are your jeans miraculously waterproof?"

"Um. No, seriously, Lin. I know I'm the uninhibited exhibitionist of the outfit, but I draw the line at nudity on the public roadside."

"You can't keep wearing any of that. You'll get pneumonia or something. We've still got, I don't know, five hours, maybe more, to go. Strip."

"Find me some clean clothes, then. I'm going to the woods."

"Nobody's going to see."

"Allow me to preserve my modesty, my good man."

"Yeah, well, don't fall into anything."

"This is probably the only heffalump trap in the neighbourhood. Surely they wouldn't dig two so close together."

Lindsey roots through the dufflebags and backpacks, turns up a change of clothes. Finds a roll of paper towel shoved under the seat. They have one unopened bottle of water plus a two-litre camping jug, and Thomas is starting to shiver in the autumn air.

Lindsey opens a back door. "Just stand behind this and strip," he orders. "Be quick, or someone will turn up."

Thomas makes a face and hauls his T-shirt off. He really did go down flat in the puddle; mud to the skin. Boots, socks. He bundles everything in on the floor of the back seat.

"Good enough? Give me the water."

"No way."

"You're enjoying this, aren't you?"

Lindsey considers. "I think I am."

"If you tell Frankie I'm going to have to murder you."

"I'm already composing the email. Maybe I should take a photo."

"No, you shouldn't. You really shouldn't."

"*Strip,* Thomas."

"I mud-wrestled a Ford, babe, and the Ford won," Thomas remarks, undoing his fly, peeling out of his jeans and underwear together, handing them to Lindsey. He drops them on the floor with the rest, handling them with fingertips. Brown with mud, and dripping.

"Shut your eyes."

"I'd rather you shut yours, to be honest. I'm really not at my best … "

Thomas yelps, Lindsey dribbling cold water over hair, face, shoulders, chest … everything muddy. Which is everything. He'd been thinking only that Thomas needed to not be sitting in soggy clothes for the next five hours, especially since he always worried so much about his voice and catching colds, took vitamin D year-round trying to prevent them, but that fine silt really did go right through to his skin. "Turn around. Okay, and let's see your face again."

Lindsey empties the last of the jug over his hair. It's a slight improvement.

"Oh God, that's so cold! Is that an engine?"

"Yes, here."

"I don't want paper towel, I want my pants." But he's drying himself off—plenty of mud left, unfortunately. "Pants! No, underpants, don't go all American on me—quick!"

He's on one leg, hauling a clean pair of jeans on, steadying himself on Lindsey's shoulder, by the time the first of the convoy goes rumbling past again.

"Guitarist arrested for indecent exposure. Almost."

"Any publicity is good publicity, right? Give me the paper towel—we need to clean the windows. And the lights. Maybe we should run through a car-wash as soon as we get to civilization."

"In Pohénégamook?"

"We're not going to Pohénégamook, Thomas, we're turning around and following the army to Oromocto."

"Do you suppose they realized in time, or did they get turned back at the border?"

"No gunfire," Lindsey says. "Thomas?"

"Yes?"

"Thomas, I love you dearly, but—it's my turn to drive."

"Yeah, okay." Thomas plays with his phone, plugged into the car stereo, till he turns up Rush.

They wait until the army has passed, then follow docilely after it, stopping at the first gas station they come to for hot chocolate. Thomas is still damp and shivering, despite the heat being turned up full. The army's had the same idea.

"Been off-roading?" some little guy with stripes asks them cheerily, looking the Focus over, more admiring than disapproving of the mess. "You boys need a Jeep for that."

"Next time," Thomas says.

They finally lose the army when they stop for sandwiches and coffee in Edmundston, eating them while they run through an automatic car-wash, because a wheel is making a strange noise and Thomas, familiar with so many of the horrible, expensive

noises cars can make, says he hopes it's just mud inside somewhere, nothing worse. Seems to be the case. It's quieter, after.
Thomas takes the wheel again at Perth-Andover.

But now Lindsey's driving the last leg, Route 102, the old
river-road to Gagetown, eyes strained for deer, moose, bear—
all the things that leap out of the trees at you along here. They
could have gone almost to Gagetown on the Trans-Canada
but once they were in Oromocto he couldn't find his way back
to it. Oromocto exists solely for the military base; its signage
seems designed to confuse the Germans, or the Soviets, or
whoever it is they think likely to invade. Not so distant thunder. Clear sky. The base is mostly an artillery range. Night
firing practice.

"They're keeping up their skills for the Western Front?"

"Something like that. There's always helicopters, too, up
and down the river. And water-bombers, after they set the
woods on fire."

"That happen often?"

"Almost every summer, if you can believe Carleen."

Gagetown's quiet, dark, nobody out under the streetlights.
It has a gas-station, a marina, a pub, a fairground. No library.
A ferry over the river, but rumour is the government wants
to get rid of half the river ferries, Carleen says. They've taken
to shutting some of them down for the winter, even though
the fire departments count on the bubble-lines that keep
the crossings clear of ice for open water to fill their pumper-
trucks. Carleen, again. She has opinions. The main industry is
half a dozen potters. Tourist village. Very picturesque. It pretty
much shuts down for the winter too. Big black locusts tower
over Front Street, silver maples and red line the river, leaves
yellow now, and scarlet. No guests. The season's over, and

Mom actually gets boaters as much as people arriving by car. Only Mom's Suburu and a battered Ford pickup that must be Carleen's in the gravel parking lot.

"Nice," Thomas says.

The lights over the front and side doors are both on. There's a narrow flowerbed along the foundation, filled with frost-dead impatiens, and a couple of potentillas flanking the door. Needs work. Lots of work. Some old peonies and lily of the valley along the back, though, facing the river, if he remembers right, and a big rugosa rose by the deck, where the guests can have morning coffee while ignoring the view in favour of their phones.

"You made it!" The side door's opening. Carleen. She comes to meet them at the car, alone. No dog, these days. Not even a cat. Apparently Mom has a couple of budgies.

Carleen's wearing scruffy jeans and a long hand-knit sweater. Her short hair's her natural brown, a colour he's almost forgotten, only a streak of green. Smiling. No hugging. They don't do that sort of thing. Not to hug her, when he hasn't seen her in person since last winter when she brought the stereo up to him seems, well, weird.

To hell with it. He's turned into a Gorev. He hugs her. She's startled, then laughs and hugs him back. Not so thin and bony as she used to be, even last winter when she came up to Kingston, which is good. She looks well, really fit, happy. Seems she's making the same judgement of him, stepping back, but keeping hold of his hand.

"You look good, Lindsey. You do! Someone's looking after you."

"That'd be me."

"Thomas, hi!" He gets an assessing, and evidently approving, look, a nod, a grin. "I've got all your albums. Both bands, I mean. Last birthday. Whether I wanted them or not. Luckily I like them. Did you bring your guitar? "

"I brought a guitar."

"He always brings a guitar. At least one."

Thomas holds out his arms, a question, inviting. Carleen laughs, a little embarrassed, maybe, but steps into them.

"Careful," Lindsey says. "He's probably still damp. This afternoon he was face-down in a very deep mud puddle in the wilds of Quebec."

"Why?"

Thomas shakes his head, letting her go. "Pohénégamook," he says. "It's best not to ask, really. Would anyone mind if I did some laundry—is too late at night for that?"

"Sure. It won't disturb anyone, if that's what you mean. There's only us, and the old summer-kitchen's a laundry and mud-room now—we can't use the cellar for much, since we get water down there every spring."

"Mud-room's what we need," Lindsey says. "And a shower."

"How close is the river?" Thomas asks.

"Twenty metres or so. In summer," Carleen says. "Back door in spring. If we're lucky."

"And unlucky?"

"Dining room. No, that's never happened, not since we've been here."

"You'll jinx yourself, saying things like that, won't you? Lindsey says you're off to Bolivia soon?"

"Next month. Working for an NGO, sustainable forestry."

"That'll be an adventure."

"And a half! Let's get your things. I made up your room for you. Lindsey, did you tell Mom you were bringing Thomas?"

"I told her I was bringing a friend."

"Right. Really, Lindsey—"

"Oh, you made it."

Mom, in the doorway now. Wondering where everyone's got to, he supposes, since they're all just standing around at the car, nobody making any move to grab the luggage. Her sweater's hand-knit too—Carleen did say she'd run out of rooms to wallpaper. The same hairy yarn as the cushions Carleen sent him. It works better as a sweater. New hairstyle, blonde highlights in it. Blending in where she's getting some grey, he realizes. Not much changed, otherwise. Doesn't really look her age at all. He'd expected her to be—older, somehow. But he's thinking of Thomas's parents and Uncle Henry and Uncle George, half a generation beyond. She looks—forty, maybe. He thinks she looked older than that, those first years after Raleigh and Dad died.

"Why's everyone so surprised we made it here?" Thomas stage-whispers behind his hand.

"On the evidence, shouldn't they be?" Get it over with. "Mom? Mom, this is Thomas." He takes him by the arm, tows him forward. Doesn't let go.

"Oh yes," Mom says.

Hands entwined now. He doesn't know why he's so nervous; it's not like she'll care. It's the unspoken, well, that explains a lot, that he's flinching from. Because it's there, and it doesn't. Not anything, really.

"You're new," she says to Thomas, cheerful, not accusing.

"No," Lindsey says. "He's not, really."

"Better get your bags and come in," Mom says. "Have you had supper? There's lasagne ready to heat up. Carleen said you were vegetarian, Thomas? It has cheese, but she thought that was all right."

"That's great, thanks," Thomas says. Doesn't object to the cheese. Well, he wouldn't. A nicely brought-up child, he'd say, and he likes cheese; it's not rooted in his old meat-phobia, just a discipline he enforces on himself, eating it so rarely. Lindsey hopes for his sake it's good cheese, worth the fat.

"You already told her?" Lindsey asks, cornering Carleen alone by the car.

"Sort of. I mean, you knew she's wasn't going to mind. I don't know what you've been being so evasive about it with her, all these months. She asked. She said you'd gone even quieter than usual in emails, was that good or bad, were you seeing anyone these days, you said you were bringing a friend but not what sort of friend, were we making up one room or two for you? That sort of thing. So eventually I just said yes, it's his boyfriend but he's being all stupid and shy, for some reason, and I didn't know why because Thomas seemed really nice. And she said, oh good. And I said, he's a vegetarian though, and she said, oh dear."

He laughed at that. But, "I wasn't being evasive." He hadn't been. Had he? Hadn't been talking to Mom much at all. But he didn't, anyway. They'd never really had much to say to one another. "It's just—I don't know. I just don't know. They always go on—they make me feel there's something wrong with me, whatever I do. All the time."

"Mom doesn't."

Well, she didn't stop it.

"Anyway, you don't have to come to Dartmouth. Last I heard, we're going up Saturday night, coming back Sunday afternoon. Just say you've had too much driving."

"That's the plan."

"I wish I had that excuse, but I can't really get out of it, not when I'm heading off to Bolivia for a year at least. Anyway, I want to see Piper and the boys. You'll come to Grandma and Grandad's, though, on Monday?"

"Of course. I want to see them."

"Will he eat turkey?"

"No. We'll bring some kind of egg dish or something to add to the table, it'll be fine. Or there's this curried chickpea and sardine salad thing he does, don't make a face, it's great. He's an amazing cook."

"You've said. In fact, he's about all you talk about, you realize."

"Really?"

"Yes." She hugs him again, startling. Grabs a bag out of the back of the car. "Come on. We've left him to Mom's interrogation long enough."

All in all, it's not as bad as he's been thinking. But Thomas can talk to anyone, and Mom seems genuinely interested in hearing about the band, doesn't feel as much of a need to update him on the doings of Makayla and Julie as usual, as if she thinks he might somehow care, as if small childhood mis-understandings are long forgotten. Makayla's an elementary school teacher and his personal opinion is that she shouldn't be left alone in the same room as a child; his impulse is always just to leave the room himself when her name's mentioned. But once Mom gets off onto family doings, as she inevitably does, the novelty of a musician in the house exhausted, it's Piper's place on the Nova Scotia provincial women's soccer team she's telling them about, and how Zack is hoping to make some big hockey tryouts, though Darren, at St. Mark's, has given up hockey in favour of Fine Arts, of all things. Photography, not cubes. Piper and the boys are all right.

He and Thomas and Carleen go out the next day to wander around Gagetown and Thomas decides to do all his Christmas shopping, pottery for everyone—he has so many people to get presents for, a daunting expense even when it's all just pairs of the pretty little wine-cups. Apparently they're all from him and Lindsey together, though Thomas laughs and says, "No way, not your fault I have so many relations real and honorary," when, realizing that, Lindsey offers to help pay for them. They take the soon-to-be shut down ferry over the river to what Carleen calls Scovil's, not a village, just a couple of barns, no house, and the prettiest road in the province, he's always thought, drive along the north side to Jemseg and back, enjoying the scenery. Walk around town some more, exploring, have a beer watching the river and the nearly-empty marina from the back deck of the pub, the Old Boot, which has half an actual old sailing boat called the *Old Boot* as its bar, go down past the Victoria to the boat-launch ramp and play with someone else's dog that turns up wanting sticks thrown. It seems to live nearby. A little girl comes out of a house, waves and shouts hello to Carleen, calls it home for supper. Everyone says hi; everyone seems to know Carleen.

Aside from getting introduced to too many strangers, Lindsey's actually enjoying himself. Seems like Thomas is, too. And Raleigh's silent. Hasn't said a thing since they left Kingston. Maybe he stayed behind.

Yeah, someone had to look after the worms. It's a Raleigh kind of joke, but it's just himself, thinking what Raleigh might have said. Not that voice. Lindsey isn't missing it. Is he?

Save it up, the happiness. Sunshine held close. Strange Pilgrim Road is going to be in Europe most of the winter.

Though it seems taken for granted that Lindsey'll keep showing up for Sunday dinners with the Gorevs and Uncle Henry anyway.

He's family.

The Gorevs were family, and even the Parks. What was his biological father, really?

What Isabel had said? Just a sperm?

He might be a face in a yearbook. But what difference would that make? Still just a sperm, in the end. An accident.

Nothing bad. Dad said so. A nice guy. They just weren't in love.

And what were the chances he'd even recognize anything of himself in some little square of grad photo? Or a nose, an eyebrow in a club group shot … There's nothing of Mom in his face, his build, nothing to say he's hers at all, not that any of the Quinlans have ever been able to see, and they loved to pick at it, at him, looking for it, when he was little.

He could narrow it down, anyway—exclude all the blonds, anyone short, fat, pale-skinned … ?

When he and Bunny returned from their morning run, Thomas was drinking tea on the couch, with the yearbooks beside him, one open on his lap.

"Morning!" Thomas fed Bunny a crust of toast that he'd saved on his plate, before she rushed to her food bowl, her breakfast ready and waiting. So was Lindsey's tea, poured and still steaming.

"Shower," he said, but he took it and sat down anyway. "Not quite so hot today, but still … "

Resolutely pretending he didn't see the yearbooks, as Thomas cleared them away to the coffee-table.

"All right this morning?" Thomas asked. "Would you rather I put these away?"

"Why?"

"We can put them in the bookcase, leave them for another time. Forget them entirely. Whatever. Whatever you want."

"Why, Thomas?"

"Because it's none of my business, really. And I shouldn't be pushing at you about it. Tank, like they say. I think I'm learning to restrain myself and then I just decide, this is what's good for him and I don't think, what does he want, not what do I think he needs. You know."

"I'm fine. I'm tired, okay. I didn't sleep much. But I feel—I feel okay. It's—the thing with Raleigh. At least I know. I think I understand. That's—I think I needed that. It doesn't change anything, and it does. You know? Does that make sense?"

"Yes."

"So. Why are you suddenly going guilty about looking in the yearbooks?" Because Thomas hadn't been feeling it was none of his business enough not to start looking at them in the first place.

And that was a bit—stressing.

"Because it's personal, and private, and none of my business, it's between you and your mum."

"Me and my mother and some guy. What, Thomas?" Long swallow of tea. "Okay, did you find some grad photo with little hearts drawn around it in sparkly ink labelled, father of my baby?"

He could say that. Carefully, pretending it was casual; he could say it, make a joke. He held out his mug and Thomas topped it up.

"No," Thomas said.

Something washed through him. Emotion. Heat. Uneasy in his stomach. Relief.

Disappointment.

Thomas put an arm around him, pulled him closer. He let himself be pulled.

Mouth dry. Swallowed more tea. His stupid hand was shaking.

"T-Thomas?"

"It's this. It was in the fourth-year one. Just stuck in the middle. Do you want to see?"

No. "Yes."

A printed paper, folded, stuck like a bookmark in the one yearbook still on Thomas's lap. It wasn't the page that mattered. It was the paper itself.

Program. A concert programme from the yearly St. Mark's Performing Arts series. Touring musicians, dancers, not just Canadian but international too, things you'd never get to see but in a big city, otherwise.

"Look at him, Lindsey. It could be you."

This one was the Generalife Guitar Quartet.

Two men, two woman, formally dressed and standing together against some vaguely-familiar backdrop: arches, slender pillars, a long rectangular strip of water. Guitars in cases at their feet or leaning against a pillar, smiling, relaxed, casual in contrast to the suits and full-skirted dresses, as if they've been captured by a quick snap, a pause on their way to set up in the garden. The men—one was short, dumpy, cheerful-looking—it was the other, the tallest one of the four. A dark and handsome stranger ... Did Lindsey look like that? Really? No. Though that narrow blade of a nose was familiar. A smile that looked open, easy. Confident. That wasn't his. The man's hair was black, curly, layered, long in back, past his ears but not to his shoulders; he didn't have a beard but just that deliberately unshaven look. So very—eighties. And he was young, surely he was young. They were all young, they were kids, even the stout man, who was the oldest of them and probably not even thirty.

"He's not—" His voice was cracking. "He's not that like me."

"Not quite a mirror but—he is, Lin. He's so, so like you. Look at his smile, look at the shape of his jaw. Look at his nose. His eyes, Lin, his eyes."

His grip was creasing the paper. He hadn't realized he'd even taken hold of it.

"Here," Thomas said. "Let go. There are bios inside."

The date. It might all be just—1987. Friday, December 4th. Taylor Hall. 7 p.m.

"It's right," Thomas says. "The timing's right." Mind-reading. "Here." Lindsey managed to relax his hands, enough for Thomas to take the programme back, open it up. Individual photos, like postage stamps. Perversely, he read everything else on that page first, though Thomas was practically quivering beside him, like Scooter when he was waiting for someone to hurl a stick out into the lake. The group was formed as a trio in 1984 by Andrés, Sampedro, and MacWhirter, alumnae/i of the *Conservatorio Profesional de Música de Andalucía,* with Olivares joining to make a quartet only in 1986 … toured widely in Europe … first Canadian tour … The woman were Estela Andrés Paz and Paulina Sampedro Laviña and they were from Seville and Barcelona; the other man was Robert MacWhirter. From Glasgow. The dark—boy, he was a boy—he was Spanish, like the women, a native of Granada, and his name was

Antonio Olivares Garcia … and it looked like those were the surnames, those second names, not middle names and …

Not quite a mirror. But that face he knew better, that more formal headshot. Not smiling, just looking out at you, serious, a—maybe a hint of amusement.

You have the most seductive eyes, Lindsey Quinlan.

Guess Mom had thought so.

Thomas was trying to move his hand, to see the actual program on the facing page.

"Sanz, Dowland, Weiss, good old Anon. Mostly early music." That was Thomas, babbling. Because Lindsey wasn't saying anything and Thomas had to fill up the silence that was making him nervous, making him worry, Lindsey worried him so much, sometimes, he knew he did. "And after the intermission it's Sor, nice contrast. Practically modern."

That's probably a musician-joke; right then he just didn't know. Or care.

Antonio … Olivares? So … ? So.

Lindsey … Olivares?

No, that wasn't him. He was still Lindsey Frederick Quinlan and if none of it ever quite fit, some stranger's name didn't either.

But. A father, not just a sperm any more. Already. A way of smiling. Looking at him out of that photo.

"Clearly you Quinlans have a thing for guitarists," Thomas said. Babbling. Mind-reading again.

A musician.

And that's what they said about musicians, wasn't it? One-night stands, pick up a fan after the show and gone in the morning. Seventies rock-star stuff.

Thomas wasn't like that. And anyway, classical musicians

… more sober, more serious, more respectable … sure they were.

"I need to go for a walk," he said.

"You just got back from your run." Thomas took the programme from him. "Remember?"

He hadn't, actually. Remembered, that was. Remembered now; sweat-sticky, chilled. Hadn't eaten breakfast yet.

"Go take a shower. Just—it's okay. Just think about things. There's nothing you have to do. Nothing that's going to happen, unless you decide to do something. It's only—now you know. Just someone she met, like your dad said, right? She kept the programme, to remember. There aren't any other programmes stuck in the book, just the one. It must have been a good memory. She wasn't lying to you about that, she and your dad." And, maybe he was thinking of Isabel and Ricky, because it came out too intensely, a protest, "He looks nice."

He'd have been gone by the time she found out. Back to Europe, probably. And anyway—

It was my problem …

"Shower," Lindsey said.

He stood too long under the water, letting it pound on him, a rain-drumming white noise that didn't quiet his mind.

There was toast, when he came out, dressed, hair just towelled, which always made the curling worse, but Thomas liked that anyway. Toast and poached eggs, and fresh tea, and Thomas hovering casually.

"Don't you have hits to write or something?"

"There's another singer coming. Someone Anicky found. He won't be there yet. I'll show up when I show up."

"I'm fine, Thomas. Go on."

"You come too. Bunny'd like to visit Scout. Bring whatever

it is you're reading today along, and we'll get Isabel when we're done and invite ourselves to Mum and Dad's for a swim, use their barbecue."

"You can pick me up when you come back for Iz, then. Don't hover. I'm fine. I'm just going to—I just need to think, okay? Some peace and quiet to think in. Sorry," he added.

"I'm sorry," Thomas said. "Okay. Text me, if you want to talk. I'll leave it on to buzz, call you back, I promise."

"I know."

He got Thomas out the door eventually. Sat down, got up, fed the worms, took the rest of the compost out, picked a handful of peas he could throw into something for lunch, and some lettuce, washed the dishes. Paced around. Bunny watched him worriedly. Brought him her rope, so they played tug for a little. How to make the human feel better.

"Get it over with," Raleigh said. *"Call her."*

"And say what, exactly?"

"I don't know. Try, I sort of stole your yearbooks and found the concert programme and why the big mystery, why didn't you just tell me all this years ago?"

"Oh for God's sake, stop nagging me."

He flung himself down on the couch. The programme was on the coffee table, still lying open and he shouldn't leave it there, Bunny took things like that off to chew up in case they turned out to be tasty, or fun, or best of all, something that would make the humans chase her.

Got his phone and took a picture, close up. The one face, near as he could make it; the one bio. Emailed it to his mother at both her addresses, the personal and the inn.

Send with no subject? Nagging program. Damn it, just send when I say send.

It went.

Sat back, feeling shaky.

Waited.

Waiting grew stale. He tried to read his book on setting up a small business. Couldn't. Tried to read *Wintersmith*. Not even that worked.

Email. Only Dodger.

>*The Bells' landlord says yes and he's delivering the shingles this morning. We're on. Get your hammer.*

Anicky, fed up with her leaking roof and her landlord's delays, had told the man that if he bought the shingles, they'd do the work in return for a cut in the next month's rent.

>*They've gone to the studio.*

She must be sitting right there. Dodger had never taken to texts.

>*I know, but you and I can make a start. I could use a hand loading my scaffolding. I'll come in to pick you up about ten-thirty.*

Well, he could use Anicky's wifi, keep checking his email on his phone. Lindsey went to change his clothes again. Gardening clothes, appropriate for roof-shingling. Sneakers that wouldn't slip, laces double-knotted. That broad-brimmed canvas hat that Frankie kept threatening to steal and feed to badgers, though where she thought she'd find a badger he didn't know. Just because he went so brown in summer didn't mean he couldn't burn, and up on a roof … Dodger was probably serious about the hammer. He found his hammer, and a pair of work-gloves that weren't stiff as steel gauntlets with mud. Bunny considered stealing them.

Got Bunny's tie-out chain, and put her seatbelt harness on her, ready. What was he thinking? It wasn't even ten, yet.

Email.

From Mom. Oh God.

"For God's sake, Lindsey, open it. You're just so …"

It was going to be nothing. She was just going to ignore it; it would be telling him that Carleen had sent some more photos of the new village she was in, and all about the old man with the hens he was so proud of, as if the photos and the newslettery-type email, Carleen's adventures in Bolivian forest restoration episode thirty or so, hadn't been cc'd to him and Mom both.

>Where on earth did you find that? I'd forgotten all about it.

And then,

>Are you home? Do you want me to phone you?

He replied. Nothing but,

>I'm home but going out before lunch.

Waited. And while he waited …

Browser. Quotation marks:

>"Antonio Olivares Garcia"

Apparently not an uncommon name.

He added,

>"guitar"

And in a new window, searched on the quartet. Looked like they'd disbanded in the early 2000's. Estela and Robert were fairly prominent in the early music scene in Europe. Paulina didn't seem to have any online presence connected with the quartet except in old mentions of its existence. Retired from music, maybe. And there was Antonio Olivares again …

Back to the other windows. Professor. Hochschule für Musik Frohnau. In Germany. Berlin. A bio page.

All in German. Why couldn't it have been French?

Spanish. Carleen had been frantically studying Spanish before she went to Bolivia; she'd probably left her CD course at Mom's. But the library would have that sort of thing, too.

Mom didn't speak Spanish. Antonio must speak enough English. Enough for—yeah, well, okay, maybe you didn't need much. Humans would always find a way to get on with making more humans, wasn't that a Pratchett quote of some sort? Misquote.

Or maybe they'd used French, or …

Anyway … He wasn't about to phone the man up in his office in Berlin. Lindsey ran the webpage through a translator site. The Hochschule was a—"college of music" was probably a conservatory. Born in Granada in 1961. So he was twenty-six when—older than he looked in that programme photo, only two years younger than Lindsey, which he'd say was old enough to know better, Antonio hadn't been some kid. But still, that wasn't so bad, Mom had been … well, almost twenty-two, an age difference the same as her and Dad, actually. Studied at the Conservatorio of Andalusia, member of the Generalife Quartet from 1986 to 2002, then part of a duet for several years, then teaching, still performing as part of Trio Frohnau … Some stuff about his particular interests in music, the courses he taught, it looked like, though the translation seemed to get a bit muddled or convoluted at that point. He'd written some music, too?

A photo, sharper than the ones in the old programme. Colour. His hair was shorter, but not fashionably short and that had made the curls go wild. Thomas would like it. Clean-shaven. Going grey at the temples, silvery, but not creeping back, something Thomas already worried about; Dr. Gorev was a bit thin on top, and the bishop looked like he had a tonsure, so he was getting it from both sides. Nothing you could do anything about, Lindsey told him, and felt that perhaps amid everything else, feeling you were glad you had a chance of keeping your hair was bit … strange. That skittering *I don't want to think about the real stuff* thinking kicking in.

Antonio was a handsome man, he could see that now. Thomas always said he … Lindsey just didn't see it. Not in himself. All eyes and hair he could feel safe hiding behind, and awkward arms and legs, wrist and ankles hanging out of his clothes until he discovered that good thrift stores actually had a wider range of sizes than the cheap department stores where he couldn't afford to shop anyway …

More to the point, Antonio Olivares Garcia looked—yeah, a professor he'd like to have. Someone with a sense of humour, could you tell that from a photo, why did he even think that? Someone—who looked like they'd care about what they did, whatever it was they were doing.

He was making things up. You couldn't tell that from a photo.

Antonio held a guitar, not playing, but upright, arms around it, neck against his cheek, a posture so familiar, Thomas would hold them like that, curled up in a chair, talking. Casually dressed, blue fisherman's sweater. Wedding ring, thick gold. But on his right hand, resting on the guitar, not the left … Looked like a wedding ring, anyway, third finger. Maybe that was the proper hand for them in Spain. Or Germany.

There might be—he might have … brothers. Sisters.

"You've got a brother. And a sister." Raleigh was very quiet.

"I know." He could have more. It wasn't as if you could only have one.

Stepmother. A wife who didn't know her husband had gone and gotten some girl pregnant, far away in Canada. Maybe he hadn't been married, then. Couldn't see a ring on either hand on the group photo on the programme. Why was he worrying? It was not his problem; he hadn't even existed yet, he wasn't responsible for, for any of it.

Be fair, the man might have a husband. Could you, in Germany?

Don't look that up. Stop. Just—stop. Right now.

"What are you doing to do now?" Raleigh asked.

Lindsey sighed. "Yeah," he said aloud. "I don't know, Raleigh. I don't know."

Because.

There was an email address. He wrote it down on the programme. As if the whole website of the *Hochschule* might vanish if he looked away from it.

His hand was actually shaking.

The band was going to Germany.

And what was taking Mom so long to call, anyway?

The band was going to Germany.

To Berlin? They'd gone to Berlin last year. Of course they'd go to Berlin, if they were in Germany. Thomas said, he liked Berlin. He said, he wanted to take Lindsey to Berlin, someday. He said—

He never had gotten around to getting a passport.

New window. Applying for a passport ... photo requirements, fee ... Another tab. Airfare, Toronto to Berlin.

"It's probably not actually easy for her, either," Raleigh said.

"I'm not sure I care whether it's easy for her or not." Lindsey was suddenly angry. "Why couldn't she ever just say*?"*

And the phone rang.

"Now you can ask her," Raleigh said.

For a moment he couldn't answer, couldn't get up, it was a

cordless and the base was over by the door and to walk across the room—the answering machine was going to kick in. He ran for the receiver, Bunny leaping around his legs, yapping and then going into her *Whoo-whoo-whoo* excitement howl, fool dog.

"Hello?" And if it was a telemarketer—

"So," Mom said.

And he had no words.

"Lindsey?"

"Mom."

After a moment she suggested, "Or we could talk about the weather."

"That's my father," he said.

"Well, yes. Technically."

"Technically!"

"Jonas—"

"I know! Dad is—Dad is always going to be my dad but this guy was my father and why wouldn't you ever tell me, why couldn't you just tell me his name, tell me about him, why did you let this go on, all my life, everything they said, all the going on and on at me that I didn't belong, I wasn't right, I didn't belong in your damned screwed up family, I didn't look right, I didn't think right and—"

"Nobody ever said—"

"Your fucking mother did, does, every time she looks at me. And Tanya, and Makayla, all my life, every fucking summer was like that until Dad bought the cottage and—"

"Lindsey … "

"They tried to make me think my real father was some kind of rapist, they said—"

"Lindsey!"

Oh God, he's crying and shouting and swearing on the phone at his mother, and—

"Lindsey, nobody ever—"

"They did," he said. "They did. Makayla did. She, I had to, all the time, she would, I had to let her do what she wanted, she hurt me, she said she'd tell her mother I'd—that I was like him, if I went against her, she'd—that's why Raleigh hit her, that time, at Easter. Because I couldn't. She would have said I—"

"Oh Lindsey. Lindsey—no. No, no, no. He was—Oh, Lindsey."

Silence. Bunny was licking salt off his face, her ears folded back, upset.

"I used to get a season seat for the performing arts series," Mom said. "Me and my friend Kim, we'd go together. I think you've met her, once or twice, when you were younger? Maybe you wouldn't remember. She's out in BC these days. She was in music, and there'd be a reception, after, for the performers, in the music department or in the art gallery. Wine and crackers and cheese, that sort of thing. I'd go along with her … " Nothing more about Tanya and Makayla. Of course not. Because she didn't know how to deal with that, she hadn't then and she didn't now, and so she ignored it and he was a grown man, it was too late for her to defend him anyway, so let it go.

"Sometimes it was boring," she was saying. "All the profs talking to the artists and the students standing around eavesdropping and wolfing down as much food as they could. But sometimes the performers were really interested in talking with the students, treating them like real people. And after the Generalife played, we were in the art gallery, all this music talk going on. There was a photography exhibit, just local landscapes and buildings, and he'd—Antonio—he was really quiet, like you, shy, I think, he'd wandered off, looking at the photos, and—I don't know, he looked sort of interesting and—"

"Interesting."

"Lindsey." And she laughed, suddenly, "Lindsey, he was— hot. Awesomely hot. But it was the other guy and one of the women that the music students were all hanging around, they were both those happy, exuberant sort of people, always the centre of a crowd types, and the other woman was having some sort of intense technical discussion with one of the voice profs about something. Antonio ended up all on his own. And I sort of drifted off after him, and started telling him about some of the places in the photos—he was really interested in the architecture, the wooden buildings, so different from things in Europe, he said, and we just—we talked. His English was okay. We talked about Nova Scotia, and about Granada, and—he wasn't that much older than me, maybe I was more interesting, babbling on about local history, how it must seem to him coming from Europe that nothing here was very old at all. Maybe I was more interesting than a bunch of professors and music students who wanted to have the same conversations he'd been having at Memorial and Dal and wherever else they'd been playing. I don't know. There was just—there was something. Really—do you know what that's like? I wasn't someone going to parties and just looking to get some guy into bed. I wasn't some kind of slut, which is what—"

"What Aunt Tanya said." He knew that, suddenly. Of course she would have. Maybe implied, maybe in so many words.

"It was just, out of nowhere—oh lord, this guy. His eyes.

And he was so sexy, a real fox, but not swaggering with it, and sweet, he was sweet. And he was laughing, not laughing at me, I was just, we were laughing. We were happy. Out of nowhere. Looking at me, like he really saw me, and he liked me. Like he was so—so delighted to find me there, in that art gallery with him. Do you know what that's like?"

"Yeah. Yeah, I do."

"So everyone started to drift away. Kim had gone without me. She said, after, she said she looked into the room we were in and decided the last thing I wanted was an interruption. And Antonio and I, we were—we hadn't even touched one another, but it was so intense, just standing there with him. And one of the women, his friends, came in to where we were and said something in Spanish about the hotel—they were going back to the B&B, I guess. It was that one that used to be called The Merganser. Very nice. And he said he'd walk. And she smiled and looked at me and said something else, kind of amused, nice, I mean, not snarky, and went off. And he just, he touched the back of my hand and said, I should walk you home, Tricia. And we were just looking at one another. And out of nowhere I said, Or I could walk you home."

"Mom."

"I know! It just—came out. And I'd only had one glass of wine. And somehow we just—we just went, without saying anything more. Holding hands. Except we kept stopping to kiss under trees. And we stopped at the drugstore, luckily one of them had started staying open late on Fridays and Saturdays that year, or I don't know what we'd have done, because I'd—I'd never been good at that kind of thing, boys, stuff, I'd broken up with the only serious boyfriend I'd ever had the spring before and I hadn't been missing him, I wasn't on the pill, and he—Antonio, he wasn't some gay Lothario type—"

"Mom!"

An actual giggle. "Whatever that means. He wasn't sleeping his way across the universities of Canada, your father. He wasn't like that. Not carrying a condom in his wallet ready for the next undergrad to cross his path."

"And they were closed."

"We got in as they were locking the door. It was … " She paused. "Yes, it was the single most embarrassing moment of my life. Rushing in the door at the last minute to buy a package of condoms. And—oh God, Lindsey, so many kinds and me thinking, I don't know, the guy's supposed to look after this, is there any difference between them, really, can't they just make it easy?"

"Mom, I don't need to—" But he'd gone from tears to laughing. Practical, planning, sensible Tricia Quinlan dithering in front of the condom selection.

"No, let me tell the story. You want to know."

"I—okay, I want to know."

"So there I was, standing like I was stunned, and frantic that Antonio would think I was changing my mind and I was only paralyzed with not knowing what I was meant to be looking for and he seemed to be assuming, I guess, that maybe I had some preference, that I knew what I was doing. Sweating, and thinking, Oh lord, my deodorant's failing, I'm going to reek."

"Mortal embarrassment. Because you're convinced when you go back in a day or two to buy a bottle of aspirin that they're looking at you, and snickering, and thinking, how did it go, dear? And it's always some middle-aged lady."

"This was the man with glasses. And the moustache. The

pharmacist himself. All the cashiers had gone home. I wouldn't have minded so much if it had been one of the girls."

"Oh, that moustache. He was still there when I was. So was his moustache. He waxed it into points."

"Yes, in my day, too. And Antonio—you're so like him, Lindsey. Not just your looks. He was really quite shy. About everything, really. So shy and formal, maybe being European, maybe being a classical musician, I mean, he was wearing a bowtie, probably that does something to you, just putting on a bowtie and a cummerbund—and, and gentlemanly. So he was all flushed, embarrassed, too, as much as I was, because the pharmacist was standing there jingling his keys trying to pretend he wasn't annoyed, or—probably he was laughing his head off, inside—And I just grabbed a box at random and Antonio was all gallant and insisted he must be the one to pay, and—I've always thought condom vending machines were such a good idea. They should put them on street-corners in small university towns. Though I'd wonder about the quality."

"Yes, well, Mom, quality … "

"And yes. Lindsey. I'm sorry. It's not what you want to say to your son, is it?" She was laughing again. "I'm sorry."

"The condom broke."

"Like an elastic. Snap. I mean, we though it was okay, we thought we were okay, we, uh, we hadn't—we got right apart and we got another one on and—"

"This is really more than I need to know, Mom."

"—and carried on," she said. "Laughing. Because it was so funny, really. I mean, *snap!*"

"Mom!"

"Well, it was. And he was so—I loved him, that night, Lindsey. I mean, sure, I didn't know him, not really, but the things that mattered for that night, I loved him. We weren't either of us looking for anything else. It was—it was a good night. And in the morning we took a shower together and he wanted me to stay for breakfast but I thought that was going to be a bit awkward, with the other guitarists. I guess I didn't want them thinking I was some kind of groupie who hung around parties trying to pick up musicians. So we exchanged addresses and kissed goodbye and I went off home—I had an apartment with Kim and another girl that year. And slipped in before they were up. And told Kim we'd walked around town and necked a bit on a bench in the park and that was it. Well, eventually I told her what really happened, obviously, but she never told. She's the only one who ever knew who he was."

"Did he write to you?"

"Oh yes."

"Did you write to him?"

"At first."

"But you didn't—"

"I didn't tell him I was pregnant. And that was the last thing he said to me. Well, and thank you. As if I'd given him something lovely."

"You had."

"It was quite mutual. No, he said, when I was getting ready to leave, something like, about what happened, if there are consequences, you will let me know, you must let me know."

"But you didn't."

"No."

"Why not? Mom, he was—"

"I—he was in Spain. He had a career. We weren't—we'd had a wonderful night but that's nothing to change someone's life like that for."

"It changed yours."

"Well, yes."

"But he should have helped you. It sounds like he was the kind of guy who would have."

It sounded like he would have wanted to. Would have wanted to know, to know his child, even. Maybe.

Wishful thinking?

"I didn't want to do that to him, make this claim on his life. I didn't want to seem like, I don't know. Like I was trying to get anything from him. It was just an accident."

"I'm not an it." He was angry again, all of a sudden. "I've never been an it."

"Well," she said thoughtfully. "There was a time you were. You're an adult, I can say these things. There was a time you were—just something I had to make a decision about. Something that had happened to me. It wasn't easy. It wasn't easy at all."

"Why did you keep me? Why did you even *have* me?"

And she didn't say, what a thing to ask. Paused, considering the question.

"I don't know, really. It just … in the end it just seemed like I wanted to. Because we'd laughed together. Because I'd been so happy, all that night. And he had, too."

"What *did* you tell him?"

"Well, nothing. I just … I just didn't tell him anything. I went for a long time without writing to him at all, because I couldn't think what to say, especially later, when I had you kicking away inside me, a real thing and not just a sort of, is this really happening to me? You were such a kicker. Neither of the other two were nearly so bad. I thought you were going to turn out some sort of soccer player or something. *Real*

Madrid. But I sent him a note when I was getting married. And he sent us a nice card, congratulating us both. And that was that. I didn't show Jonas the card, which was—I should have. But I knew he'd know, your looks even when you were a baby, and the Spanish name and all, and—I wanted him to feel like he was really your father. Which he did, so—it was silly of me. I didn't even keep it, though now I wish I had. But I don't suppose Antonio's at the same address, after all these years," she added.

"He's a professor at a conservatory in Berlin. I have his email."

"Oh. Right."

And there they were.

"It's up to you, what you do," Mom said.

"Yes. It is."

"I liked him," she said. "I'd have liked a chance to get to know him better."

She would have? What about him?

"But I loved your Dad. I didn't marry him just because I had a baby to look after. And part of why I loved Jonas, was he loved you."

"I know, Mom."

"Tell him—if you get in touch, tell Antonio I hope he understands. I didn't want to mess up his life." An unspoken 'too' there, or was he imagining that?

"I don't know what I'm going to do."

"Well, you can call me, you know. Whenever you want to talk."

"Mom. Mom, did you know, Raleigh was—I think he wanted to quit St. Mark's. He wanted to study acting."

"Raleigh did?"

"Yeah. I—I took his books, remember."

"Oh, right."

"He was planning to apply to the Performing Arts school in Montreal. He-he was going to tell you guys at Christmas. I think."

"How strange. He always said he wanted to be a doctor."

No, Mom. It was you said that. I'm pretty sure it was you. He just wanted to—to do what he thought you wanted him to do. To please you. But he didn't bother to say it aloud.

"Well," she said. "People change."

"Yes," Lindsey said. "They do."

"Call me if you want to talk."

"You said that, Mom. I will. I've got to go. Dodger and I are shingling a roof today."

"It's hot up there, isn't it? Don't get heatstroke and fall off."

"No, Mom. Anyway, it's only Anicky's mini home. Not too high."

"I suppose. Take care."

"You too, Mom. Bye.

And that was—

He pushed Bunny off his lap—he'd ended up the floor, back against the couch, and a human on the floor was a human who wanted to be sat on, apparently. Maybe she thought she was a cat. Went to make a cup of tea, dog trotting at his heels. Maybe there'd be biscuits. Bunny's philosophy of life.

What else did you do but make tea? He'd been hanging out with the Brits too long.

Oh God. A defective condom.

Because we'd laughed together.

Dodger Smith was closer to seventy than she liked to admit,

and until a couple of years ago, had apparently ridden a Harley from spring thaw to first snow, which, Thomas said, had made the weekly egg delivery a bit of an omelette roulette.

Little old lady with a chainsaw was inaccurate on several counts. Five foot eleven, she had said indignantly, when Thomas made some joke along those lines to Lindsey, the first time he introduced them. "Which is taller than you, young Tank. And old is relative."

"While you're only an honorary old relative."

"I'm your first cousin twice removed."

"They keep removing her, but she keeps coming back," Thomas had whispered behind his hand.

Close like friends, choice, not mere relatives, as if age notwithstanding she were another one of the gang, with him and Isabel and the Parks and Bells. Thomas seemed to have gotten her energy as well as her name, godmother's christening-gift. Why Smith for a middle name? Lindsey had asked that, early on. Because Thomas just didn't look like a Mary Jane, and his father had drawn the line at Dodger.

"Why are you called Dodger?" Lindsey asked. Nail. Strike—strike. It made a rhythm, a drumbeat. Sun pouring down, liquid heat, the black shingles drinking it, throwing it back. They weren't stripping off the old ones. Only the one layer, and the roof below was sound, or so the landlord claimed. There were too many crumbling away at the corners, curling up or outright missing after the winter; the Bells would have had leaking in more than the bathroom as the summer went on, if only there had been rain. He felt like some sort of amphibian, skin slick and wet. He kept a sidelong eye on Dodger, wiry arms bare and sun-spotted, wild white hair sticking to her face, the back of her neck, under a floppy paper-straw hat meant for lounging about on one's deck looking genteel. Vague thoughts of first aid for heatstroke, for whatever might strike down little old ladies who did strenuous physical things on broiling on roofs in the sun. "If you don't mind my asking," he added. "Was it like Tank, something your brothers and sisters stuck on you?"

"'M'n on'y child," Dodger said, around a mouthful of nails. She spat them out into her hand. "Sad, really. My parents always wanted grandchildren, but … " She shrugged, sat back on her heels, wiping her face on the tail of her shirt. "No, Dodger. Why am I Dodger? You'll laugh. I was six. I hated Mary. And Jane. And Mary Jane was worse. Perfectly good names, of course, but they just weren't me. I tried Charlie, and hmm, what else. Oh, Pepper, I tried being Pepper for a week or so. Neither took. Names are strange, aren't they? Mary Jane—no hyphen. My parents always used both names, though at school I was plain Mary—it was like a pair of shoes the right size, but—you put your feet in them and the shape's wrong. They're not yours. You know how that feels?"

"Yeah." And not shoes, either.

"I had an aunt, a dear old lady down in Dorset. She kept a spotted pony. And the pony was Dodger. A contrary beast. Good tempered, but contrary. Could open any gate. Favourite food was roses. And one day, I just realized, I'm Dodger. My parents were amused. They thought I wanted to be a horse. But it fit me, and they got used to it, and at school, too, though of course I had to tell every new teacher I wasn't going to answer to Mary. Once I rose to the giddy heights of head-teacherdom and got my very own brass name-plate for the office door, though … Well, you've seen it."

Screwed to the front door of her church, brass cloudy with

lack of polishing. *M. J. Dodger Smith*, it said.

"I found my father today," he said. He hadn't meant to. He wanted to tell Thomas, first. The whole story. Give that to him, a piece of himself, an offering.

"Oh? Good?"

"I—guess. I mean, I didn't find him, personally. I found out who he was. It was just one of those things, a—a one-night thing, a happy one-night thing, two people and consequences they didn't intend. He doesn't know about me. He's in Europe. Germany. But he's Spanish."

"Do you think you're going to get in touch?"

"I don't know. I don't know what—he's probably married, he probably has a family. He's probably not thought about my mother in years."

"What would you want? If you were he?"

"That changes, doesn't it?" Lindsey went down to the scaffolding, heaved another bundle of shingles up. "I mean, there's points in your life you'd be—be trapped by it, wouldn't you? Look at Ricky's reaction. He's gone down to the States somewhere, did Isabel tell you? Running away to be sure no one comes after him for support, is what it looks like, though she says she doesn't want to do that anyway. But I'm not a child any more, I'm not—something that he has to be responsible for, now. I wouldn't be turning up wanting anything from him. Just to—to know him."

"I imagine one would feel differently at different points in one's life," Dodger said. "Thirty, fifty, seventy … At thirty, when you have your own young children at home, maybe—maybe it would be most difficult then, for you, for your partner. But fifty, that's a bit different, and seventy. If—obviously I wouldn't have a child I didn't know about, but if I'd ever given a baby up … at this point in my life, if they turned up, I'd want to know them."

"Did you?" he asked.

"Good lord, no. I was never that into the opposite sex." She grinned. "And now it's well past noon and time for lunch."

Bunny had barked at them for a while, either outraged that they were up where she couldn't go, or demanding they come down where it was safe, but eventually, after digging herself a pit and knocking her water bowl over twice, she had settled down to sleep under the lilacs. She woke when they climbed down, greeted them with a howl, bouncing at the end of her chain. They fished the key out from under the planter of geraniums, his birthday present for Anicky, let themselves in to eat in the living room with a tall pedestal fan going. A little cooler. Lemonade and egg and ham sandwiches. Lindsey fed Bunny the crusts, making her practise her sit, stay, come, lie down, to earn them. He was feeling the work in his shoulders, his back, neck. Not sore yet, just that knowing that tomorrow your muscles were going to let you know they hadn't been in shape for this.

Checked his phone. Nothing from Thomas. Maybe things were going well with this singer.

"So how's your new venture coming along?" Dodger asked.

For a moment he couldn't remember what she meant. Couldn't think of anything but his father.

"Oh, the landscaping?"

"You starting something else too?"

"No, no. The courses don't start till September. I'm going to set up a business soon, though. Not wait till I'm done. Start seeing what work I can find, even if it's just, I don't know, weeding while people are on holiday, whatever. Register as a provincial corporation. Sue says that's the best way to do it. Go at it professionally from the start."

Though the flaw in that plan was that with no rain and the bricklike clay of this region, if you'd weeded when things were first popping up in the spring, you really didn't have to do much for the rest of the summer. Nothing stood a chance of germinating. And lawns didn't grow much either, except for people who thought they could get away with ignoring the watering ban.

"Incorporate, yes. Always listen to Susannah, about things like that," Dodger agreed. "How are you off for equipment?"

"I've got a spade."

"And ... ?"

"Pruning shears. A trowel. One of those long prong things for dandelions and thistles."

"Wheelbarrow?"

He shrugged. "Where would I keep it? I've got to start with what I can do, which is lug things around downtown on foot, mostly. Borrow the car when I can."

"Ah," said Dodger. "Right."

Yes, he was worrying. Mom helping with tuition, an allowance for living expenses in the fall, that was one thing. He couldn't see any way around it; he was going to have to get a bank loan, buy a little truck like Dodger's or something, and all the equipment a garden caretaker would be expected to have. Too bad Carleen had sold her pickup before she went to Bolivia. To buy something decent when he had no money coming in ... A bank wasn't going to go for that, no matter how sensible his business plan looked on paper. It makes sense, Susannah Park had said, reading it over for him, but—it's not the kind of thing banks like. Because the city hardly lacked for lawn-care, and it was either the big chemical-pushing chains, cancers gratis, 2,4-D or glyphosates or whatever flung all over the sidewalks for dogs to snuffle up, for God's sake, or some guy from Odessa with a pickup truck and a tractor and he probably drove the schoolbus too and the lawnmowing side-line didn't even make it onto his taxes ... Where was Lindsey going to fit in between them, how was he anything different? He didn't have the name-recognition and advertising budget of one and was going to have to charge more than the other. And sure, the real plan was design, but you didn't come out of nowhere and say, hey, let me think up your garden for you and he had to show he was there, in the mud, as it were. Also banks didn't let you say, I can pay you back in summer months but not winter ones.

He was going to end up with a real beater of a truck, some-thing parked in someone's yard with a sign in the window. Though he'd probably have to borrow money even for that. And a junky truck was going to mean endless expensive re-pairs; he was no mechanic. Better a junky truck than a junky mower that would be breaking down in people's yards; that really wouldn't impress. That was where his money, not that he had much, was going to have to go. Equipment. See if Mom could make a loan on top of supporting him through the coursework ... ?

It was going to have to be his house-fund. And even that wasn't enough.

Jobbing gardener. If it were a nineteen-thirties mystery, he'd be either the red-herring working-class suspect who of course didn't do it because that wasn't interesting enough, or someone's alibi. Or the one who discovered the body. The chorus girl wife from London, dead in her elderly husband's shrubbery … Was there ever a series where the gardener was the detective? Brother Cadfael, of course, one of his comfort reads, a place to escape to for so many reasons … Cadfael was hardly a jobbing gardener, though.

"Well, I have a proposition for you," Dodger said. "Or two, actually. One: I have a shed full of tools, small equipment. Lawn tractor. I have a proper tractor, even, should the need for one arise. Anyway, you come look things over, see what I've got. You might want to get other things, of course. Electric lawnmower for small city yards? It's not ideal, where I live so far out of town, but you can't lock it all down in your stairwell like Thomas's bicycle. Anyway, you can make use of what I have."

"Really? Dodger, thanks. That'll be such a big help, getting started. Are you sure—?"

"You've seen my yard. Aside from vegetables, how much gardening do I do? I don't even know what I have; most of it just got dumped on me when the people across the road moved out west. So, proposition two: I've spent the last twenty years pottering away at my church, and it's pretty much finished at last. And I know young Tank is worrying I'll just curl up and get old now, without anything to do. Which is ridiculous. There's always firewood to cut and donkeys to fuss over and tomatoes to turn into chili sauce … you get the idea. I'm not done yet. But I look at that crunchy dry lawn and think, I don't know where to start. I've stuck in some random things over the years, roses and peonies—I like peonies. But then I don't have time to weed them and they get to fight it out with the thistles and they don't always win. And they look like someone just plunked them down wherever she happened to drop them when she got them home. If it's left up to me it's going to be more random lumps of things. So. How about it?"

"You want me to dig out your thistles? I'm not doing herbicides for anything short of poison ivy."

"Dear lord no, no herbicides. Thomas would revert to childhood and have one of his famous tantrums. Not just thistles, Lindsey. A job. Seriously. I'm not one of the filthy rich but I can afford a few luxuries and I think a gardener's one of them. I want to hire you to make me a garden. Well, and do some general handyman-ing, I suppose. There are always things need doing that take more than two hands. I've got to get my year's hay from Gordon-down-the-road and there are some dead ashes in the pasture need to come down before they fall on some silly ass. But mostly, I want a garden. I want a proper garden, so I'll have garden magazines as well as old house magazines after me for feature articles."

"Has someone written about the church?"

"Not yet, but a girl can dream. How about it?"

"Yes! Sure! I told Thomas I'd be a roadie at the Mud Festival at the end of August, but—"

"Time off for festivals," she said. "Naturally. We must support the arts."

"I'll have to get Thomas to drive me out—how early are you going to want to start?"

"Earlier than that slugabed will be up. You'll be wanting a vehicle of your own anyway, for your gardening. And what are you going to do in the winter? Snow removal? You'll want a truck and a plough for that, probably. You could borrow my tractor and blower but you can't travel far with that and everyone out my road has their own tractor, pretty much."

"I've been thinking about that," he said. Well, snowploughing hadn't crossed his mind but she was right, he needed to think about winter work, too. Since nobody was actually going to be paying him to spend days or weeks merely designing their gardens for them. Not yet. Well, other than Dodger, which was kindness and nepotism and—that was how you got started in this kind of thing. Beg and borrow. Get the practice, get the portfolio.

Things to look up. How to do snow removal. Could a lawn-tractor fit in the back of a truck? Probably not with a lawnmower too. Anyway, the box would be too high, you'd need a super-long ramp. That meant a trailer ...

Snow removal. Quinlan Landscapes. We also clear driveways without ripping up all your shrubs ...

"Well, if you need to borrow money, come to me, all right? I might be able to help you out a bit."

"Dodger ... "

"You won't be the only one in the clan I might have made a bit of a loan to, over the years. And—" she downed the last of her lemonade, "—Thomas is—" A shrug. "Young Tank is very dear to me. And you to him. So. Let's get back at this roof. We'll show these layabout musicians what a real day's work looks like, if they ever condescend to turn up. And Lindsey?"

"Yes?"

"You're supposed to ask what I'm offering to pay you. Or tell me your rates. Are we doing this by the hour? Do you have estimates of hours per project? Rates for stages of a project, estimated hours per task? Are you buying things and billing me for them or just telling me what you want and leaving it up to me to produce it if I want it? How are you working it? I know Sue and Laura and probably all those dreary business books you've been lugging around didn't let you get away without settling all that."

"Oh. Right. Yes. Well … "

"You can't go into business as a tradesman and get embarrassed asking to be paid for your work. People expect that from artists and they take advantage of it, but no one ever figured a plumber should be hesitant about asking to be paid. Trust me, they're not hesitant at all."

"Okay."

"Even an artistic tradesman. Stand up for your skills."

"I don't have any yet."

"No, no, no. You're not selling yourself with that. You do. That's why you're doing it and not me. Of course it'll all be an apprentice-piece, to start off. Of course you'll make mistakes and we'll wonder why on earth we did whatever it is we're regretting. A practice run. That's okay. I know I'm not hiring Humphry Repton. And I'm family. I don't mind you giving me a bargain price." She grinned. "Well, you'd better come over tomorrow to look at what's on the ground, and we'll sit down and work out how to do it."

"The gardening or the paying?"

"Both."

Mid afternoon before the band appeared, the Focus and Frankie's little Hyundai and Uncle Henry's Kia in close convoy. Not a lot of chatter. No excitement. Just a kind of tiredness. Lindsey didn't need to ask. Did, of course.

"No go?"

Anicky shook her head. Frankie grimaced.

"No," Thomas said.

"He wasn't bad," Kevin said. "He'd do. Voice-wise. If we didn't have Thomas. But—"

"Face it," Anicky said, "anyone who sounds better than

Thomas is already with a serious band. We're not going to get anyone better than him, just different. Someone who can sing as well as Thomas and hold down centre stage, that's what you wanted. If you don't want that, then admit we're fine the way we are."

"He wouldn't have worked out," Kevin said. "It's not just the voice. It's the chemistry."

"That last guy was okay. Nice voice, but no life in him," said Frankie. An air of changing the subject, almost? "Too careful."

"So was that woman we met in Peterborough—okay, but too, I don't know." Kevin shook his head. "Restrained? You hear a lot like that. It's like they don't want to really use what they've got."

"Or when they try to reach, you hear they can't," said Frankie. "They're the vocal equivalent of the guys that know a few chords and can play them fast and loud and the kids go, ooooh, cool, but ask them to do anything else and they're like, hey, I never said I was Jimmy Page."

"If they've heard of Jimmy Page," Kevin muttered.

"They don't bloody know how to sing," Thomas said. "They think because they can hit the right notes—if they even can—that's singing. They don't know how to *breathe*."

"Dylan today was—" Anicky began.

"Oh, he could sing, anyway. He wasn't bad. I didn't say he was—he was just—" Thomas turned on his heel, walked off.

Kevin watched him, frowning. Took a step as if he would follow, looked over at Lindsey.

"That bad?" Lindsey asked.

"Two cats," Kevin said.

"Just let him sulk and get it out of his system," said Frankie.

"You too, big sister. Pound some nails. You'll feel better. I know auditioning Dylan was your idea, but I thought he was a bit of a prick too. Okay, Dodger, do you want us all up on the roof or what?"

"So Dylan can be abrasive," Anicky said. "He's not the only one."

"If we're all getting on one another's nerves after a single day with him, he's not the person we need," Kevin said. "Just forget it. Let's get this roof on."

"Done my share for now, I think." Lindsey handed Anicky his hammer, went after Thomas, who was under the lilacs, crouched down and tussling half-heartedly over a stick with Bunny. He didn't look up when Lindsey came over, leash in hand.

"Hey," he said. "Come for a walk."

"It's hot."

"Yeah, so?"

Thomas sighed. "They mad at me?"

"I don't know. What did you do?"

"I didn't do anything. Except say no."

"Right. Come on. Walk. That means you too, puppy, and nobody's going to carry you. You're too big for that now." If they'd been at Dodger's they could have headed for the sugarbush, her maple woods behind the donkeys' pasture, back along the brook. There was a peace there, water chiming over rocks, the shifting light through the leaves … Pasture behind the Bell's but there was a bull in with the herd of beef cattle. And once, when some vandal ATVers cut the fence, in the driveway. They wandered down the road instead, Bunny plunging in and out of the weed-grown ditch, nose down, tail up and wagging steadily. All was right with her world, outside with both her humans and lots of things to sniff.

"Anicky thought Dylan was the one. Someone she knew at university, I guess. Another teacher, sings in a weekend blues band up in Ottawa. I don't mind someone who's damn good and knows it—"

"Not mentioning any names."

"Lin ... Okay, that's fair. But someone who's damned good at one thing and thinks that gives them the right to lay down the law to everyone around them about things they know nothing about, someone who thinks that makes them some kind of superior human being—and someone who's only averagely good but thinks they're some undiscovered genius and don't you dare say a word—"

"You're way beyond averagely good, even I can hear that."

"—and talks down to everyone like they're a bunch of over-ambitious teens jamming in the basement for the first time ..."

"Did he?"

"A bit of that, yeah. Putting down the studio, even, and seriously, okay, you can't judge but it's pretty much up to professional standards in the things that matter, in the results we can get. Just because everything's a bit knocked around and third-hand—it's good where it matters. Kev's put so much of himself into building that up and he could find work, you know, if he went off to Toronto, recording engineer, I don't think there's much they could teach him even if he did go to do that course he was planning on, back in high school. And you know him. So polite. Just gets quieter and quieter. And, too, Dylan was—I don't know how to put it. Kind of always, lining up with Anicky, not that we were fighting about anything, but somehow putting himself so it suddenly felt it was,

was them and us, some kind of tension in everything, not the usual kind of 'arguing things around till we get where we want to be' thing but something—something artificial, like he had to prove something, when what he needed to be proving was that he could sing and work with us and, and fit ... I don't think she even saw it, honestly. Frankie did. And you know her, she started getting a bit—" He made a sort of snarly-tooth gesture with his hand. "Snappish. Going out of her way to provoke him."

"He's got a thing for Anicky?"

"You think that was it?"

"Sounds that way, and—no surprise if he does. She's pretty striking."

"If you're into that sort of thing. Or were you leaving me an opening for some sort of bad joke about pretty drummers striking things?"

"I wasn't, but feel free to make one."

"Not in the mood. Okay, but if an old school friend you have a crush on—he really does not know her very well if he has hopes there—invites you to come jam when you're in town and says, by the way, we're kind of thinking about adding a vocalist, you don't impress her by hinting the rest of her gang's not quite up to your standard. If you really thought that, you'd make some polite 'It's been nice but not really my thing,' comment and be off."

"Some people don't know how to, how to brace someone up, without running everyone else around down."

"I suppose. Lindsey—am I arrogant?"

"How do you mean?"

"It's a yes or no thing."

"Not really. Arrogant, how? I mean, you know you're good,

but you're not—you're not all about how nobody else is good as well. You don't think the world owes you a living just for being good—"

"I think it owes me a living for working damned hard at what I do, since people apparently like what I do—it'd be nice if they paid me for it."

"Well, yes. Anyway, arrogance is like, I'm damned good and therefore you don't matter. Not, yes I'm damned good, so come on, keep up."

"Oh God, that is arrogant. Am I like that?"

"Not—no! I mean, yes, you are, a bit, but not in a bad way. It's not, come on, keep up, as if you think they *can't*. It's more, come on, keep up, I know you can. Like, if they can keep up, they can push you and you'll all be better than damned good together. In the aggregate."

"Oh God, Lin."

"And you do—I watch you guys, Strange Pilgrim Road's not a dictatorship. It's not like anyone's in charge or thinks they're supposed to be. Well, I guess when push comes to shove it's you in charge, or you and Kevin, but for general things … Look, let it go. It doesn't matter if he was good or wasn't, if he's just going to irritate people, you don't need him. You've got four good people, you all get along most of the time and nobody throws things—"

"Cushions."

They did. Sometimes Lindsey thought about donating his mother's horrible hairy, beady-eyed ones, the two that had survived Bunny, to the cause. There was an assortment of little throw cushions that had been collecting in the studio over the years, carried off from various family chesterfields. They nested on the battered old couch at the foot of the basement stairs , got beaten on the floor, on the walls, howled into, bitten, hurled—into corners and at people, accompanied by language that you'd take for the end of band and friendship itself, less often at the boards or the drum kit or keyboard setup. Never the guitars.

"Cushions are a necessary outlet. They don't count. They're probably why you're still all friends. Thomas, look, I'm supposed to be the obsessive one, right? Just let it go. If the others really think you're being arrogant, making it all too much about you, they're going to say so."

"Kevin would never say anything."

"Kevin's your partner. Your brother. He loves you and—"

"Lin—"

"No, he does. You said it when we started, and it's okay, I know it's not like that, I really do. And he knows what you've got between you and I don't think he'd stand back and let you break it by going all, all diva-like, isn't that your word for it? All like that on him. So if he's not telling you you're being unreasonable, you're probably not being unreasonable. And trust Frankie to knock you down if you start getting uppity. Thomas, seriously, if you're getting so tangled up thinking about this you can't see yourself clear—just ask them. Okay?"

Long sigh. Thomas scooped up a stone, hurled it ahead of them, into the ditch. Bunny looked up in alarm at the rattle in the dry weeds, gave them a quick glance. Humans not panicking, not a monster, nothing to bark at. Everything good. Back to letting her nose lead the way. "Yeah. Right. I don't know. I just wanted to fix things and now everyone's all—jittery, somehow."

"I shouldn't have said anything. What do I know about it, anyway? Why did you even listen to me?"

"Because you were right. Nail on the head and all. It's just—finding what we need, finding what I want—there's no one with that, that *thing*. That magic that's what we need."

"Wanted," Lindsey said. "Singer with magic. Right. Are you holding out for the ghost of Mercury or what?"

"Something like that, I guess."

"Well, good."

"Not really."

"Yes," Lindsey said. "Don't settle for anyone who makes you less, collectively."

"Honestly? Like, if you weren't sleeping with me, you'd still think so? You'd never heard of us before."

"Yeah, well, I had, actually. I just didn't listen to you, because other than Krown Imperial, I didn't listen to much that was recorded by anyone who came along after I was born, back then."

"Back then! Long, long ago—weird, what's it been, a year and a half? Seems like forever. In a good way, I mean. Ah, Lin, sorry, I should have asked right off. The thing, your father. Did you email?"

"Email—*him?*" What did he even call him? Antonio? Professor Olivares? Herr Professor Olivares, or was it Señor Olivares even if he lived in Germany … ? Stop. "God, no. What would I say? I told Mom I'd found the concert programme, though. So she called me. We—we talked."

"Good? Bad?"

"Good. I guess, good. I—" Actually, Lindsey couldn't think when they'd last talked like that. Without restraint. Without—him wondering if she was even hearing him. "Good," he repeated.

"And? I mean, only if you want to tell me."

"I want to tell you. But it's—you know, now that I've had time to think about it—it's the Fine Arts party all over again. Except it came first, obviously, but—"

"Fine Arts party?"

"Hallowe'en? You do remember. You practically ran over some guy, charging down the stairs, and backed him into a corner and—"

"Oh, that. I vaguely recall that. What did it have to do with Fine Arts?"

"It was—oh, God, it was the same building, even. I mean, not the same part of it, the actual art gallery's separate with this sort of glassed-in café space between—maybe it was two buildings in Mom's day—"

"Now you're babbling. Sorry, you were conceived in the same building we met in? At a *party?* I've met your mum and I wouldn't have thought—"

"No, it was the Merganser."

"Okay, ducks are involved, how? I know your family's strange, Lin, but—"

Arm around Thomas, hand over his mouth. Laughing. Bunny oblivious, sniffing a thistle. "Be quiet. Just be quiet, Thomas. No, they met at a reception after the concert, in the art gallery, and it was like when we first met, she said—she didn't say that, but what she said, it was, he was young and gorgeous and interesting and nice and—and anyway, his friends didn't come along and drag him away, they came and said, 'Carry on,' or possibly just, 'We won't wait up,' she doesn't know because they were speaking Spanish, and went back to their B&B. And—so did she and Antonio. And things happened."

"And here you are. Right."

"There was … a last minute rush to the drug store followed by a certain degree of latex failure."

"*I* was found under the rhubarb, or so Maddie told me. Sounds a bit more hygienic, all things considered."

"And here I am."

"And she didn't tell him."

"She decided on his behalf that they'd had a lovely time and that was that, he didn't need to know there was an epilogue."

"Ah. I don't think that was right."

"No. But, that's Mom. Her problem, her solution."

"But—Lindsey—Lin, did your mum ever get you music lessons? Piano, even—anything at all?"

"Not really. I mean, we did recorders in elementary school. I was in the choir a couple of years. But I never wanted to play anything, not—nothing like you, the way you have to be making music. I just wanted to listen."

"You've got such beautiful long hands—" and he caught one, made Lindsey flatten it out over his own. "It's just so—" Fingers laced. "A waste. You should have. You should have had that."

"Thomas, it's all right. I'm all right."

"Are you?"

"Yes."

"*Liar,*" *Raleigh whispered, somewhere, faint.*

/Five/

He hadn't emailed his father. He would. Just—not yet. Wrote drafts of letters, deleted them.

Are you all right, Thomas had asked, a couple of weeks back, and he had lied, because he always lied about that, and he hadn't been then, though he'd managed to pretend, even to himself. Because of course he was, he should be.

Not all right had grown, quiet, stealthy, swelling within him, and he hadn't been then and he wasn't now. All—shattered-feeling, like he was a kaleidoscope in slow motion, not settling. He could ignore it, some of the time. Sometimes. And sometimes it was almost a panic, surging up from somewhere deep inside, going to drown him if he so much as glanced down into it.

It was edging towards ... something. Almost like after Raleigh died. And Dad.

This wasn't that bad. It wasn't.

He didn't actually remember a lot of his fourth year. Or his grad school years. Things like music, movies, what had happened in the world, on the news ... as if he'd just been shut

265

off. Everything outside himself just noise that didn't register. People. The people he'd lived with, yes, that handful he still remembered, but even people on his own floor in the biology building, in his own lab … that red-haired guy who'd had the cubicle back to back with him. Name? Gone. And everything else about him. But they'd talked. They'd drunk coffee together, talked about … he didn't remember what. And it was happening again, that feeling of being … pieces of himself, drifting, unconnected.

He wanted Thomas home. What could he tell him? He was glad Thomas was away.

"*Stop,*" *Raleigh said. Over and over.* "*Listen. See it, see what you're doing to yourself. Don't you see? Look it in the eye. Breathe. It's the anti-Lindsey.*"

The anti-Lindsey wasn't him. He wouldn't let it be. It was a thing, stalking him.

"*Talk to Thomas,*" *Raleigh said.* "*Tell him.*"

"*Tell him what?*"

August, now. When he turned the page, it would be there. Note on the calendar, like a deadline.

?doctor?

He had his bed to himself. The band was off again, a short tour, small festivals and a string of bar-gigs, heading west, Toronto, Kitchener-Waterloo, Barrie, Chicago, down further into the US from there. Zigzagging all over points in-between. They didn't talk on the phone much. Email whenever Thomas found there was wifi, or chat when they were both online at the same time. He followed their adventures on Twitter, too. Which was odd, reading about Ivan, the bits that had Ivan, because at first Lindsey kept forgetting he was with them, that he existed at all. He'd barely had time to get to know the new guy and they were gone.

Ivan Shawcross. Shakedown cruise, they called it. They'd had a couple of weeks working on their old material, a few of the new things, long days and sometimes frazzled and Thomas showing up exhausted at weird times and taking his bike out in the heat because he was working off frustration or temper or something and couldn't get at his rowing machine—but that was the first week, them all settling in to one another and he kept at the same time saying no, it's good, it's going to be good, we're good, it's just—we don't have *time*.

And Ivan's mother was unhappy, and during that first week of their rehearsals had actually phoned the studio up—or rather, called Henry Park's number, which Ivan had unfortunately given her as the studio's—and yelled at Thomas. Who hung up on her.

Apparently Ivan had, several days before, stopped answering his cell when he saw it was her.

"She's, um, a bit overprotective," Ivan had said. "Sorry. I'll talk to her."

Only child. Parents long divorced and his father out in St. John's. He still lived at home. He'd turned up with a rusty little Honda hatchback that he'd bought only the day before and a sleeping bag and foam pad from his Boy Scout days, ready to sleep on the studio floor or in his back seat if need be. Thomas gave him the spare keys to his room on Aberdeen.

"Sorry about Mom." More than once, Ivan had felt he had to say that. "I speak and it's in one ear and out the other, just noise, unless I'm saying what she wants to hear. So I just don't bother arguing, these days. I told her nothing was decided, this was just something for the summer. Look, I'm really sorry."

Ivan's mother kept calling, demanding to talk to him. Kevin

blocked her; his father wasn't their receptionist and shouldn't have to deal with that.

So everyone was on edge, even though it was supposedly all just a trial run and Ivan wasn't committing to anything. While Laura frantically tried to get everything adjusted for the expanded lineup, paperwork, visas, increased payments where that was possible and mostly it wasn't. Ditto the paperwork needed for Ivan to work in the States; not enough time, it turned out. So they had abandoned him when the tour crossed the border. He had gone back home to try to smooth things over with his mother, but down in the States, Strange Pilgrim Road were getting questions, like, where's Ivan—? Because the wake of chatter their Canadian gigs had left online these past weeks was pretty consistent in agreeing, he was bringing something new, and it was good.

Something they'd been missing.

Gorgeous voice.

Maybe just as well he gets some time off to think about things, Thomas said, one of their email exchanges. Time to step away and ask himself, was this what he wanted? Because we want him but he's on track for a career in opera or something and oh lord, his mother ... They were stealing the guy from some weekend student cover band in Toronto that his mother told him he was supposed to be quitting anyway, and he was facing—quit his studies and join them, or say no and be a good boy and go home.

Though Laura swore about that and said the sooner she *knew* the better for their European plans or he wouldn't have his visas and permits then, either.

Nice enough. A little guy, kind of fidgety, but also with that slightly diffident shyness that ended up being charming and making you feel like you should look after him. On stage—he flung that off like a unnecessary coat, and gathered the audience in, total control.

Curly light brown hair and intense brown eyes. A bit startled by it all, at first. Not least because he'd had *Mademoiselle Bell* for grade nine French. But he was a fan, and he'd come to try out when they'd gone to Toronto for a few days and passed word around they were thinking of maybe auditioning someone to take over lead vocals, and one of the guys from Exit 369 who was still speaking to Thomas was seeing someone who knew someone who knew Ivan and told Thomas the Shawcross kid was what he wanted, told Ivan he'd better show up … something like that. And Ivan had figured, why not.

And Thomas, before any of them—had they all been too cautious to say, till they saw how he reacted?—Thomas before any of them said, "Yeah. He'll do." According to Anicky, who also said, "Which was, under the circumstances, practically running around screaming and setting off fireworks."

And Kevin said, "He's good, he's very good, and he's got the right feel for the songs which maybe matters more."

"And he's not all, Uh, are you sure no one's going to think I'm gay if I sing this … " Frankie had said.

"If he can get along with us—"

"If he can learn to say 'Anicky' without that sort of, um-pause where you know he's editing out 'Mademoiselle'—"

"He's got it," Thomas had said, in private, when he first got back from Toronto and Ivan was safely installed at Aberdeen for the night. "What you said it was I wanted, Lin. The right magic. And he seems like a good guy, too."

"And cute." He was being stupid.

"Idiot," Thomas said. "Not my type in any imaginable

way. Frankie, however—oh God, that's a problem I hope just doesn't come up. But here, listen." Just something recorded on his phone. "What do you think?"

Yeah. A *voice*. God. Made for them.

They had magic. A bit rough. First experiments. But you could hear it … something was going to be born.

And *not my type in any imaginable way …* he couldn't pretend that didn't make him feel better.

"You are so insecure," Raleigh said. "You trust him."

Of course he did.

They lost their exhaust system on the 407. Frankie and Jon had food poisoning in Windsor, not too serious but still, a bad couple of days … The van was way too crowded. The PA they'd rented for one gig didn't show. Frantic last-minute scramble and much swearing, because there was no way Kev and Jon were putting up with the lousy house equipment. Laura in a rage on the phone much of the next day. Got their deposit back. Their feed made it funny. Lindsey got the uncensored version.

He hadn't had his phone and internet disconnected. Thomas had left a handful of fifties on the counter under a coffee mug, the day the band went. Sticky note. *This'll help with some bills.* Lindsey had already switched to just a pay-as-you-go cell plan, kept data turned off. Didn't get into long conversations by text, at whatever it cost a go. Had to talk to Thomas somehow. Waited for those moments when chat showed him Thomas was actually online, some Tim Horton's parking lot somewhere, more often than not. Then they could talk.

Hard, sometimes, to find anything to say. Easier to let Thomas lead the way.

Did he notice?

Why don't you call up Ivan? Thomas asked, when they were down in the States and apologizing for the visa delays that meant they didn't have their singer, as though it was already decided, he was an absence, not an extra. Run up to Toronto, hang out. Rescue him from his mother for the day.

He didn't.

Didn't sleep well, bed to himself or not. Blame the heat, though the fan on the floor made it bearable.

Bought some frozen microwave dinners. Macaroni and cheese; alfredo with broccoli. Canned ravioli; canned baked beans. Too hot to cook, he told himself. Too tired.

Too chewed up inside.

The anti-Lindsey had grown teeth? Just when he'd begun to think he'd figured it out, found his way through.

"Send the damned email," Raleigh told. "Do it and get it over with. Just say it. You're my father, I exist, hello. What's the worst that can happen? He doesn't answer, or he writes back and says please don't contact me again. And there you are. At least you'll know, and you'll have lost—nothing you already didn't have anyway, so then you can shrug him off and forget about it. Go on. Don't look back."

"I can't. I can't just—how would you feel if you got an email like that?"

"This isn't about how he feels. It's about what you need."

"I don't need this right now. I don't have the energy to deal with this right now."

"Then stop thinking about it. Put it away for later."

He couldn't. He couldn't put anything away for later. Later kept rushing up at him. August already.

He wasn't sure how he could pay the bills. Work for Dodger would dry up as fall passed into winter. He'd have Mom's allowance, but … at his age.

It would help. The hydro bill would go up once he had to have the heat on. And he didn't like having to do that. Take Mom's money. Didn't want to. But service jobs, cash register clerking … he broke down entirely, ended up in the bathroom, throwing up, thinking of that. Crying.

Loathing himself. He could do it. He'd done it. It wasn't so bad, it shouldn't be, it'd be just while he did his courses, just till he found some garden work in the spring again …

Something wrong with him. Everyone else did that kind of work. Probably most didn't enjoy it.

They didn't feel customers' eyes were claws, shredding at their skin, at their self.

He couldn't. He just couldn't. He'd fall …

He was falling and if he did that, ended up in the mall, not even a window to look out, he'd—hit the ground.

Other ways to save money?

Thomas hardly ever spent the night at his own place. Maybe they should just … share.

Live together?

"Ask him."

Thomas wasn't the one who held back, stewing over things. He'd have said, if he thought they should really move in together. He kept his Aberdeen place and his driver's licence gave his parents' address. An escape clause, a way to just fade out of the relationship … Thomas had never mentioned living together other than back when Lindsey had first lost his job. He'd been joking, then.

Lindsey was probably hard to live with. He couldn't blame Thomas for being careful, leaving a back door open. The place was a bit claustrophobic, maybe. Overgrown.

Thin out the plants? And he was obsessive about things, moody—depressive—

Not quite … right. Maybe it showed, sometimes. It had to. Especially now.

"Don't start that," Raleigh said. *"He's been living with you practically since you met. Just brought over his guitar and his housecoat and never left. Whatever you are, he likes it."*

"That's not living with. That's just—making sleeping over more convenient."

"For God's sake, Lindsey, don't be so—"

"Don't."

"Stop listening to it, that anti-Lindsey. Don't let it wake up again. Dig a hole and bury it. Obviously you're living together. He doesn't want an escape clause. He wants to be with you. Maybe he isn't sure you want him moving in for real, filling up your space with his clutter, did you ever think of that? Maybe you make him not sure, so he keeps the Aberdeen place for that, to make you feel safe. So that he feels safe, if you say one day, don't keep leaving your stuff here."

"I—now who's being the anti-Lindsey?"

Raleigh shrugged. Just off to the side, almost not-quite out of sight, if he looked.

Curled up on the couch, afghan over him despite the heat. In the dark. Living room fan going. Bunny twitched, yipped in her sleep. Chasing dream-rabbits. She'd taken off after a cottontail in the donkey-pasture, lost her off-leash privileges again.

Anti-Lindsey.

If Raleigh was—

—what he was.

Not a ghost. Not real.

A … a shadow-self, grown out of memory and loss and need—

—then what was the anti-Lindsey but Raleigh's dark shadow? A thing grown in him over long years, just as real, just as true a voice even if he didn't pretend—it was pretending, a child's imaginary friend, Raleigh's voice in his ear, no, in his mind—was it something he could try to make separate from himself? Was that what it was all along? A monster born of himself, umbilical-feeding off everything that hurt.

So could he try to see it there? Shadow, darkness, monster leech? Say, this is not me, this thing?

But that felt like a lie. It was him, and Raleigh saying, it's not you, it's the anti-Lindsey …

Didn't feel like truth.

The anti-Lindsey was him.

Raleigh … remained Raleigh. Separate. Real. Angry at him, those sleepless nights.

Thomas's phone buzzed and it was Lindsey. Lindsey never phoned, too expensive, and his first thought was—something bad. Bunny.

"Lin?"

"Oh, hi." As if surprised he'd answered, but that was Lindsey, always went awkward on the phone, even with people he knew.

"What's up?" he asked.

"Not much."

"You okay?" Just the sound of Lindsey's voice—he missed him so much. But couldn't enjoy it, because Lindsey, telephone … "Something wrong?"

"No. No. I just wanted … " Lindsey trailed off. "How's the

trip going?"

"Same as usual. Nothing too alarming. Good crowds. We're not playing this evening." Obviously, it was after eight. "We're camping tonight." Narrow townhouse and small children—less imposition, less hassle all round, to put up the little backpacking tents, on a fine night. Someone's backyard, friend of a friend, fan, something like that. Laura looked after that sort of thing. "Some suburb, somewhere."

"In summertime."

"Something like that." Shrieking. Children racing around an inflatable wading pool, whacking one another with foam batons.

"I've—I—I've got another job," Lindsey said abruptly.

"Oh." Damn. "Lin, love, you don't need to do that." He should have—"Look, if the work for Dodger's not enough to make your rent and all, I can help, you know. I will. I—"

"No, no, it's not that—it's okay. It's just—"

Anicky tapped his shoulder, passed him a hamburger bun holding a barbecued portobello mushroom cap and zucchini. Rolled her eyes. She knew his opinions. The sort of thing that people who weren't vegetarians thought vegetarians wanted to eat. Because who needs protein. But these were nice people, whoever they were, he should have been paying more attention, Greg and Lisa, Greg and Lisa who … ? And beer. The beer was okay, for American.

"—we went for a walk after we got back from Dodger's today. Bunny and I, I mean. And there was this old lady. One of the old ladies who used to come into Clare's. I didn't recognize her, but she knew me."

Of course she would. Lindsey's wasn't a face you'd forget.

"She lives over off of Johnson. She was sitting up on her

porch. We got talking. She can't really look after her yard any more herself. Arthritis. Bad. Her hands are like claws and she can hardly walk. Her son's trying to get her to move into an apartment but she'd miss it, she says. Her garden. She had some company that was supposed to be doing it and they cut down her clematis with a string trimmer—not one but three of them, up the side of her porch. And then tidied the vines away as if they'd never been there. As if she wouldn't notice or was senile and wouldn't remember they'd ever existed. And they dig little trenches around the edges of her flowerbeds and call that weeding, but leave maple seedlings and couch-grass all growing up inside. Do you know what kind of root system a Norway maple gets just in its first summer?"

He didn't. It wasn't the sort of thing he'd ever considered. But when Lindsey said it—it was interesting. That Lin knew these things, the complexity of these things, and they mattered.

"And if you don't get the roots out they'll just keep coming up and coming up and getting bigger and deeper and tougher no matter how often you cut the top off. But it was the clematis thing that did it. She lost her temper and told them not to come back. So. First client for Quinlan Landscapes, I guess."

"Second."

"I wasn't counting Dodger. Dodger's thing won't be something that'll keep me going through the summers anyway; it's mostly a fall and spring thing, building a new garden. It'll just be yard-care stuff for her, too, in-between. And the old lady— Mrs. Steinberg—she's going to mention me to her friends, she says. She's not the only one could use some help around the yard."

"Well, good. That's good. Isn't it?"

"I—I told her my name—my name was Neill."

What?

"Why?" Wait, that sounded a bit too—"I mean, uh … "
Thomas didn't know what he meant.

"She's writing cheques to Quinlan Landscapes, not me; it
doesn't matter if I'm not legally Neill."

"You going to eat?" Frankie. He'd only had a single bite of
the mushroom-bun. Remembered he had it in his hand, took
another mouthful, then couldn't answer Lindsey's silence but
with a sort of stuffed-mouth grunt. "Here," said Frankie. Plate
of some kind of macaroni salad balanced on the deck railing by his elbow. Red peppers. Little squares of bright orange
cheese in it. Well, it was protein, of a sort. "Is that Lindsey or
Isabel?"

He waved her off. She made a face, then, suddenly serious,
"Is it Iz? Is everything okay?"

Swallowed. "Fine, no." Shooed her away. "Um, no, sorry,
just Frankie. Sorry about that, eating supper. I mean, yes, of
course it doesn't matter what you go by, if the cheques go to
the business."

"If Dodger could be Dodger most of her life, even when
she was a headmistress, I don't see why I have to go on being
Lindsey. And lots of people decide to change their names, or
parts of their names. Freddie Mercury. C.S. Lewis. Most of
Rush, right?"

"Oh. Right." He must sound stunned. Or like he wasn't
listening. It was just—he wasn't even sure what it was. Just—
Neil—where did that even come from?

"I don't like Lindsey, I never have. It's not the girl's name
thing, maybe it was when I was a kid in school but it isn't
now. It's just—it doesn't *fit*. It never did. And I can't be Freder-

ick, that was my Grandfather Quinlan and anyway Frederick's worse, even less myself."

"Oh." Stop saying 'oh.' "Why Neil?"

"With two l's."

How did he hear the lack of the second l? "Okay. But why Neill? I mean … Is there any particular reason?" Was he going to be Neill this week and … and Alex next? Because that could get kind of confusing, and—was this really to do with names at all, or something else?

A pause. "It just—it just came to me. I know that doesn't make sense. I mean, it's been in the back of my mind. The name thing. Dodger. Almost like, I'd been wondering without even thinking about it openly. If I … if I was going to call myself something else, what? And you think about names and none of them are you and then—yeah, I just said, when she said, I don't think I ever knew your name, dear, I said, mostly I go by Neill."

And that was Lin, yes. Awkwardly renaming himself because to say outright "My name is Neill" would feel like he was lying.

Not Lin. Neill.

"Neill for—good, then?" he asked, gently. Carefully. Not to sound like, well, he was dismayed. But he liked Lindsey. It was different. It had character. *It's Lindsey, labcoat bloke says,* under the tree by Summerhill, and it was ringing in his head: *Lindsey, he was Lindsey, of course he was and he'd found him after all this time …*

He thought Lindsey suited … Lindsey.

That was a bit like the way Maddie used always to say he should wear green, green suited him. But green was meaningless. There was green and there was green, and sometimes it was yellow and sometimes it was brown, and who knew, that might not even be what other people meant by brown, since quite a lot of brown, like faces, looked more like yellow, and how was he supposed to know the difference? What suited whom was pretty damn subjective and … who was he or anyone to say what suited … Neill?

"Neill for everyone?"

Lindsey—Neill—was silent a moment. "I'd—I'd rather."

"Okay. You want me to tell the rest of the gang?"

"Yeah. Okay."

Which probably meant, please.

"You know it's going to take us a while to get used to it. Just—be patient, if we screw up."

"Yeah, of course. Me too, really."

"Two l's."

"That's important." And he laughed at himself, Neill did. That was good, and Thomas breathed a little more easily. "I don't know why, but—"

"Of course it is. Neill."

"Yeah."

"Just trying it out. Okay. Neill. Hm. Maybe."

"Maybe what?"

"Maybe you look like Neill."

"You think it's stupid, changing my name?"

"No! I don't. I mean, I like Lindsey but it's not me wearing it, is it? I *hate* being called Tom. I always have. There's nothing wrong with the name. It's just not me. Thomas is. Tank is, even. You don't call me Tank but I kind of like that you don't, really. It's like Thomas is underneath Tank and you see that and—never mind, this isn't about that, what I mean is, I understand it. I'm just used to you being Lindsey. You've formed my idea of Lindseyness. That's all. Like I said, it'll take us all a while to get used to it. But we will. People do. Like you said, people change their names all the time. Legally and informally both. I mean, look at Dodger. Who the heck is Mary Jane Smith? I don't even know her."

"Okay. Thanks."

"Lin, you don't say 'thanks' like I'm doing you a favour, you've got a right to—oh hell, sorry. Sorry, sorry, sorry. Just give me some time."

"Hey. Thomas." Very quiet. "I—I didn't say I didn't like Lin. I can be—I'm still Lin. When it's just you and me, when … I'm—nobody but you's ever called me Lin." Almost a whisper. "I like it."

And that was a warm thing, like lips brushing his neck.

Later, he would think that maybe right then would have been a good time to say some of the things that were in his mind, that he'd thought didn't need saying, to head off that snarled knot of anxiety that was growing in Lindsey—in Neill. Once they were home, and rested, and the Mud Festival was out of the way, he was going to do it. Tell him. I'm giving up the house on Aberdeen. Let's look for a place together, let's— think seriously about our future. Should have said it then, but he didn't, because L-Neill was sounding stressed enough as it was and—nerving himself up to call and actually tell him the name thing, not waiting for him to come home, to say it, stammering, hesitant, pretending to be off-hand—for Neill that was practically shouting, and he didn't want to stress him worse and any kind of change seemed to stress him.

Shouting, yeah. And he didn't hear it then.

Help. A whisper.

❦

Climbing up, a little. Slipping back. He felt like he could be Neill, and then he didn't, the anti-Lindsey growing stronger, pulling him back; changing his name didn't mean he could hide from it after all, put it aside from himself and say, you are not me.

"You're not crazy," Raleigh said, *"but you're doing a good impression of someone trying to make themselves ill."*

He and Bunny were back from their run, and he had showered, was eating breakfast and looking at trucks on Kijiji yet again when Thomas wandered out from his own shower to join him, damp and blurry. Up early, but he'd only gotten back the day before and he was always jittery, exhausted and restless at once and taking naps at weird times, for a few days when he came back from a tour. Probably wanting to go over to Aberdeen to burn it off on the rowing machine, which he couldn't do because Ivan had turned up the day they got back and was staying there again.

And Thomas was finding other things to do at night, which usually meant sleeping in for both of them …

He was going to be late getting out to Dodger's. He'd forgotten, Isabel had the car at her place again.

"Ow," Thomas said, leaning on his shoulder. Looking at the prices, he presumed. That was what he was feeling. Ow.

"Yeah. This one looks good, though. It's older, but the mileage is pretty low." One of three that he'd saved. Nerving himself up. *Contact the seller …* It didn't commit to anything, asking if the truck was still available. It was just … there was no way around it. He would have to go out, test drive them. People always wanted to haggle over vehicle prices, didn't they? He couldn't do that. He wanted to just find it listed somewhere, say, that one, click and have it show up at his door. No human interaction required. And he didn't have the money.

"Cars are cheaper," Thomas said.

"A car won't be any good to me."

"No, I know. I just mean, I wasn't really thinking about what it would cost. How are you planning to manage it?"

Neill sighed. "It's my house money."

And the house money wasn't enough. He hoped Dodger was in earnest about being willing to make him a loan.

"House money?"

He had never told Thomas this. It was … why should it feel like a secret?

Because it was private. Because it was a dream. A fantasy. Because if he talked about it, it made it obvious it was all too hopeless and unrealistic, living how he did.

"I've been saving for a down payment. Every paycheque." Every EI payment, too. "One of those tax-free savings accounts. Since I left Queen's."

Made it a rule. Fifty dollars. Or more, if he could. But in the summer, when the hydro bill was lower, he always tried to make it more. No indulgences, until Thomas came along and then there were evenings with wine and going out to the SandWitch and he couldn't let Thomas pay all the time. Gas for the Focus. He couldn't live off Thomas, who was generous without thought.

When there was Christmas money or birthdays, the house account was where it went.

"I wanted—I want to get out of town. A house—I don't care if it's even a mini home, so long as it's got a bit of land, some space, somewhere to walk, to go for a run and not have to see people all the time. I just—I know it's stupid, it's never going to be enough, I can't make enough for it ever to be enough, but—" He shrugged, looking at his hands, the keyboard, not the screen, not Thomas.

But there were times, especially those first couple of years at the flower shop, when that was all he had to keep getting up for. Times when the lake was cold and grey again, and the waves off the rocks were hypnotic, and he had to tell himself that someday at least he'd have his bit of land, he'd plant things that would last, and make some shape of peace and beauty around him that could endure.

"It'll have to go on the truck. Truck and a utility trailer, so I can haul the lawn-tractor around, assuming I can get clients for that." Snowplough, and that just seemed—ridiculous. Him, one of those guys who went roaring around at six in the morning, clearing people's driveways so they could leave for work. Higher education, right.

And there'd be no saving to restore it, when he was having to pay back loans, even from Dodger, and keep buying new equipment, and repairing the truck, and … he was never going to get there, not even some two-bedroom Kent home prefab, or whatever the Ontario equivalent was. It was always going to be something seen, out of reach, a carrot dangling in the future forever.

This morning, these past couple of weeks, he couldn't even believe in the business making enough to buy groceries. People didn't care about real gardens; they just wanted a little kidney-shaped blob in front with two carefully spaced hostas and a potentilla surrounded by several square metres of black-dyed cedar chips. And someone to mow the lawn for them and get rid of all those nasty bee-filled patches of clover.

"Seriously? On what you made?" Thomas was still frowning at the screen. "And then you've been saving in the tea-tin for Isabel on top of that? I didn't know."

He shrugged.

"Well, good. But spending it on a truck—"

"I have to. I can't get anywhere with this plan without a truck. I don't want to be someone's employee, I want to work for myself, and I need the truck for that. If I can't work … "

"Yeah. I know that one. Takes money to make money. That first CD … But don't empty out the account entirely. Is it even enough?"

"No." Not nearly, even for the truck that he thought was the one he'd have to go for, which was the worst of the three he was looking at, not the low-mileage one, which was in the middle, trade-off of age and mileage. Reluctantly, he said, "Dodger said I could borrow from her."

"Bank of Dodger, yeah. Guess where the first CD money came from. And some of the second. And we've managed to pay it all back, which I'm not sure she expected. Nice to be surprising. She likes you, you know."

"I don't like doing that."

"She wouldn't offer if she didn't mean it, but look, you don't have to borrow, even from her. I'm not entirely broke, you know. Or I won't be. Have you been listening to the radio? Of course not. In the brief moments when they're not playing The Hip, Tasha's single's getting some airplay. It's one of the ones I'm co-writer on. That means royalties, you know. She's going to be interviewed on *q* on the CBC next week. And it's up there, climbing the ranks on iTunes and the like. I mean, hard to say how it'll do when the numbers come in, but—I'm feeling optimistic. Fuck the pirates. I'll buy the truck. You get your trailer."

"Borrowing from you's worse than borrowing from Dodger. At least I know she can probably spare it."

"Not borrowing, love."

"I can't take your money."

"Not taking it. Just—helping. Why can't I help?"

"You've got that album to record at some point. You said, it was already getting to be too long since the last one, people were forgetting you. You need to do that. And you lost money on the tour."

"And it takes money to make money, yeah, but we almost broke even which is good, considering we hadn't factored Ivan in and—like I said, there's money coming in. Me money, not band money, though me money always turns into band money in the end anyhow. But really. There's money, or there will be."

"I can't, Thomas."

"Why not?"

"Because I'd owe you and I couldn't pay you back."

"You wouldn't have to. I said, not a loan."

"I can't take your money." He had already said that. He heard his voice going tight.

"Don't be so stubborn about it. Why can't you?"

Because. Because Thomas was—because he couldn't, because Thomas might be gone, next month, next fall, an email from France, met someone who's not a neurotic depressive sorry this isn't working, because he was writing songs with someone like Tasha Meyer, he was turning down touring with someone as big as Tasha Meyer was getting, he was going to make it, he and Strange Pilgrim Road, they were going to be someone, be big, and Lindsey was small and awkward and an embarrassment to someone like that and it wouldn't last, it wouldn't work, he didn't belong in that world, he had turned into some kind of minimum wage labourer and it was all he'd ever be, mowing lawns and clearing driveways and what did anyone expect, he'd never been good enough, never figured out how to fit, wherever he was—

"I can't," he said. "It's my stupid business idea, my problem, not yours. I'll figure it out."

"Neill—"

"I have to go. Dodger's expecting me. Bunny, come. Walk-time."

He had to walk over to Barrack Street to pick up the Focus at Isabel's.

The irony did not escape him. It was Thomas and Isabel's car he drove.

Still sponging off other people like a student and he was nearly thirty.

"Neill—damnit, what are you angry about? What did I say? What's *wrong?*"

—with you?

But Thomas didn't say that.

It was just there, it always was.

Thomas had never said it.

Neill didn't answer anyway, far enough down the stairs he could pretend he didn't hear. Thomas ended his pursuit at the door.

Dodger's church was more a sort of limestone cabin, with a bit of a pasture and a stony maple woods added on to it at some point from a neighbouring farm, a brook lined with black willows, a waterfall, even. No manse, no graveyard, no steeple or stained glass—always part of some larger parish. You went into the front porch through the original split doors, black hand-forged hinges, doorway a Gothic arch. From there into the kitchen and dining room, under the loft sleeping area, with a combined bathroom and laundry-room off to the side. That part was all raised up a foot above the rest, and the new floor tiled in dark blue. Down two shallow, broad steps onto the original floorboards, scarred with years, glowing golden when the sun slanted in. Original wainscoting refinished to a natural dark amber; restored white plaster of the walls above. Pictures, mostly little watercolours of what looked like Mediterranean landscapes, the south of France or somewhere like that. Holiday souvenirs?

The thoroughly-insulated and high-peaked ceiling was painted a palest blue; fans turned all the winter to push the heat down. Armchairs and couches that all went together, warm burgundy and gold, a couple of the old pews now ranged along the wall, made comfortable with cushions. Bookcases, cabinets with odd knicknacks. Big stereo, of course. Gothic-arched windows, three on one side, two on the other—the third in the bathroom. Another, broader and higher, at the far end, framed a view of the big white oak in the pasture. 'The far end'—the sanctuary, it's called, you unbaptised heathen, she would say, where the altar had been, with the woodstove on its stone hearth offset, new chimney rising beside it, and another pointed door into what she called the vestry, which was a side porch, full of coats and boots, the woodbox.

Up in the loft the bed looked out through a round window over the front porch, with a wrought-iron railing to keep anyone from falling through it, since it was at the loft's floor level, and the points of the first two windows rose past the floor, into the loft, with railings like the round window.

It was … all very Dodger, somehow. Comfortable. Odd. Shaped around her.

She'd bought the church, falling into sorry disrepair, from a sculptor, who had built a big hip-roofed garage like a small barn and lived with his two kids over that while using the church itself for a studio, letting it continue to fall down around him. Dodger had apparently begun by repointing it all over several years, working alone on a scaffolding, consulting heritage building experts, mixing her mortar herself. Younger, then.

Watching over her godson, that was the impression Neill got. As if she felt that somehow she'd had a part in dragging him back from death's grip and if she turned her back, went home to do whatever retired head teachers did for amusement in England, he might slip away. She was fond of Elizabeth Atkinson, and of Isabel and Maddie and James, but Thomas was hers.

She likes you.

"Bad day?" Dodger asked, when he came in, mid-morning, to refill his steel water mug.

It showed. "Tired," he said, not looking at her, and went off, back to digging the line of the rose hedge along the ditch, inside the old split-rail fence, a trench into which he'd work some well-rotted donkey-manure and old leaves. It wasn't spade-work, but spade and pick-axe, sometimes. Probably wouldn't get any actual roses in till spring. Rugosa hybrids, they would be, mostly. All colours. They would come into bloom not long after the lilacs finished, and the lilacs—there were a quarter acre of them, behind the garage. Run wild, naturalized. A lilac forest, fit for unicorns. The scent, lilacs followed by roses … It was going to be a garden of perfume from May to July.

Most of what he had done so far was archaeology, almost. Digging out the entrenched and vigorous weeds, finding what still struggled in old flower beds, finding the shape of them in traces, things lost in a jumble of wormwood and golden-rod around the down-swept branches of a giant crabapple by the vestry, in front of the three-walled woodshed. Perennials, bulbs, lost but still surviving, things Dodger didn't even know were there. Rhubarb, indomitable. The crabapple was the biggest apple tree he'd ever seen, nearly the size of a maple, white-flowered in spring, astringent yellow-fleshed fruit. Dodger made a dark amber jelly.

Whose flower beds had they been? The artist? Not likely, since he hadn't bothered to maintain anything else. Parishioners planting cinnamon roses and phlox to brighten their churchyard long ago? The hippies, who'd tried to farm? They'd lived in a camper, kept goats and a horse in the church, one of Dodger's neighbours had told her, which explained why part of the floor was so bad she'd just raised the kitchen up. Spent their winters in town, apparently, until they gave up, moved to Toronto, became yuppies instead.

He liked the old remnants, whoever had put them in. Planning new beds to work with those old survivors. There'd be curves of colour, of shades and textures that even Thomas would find pleasing to the eye, an undulating bank of mixed dwarf conifers, harmonizing the lines of old stone church and grey cedar board-and-batten garage and barn and henhouse. Everything would blend together, even the naturalized lilacs and the maple woods beyond, where in May it looked like snow again, the drifts of trilliums. Last week he had made a start on cleaning out the edges of the lilacs, to make them look more tended, getting rid of burdocks, thistles. Eventually, a shore of lilacs—things like Solomon's seal, daylilies, delphiniums, Michaelmas daisies, ornamental grasses, would lap up against them in waves—some clumps of asparagus would have a place too—paths curving through … well, that was the plan, anyway. Dodger liked all those old-fashioned, cottage-garden things that didn't need a lot of fussing. Peonies, daylilies, dwarf conifers, in front of the church. His Japanese maples would find a place, although they'd need a nursery bed at first, to get big enough not to fall victim to a careless hoe, and the soil would need to be acidified a bit …

"*Better?*" *Raleigh asked.*

Yes. He felt better. Calmer. Mind-walking gardens yet to be. Shirt sticking to him.

"*So.*"

Dodger, wearing her paper-straw garden hat, was thinning her carrots over in the big vegetable garden, Bitter and Lager watching over the fence, waiting for handfuls of thinnings to be tossed their way. Bunny was tethered in the shade, stalking something, pouncing—grasshopper, he hoped, not bumblebee.

"*You should call Thomas.*"

He was just tired. Too tired for this. Too tired for Raleigh.

Maybe it was the day-length, lowering towards autumn. It was always worse in the fall. And March, it got worse in March, sometimes. Day-length, that was all.

Try taking St. John's wort, the internet said. Maybe he would.

That wasn't even a fight. Thomas didn't fight. He didn't get mad.

"*Yes, he does.*"

He got mad about things, not people. Got mad and went away, came back trying to understand, to figure things out. He'd do that now. As if Lindsey—

"I thought you were Neill. Make up your mind."

—were some sort of puzzle to figure out, as if, if he could give them both space, some calm to think in away from Lindsey's stress, he would see his way to what was underneath and everything would be clear and all right again.

It wouldn't be. It couldn't. He couldn't see what was wrong. Because there wasn't a thing, a wrong thing to fix, was there? There was just—him. With all these pieces flying, falling, and everything too far away to reach, and going grey and dead—

"That's not you. That's—just a piece of you. A place you've been. You can't let it make you be it, any more," Raleigh said. *"You have to talk to him. Lindsey, Neill, you have to talk him, or you'll lose him. You will. Heaven and hell and wild horses couldn't pull him away from you, but all you have to do is turn your back and walk away. All you have to do is show him you don't want him."*

"I do."

"He tells you he needs you and you just—you just worry he doesn't. You don't answer, what he shows you. You don't let him see how you need him."

"I don't know how." He whispered that, even to Raleigh.

Aloud, he said what else was there, a truth in him. And in speaking, the peace of the garden planning was like everything else, broken pieces, falling away out of reach and he was drowning, reaching for that place again, and couldn't catch his breath—

"He'd—not like me. If he really saw me. Inside." Words for children. *I don't like you any more.* There was nothing in him, nothing underneath, that someone like Thomas would want, if he knew, if he saw. Just some knotted up, ugly, wrong thing, alone.

And he was talking to himself. Out loud.

Bit his arm, hard, hard till it hurt, a red welt that was going to leave a black bruise.

Fuck.

He hadn't done that since he was a kid. And those first months after Raleigh died, rocking, crying silent, voiceless, huddled in the muddy-mustard-coloured institutional arm-chair in his residence room at St. Mark's.

And it was going to leave a mark and this wasn't long sleeves weather and he didn't burn now, brown as he was and outside all summer, people were going to ask why he was wearing long sleeves, a fucking bite mark on his arm and how was he going to explain that to … everyone.

To Thomas.

He leaned there, head on his hands, spade standing in the earth. Eyes shut, hot with tears. He couldn't—

Just fucking do it.

That wasn't even Raleigh's voice.

Left the spade, the pickaxe. Took his mug, went back to the vestry. Changed his steel-toed workboots for his sneakers, methodical. But his hands were shaking. Left his gloves and canvas hat on them, put the mug by the sink, got Bunny's leash and retrieved her. Detoured to Dodger at the far end of the vegetable garden.

Dodger wiped her face on her sleeve, leaning on her fork, caught Bunny's paws on a forearm as she bounced up.

"Down," he ordered, twitching her back. Sometimes she remembered. Sat to be patted.

"Should have done this back in June," Dodger said. "Take some of these bigger thinnings, will you? Ask Thomas to make that lentil and carrot soup he does with cumin and ginger, and send me some, if he's got time."

"Sure." His voice sounded fine, didn't it? "Um, Dodger, is it okay if I take off for the rest of the day?" They kept track of hours on her kitchen calendar. Not very formal.

"You look like you probably should," she said. "It's too hot for all that digging. Of course, go when you need to."

"It's not ... I need to see Thomas about something." As if it mattered, as if he were malingering, if he went and left her thinking he wasn't feeling well or had heatstroke or something.

"Everything all right?" Dodger asked.

"Yes." No. "I—" Shook his head. "It's okay. I'm just— things are difficult, sometimes. For me. Everything is." Voice cracking. God damn it. "I—sorry. I just need to talk to him. To—"

Something Thomas told him once, that he said was a Dodger quote of some kind. There doesn't have to be someone bleeding on the floor for it to be an emergency.

Message he hadn't got at the time?

Dodger put a hand on his arm. "Neill," she said. "Look, love, don't think I'm being a nosy old coot, but—if ever you want to talk, if you need to talk—sometime, now, tomorrow, next month, next year—ever—I can listen. Not for Thomas's sake. For your own, all right?"

He nodded. Didn't protest.

Raleigh stayed quiet as he drove back to Kingston. His shoulders ached, his wrists. The bite on his forearm. Dodger had seen. Of course she had. He didn't even have a long-sleeved shirt thrown in the car he could cover it with and he was chilled, sweaty T-shirt, the wind through the open windows.

What was wrong with him, anyway? Not generally, he had an answer for that and there wasn't any easy solution. Right now, here, today, what was wrong?

He was trapping Thomas. He was being needy, dependent. He was forcing Thomas, somehow, obligating him. Taking where he had nothing to give.

Taking what he could never repay. Not money, but support.

Doing what Megan had done to him, what Megan said he had done to her, manipulating her, and he didn't think it had been him, what she accused him of—

—but of course it had been, of course he was the one in the wrong, maybe he was—

Just stop. Breathe.

There. That was … the shape of it. The fear. Wasn't it? Was it even real? Was it him, or was it the anti-Lindsey, twisting everything into predatory shadows?

Drove up Danbury Road and hesitated. Didn't even pull into the driveway, just parked on the street. Walk in. Uncle Henry would be at the shop. Go down to the studio. Everyone looking at him, wondering. He called Thomas's cell. It was going to go to voicemail; he wouldn't answer, not in the studio, unless they were taking a break and—

"Hey, Neill."

"Hi."

"Hi, yourself."

"I was just—" He rubbed at the mark on his arm. Sore, of course it was sore. Hurting was the point. Like, chew off your leg and you can get out of this trap, hurting.

He was too much of a coward to have ever taken to knives.

Sick.

"Can we talk?"

"Right now? No, of course. Hang on."

He could hear a muffled voice, hand over the phone, Thomas speaking. Making some excuse. Then, "Okay, just wait, I'm going upstairs."

"I'm outside."

"In the shade, I hope."

"In the car, I mean. Here. There."

" … and everywhere. Oh, wait, got you. Here as in Danbury." Thomas at the bay window of the lower living room, pushing the vertical blind slats together. Waving. Phone disconnected, and then he was coming out.

"Hot out here," he said, sliding into the passenger seat, twisting around to scratch Bunny's ears. "Want to head home?"

"Do you mind?"

"Whatever you want."

Easier to just drive around. To find words without looking at Thomas. Eyes on the road. He headed out to Princess Street, driving in silence. No music. Cataraqui. Turned left and went up Sydenham Road, brick church on the left, limestone one with its offset steeple on the right, surrounded by the big graveyard with its arboretum-like groves of old trees, over the 401, away from the city.

He couldn't find words. Mouth too dry to shape them. Driving and driving in silence and this was—

"I didn't mean to push," Thomas said, slouched in his seat. "I just—I upset you and I don't know what I did. I'm sorry."

"No!" he said. "Thomas, I didn't—it's me, it's not anything you did, it's—Raleigh says—Raleigh said I had an anti-Lindsey in my head and he doesn't, he can't believe in anything good, that voice, the anti-Lindsey."

"Anti-Lindsey. Yeah. That's a good name for it. And it's got your grandmother's voice."

"I—" *Oh.* He knew. Thomas knew. "I try not to listen to it but—it's there. And I-I get—I get sick. It's like I'm panicking, like I'm trapped, that it can't be real, the good things can't be real and I'm trapped and drowning in all this hate and it's me, it's just me, trying to destroy everything good because it's not real and it's not true and it won't last and I just want to run away before it all happens, and I know it's not true, what I'm thinking, I know that the good things are real and normal and just—but I know it and I don't believe it, there's all this poison telling me it's not and everything's wrong and it's my fault it's that way. Megan, Megan said it was me, all the time, everything that was wrong was me and all the things she did, she wouldn't listen, everything was all about her, all the time, and I was always being selfish, not listening, only thinking of what I wanted, talking over her when I couldn't say anything without her contradicting it, challenging it, denying it, taking up all the space in the room, living off her she said even and it was her, she was even subletting her bedroom and living in mine but—everything twisted around, I know it wasn't me, but I can't—am I doing that to you, making you feel you have to carry me, so you're going to want out, you're going to—I'm not the kind of person someone like you wants to be with, I can't be, I try and I'm not right, I'm not normal, they always said so, it showed, when I was a kid and I can hide mostly now but it's still there, I just can't, I can't deal with things, I fake it and—"

"Pull over," Thomas said. "Pull over, Lin, before you put us in the ditch, okay?"

So he did, blinking, and Thomas undid his seatbelt and untangled himself from the shoulder belt, scooting over as far as he could, holding him. Bunny popped up in the back seat to see if they'd arrived at any place interesting.

He was shaking. He wanted to throw up.

"Poison's a good word for it," Thomas said. And, "You know depression's another."

"Yeah." Whispered. "I know."

"Okay."

"It's mostly not that bad."

"But you've got to deal with what comes in the bad spots between the 'mostly,' Neill."

"I know. I'm trying."

"I know."

And it was good just to have his eyes shut, to have Thomas stroking his head like he was a dog scared of thunder, but they were parked on the shoulder and cars were zipping by—"You want to drive?" he asked.

"I think I'd better, okay?"

Neill got out, went around, and Thomas hoisted himself over the emergency brake, adjusted the seat forward a little, tilted the mirror.

"I thought I was doing alright," Neill said. "Since the spring. On top of things. And then I just panicked and fell apart."

"Because I said let me buy a truck? Or something else?" Thomas looked at him and Neill wished he wouldn't, that he'd keep his eyes on the road. "Is this about your father?"

"Don't just say no." That was Raleigh. "Think."

"It might be," he said. "I think … I don't know, Thomas. I think it's like, everything that should be just, normal things to worry about, they weigh too much, and if I don't set them— sort of off to the side where I can look at them a while and get used to them, and figure them out, they just—I can't carry them. If I've got time, if I can make a plan, then it's okay. Mostly. I think. But I can't make a plan about that. About— Antonio Olivares. I don't know what I should do. I don't know what I *want* to do."

"I was really worried when you lost your job."

"Oh."

"And yet I hated seeing you doing that job. It ate you up, all your energy. So. I was glad, you did so well. Figured out what you could do that you wanted to do, found a way to do it. I've been so glad for you, seeing that. God, does that sound condescending? I mean, seeing these plans you're making for Dodger and how it's all going to become real—that's beautiful. That's making something that'll last, bringing beauty into the world, and if we can't do that why are we here? And it should give you a portfolio you can use, once you've got your courses done. Even if you do have to work for some other landscaper for a few years—you'll have this to show what you were capable of even before you studied it."

"I hope it'll be all right."

"It will. You can see the bones of it on the ground already. The lines. When you talk about it and start waving your arms around—"

"I don't!"

"You do! Okay, look, let's set aside the thing about your father for a bit. It's not something that's going to change dramatically if you don't deal with it right away. Let's—deal with you. This. Today. I've told you about Uncle Henry and his breakdown, haven't I? And what that did to Kevin? I don't want you to end up like that. I want to help you head this off."

"I'm not—" *That bad ... ?* He rubbed his arm.

"You do that to yourself?" Thomas asked.

Hand closed over the red mark.

"Because I know I didn't and if it was someone else I'm going to have haul him out to a back alley and beat the crap out of him."

"Thomas!" Oh God, he was laughing. "Yeah. I'm sorry. It just—I don't know. It helps. For a moment, it helps. I used to—I haven't, in years. I just—when everything's breaking, you want to—to have some hurt you can—can localize, I don't know, I don't understand it."

"Okay. So you think you should see a doctor?"

"I'm pretty sure I don't have rabies."

Thomas just eyed him.

"Keep your eyes on the road!" Neill sighed. "I don't know. They—I tried, once before. And she just wanted to throw antidepressants at me, didn't want to talk, figure out if that was what I needed. She thought it was all about sex and it wasn't, but I couldn't explain, I couldn't even find the words for myself. So—not a success. I'd rather try, you know, sorting it out, figuring out how to deal with it, teaching myself how to carry it, without that. If I can."

"Yeah, makes sense but—I don't want you finding out you can't when I'm in Frankfurt or some damned place, you know? I don't want you lying to me in emails and then—not answering some day."

"Thomas!"

"I'm serious. This is serious."

"I'm not that bad."

"People aren't, until they are. You're in remission, until

you're not."

Neill looked away, watching out the side window. A bit of swamp. A woods, mostly dead ash trees. Old pasture filling up with junipers.

"I talk to Raleigh," he said. "Sometimes that helps."

"You did not just say that."

"Shut up, Raleigh."

"Ah," Thomas said.

"Ever since he died. That winter. It was—I was really bad. I couldn't—I went to my classes and I did everything I was supposed to, turned in my labs on time, never missed a deadline, went home on weekends, five hours each way on the bus, because Dad thought that would be good for Mom and Carleen. And I wasn't sleeping, and just wanted to scream and hurt people whenever they tried to talk to me, everyone saying, they were so sorry and they understood how I felt and they didn't, how could they? And pretending, everyone at the same time pretending everything had to be normal, because it was embarrassing for them to not know what to say. And even worse, all the people who didn't know—everyone knew he'd died and how he'd died, there were only about two thousand students at St. Mark's so everyone knew someone who knew one or the other of us and people kept talking about it—but lots of people didn't know he was my brother. We didn't look alike, we didn't even have the same surname, and they'd not know and think I was a weird guy who'd just gotten weirder, a freak, and what the hell was wrong with me anyway. I ended up just screaming, really screaming, losing it, at some guys in the basement rooms, they were playing music too loud in their section's lounge one Saturday, under my room, and— they thought I was nuts. And I was doing this to myself—"

Angry swipe at his arm, as if he could erase it. "All the time, just black and blue all up and down both my forearms, my wrists, the backs of my hands even, where it would show and nobody—"

"Nobody asked."

He shook his head. Not even Dad. Nobody noticed. Nobody heard.

"And I started talking to Raleigh."

"Does it help?"

"He's a lot more sensible than I am, sometimes." Neill considered. "More sarcastic, too."

Thomas snickered. "What's he think of me?"

"Don't—"

"I'm serious. Well, I'm not making fun of you, anyway." And then he was serious. "Sorry. I need to ask this. You know he's—"

"Of course I know it's not real. Even if I hear him, even if I almost think I see him, it's not real."

"Do you hear him?"

"At this point, you should lie."

No. He shouldn't.

"Yes."

"Ah."

"Makayla always said I was crazy. Raleigh said I wasn't. I mean, really, Raleigh himself. He got really mad at me about that once, in high school. And it's always seemed … like that's there. That maybe she was right, what the aunts said—I was just kind of a hysterical kid, I think, always getting freaked out by things that if people'd just given me a little more time, it would have been fine. It was panic attacks, a child's version of them, I can see that now. I wish someone else had, back then."

"Sounds a lot like my tantrums. Same thing. Screaming panic at the world."

"Yeah. If I'd learnt to understand them then, manage myself better … But anyway … it's always seemed as though there's a bit of, 'Yeah, they're right, of course they're right.' That whisper. That of course I'm crazy, because I can't be normal and if you're not normal then what are you? And then with Raleigh, this thing with Raleigh, in my head … that doesn't make it any better. I know it's not some delusion, I'm not that kind of mentally ill. I know he's just—something I need to make inside myself, so I can … so I can step away and hear myself think."

"Does it help?"

"Yes."

"I had—when I was sick, when I was in hospital, obviously, but some of the time when I was home, too, they wouldn't let Kev come see me. Germy kids, you know. So I had a sort of imaginary Kevin, for a while. He was sick, too, the imaginary Kevin. Which was kind of weird and twisted, because we'd have these adventures together, I'd make up these stories, desperate things full of fighting and goblins and swords and guns and caves and drowning—he always died in them. So I didn't have to, I suppose. I've never told Kev about that. Probably best I don't. Um, I don't mean that's the same thing. Just—he felt very real, the other Kevin. And he existed because I needed him, maybe making him allowed me to see something in myself. Take my fear and put it where I could see it. I couldn't believe in God, you see. Awkward, in a religious family, when maybe you're dying. It was really strange. I was so young to be coming to that sort of conclusion but—it was so obvious. Jesus, of course, he was real once, somewhere back in time, a wise man who said some good things. But God the Father Almighty, maker of heaven and earth and of all things visible and invisible, some afterlife—no. And I couldn't tell them because it was making them all feel better. I had to protect them from being upset by not letting them know I knew what they were saying wasn't real. This secret I understood that I couldn't tell them, to protect them from feeling bad. And I was so tired, so deadly tired, and so alone and scared. Sorry, I'm not sure what point I was trying to make, now."

Neill swallowed hard against crying outright. Wanted to hold that scared and lonely child. Who was driving and he didn't need to put them in the ditch. Put a hand on Thomas's arm, shyly. Thought, it was that kid he was holding, every time Thomas woke them both up with a nightmare.

"It's okay. I—you don't think I'm crazy."

"That. Yeah. Okay. So I guess, look, can we deal with this together? Is there a way I can help? Is there a way we can deal with this so I'm not scared, when I go off and you're alone for weeks or even months—because that's going to happen. It's got to happen, it's—"

"It's what you are, I know that."

"And I know what you mean, about not wanting them just to throw medication at you. It worked for Uncle Henry, but I think it was the rest of it, maybe, getting help learning to deal with it from inside himself, really made him better in the long-term."

"I kind of—okay, I promised Raleigh I'd make a doctor's appointment if I wasn't doing better by my birthday. That was last spring."

"Are you?"

"I thought I was." He leaned back, shut his eyes. "Oh God,

Thomas, just by telling you—it feels so—I feel so light. As if everything's all washed away now."

"Hey. I'm good for some things. Do you even have a doctor?"

"No."

"Okay. Tell you what, I'll get you in to see mine. She's good. She listens. You talk to her. Tell her this. All this. Maybe not about talking to Raleigh. I'm a poet. I get metaphors. Doctors don't. Just, tell her about how you've been coping. And sometimes not coping. How long you've carried this. And what you're afraid of, crashing, and reluctant about relying on medication, and—you don't have any supplementary insurance, do you, that would cover prescriptions and counselling, that sort of thing. Damn."

"Do you?"

"I actually ended up getting it through a program that's a coalition of writers' groups, not musicians. But as a songwriter I was eligible. An artist. It's a guaranteed thing, no penalties for pre-existing conditions, yay. I wonder if I could add you on as my spouse ... probably not by next month, we haven't been living together long enough to be official."

"We're not technically living together at all."

"Oh."

"We'd have to have the same address, file our taxes together, for that. And it's three years for common-law in Ontario." He'd looked it up, afraid, when he was sharing a room with Megan.

"Oh, fuck, Neill, just—did I do this to you? Look, is that part of it? Because seriously, I was going to say, we should look for a place together, someplace bigger, once the festival's out of the way I was going to—did you think I didn't want to make this—make this serious?"

"No, I —" Long sigh. "I couldn't tell. I can't trust what I think, you know. Because some days it's okay and some days it's the anti-Lindsey doing the thinking and he doesn't know why you like me at all."

"He's an idiot. We'll come back to that. About the doctor—I'll get her to take you on as a patient. You tell her what's going on, where you are. You and she can—work out what's best for you. But it means you've got a doctor who knows, it means if you start to feel—"

"Like I'm falling. Like everything is too heavy and I'm too far away."

"Is that how it feels?"

"Sort of. Sometimes. Kind of, dead and screaming, both, too. Sometimes."

"Okay, if that—then you go to her. Whether I'm around to nag you in person or if I'm on the road and it's by email or whatever, you'll have a doctor who will see you, who will know. Okay?"

"Yes."

"Good. And you are not to worry about what things cost, things OHIP doesn't cover. Prescriptions, therapy, if you decide that's the way to go. Whatever. Not when it's your health. We'll manage. And—where the hell are we?"

"I have no idea. You're driving."

"Somewhere ... Perth Road Village? How did that happen? I'm going to turn around before we end up in Ottawa. Okay, so, the rest of that is, you promise me, seriously, solemn oath, you promise me, you won't mess around with this, you won't start hurting yourself again. You start feeling this thing growing on you—you start feeling like that, even a little, *you will tell me.* You'll phone, you'll email, whatever, we will find wifi and use Skype or something in Europe whenever we can, you will be honest and tell me, and we'll work out what you should do, and if I tell you to go to the doctor you will. Okay?"

"Bossy."

"Yes. Promise."

"Yes. I promise. Thomas?"

"Here."

"Thanks. I will. I try. I really do."

"I'm so scared of this, Lin."

"It's okay, Thomas. I'm okay. Mostly."

"Now?"

"Better, now."

"So we can buy ourselves a truck?"

"We can buy ourselves a truck."

They went home, and one of his garden notebooks was open on the kitchen table, a poppy-spattered mug sitting on it. Disorder, demanding attention, that would have been, if he'd come home alone.

"Oh," said Thomas. "Right. I left that in case you got back first. You might as well read it."

A page written in dark, soft pencil, Thomas's scrawl and for a moment, even with Thomas there, his head in the fridge now, Neill felt that apprehension. You didn't leave people notes unless—

1) You are an idiot. (No, you're not. Idiot.) And I love you.

2) You are not worthless, which is what you seem to think whenever you get into this state; you are weird and smart and deep and you make things beautiful and when I'm with you I'm not scared of the dark and I remember that Thomas exists underneath Tank and Thomas is scared of the dark and you

will always find me there, and I know you've hurt so long you think that's how it's supposed to be, but it isn't. You don't need to hurt. You're not supposed to hurt.

3) And you are beautiful. And when I am rich and famous and we are old and bald and crotchety codgers, you will still be beautiful and we will buy expensive trucks together.

4) I want you forever. In case 1, 2, & 3 were not clear. I need you.

5) I'm borrowing the money from the old folks and remember I'm a co-writer on Tasha's single and that means money and it's playing a lot; I can start paying them back when the royalties for "Sweetest Summer Lie" come in I hope so go buy us the damned truck and once I pay the folks back we can start adding to your house money together.

6) Don't deposit this cheque till tomorrow; I haven't actually gotten the money from Dad yet.

Cheque. Corner sticking out from beneath the notebook.

That's not going shares on a truck, that's—does Thomas seriously think this summer song is going to earn him—

—it's been coming into his head, off and on, since Thomas first played it for him. "Sweetest Summer Lies". Too pop, no bones, notwithstanding.

"Dancey with shadows," Raleigh says. *"Very Pet Shop Boys, really, if you'd just listen without prejudice. I think you maybe have a thing against the higher end of the female vocal range, actually, and you should maybe think about that."*

"Sorry, what?"

He did not need irrelevancies from Raleigh right now.

There were seven points on that page of notes and the last had been erased, but Thomas obviously hadn't found the good eraser; it was smudged, smeared ghost-words, and they said,

7) Please take it. You make me feel like you don't—

And then the erasing got violent and he couldn't decipher the last two words at all.

—want me?—trust me?

He did. He just couldn't—

It was himself he couldn't believe in sometimes, in being wanted.

"Not much in here for lunch," Thomas said, and arms went around him, head leaning between his shoulders. "Last night's leftovers or are we saving them for supper?"

Which reminded him he'd left that basket of thinned carrots in the back of the car in the heat.

He turned around within those arms, pulled Thomas closer. "Are they expecting you back?"

"In the studio? No, I told everyone we were through for the day, go home."

"Not really hungry. Too hot. Too tired. Just honestly tired. I haven't been sleeping much."

"Yeah, I can tell."

"Sorry."

"Sh."

Curtains closed against the heat. Cool off with a shower, take a nap … with Thomas, preferably.

Thomas. It was easy to think of him as something buzzing like a bee in the sunlight, full of music and chatter, and to forget he—he was miles deep underneath that, watching, and thinking, and all those songs with bones and shadows in were coming out of the dark, the fear, the watching, trying to make sense of a baffling and frightening world. He watched. He saw things.

"You make everything make sense," he whispered. "And I

don't have anything to give you back."

"You are so worried about not being good enough or cool enough or deserving enough or real enough you don't even notice how I lean on you. How you are—some kind of shelter I can crawl under." Holding hard, as if something was trying to pull them apart. "You're like this—this garden, like your flat, this place where I can be quiet and—just pay attention. I need you. And that's not the point, anyway. It's just, together we're right. We don't have to say this balances that, this trades for that between us. It's us. We're just us, holding on to one another, okay? Because that's what we want and what we need and where we need to be."

Neill was all long wet hair and cool skin, and they were both too tired, too quietly drained, emotionally, to want to do more than just lie there, touching. It was good, being there, like that, and the soft rush of the fan was like distant running water, almost. And there was something Thomas wanted to say, but was it the time, and if it wasn't, then when, and—

"Hey. Tell you something?"

"Listening." Neill's eyes were shut and his hand was tracing slowly over Thomas's back, up and down his spine, the edge of his shoulderblades. And if he kept that up the idea of *just a nap*, just lying here resting, maybe falling asleep, which they both needed, calm and stillness, was going to go out the window.

And then they'd need yet another shower, right.

"Okay, look. This isn't about—today. It's not some thing that's me thinking, oh God how can I cheer him up, don't let the anti-Lindsey ever start telling you that."

"I don't need cheering up."

"I know. And this isn't some—don't you ever let the anti-Lindsey take this, this coming now, and twist it into something against you, okay? Promise. This isn't some—some panicked thing on my part, this isn't some bribe, or consolation, or insurance convenience, or—or anything but what it is. Because I've been realizing this for a while and it's big and it's sort of, oh, obvious but I've been holding onto it, just sort of, getting used to the shape of it like an interesting stone in my hand and … so promise."

"Not sure what I'm promising." Neill opened his eyes. "But okay."

"So this isn't about that, today, what we've talked about, except that—except that I'm realizing I need to do more of this, this saying things that need said, too. Not be second-guessing you, deciding what'll make you anxious and what not, deciding to wait on things I want to say. So, this is something that's been in my mind, this summer. Thinking about this. Realizing this."

"This which?"

"I guess it's sort of about us looking for a bigger place together."

"It's kind of late now. Students'll have grabbed everything. But we should look. Maybe out of town?"

"So, yeah. Okay. It wasn't really that, even, what I was working up to. I mean, yes, definitely, let's do that, but—"

"You're sounding like me." Neill rolled up on his elbow. "What?"

"What I've been realizing I want." Tracing along the line of his beard, two fingers.

"A bigger bed?"

"That, too. You, Lin. For real and for ever and—look, how

would you feel about getting married?"

"Married? Us, you mean?"

He could have said, *No, me and Anicky, obviously us, or Who else, or* … But all he said was, "Yeah."

Silence, then, and he couldn't read Neill's face even, just blank, like that look by Summerhill, this lunatic on a bike coasting down, hailing him like a long lost lover …

Then it was like the sun coming out all over again.

"Thomas. God."

"Only where guitars are involved. And one or two other things, maybe—"

Silenced, mouth on his, and then pushed up on an elbow again, looking down on him. That smile.

"If you—yes. Thomas … " Touching his face, like he's not sure he's real. Fingers. Lips. "Yes."

"You've bought a truck," Dodger said. Walked around, looking, approving. It was a Toyota, like hers, which always seemed to last and she did keep buying the same make, so that must mean something, Thomas said. It was the older model, lower mileage one, the middle one of the three Neill had been considering, but the first choice, newer and most expensive one had had a lot more stealthy rust on it, when you actually crawled underneath, which they had done.

"We did," Neill said. "Um, sorry for cancelling yesterday too. It ended up taking most of the day. Testing them, hashing it out over coffee, pros and cons, which we really wanted, getting insurance and all that sorted out. Figuring out how to drive it."

"Standard," Dodger said. Chuckled. "First time?"

"Yeah. You noticed."

"You'll get smoother. Neill?"

"I know."

"It's pink."

"Yes."

"You bought a pink truck."

"Officially it's 'light red'. And something about sparkles, but the vet we bought it from couldn't remember whether it was called pearl or metallic or mica or what, so Thomas is calling it the sparkly truck." As in, What colour is the truck? I can't tell but who cares, it's sparkly. *And something sparkly is traditional, under the circumstances …*

"True. But light red … "

"It's a—sort of orangey pink, don't you think? Like sodium street-lights. Anyway, technically pink is light red."

"Does Thomas realize?"

"He says maybe it's taupe. He says it very seriously, so I'm pretty sure that's a joke."

"Taupe? Who even told him there was such a thing? Well, I won't tell him pink if you don't. I assume he has some deep-seated Kindergarten trauma about getting colours wrong; James never got fussed about it the way he does, even when he went through the usual sort of fashion-obsessed phase in high school."

"At least it'll be advertising, of a sort. I'll be 'that landscaping guy with the pink truck.' Dodger … Dodger?"

"Neill?"

"We're sort of—engaged. Thomas—Thomas said I should tell you."

/Six/

Mood:
Pet Shop Boys, "Liberation"
Crunch of dry grass; goldenrod like flame

The highlight of the band's summer was usually the Hard Rock Mud Festival, which was a ridiculous name and the music was never all hard rock. But this year the mud was likely to be rock hard.

It was happening less than a week after would be the one music event the entire country talked about. The Mud Festival was always the last weekend of August. It was traditional. It was theirs. But this year The Tragically Hip was touring, and it wasn't a farewell tour, no, they weren't calling it that, but their singer was dying and everyone knew it for all the upbeat blah blah blah brave battle talk. And they were *the* band, Kingston's band, Canada's band—

"Why does no one ever say, yeah, what about Rush, when people say that?" Frankie wanted to know.

"Nickelback?" Anicky murmured, and Thomas mimed throwing a cushion at her head, mimed because they weren't in the studio but at the SandWitch and there were no cushions.

Everyone was loud, full of fries and sandwiches and craft beer of choice, except Isabel, who was making do with or-

313

ange juice and tonic water. Emily, Laura, Sue, Jon—the whole gang. Ivan, sitting between Frankie and Isabel and looking like everyone's little brother. Stefan and Michael had both wandered over from bar and kitchen to squeeze in for a bit.

Still a bit weird, a bit dizzying, wait wow what, really? They'd told them. It was true. They were serious. Fiancé. Thomas kept saying it. "Hey, fiancé … "

"Idiot," Neill said, and missed whatever he was aiming for, kissed his ear. Slumped back in the corner of the booth, laughing. He was just nicely drunk enough to be relaxed, to slacken that overwound tension that was so much a part of him.

Neill was so sweet when he went like that, and it didn't always take a couple of pints to do it; he *could* relax; he could let that tension go. Thomas had seen it more frequently over the past year, especially this summer. Just the last few weeks had been rough again. But it was going to be like that, always. Up and down. That was okay. They were good.

Wanted to tell him so, take him home and make him know how much he mattered, all over again. But everyone was having a good time and this was now, this was good. Neill put a long arm around him and Thomas leaned back against him, swung his legs up over Anicky's lap, and Laura's.

They weren't going to mess around, drag this out. Just get married soon, quietly, no fuss. And next summer have a hell of a party by the lake in Mum and Dad's backyard, everyone, all the cousins and aunts and uncles, his, not Neill's except they'd invite the Kavanagh cousins, they were okay, Carleen would be back from Bolivia then, Neill's mum would come up, the bish and Nan would come over and Grandad would no doubt insist on some kind of blessing, which was okay, God could drop by if he felt so inclined and maybe like the bishop he'd bring his mandolin. The C of E wasn't there officially on marriage yet but it would catch up in the end, Grandad said, if he had anything to say about it. The Canadian Anglicans were more disunited. They couldn't have a church wedding here in Kingston but in the next diocese over, in Toronto, they could and no, they'd told Mum, no, they weren't going to do that, Neill, ancestrally Catholic, wasn't even baptised and Thomas had given up religion himself ... He wasn't going to outright lie at his own wedding, like he did at his confirmation, all spiffy in his first suit and tie ...

So much simpler, this way. No tie required. October. And Neill said, Hallowe'en. Which was a Monday, this year, not a popular day of the week for weddings so no problem getting that date. And they'd have two weeks before the band headed to Europe; they were going to take Bunny and go off in the truck, rent a cabin on some little lake for a few days.

"Why on earth are you getting married on Hallowe'en?" Frankie wanted to know.

"'s'when we met," Neill said.

"Can I wear a costume?" Anicky asked. "I want to come as a pirate."

"Princess," Emily said. "Pirate-princess."

Ivan began to sing " ... for it is, it is, a glorious thing, to be a pirate-queen ... "

"No pirates," Neill said, stern.

"Oh, you have to wear your labcoat," Thomas said, and went off into giggles. Neill pulled him over, muffling him against his chest.

"I thought it was in the spring you met," Frankie said. "I'm sure it was in the spring, because we were just back from Quebec, the time we had flat tires two days running. You were so repulsively giddy for weeks, Tank. Lindsey this, Lindsey that—"

"No, no, no, hah, didn't I say, didn't I ever tell you—"

"He told everyone else and their dog," Kevin said. "He must have."

"I met him years ago. Years and years and years and—before I ever knew you, Mouse."

"Eight years ago," Neill said. "You were just a baby, Frankie."

"Baby! Do the math, Mr Scientist-guy. But wow, guys, eight years. I did not know."

"Probably because you weren't paying attention."

"Of course, Tank didn't actually get his name. He spent *years* mooning over this guy he'd kissed in a bathroom—"

"It was a hallway!" Indignant and in unison, which sent Thomas into more giggles.

"—a hallway, they claim, when he was too high to think of getting his number or even asking his name—"

"Let's not get into that," Thomas said, and Kevin smirked at him.

"You didn't even ask his name?" Ivan said. "Wait, wait, I want to hear this. How'd you end up meeting again, this is a story ... "

And the evening wound along. Laughter. Friends.

"So seriously," Isabel said, and it was later, getting late. "Not to change the subject, but we're going to this thing, right? All of us? It's important."

This thing, right.

The last concert of The Hip's tour was Kingston, their hometown. And it was the week before the Mud Festival and it was sold out within an eyeblink of the tickets going on sale.

Kevin knew because he had tried to get tickets; okay, it wasn't the style he wanted to play but to listen to, he actually liked them now and then, he said. Defensively.

And the people who couldn't get tickets weren't going to say, oh well, let's get a weekend pass to the Mud Festival instead. And mostly, it seemed that even if The Hip was not your thing, you were still—it was still *the* music thing that was on everyone's mind. The local media weren't mentioning anything else that was going on. The national media hardly were. Which was nice. Drove that foul nutter who was running for president in the States out of the headlines for a bit.

Surely even Americans wouldn't vote in someone like that.

Of course people'd thought that about Ford, too, in Toronto.

The concert, the last concert. Ever. It was being broadcast nationally, TV and radio. The city was going to livestream the concert downtown, market square, massive LED screen on the backside of city hall. Kingston's band for Kingston's people. But it would be outsiders pouring in too, and not just from Napanee and Gananoque. People from right across the country. From overseas, even. Everyone would be all festivalled out by the next Friday; no money, no energy, no emotion left.

Thomas was just being cranky. and he didn't want to feel cranky. He would play to an empty bar so long as the bartender made a pretence of listening; he'd done it. You're there to play; you do your damnedest because if you don't you're a lie. But it would be nice to have a crowd with some emotional energy left for the rest of them. And some money to buy stuff. Buying stuff was good. He had a husband and a dog to keep. He grinned at no one in particular. Oh God, he was a grown-up. He was getting married.

Neill's hand was on his ribs, under his shirt, and it was really getting to be time to go. He didn't want another pint, wanted to hold this light, this bubbling golden evening, make it go on forever.

They would have to take Bunny for a little walk around the block when they got home. It was a Rule.

And Neill's breath was in his hair, and his hand—yeah ...

"Time we were heading off," Thomas said, his hand over where Neill's lay under his shirt, fingers spread on his skin, below his ribs. "Dogs to walk, someone's got to go off landscaping early ... Guys, thanks. Thanks for coming out. Thanks for being here."

Jon and Emily decided they were off as well, and the Bells were staying in his room on Aberdeen, Ivan had said he didn't mind, they could have the bed, he had his sleeping bag; the three said they'd walk with him and Neill as far as Neill's, and Kev came into town with the Bells but was getting a taxi back to Bayridge—he said he'd drop Isabel off, and Laura and Sue as well ... So Susannah made Frankie unknot his shoes, kind of her because he'd completely forgotten what the kiddo had done, and they all dispersed, and it seemed it was decided and maybe he'd missed the decision being taken, distracted, lost in the rise and fall of Neill's chest under his head and the new roughness of Neill's calloused palm against his skin. Working man's hands. Which was distractingly erotic, somehow.

So. They were going to the concert, The Concert.

And he had the PRS at Neill's, *at home*, lovely sound, *home*, and half a wordless thing floating in his head, where it had been for days and he couldn't work it out, find its right shape, but that wasn't for tonight.

Tonight was Neill's.

The city had pretty much ground to a halt. They weren't within the zone of closed streets, even Isabel's flat over on Barrack, but it was a near thing. Neill hadn't bothered to go out to Dodger's yesterday; wasn't worth it, the gas he'd have wasted sitting in traffic, trying to get home.

Not into collective emotion. It seemed … a lie, anyhow, when Thomas didn't share it. Couldn't. He'd honestly tried, as though it was some fault in himself, some—insult, almost, that he didn't want to make. He was sorry the man was dying. He was sorry they weren't likely to be making more music. He was sorry for the band, for their families, for all the people who were genuinely hurting, anticipating the loss of something that mattered to them, and deeply, and even for all the others just getting caught up in the emotion because it was a great collective thing, a belonging they could fall into. He certainly didn't deny anyone their right to grieve, to celebrate and mourn at once, a wake for the living. He'd *hurt* when Bowie died, a deep ache, something personal lost. And James couldn't get why that bit of banter on the Wembley recording made him cry, first time he watched the DVD, really saw it. Supposedly not, but had Mercury known already? Suspected, at least? Had they all? Sometimes he thought they must have. *Keep doing this … till we bloody well die.* Something like that. And into "Who Wants to Live Forever?"

He'd never say this unbelievable mass of people shouldn't be here, caring. But it still wasn't his thing, his music. So why was he needing to be here taking up pavement space?

Because we're here, this is home, this is … something that matters, Kevin said, and it wasn't Thomas's thing, or—Neill's, or Anicky's, but Kev liked them well enough, not fanatic but something he'd put on at a barbecue; it was one of the things their tastes didn't overlap on, like Viking metal, which he had a bit of a thing for, secret vice. And Frankie said they were okay, and Isabel had all their albums and was a bit disappointed that when part of Barrack Street had been renamed The Tragically Hip Way it hadn't been her part, not that she'd been living there then or ever had a notion she might.

But my God, what a crowd. What a ... thing. They were a lake, an ocean, filling the streets, the market square, washing up against buildings. Stirring with currents and eddies. Some just standing, fixed on the screen. Some in motion ... seeking a better vantage, toilets, food ... A cooler place to stand. The sun had set around the time the concert began and now the evening was cooling off, a little, from the near-thirty of the afternoon, but the pavement and brick and old stone walls held the heat, flung it back up at them. He kept an eye on Isabel, but she seemed all right so far. Not weighed down with baby yet, just a bit tubby if you knew where to look, a bit plumper all over. Getting that habit of standing with a hand on her belly, communing with the critter. Kevin kept close by her, too. Frankie and Ivan and Anicky, the quest for sausages ... lost, lost, never to be seen again ... The pressure of the crowd, some gang of bodies trying to join another, squeezing in, washed them up against the railings of the Olivea's patio, petunias being crushed against his back. Crazy. Neill and Kev had their arms out, shielding Isabel from that surge. He was getting cut off, edged away. The restaurant had bouncers at the door, defending the space. No, sorry, someone was being told, you can't just come in for a beer, we're not a bar, we're not a public toilet, we're full to capacity ... People were standing on chairs on the narrow patio, their plates forgotten, craning to watch the screen.

Thought he'd seen Trudeau out in the crowd, even.

"Come on." He squeezed through to Neill, let himself be pushed up there. Someone pressing up against him, not Neill. Big woman, swaying to the beat, eyes half closed. He edged away, took a swig from his water bottle—healthy Belgian summer beer, full of electrolytes and a hint of orange, thank you, Frankie—tugged at Neill's arm. Neill caught Kevin, Kev caught Isabel, and like a daycare on excursion they wound away, human chain.

Times like this he remembered he wasn't short; it was just his crazy tall Viking Rus, Viking Yorkshire family and his taste in men made him feel that way. He could actually see over most heads.

Tank engine, towing his little train of carriages. Resisted the sudden urge to make chuff-chuff noises, but let an insane cackle escape. Okay, so where was he going? In search of the strayed and lost? The Bells and Ivan had swum off in search of food a couple of songs ago.

He hoped the SandWitch and Brew was making a good thing out of this. They were a street away, just below the zone given up to foot traffic only. A TV-free pub, but they'd brought in screens for the event. Who hadn't? Even the Seoul Kitchen was expecting to be busy all night, and more so once the concert was over and all those thousands of bodies found themselves reluctant to just go home. He'd offered to work, but Uncle George said, no, you're a musician, you want to be there. Sue and Laura and Emily, all three drafted for the night, hadn't got that offer, but they said they didn't mind, they'd hear it, they'd have the radio on. And Jon, who would have minded very much if he'd missed it, was working at the venue itself, the K-Rock Centre, one of the many part-time gigs with which he kept himself afloat.

"Where are we going?" Neill asked, voice raised to be heard, leaning into him.

"Anicky?"

"Can't see her. And I've lost Kev and Iz."

"Where?"

"Don't know. Kev said something I didn't catch and they were gone."

"The tug of the current, a fading cry and his desperate hand closed on—nothing. At least they're together."

They halted, looking around. Blonde head and black … ? Nope. No Bells and Ivan, either. Well, Ivan had the keys to Aberdeen. Still had that lease—but he had students in all the rooms and it would be too much for just the two of them anyway, and they didn't want to start life officially together sharing a kitchen with a bunch of kids. Also it was too dark for the plants. Neill had been looking but no luck yet with finding a bigger place. Tricky, with a dog, the time of year.

He needed to go over tomorrow, get some more clean clothes. Or maybe see how many of the laundry baskets would fit in the bottom of the wardrobe and move the whole thing, though where it could go under the steep eaves of Neill's ceiling …

Maybe Ivan would want to take over the whole renting and subletting arrangement … But was he capable of putting on the stern elder mask of authority and making the students actually cough up their rent money? Maybe he'd better just keep the lease himself and sublet to Ivan as well …

"Alone at last," Neill said wryly. Took a long drink from his water—or what-have-you—bottle. Frankie had rounded up all the steel water bottles they usually took along on road trips, filled them with beer, saying the police, security, would never check, not if people weren't being a problem. Marked a couple with masking tape. Lemonade for Isabel.

"What now? Want to text? Send up a distress beacon to rally the troops to us?"

"Not really. They're big kids, now."

Lots of real kids here. Codgers. Okay, maybe not codgers. Lots of the middle-aged. Bare arms and legs.

Music.

Dry event, the city had said, wink wink, everybody bring your virtuously reusable water bottle along. No smoking, either, but the air was heavy with the smell of pot. Ah, the good old days, Toronto, all that was missing was stale deep-fryer grease and the tang of an uncleaned rabbit hutch. That's what Ronnie had wanted of the Exit, to be the next Hip. Who knows, they might make it someday. Still around. Best of luck to them.

We'll see who makes it to the Junos first.

Stop with the cranky, Tank?

Swaying. Singing. Everyone singing. They all knew the words, or it felt that way.

He felt very—unCanadian. He didn't know the words to this one. To most of them. They'd never really caught him, the ones he'd listened to. Couldn't catch them, either, don't think snarky thoughts about that. That was a stage presence, though. Man beside him was crying.

Sardines in a tin.

Hand on his waist. Neill, behind him. Thomas leaned back against him. Glad he was there.

He didn't belong here. Didn't get the feeling Neill felt he

did, either.

This wasn't the language they spoke.

But yet there was something in the night, the crowd, even for him, for them … a truth. To be witnessed. But from outside. He was still outside. That they were outside was part of it. He …

Turned to look up over his shoulder. "You bring one of your notebooks?"

"Notebook? No."

"Damn. Pen?"

"Maybe." Neill twitched his backpack around, felt inside, checked pockets. "No. You can have a granola bar, an apple, or another water bottle with actual water, but—okay, pencil."

Thomas took the pencil, considered his arm, only surface he had to write on. "You always have a notebook," he complained.

"I was trying to lighten it from all the useful stuff that wasn't going to be useful at a concert. Why do you need a—"

"Turn around."

Pencil on white T-shirt. Would that even work? Nice firm back but not an ideal writing surface nonetheless, and in the dark he couldn't see if he was getting anything coherent down or not. Words, sounds, broken sentences, riffs and thoughts suddenly swarming half-formed—Hell, what did he have a phone for?

"I am so bloody analogue sometimes." Phone. Recording. Leaning over it, head bowed against Lin's back, and if the people around thought he was breaking down, fine, fair enough, it was happening. Did the music come first or the words, people'd ask and usually it was the music but sometimes the words sat waiting, scribbled in notebooks, in the margins of novels, till the right sounds found them, and sometimes they grew together, sometime they demanded one another, came rushing, torrent to drown all other thought, no need to hunt, to lie in wait ... Eyes closed, shutting out the noise, the surging sea, just chasing the words, fast, before they vanished, singing the half-broken snatch of a melody that had nothing to do with the music pouring down on them like rain, the thing everyone around was singing, not sure if that was going to be audible in the end, just named chords then, feeling them in his hand, in his chest, ears, desperate, this thing, this fluttering half-born critter of a song drowning under the sound of the population of a good-sized town, all singing.

"Lin, you mind—?"

"No. Let's go." And that was all that needed said, no pointless words to jar the thoughts loose, the sounds that struggled together. Did text all his strays:

>*Bailing out got to go write something. Love & kisses. T&N.*
>*Ok see you brunch.*

Anicky's acknowledgement, and from Kevin,

>*Don't wait up. Will crash at Izez.*

Good. He wasn't ready to throw this even at Kev, yet. Let Neill do the threading through the crowd, keeping close in his wake, till they were past Clarence and the great herd thinning to smaller islands, bodies in motion, laughing, calling, lots of activity down by the SandWitch, and still the songs carried, the reek of pot and sweat in their clothes, their hair, the bodies around them, like they were emerging from the sea, the song. The breeze off the water felt cold. Moon, almost a full moon, silver through scraps of cloud, climbing overhead.

Another block and they were home, and Bunny, in her box, barked warning at the sound of keys in the door, howled—

whoo-whoo-whoo—welcome at a familiar voice hushing her.

The PRS was still here; he'd been carrying it back and forth a lot lately, chasing this thing he'd finally caught, maybe, or maybe this was something altogether different. The baby amp plugged into his computer. Listening to what he'd got on the phone, which was mostly muttering and noise, and Neill's shirt was all sweat and a half-legible word—didn't matter, it was still all there, seething—

Neill just touched his head, smiled, got Bunny's leash.

He had the headphones on when they came back, lost in it. Shutting out the faint thunder-rumble through the windows from the concert, the hum of the fans. Talking to himself. Bunny went to her box on principle, since a guitar was out. Neill gave her her bedtime biscuit, shut her in. Wandered off, came back with two glasses of wine, the bottle. Warm, thick, dark. Put it within reach, went to curl into the armchair. Just the nightlight in the bathroom, the lamp in the far corner, catching the shape of him, watching.

And finally. Done. Done-ish. He and Kev would throw it back and forth; the final thing would have all of them in its shaping; he could almost hear the drums, *there*—but it would do, it would keep, not evaporate now. Unplugged head-phones, left everything recording, never mind disturbing the kids below, they were probably at the concert anyway, upped the gain a little, went straight through, music alone, spinning out melody over chords, and then again, voice raised, squint-ing at the page where he'd scribbled words fast as they came.

No Passing Bells (Ain't Down, Ain't Dead) …

"God, yeah," Neill said, when it all died to silence. Came over. Wrapped in around him, careful of the guitar, the amp, the computer—the wine bottle too close to all of them.

"It's okay?"

"Thomas." Head against his, breath against him. "Yeah. *Okay.* Sure. You could say that."

"Good." He drained his glass. "Right. Finish the bottle?"

"No. Come to bed." Neill was leaning to screw the cap on one handed, not letting go of him.

"Shower?" he suggested, because he was sticky and smelt like other people's smoke and—

"No." Neill was turning down his gain, the volumes, switching the amp off, taking the guitar.

"Don't leave that on the couch—"

"It's fine."

"Bunny—"

"She's in her box."

Didn't protest being led away. The guitar would be fine, the files would upload to the studio's cloud backup … detour to put the wine in the fridge and he was being most thoroughly kissed, up against the cupboards, drawer-pull digging into him.

"Lin," he whispered. "Hey."

"You have no idea—" Breathless. Shirt off him, right there. "—how beautiful you are."

"Hey, Lin." Sometimes love was something like awe.

Asleep, and dreaming of music, of swimming, dark water over him and music he could only half hear and it wasn't panic, it wasn't drowning, because Lin was there and they were swimming together, two bodies hot against one another, rising through the cold water … He woke up blurry, annoyed, because he couldn't quite hear the music and it was turning into Westminster chimes of all things—

Which was Linds-Neill's phone, and the clock-radio on the upturned clementine box that did duty as a nightstand said 3:42.

Neill growled and reached over him for the phone. His own, habitually set only to vibrate when they'd been in the studio so much, began buzzing on the wood.

Both—Oh God that wasn't good.

"Frankie?" Neill.

"Thomas! God, I thought you were never going to answer."

"Anicky, what's—"

"Oh God, no, okay, we'll come. Thomas, Frankie says—"

"Thomas," said Anicky, "your house is on fire. Thomas, it's okay, everyone's out, the smoke detectors went off, we went out and and yelled up the stairs, the kids are all out and all their friends—you couldn't sleep through that, Thomas, are you there?"

"Frankie says your house is burning, not your folks', your house on Aberdeen, they've called 911, everyone's safe they think—"

Sirens. There were sirens, he could hear them out the window, through the phone. And half the streets were blocked off, still, but they'd be letting emergency vehicles through, the crowds would have mostly thinned away, surely—

L-Neill crawled the rest of the way over him to the floor, turned on the light, then the bathroom light. Back looking damp and grim, hauling open the dresser, finding them both clean clothes, underpants and T-shirts, anyway. He had a hasty wash himself, wondered if a water bottle of unknown beer and a single glass of wine had worn off, could they take the truck, but it would hardly be faster and they'd get in closer on foot, found his jeans abandoned on the kitchen floor …

Landlord's phone number—no, call once he knew what was going on.

Someone too drunk to operate a toaster, probably.

Nothing worse.

More sirens.

"It's okay, Bunny. We'll be back soon." Reassurance. Bunny merely looked peeved, a dog who suspected her humans were going for a night-time adventure without her.

Unreasoning desire to make sure the smoke detector here was working before they left, leaving Bunny and the PRS behind, but Neill was the sort of person who changed batteries religiously.

He phoned Isabel as they headed down the stairs. Because—they wouldn't have gone to his place, further from the market square than any of them, they wouldn't, they wouldn't be there without Anicky knowing, how could they, but—

"Iz, you okay?"

"Tank? Thomas, what's wrong?"

That voice was manifestly not Isabel's.

"Kev? Where's Iz?"

"I'm right here." Blurry, cranky, I really hate people waking me up Iz-voice, thank God. "Tank, are you—has something happened?"

"No, I wanted to be sure you were okay, sorry. Sorry. Just, Anicky says my house is on fire and I—I had this stupid idea you might have gone there, I—um, sorry, is Kev there?"

A sort of silence. There was breathing. Possibly whispering. He grabbed Neill's arm, mouthed, *They're in bed?* and got a puzzled look, incomprehension.

"Really on fire?" Kevin asked. "Seriously? Frankie didn't just make tea in the microwave without putting any water in the mug again or something?"

"Kevin … "

"What?"

"Nothing. Okay, nothing, go back to sleep. Both of you."

"With your house on fire?"

"Is it really on fire?" Isabel had the phone again. "Oh God, is everyone out?"

"Anicky says she thinks so. We're on our way over now."

"We'll come."

"No, stay where you are. Nothing we can do anyway. Okay? Sorry. Love you. Didn't mean to, um, interrupt. Or anything. Just—okay, see you in the morning."

Disconnected.

"What?" Neill asked. "Did you think they'd gone to Aberdeen too?"

"Well, not really, but I had to be—Lin, Lin—Kev and Iz."

"Kev and Iz, what?"

"*Kevin.* And *Isabel.* He was *not* sleeping on the couch. He answered her phone."

"Kevin and—oh. Oh!" And he was grinning. "Really? I was kind of wondering."

"You were?"

"He was so angry about Ricky."

"*I* was so angry about Ricky."

"He was angry, like, like someone had just come out of nowhere and slapped him across the face angry, on top of everything else."

"Huh. You know, she had such a crush on him, along grade eight or so. Always doing annoying things, trying to make him notice."

"Thomas?"

"Lin, I love you. I do. Have I said it?"

"Might have mentioned it, once or twice. And I love you too. But Thomas?"

"Lin?"

"Your house is on fire."

"Right."

They ran, then, six empty blocks of William Street, to Aberdeen. And the sky was clouded dark. Not smoke, his first confused thought. Cloud. The air smelt of rain.

And smoke.

Not some minor toaster fire, and they stopped joking as they got closer.

"Oh God," Thomas said. Neill caught his arm.

Flames visible in the downstairs windows, the branches of the maple lashing back and forth in the billowing heat, black against the scarlet. Plumes of water rising; smoke and steam and flashing lights.

"You can't come through," an irritated police officer said, and Thomas was practically shouting, "I live here, where are the kids, is everyone out—"

"Thomas, it's okay. Frankie said they were out, everyone was out." He'd never seen Thomas like that, not in all the time he'd known him. Suddenly panicking. Losing it, out of nowhere, after all the joking on the way. Took his arm. "Thomas! It's okay."

It wasn't. There was a moment's frantic confusion, alarm in the officer's face, kids, what kids, until she figured out Thomas meant students and yes, there were a dozen people staying there, people come to town for the concert but they were out, everyone was reported to be out, there, go through …

A shocky, shivering huddle, Anicky, Frankie, Ivan among them. A girl called Bex was crying, clutching her computer, suppressing her sobs and then bursting out again, and urgent to tell Thomas something. That seemed to settle him, more than anything else. Pulling on calm, that steady reassurance that he wore like a coat. He pulled her away, an arm around her, quiet, soothing.

A choked confession.

It was her fault, she almost whispered. Was it her fault? She left the upstairs hall light on, the one that crackled and fizzed weirdly, there were so many people staying over, sleeping bags on the floor, everyone had a friend or two, the concert—she didn't want anyone falling down the stairs, getting up to go to the bathroom in the night. She thought it'd be okay, there were fuses, even if the wiring was funny all that would happen was the bulb would burn out or the fuse would blow, right, it wasn't her fault … ?

No, Thomas told her. It wasn't her fault, no. Whatever started it, even if she did leave that light on. He hugged her, handed her over to one of the other girls, who seemed to have lugged a synthesizer out, and a boy with a violin and a laptop who was wearing nothing but a striped housecoat.

Don't stop to grab anything, they tell you. But of course people did.

"My thesis," another boy was saying, on the phone to someone. "Oh my God, my thesis, I left my computer, there's only the draft I emailed you last week, my notes, all my notes … "

"A wonky light fixture couldn't do that." Thomas kept his voice low. "Could it? Oh God, I should have called an electrician myself and sent the bill to the damned landlord—I'd better tell someone official about the fizzing light. And the mice. How the hell can it be burning like this? It's brick, not chipboard."

"All that old carpet?" Neill said. "And interior walls have airspaces, even old lath and plaster walls are studs and air-spaces, inside."

"And wires. And mice."

"Yeah."

Anicky was there beside them, rubbing Thomas's back. He was still breathing a bit panicky. What Neill was afraid to do, out there with so many people around. Touch him. Comfort. Thomas looked worse than Anicky, and she'd been inside. She'd got her Birkenstocks on, but just sweatpants and a camisole, otherwise.

"Okay, Tank?" Anicky asked.

He laughed, took a deep breath. "Sorry. Sorry. Me—what about you?"

"I guess. It wasn't like this when we got out. Just the smoke detectors blaring like crazy and you could smell the smoke. And the lights didn't work. Then something went up, whomp, and all these flames started growing in the windows, just about when the firetrucks were showing up and we were all out here, everyone counting over and over, making sure—after we'd called you, that was."

"You leave any guitars there, Tank?" Frankie asked faintly.

It was Thomas's room—the roar of flames, the scarlet light. All the downstairs, his room and the common living room and the kitchen.

"Anicky wouldn't let me look—when the alarm started. Grab your bag and get out, she said."

Frankie was barefoot, in boxer shorts and the Rush T-shirt she'd been wearing yesterday, but she had both her messenger bag and Anicky's backpack. No shoes. Phones, wallets, that was probably it. And Neill wasn't wearing a coat he could offer to either. Frankie was shivering, teeth chattering. He put his arms around her. She even felt cold to the touch, all awkward angles. She huddled into him, cheek against his chest. "Thanks, Lindsey." He didn't correct her.

"Yeah, you don't look for guitars when the house is on fire," Thomas said. "Seriously, Frankie. Never. Even if you don't have insurance, you don't. And I do. And the studio does. And you do. Right?"

"Yes," Anicky said, arms wrapped around herself. "We do."

"Good. And I don't leave guitars there. Amp, though."

Neill didn't have insurance. No expensive instruments, either, but—he would do something about that this week. The stereo, all Thomas's kitchen stuff, books, records, CDs … when you thought about it, that was a lot. Some you could never replace. Something else to worry about affording. Yet more grown-up stuff.

The fire was not looking like anything left behind could be saved, but—maybe a little firelight went a long way, maybe it was not as bad as it looked? They could do quite a lot to salvage smoke-damaged things, he thought. Maybe?

Someone brought thin blankets for people in their nightclothes to wrap up in. There was an ambulance parked close, lights flashing. No one was hurt so far; he supposed it was just in case. Firefighters. Lights flashed all out of sync, the trucks, the police cars. Engines throbbed. Other huddles—people who had been evacuated from the neighbouring houses. People standing around on porches, verandas, the sidewalk. Gawking, photos, video … it was all live on social media. Go away, he thought at them. Voyeurs. Getting a thrill.

"Your icon of the guitar God is going to be gone," Anicky told Thomas.

"I liked that. Isabel was so proud of it."

"I've got a photo, somewhere," Neill said. He'd taken it last spring, to send to Carleen, when she'd sent a link to something on Brian May's Instagram.

"Oh. Good." Thomas rubbed his hand over his face. Seemed to be taking an inventory. "My rowing machine. And my coat. My coat was there. All my coats. But my bomber jacket. It's been so hot, I wasn't wearing it … I liked that jacket. It was me."

"You were wearing it the first time I met you," Neill said. "And the second."

"I thought he was born wearing it, actually," Frankie said. "Did he sleep in it?"

"Only on special occasions."

"I suspected as much." Frankie grinned at Neill, looking more like herself.

"No," he said. "Don't be picturing what you're picturing. Just don't."

"Found it on a yardsale prowl when I was in grade ten," said Thomas, oblivious. "Five dollars, can you believe it?"

"That much?" Anicky asked.

"It was way too large for me, back when I was a kid."

"It was always too large for you."

"I liked it."

"It looked like a dog had been chewing on it. It had rips."

"I *liked* it."

"We'll find you another one," Anicky said. "We'll get Isabel and go on a proper used-clothes prowl if you give us an afternoon off next week. And you can spend twenty years abusing it till it looks right."

"Okay," Thomas said. "I might need socks and underwear more urgently, and God, who cares, it's just a coat, right? Alan … poor kid."

Must be the boy with the thesis. Poor guy, yeah. Neill couldn't imagine—didn't want to, anyway. He felt panicky, just thinking about trying to feel it, losing all that work.

"Ivan—Ivan, do you have anything?"

Ivan was watching the fire with fascination. Barefoot. Pyjama pants. Windbreaker. Shook his head slowly, patted his jacket pockets. "I just grabbed my wallet and my phone. Oh. You mean clothes? At home. Not here. Winter stuff, mostly, what I left."

"We've got four days—"

"I don't need an argument with my mother, which is what'll happen if I go home now. I'll go pick up some stuff after the festival, when I've got time to deal with that. And get my computer and stereo and things. If I'm coming to Kingston to stay."

"Too long a commute from Toronto," Thomas said. So apparently that was that settled. Nobody objected. Or noticed. Or maybe they'd all begun taking it for granted. "I have one spare pair of jeans, if you don't mind taking them out of the laundry. They'll do if you roll the legs up a little, and Neill and Kev can lend you everything else. And we'll take you shopping. I hate shopping. You can't do the festival wearing pyjamas. Right." Thomas took a deep breath. "Okay. I've really got to talk to people about wiring. At least I can prove I've been harassing the landlord, if need be."

Neill trailed him over to someone official-looking who didn't seem to be doing much. But officialdom was just, yes, thank you, there'll be an investigation, wiring is always something that we look at.

"Thank you and please go away," Thomas muttered. "Okay, maybe now's not the time."

"Probably think you're an arsonist, trying to lead them astray," said Frankie. Her teeth still chattered. That blanket wasn't doing any good at all.

"Don't," said Anicky.

One of the students was in tears, again or still. Thomas went to comfort, console. Suggest, gently, what they should do next. Everyone's big brother. Everything's easier with a plan?

No flames now. Only smoke. Steam.

Names and addresses were gathered, officialdom taking an interest in them again. Who was actually a tenant, who was just a friend spending the night. Someone asking, who doesn't have a place to stay—but they were students, and there were students in all the houses around. Almost everyone had saved their phone, everyone had friends there, or arriving, taking them away, on foot, in cars … Thomas checking on all the ones he called his kids as they left, making sure they had his number, his email. And then it was just them remaining, even the gawkers mostly gone.

Well, them and the assorted uniformed types. The red lights were still flashing. The street was puddled with dirty water. Thomas stood watching, feet wet.

"Come on," Neill said gently. Took his arm. "Home?"

"Yeah." A shaky sigh. Flash of a smile. Pulling himself back together. "Home."

Anicky's car was parked on the street, trapped by firetrucks, and Ivan's was blocked into the narrow driveway. That wasn't likely to have escaped unscathed. They trudged back to Thomas's place, close together, the evacuees shivering, Frankie and Ivan barefoot. Maybe they should have kept the blankets.

Smoke in their hair.

Kevin and Isabel were waiting for them, sitting close together on Neill's front steps. Holding hands.

"Whoa," Frankie said. "Guys."

Anicky gave Kevin a thumbs up behind Thomas's back. Or maybe it was directed at Isabel.

Heh.

And finally, it started to rain.

Nobody could sleep. Bunny was ecstatic. The humans were having a party.

Thomas made pancakes.

/Seven/

Mood:
Queen, *"Breakthru"*
Mountain ash berries ripen; drifts of asters by the fence

Thomas spent two days chasing everything that needed chased in the aftermath of the fire. Landlord, to get his cheques back. His students, to make sure they were okay, return what cheques he'd got from them. Cancelling the hydro, the phone and internet. Meeting with his insurance person. Helping Ivan sort out his, for his paint-blistered car. Neill went off without them to the mall on Sunday, bought underwear, socks, for the pair of them, a toothbrush and razor and a pair of cheap sneakers for Ivan. It wasn't till late Monday afternoon that Neill managed to get him and Ivan into the truck, take them on a prowl around all the second-hand clothes places.

"Oh fun," Isabel said, calling to see how they were doing, and she and Kevin caught up with them, and then the Bells, and the practical search for jeans and dressier twill, for shirts and jackets and—"Scarves, I need scarves," said Thomas— turned into a search through Anastasia Jo's Vintage Boutique for new stage shirts.

"Why are we melting my credit card?" Thomas wanted to know. Frankie found what she was calling a flapper dress, deep red, straight down to just above the knees, three asymmetrical layers in the skirt. And that crinkly artificial fabric that was wash and wear and could be crumpled into a ball and shoved in a dufflebag and never needed ironed.

"Because you're the one getting insurance money for losing your clothes."

"I'm pretty sure I didn't lose a flapper dress. That looks cute, but are you really going to wear it on stage?"

"Why not? With comfy little boots? It'll be a look. This all black and white thing we do is getting old. Let's throw some colour other than your precious scarves into the mix, okay?"

"You do know that dress looks black?"

"I don't want to hear what it looks like to you, honestly. I want to hear what it looks like from some shiny-eyed adoring fan with a big armful of roses and a bottle of champagne. And a Mercedes. I'd like him to have a Mercedes."

"If he's young enough for you and drives a Mercedes he's a crook, Mouse."

"I've reconsidered my policy on older men."

"Frankie—"

"Relax. It's sweet you think you have to do the glowering older brother thing, but just relax. He's a grad student in astronomy, the Mercedes is old and rusty and belonged to his grandmother, and he can't afford roses and champagne any more than I can. If you all promise to be nice and not terrorize the guy, I'll even introduce you one of these days."

"They've had one date," Anicky said. "She was home by midnight."

"Good things," Frankie said, "shouldn't be rushed. I'm taking my time on this one."

Frankie got her flapper dress.

"Look," Ivan said, "Tank, you and Neill don't have to buy me clothes, it wasn't your fault. I've called my dad, he's sending me a gift card and I'll talk my mother out of a bit of cash, pay you both back. Seriously."

"You need clothes to get you through till then and you have no money," Thomas said. "Don't worry about it. Come on, we need to find you a shirt. If Frankie's going red or whatever, you need to stand out too. And not clash."

They didn't want to be all black, white, red, either, Kevin said. Anicky and Neill got serious, rattling through the racks. No, no, no, maybe. Anicky called Laura to come put her two-cents-worth in. They agreed on black pants, white dress shirts for Kev and Thomas, the sort that should have cufflinks but they were probably going to roll the sleeves, and Anicky was not going to be peeled out of her tank tops, she said, which gave them all pause, considering that image, but she promised them blue and green, and Isabel, humming tunelessly, began sorting through waistcoats, holding them up against Kev's back and Thomas's, forcing them to stand still and try them on. Black, silvery grey, slate blue, pinstriped. Paisley. Neill found cufflinks just in case, and a couple of handpainted silk scarves, water-marbled green, peacock blue with a pattern that evoked a peacock's tail. That was Thomas. And Anicky and Laura, with Stacey and Jo who owned the shop and seemed to be friends of Anicky's, all disappeared to root through "the boxes out back". They turned up a shirt, or maybe it was a women's blouse originally. Crimson. Loose and billowy, poet's, peasant's, whatever the style was. They chased Ivan into a changing booth with it, and yeah, that was going to work.

He was a bit, is this really me? about it, initially. More like, I want this but persuade me, Neill thought.

"It's us," Thomas said, and Frankie assured him, it was good.

"Okay," Ivan said. "It's got—something." Grinned. "Plus I can wear it when I go to Tank and Neill's wedding as a pirate."

"Nobody's coming to the wedding as a pirate. What is it with you guys and pirates?"

Crimson pirate. A variety of daylily.

Stacey and/or Jo turned up a couple of other outfits for Ivan too, shiny blue with a black suit jacket that had some subtle pattern in the fabric and billowy ivory with a wine-red waistcoat and you don't complain you're too hot, you delight the girls by removing layers, Laura told him and he said, guys, we're not aiming to delight only half the audience here.

And Laura conferred with Kev and Thomas and broke out the band's credit card for this round of clothes. They threw in a second twenties-evoking dress for Frankie, jade green with fringes, and a couple of striped long-sleeved T-shirts for Anicky. Very eighties Roger Taylor, Neill pointed out.

And nobody felt like the day was over. They ended up back at Neill and Thomas's.

NeillandThomas's. Savouring it.

Pizza, they decided, from that Neapolitan place. A beer or so. They brought up the set list for the festival on Thomas's computer and started going through it, what needed some attention, what to change, what Ivan thought he needed more work on. He was having nightmares, he said, where he sang the wrong set list, or where the mic wouldn't work no matter how many things they tried or he had to find a toilet just before they went on and he got lost on the way back and they started without him. He'd been fine on the Canadian leg of the summer tour. Smaller venues.

Three days.

Neill went down to the backyard, where Ivan's unfortunate car was parked, and picked leaf-lettuce, rocket, tatsoi, cherry tomatoes, basil. His water barrel had been empty for weeks; Saturday night's shower hadn't done much. He'd have to remember to carry water down before bed. Everything was going limp.

Left them to work, started to make a salad. The pizza would be there soon. Laura was setting up CDs on his stereo when he passed through. Queen. Getting everyone in the right frame of mind? Kevin and Isabel were squashed close in the armchair, but Kev caught his eye, squeezed Isabel, arm around her shoulder, left her to join him in the kitchen.

Kevin looked tired. But kind of ... floaty, happy, too.

"Hey," he said.

"Hey." They shared a smile. "Things are good?" Neill asked, rinsing leaves, rolling them in a dishtowel. Tore them up a little. Halved the tomatoes. Threw in some sunflower seeds. That'd do.

"Yeah," Kevin said, soft, like he held something small and warm and wonderful sleeping in his hands, didn't want to wake it, just cherish it there. "Just ... " He shook his head. "Why didn't I see this before? It feels like it's been there forever."

"I know," Neill said.

"Everything's right," Kevin said. "Everything's gone right."

In the living room, Ivan and Thomas and Anicky were singing, "Tie Your Mother Down."

But there was a seriousness there in Kev. Something underneath. Because it wasn't that easy, was it? And Kevin knew it. The Critter was there, a little bump you had to look for, though Isabel was wearing looser clothes than she used to, and stretchy things, and if Kevin and Isabel turned into a real and permanent thing … nobody was ever going to tell the Critter she looked like her dad.

"Can I talk to you, Neill?" Kevin said. "About—all this. You. Growing up. Your stepdad. If you don't mind. I know it's kind of personal but—"

The pizzas arrived—doorbell, barking dog, chaos. Neill held up a finger. Wait. Went to deal with it, but Thomas scooped up the fistful of money they'd all piled on the coffee table, went pattering down to take the delivery. Anicky caught Bunny before she could follow. Neill turned back to Kevin.

Kevin shrugged. "I'm happy," he said. Glance over at the living room. No wall between them, only the kitchen table, the worm bin, a couple of plants. Isabel smiled at him, turned back to something Frankie was saying. Kevin kept his voice low. "I've got this, 'Oh my God I'm going to be a father what do I do' thing happening. And Dad's all, you and Isabel at last, *Isabel,* at last. And he actually said it. I'm going to be a grandfather. But I'm scared, too. I'm really scared."

"Yeah," Neill said. "Of course. Look, you'll be fine. You've got two good families all ready to love this child, it's not like you're dealing with my grandmother, but—"

"Pizza!" Thomas carolled at the door.

"Later," Kevin said, finding the salad dressing in the fridge, a jar of something Thomas made, oil and vinegar with salt and garlic and fennel seed pounded together. "Sometime, not today. But—sometime soon? Because I'm in this for the long haul, and I know we all want to do well for the baby and we're practically one family anyway, all us Parks and Gorevs and I've looked it up, you can adopt your stepchild, but—oh God, Neill, there's always going to be that little bit of, I wish she were really totally mine, isn't there? Or not? And it'll get complicated when she hits the outside the world, people are like that, and I don't want to screw up. I don't want to screw things up for her."

"We'll talk, Kev. As much as you want. About everything, okay? Any time."

They were good. They were better than good. Strange Pilgrim Road was killing it and this, their second show, was packed. People had been talking, Twitter-noise, in the beer-tents, the food-tents, since the Friday evening set. Strange Pilgrim Road. Yeah, I heard them last year, but they've got this new singer …

They'd sold out of CDs. Laura had gone home overnight, made a QR-code poster of their links to purchase the albums digitally, had that set up when they had their T-shirts and hoodies out.

The ballcaps had sold out fastest, even before the CDs, but that could be people who hadn't had the foresight to bring a hat trying to avoid sunstroke.

And Thomas was—yeah, Thomas was free to be Thomas and it was—amazing. What was there on the CDs and hadn't come so much into the live shows, too much multitasking, he was just free and flying and he looked gorgeous and—

A fox. Yeah, Mom. I know exactly what you mean.

Ivan was not at all bad on the eyes, either. Nor Anicky, to be honest.

Not to leave out Kev and Frankie, who were handsome too even if not so much his types …

"Seriously?" Raleigh said. "And you an almost-married man."

"I'm just appreciating. Appreciating is fine."

345

They were just a beautiful thing to watch. A dance. He'd always thought that, people making music together. Paying attention to one another, holding their audience to them, making them part of it, you're here with us, we're here for you …

His phone chimed and he got a dirty look from some technician guy who was festival crew. Answered it hastily to shut it up, not looking at the number. He wasn't really supposed to be in the front of house tent, if that was what it was called—mixing boards and whatnot under a jaunty striped roof. He'd just tagged along after Jon and one of the the other guys, friends of Jon's and Kevin's who turned up because this was not something for their stripped-down travelling setup and they'd needed a larger crew. Which technically—very un-technically—included him. So he'd taken advantage of a break from managing their merch table, abandoned Emily to it, and found a place with Jon in the front of house setup, up the fenced lane where the—surprisingly few—cables ran from the stage and the security people wandered with an eye out for trouble. Back out in that runway, now, crouched down with his shoulders to the fence, a finger stuck in his other ear. Could hardly hear even so.

"Hello?" Wary, annoyed. This was "Seven Crows", off their first album and one of what Isabel called the Tank-has-creepy-dreams ones. He loved it. He loved them all. But they'd never done "Seven Crows" live before, not even on Friday. Thomas and Ivan were trading off the verses. Lovely.

"Lindsey?"

He didn't recognize the voice and his heart gave a thump, not Dodger or Mom or Carleen, and anyone Mrs. Steinberg had given his hastily-printed Quinlan Landscapes card to would ask for Neill, but someone calling about Mom or

Carleen …

"It's Marcie."

A security guy ambled up. Neill flashed his official crew-type-person tag at him. The guy nodded and went away.

Who the hell was Marcie? "I'm sorry," he started to say, "you must have—"

"Marcie Tremblay? Megan's sister?"

Megan? And for a moment he quite honestly could not think who they were talking about. "Oh," he said. "Um, yes?"

"Look, I know this is—could you turn the music down? I can hardly hear you."

"I'm at a concert," he said. "Sorry."

"Don't say sorry," Raleigh said. *"What the hell does she want? Did you even know she had a sister?"*

"They don't get along."

"This is kind of out of the blue," Marcie Tremblay said, "but Megan's going through a bit of a rough time and we were hoping—"

"Sorry, who was hoping?"

On the big screens to either side of the stage, the cameras had gone in close on Thomas for a moment, that long bridge that the guitar carried alone.

"Me and my folks. We talked it over and my mom said, call him. Because she really cared about you, you know, and things went wrong, sure, but it's been a hard summer for her and with what's happened with Logan, it would really help if you could come out here—"

"What?"

"Just for a few weeks. Try to patch things up."

"Patch what up? For God's sake, we broke up years ago. I'm getting married in two months. No. I'm sorry but—"

"Don't apologize, Lindsey, good God."

"It's just that she's really fragile right now and I think it would help enormously if you could be here. She's never stopped caring for you. She—"

"*No.*" No no no.

"—needs someone to stay with her a week or two. It's not good for her to be on her own and I had time booked off for my holidays and I've already lost a week, I've got a reservation for Banff starting Tuesday, so there's just time—I don't think she should be on her own."

"I can't. No. Did she ask you to call me? How did you even get my number? Why can't she go camping with you?"

"She and my boyfriend don't really get along. Anyway, she has to work. And you don't need to sound so accusing. I said she should call you and she said she wouldn't so I said I would. That's all. It's not like it's some plot. Look, you were close, and she never had these problems before you dumped her. You owe her."

"No, I don't," Neill said.

"Good!" said Raleigh.

"I'm sorry, Marcie. We weren't close. Ever. We were a mistake. I'm sorry she's not well, but I don't think you can blame it on me, and I can't help her. If she needs to see a doctor, get her to a doctor. You can't make someone else responsible for her just because you want to go on vacation. We're practically strangers now."

They'd always been strangers.

"She always said you were selfish. I was hoping she was wrong." And Marcie disconnected.

Oh God. He was so furious—was it fury? Upset. His hands were shaking. And he'd missed the rest of the song, and he loved it, and they were moving into the series of fast pieces that wrapped it all up and would end with "Runaway", and—

He blocked the number Marcie had called from.

Went back into the shade, lurking by Jon like a good spare flunkie. Breathe. Just breathe.

"You had to," Raleigh said. *"You don't owe her anything. You can't drop everything and rush out there because she's—"*

"What? Suicidal?" Was that what Marcie had been trying to say?

"—had another man run away from her. You can't help her. You're bad for one another. You never even liked one another, as people, and I bet it was as true for her as you. She was never happy with you."

"She was never going to be happy with anyone. She couldn't be happy with herself. She always had to find something to be wrong in me, so she could be right."

Maybe. He didn't know any more.

Nothing he could do with her. He wasn't going to drown himself as her sister's easy out from dealing with her. To give her the illusion of—was that what she was after? Megan. Marcie, both of them. Illusion of control over someone else, thinking that meant strength in themselves? Meant a justification of their own existence?

He didn't do this to Thomas? Did he? This needy, scrabbling, desperate clinging thing that couldn't even see the person under what it was clinging to—

He didn't. Did he?

"Stop it," Raleigh said. *"It's okay to need someone. It's not okay to devour them and you can't be always cringing and asking him if you're too much, or you'll end up just what you think she was, never satisfied, never reassured. Okay? Don't. Stop that*

thinking, right now.”

Anti-Lindsey. Sabotage within. Right. Stop it. He was okay. They were good. Thomas, on stage, in the screens, looked right at him. Illusion, maybe. But smile that reached even his eyes.

He made his way back to where he should be, when they came off at last, useful roadie type, shifting them off the stage, the break between sets, the next up one of the big Toronto bands. Five women. Thomas and Anicky knew them; Thomas had worked with them in his "additional guitars by" days. The Vulgar Darlings. They were excited, generous in their enthusiasm—it wasn't just Neill thinking this had been what Strange Pilgrim Road had always been meant to be.

And a dark-bearded, wild-haired older man lurking back out of the way, with a dark-haired girl of about twelve at his side, jittering the way excited kids did, and the man called, "Kevin!" with a raised hand.

Kevin handed off his bass to Neill, a sort of wide-eyed look he at first couldn't interpret, and then, whoa, that was Romeo the bass from Krown Imperial. Poster on his wall, back in the St. Mark's days.

"Oh," said one of the Vulgar Darlings women, "Yeah, Kevin, Romeo Kennedy was looking for you earlier."

"Yeah, thanks … "

"That's a good kid," the Vulgar woman said to Neill. "Wants to be a drummer. Got me to autograph her shirt."

Kevin went to met Romeo and the jittery kid, who looked like she was probably his daughter and trying really hard to be good and not rush around talking to everyone at once, just the look of her, which made Neill forget Megan and grin, and the kid grinned back. Looked over her shoulder—father distracted, shaking Kevin's hand, clapping his shoulder—kid skittered off to Anicky. Was suddenly tongue-tied.

"Um," he heard. "You're, um, you're Anicky Bell! Hi! I play drums too!"

Collecting all the drummers, or all the women drummers? Not mere collecting. That looked like honest hero-worship.

Remembered he had the bass, heavy in his hand. Knelt to its case.

"Good?" Thomas asked, leaving a couple of the Vulgar women with high fives, the black Strat he always used for "Runaway" tucked against his back.

Kevin and Romeo and Romeo's daughter had vanished.

"Oh God, yeah." Neill latched the case and stood up and they were wrapped around one another for a moment. Which Thomas might have wanted but probably wasn't expecting here and now. Heat of him, sweaty, hair sticking to his forehead, that peacock scarf, eyes bright. He might not see the green but he knew how to bring it out; today it was charcoal, ashy colours he was wearing and they really made you notice. Secrets of the stars. Get your big sister to buy your makeup for you. Mysterious little packages arrived in the mail every time Maddie came across something new.

"I've got a bit of a Megan problem," Neill said, but not until they were clear of backstage and loading their van.

"Foood," said Ivan.

"Hey, Ivan—c'mere." Anicky flung out her arms. "You were great. You're sticking with us, right? Signed and sealed?"

"Yours till Niagara Falls," Ivan said. "Hey." They hugged. Thomas got one too, and Neill. And Frankie, who kissed Ivan and said she was going to do the serious rock star thing and leave looking after everything to the rest of them, she had a date, bye.

Kris Jamison

"Irresponsible child," said Thomas. Frankie stuck out her tongue, twirled off in her flapper dress, texting as she went.

"Astronomer dude's out there somewhere," said Ivan, and went off to raid the green room, such as it was, for granola bars and water.

"Megan?" Thomas asked. Back to loading the van. Out front, the crowds had thinned, everyone taking the break between acts for food, drinks, queueing for the revolting portable toilets. The women from the Vulgar Darlings were warming up, one lying on the floor, engaged in what Neill hoped was a yoga breathing exercise and not a medical emergency of some kind.

"Her sister called me and tried to get me to agree to fly out west to look after her. Sounds like the fiancé fled."

"What, her sister's tagged you as a replacement? You did point out bigamy's not legal?"

"Yeah."

"Is she all right?"

"I'm not sure."

"You're not thinking you should go?"

"No. No, I think it would be a very bad idea."

"They're trying to manipulate you. They're trying to control you. Decode it. You're worthless so you have to prove you aren't by being what other people demand of you. Don't do it."

But if she really was in a bad way, if she really needed help—look at all the people who helped him. Who were there when he needed them. He owed—

"Them. Thomas, Dodger, Mom, Carleen, sure, all your friends, yes, you'd help, you will help, when they need you someday, and they will. People need people. But you don't break yourself running off after people who just use you as a thing. You don't

352

owe her. You can't save her from her problems. They're not yours."

But nobody had helped Raleigh. He hadn't. He hadn't been there.

"No," Raleigh said. "Don't compare her to me."

And Thomas tried—

"Thomas might want to save you from your problems but he has way more sense than you and he knows he can't. He knows all he can do is help. Walk with you. Hold your hand. Hold you when you don't feel strong enough. It's not the same. It's not. Megan always wanted someone to carry her and gave you abuse the whole time for not doing it right."

She—had. Why was instinct to deny it? To defend her?

"Because the anti-Lindsey wants to say it's all your fault, idiot. Because everything's your fault for not being born the right person. Which is stupid."

Was that it?

Thomas slid the door shut with the slam it needed to latch. Dusted his hands on his pants. "Neill? You okay, love?"

"That's it," one of the crew guys, Josh, said, making a last circuit of the loading area. "I'm taking the van?"

Thomas waved him off.

Breathe? Thomas was looking at him. Anicky was looking at them both, frowning. Ivan beside her, a couple of plastic water bottles in each hand. Gave Anicky a sort of worried look. Was he being strange? Ivan handed out water all around, without saying anything.

"Yeah." Answering Thomas. Was he all right? "I think so. Thanks, Ivan." Actually … considering. Raleigh was right. Everything Raleigh said … Deep breath. Opened his water, took a drink, realized how thirsty he was. Heat. Stress. "Nothing I could do would help her. She needs to—if anything's wrong at all and it's not just the sister imagining things—she needs to find help that isn't—something she's imagining about me that was never there at all."

"Right." Kind of a crooked smile. "You're going to call her, aren't you?"

"Oh God, Thomas, I'm sorry. This is—this should be about you guys. Forget about her. I'll deal with it, you don't have to. You were great. You were amazing and I want to hear what you did with 'Seven Crows' again—" He wasn't going to say he'd missed half of it, that stupid Marcie had picked right then to call.

"Given the number of phones I saw waving around, it's probably going to be all over the internet."

Neill made a face.

"Jon was recording. We want to hear it ourselves, talk it over, see what we should do different."

"Or do again."

"That, too."

Arm around him. This was the second show for the Vulgar Darlings, too, and Strange Pilgrim Road had played after them on Friday, heard them then. He wouldn't have minded sticking around to listen again, but he'd bought all four of their CDs, and one by a new synthpop group called Suits For Fish, too, and the debut album of a folk-metal group, Jagged Moons, for Carleen for Christmas—expensive weekend, this—and he was tired. And things needed dealing with. They walked back to the trailer, the four of them. Sauntering, him and Thomas with arms around one another; felt okay, here. Kept being stopped by people Thomas and Anicky seemed to know, he didn't have a clue. "Man, you guys were something," they said. "Great set, seriously, awesome ... "

From Exit 369, even, who were driving a van mostly fibre-glass between the rust, and stopped, slung the door open to talk on their way out, packed up and leaving. Weird realization: all these guys, they were the ones from the Fine Arts party, shoving and laughing, engulfing Thomas, pulling him away.

Surely not the same van. Looked old enough to be.

They'd never brought in anyone to replace Thomas.

"You'd be—it's Neill now, isn't it?" Thin, dark-haired guy in the front passenger seat, leaning to search him out. Dan, he knew. Album art, always that grim, cool gaze, the sunglasses, the cigarette. That was a bit—he hadn't realized he was known that way, that he'd be in Dan's awareness at all, let alone through changing the name he went by, but then, Thomas and André kept in touch.

"Yeah," he said, moving to him, away from the open side door. "Dan, right?" Offered a hand. Trying too hard? Both of them. Dan switched his cigarette right to left, pushed his sunglasses up and they shook, no power games. Tired, sunken eyes. The guy was too thin, his hand cool, bit of a tremor, holding the cigarette. Looked closer to forty than thirty, and there wasn't that big an age gap between them, couple of years, maybe. On stage, yesterday, he'd been flying, beyond alive. Not flying but falling, Neill thought, and thought, Thomas should make a song of that, and then felt guilty for it.

André and Anicky, rapid French, André making drumming gestures, Anicky laughing, blushing, which she did easily. Thanking him. Something he'd liked, obviously.

Thomas and the brown-haired guy and the dark-skinned guy who must be Brandon and Mitch were all laughing about something, and Dan was looking over at them, saying, quiet,

"Thomas looks good. He's well? Mr Health Freak, still?"

"Oh yeah," Neill said. "Always."

"Well, good, that's good. And congrats, did I say that? On the engagement. He's a good guy. Fuck, Thomas is the best."

"I know." Was that what you said to someone's ex? Hell, why not. It was truth, not smugness. "Thanks."

"We're blocking the road," the older guy driving said. Ronnie, wanting to get them apart. Ronnie the elder brother of Dan and Brandon. Ignoring Thomas like wasn't there. Bored, he sounded.

Still something a bit bullying, unpleasant about him. Maybe he imagined it. Paranoid.

"Yeah, right," Brandon said, and they all sorted themselves back to their seats.

"Look after yourself," Neill said to Dan. Thomas at his side then, arm around him again.

"Yeah," Dan said. "You too. See you round, Tom."

"Tank," Thomas muttered, but the van was pulling away then.

"He knows," Neill said. "If he could get 'Neill' right, he knows." Considered. "And he never called you anything but Thomas when he was talking to me."

"Stupid git. I'd like to—God, what can you do? There's no way to knock sense into someone like that, if the overdose didn't do it. He looks bad."

"There's a limit what you can do for someone who won't … " Yeah, Megan. He sighed. "Oh God, Thomas. Some people."

Hands finding one another, holding tight. Another straggle of musician-types tangled with them, heading for their own vehicles, probably. Everything starting to wind down here behind the scenes, while the roar of the crowd, the bass and drums of the Vulgar Darlings, throbbed in fits, louder, softer, on the wind.

He'd never heard of this lot mixing with them now, and only Ivan seemed to know them, but they were known. Accepted congratulations, traded remarks on what a great weekend it had been. Escaped. It felt like escape to him, anyway. Maybe the others. Everyone looking a bit tired, coming down off the high of performance.

"There's 'great set I think I'm probably supposed to know you guys so we'll pretend we weren't drinking in our trailer'," said Anicky, winding between parked cars, trucks, camper trailers that the festival had provided, and theirs was a gleaming silver Airstream and big enough for the lot of them, "and there's, 'great set'."

"I think they mean it," said Ivan. "Seriously. We are great."

"Ah, he's developed the Strange Pilgrim Road humility already," said Thomas. "Yeah. We're great. Sometimes. When we work hard enough at it. No resting on laurels, kids."

"Sorry," said Ivan. "Tell me to shut up if you want, fools rush in and all that and I don't know you guys like you know one another but—everything okay?"

"Me? Ex-girlfriend trouble," said Neill. "Don't worry about it."

"Ah. That one. Good. I mean, not good it's happening. But, uh, I mean, I haven't known you guys that long, but you guys are great, too. Sorry. Weird thing to say. I just—seeing people happy. Makes you feel good, doesn't it? Knowing it's possible?"

"Oh," Thomas said. "Huh. Yeah."

They needed to pack up, vacate the trailer, hand back the

keys. Laura would look after some of that final stuff. Not right yet. Time to wash up a bit, change to fresh shirts at least. Eat the last of the bananas and muffins that seemed to keep appearing as if by magic.

Deal with Megan.

Facebook. Do it in the open, so she couldn't misconstrue anything. Witnesses. He didn't use it much. Just talking to his Kavanagh cousins, mostly, and the two or three people he actually remembered from Queen's. Still friends with Megan there but had it set so he didn't actually see her.

Should change his relationship status thing while he was at it, one of these days. Married? That would be true soon enough. Maybe it would stop the dating ads. Maybe not.

Sprawled on one of the bunks. Thomas came back from the bathroom, hair damp, face clean and smelling of Noxzema and faintly, that sort of musky, floral perfume oil Neill had got him for his birthday back in May, shyly, because maybe it wasn't even Thomas's thing, he never wore cologne much, just soap and lotion, the scent of him … but he used it.

Crawled up with him, made himself a backrest for Neill. They should be packing up. Cunning Frankie, disappearing like that.

So, Megan, there she was. Pretty active in her posting, a jumble of random popular causes and the sort of cat pictures that were supposed to funny. Nothing there to worry anyone. A lot of the sort of jokes and memes that would be pretty foul misogyny if the genders were reversed. Scrolling down, into commiseration, he is a such a jerk, so sorry, you're too good for him, and that kind of thing. A couple of weeks old.

"Doesn't look like someone sinking in the deep end," Thomas said, reading over his shoulder. "But then, sometimes people don't." Sighed. Chin on Neill's shoulder, arms around his waist. "I want to say, don't, just walk away, people like that are like those insect sticky-traps, but—"

"Yeah," Neill said.

>*Hey. How are you doing? Your sister called me. Just wanted to say, take care of yourself.*

Not going to say, call me if you want to talk, no. Definitely not. You're a good person? He didn't actually think she was. Not a malevolent person. But not good.

>*Sorry if this is out of line—*

Ivan, tell me to shut up, twitch-sensitive worry that something was wrong between him and Thomas, that was a bit— you wondered what his childhood had been like, his parents' breakup, that he would watch so closely and be worried about something so subtly tense between friends, as if he needed that security, that stability around him so desperately.

>*—but if you're having a hard time, get help. This is personal experience talking, okay?*

Liar. He did everything he could to avoid outside help, didn't he? But that was different. He had—resources. In himself. Megan didn't, not that he'd ever seen. And anyway, he'd promised Thomas, he had an appointment with Thomas's physician next Friday.

>*See a doctor, okay?*

And just to head off anything—

>*Wanted to drop you a line anyway to let you know Thomas and I are getting married in October. Bunny's doing well.*

Deleted that. Just,

>*… married in October.*

Didn't want to remind her that Bunny existed, just in case. She didn't know the dog's name anyway.

That said everything about Megan, didn't it? She hadn't even told him what she'd named the puppy. Maybe hadn't even named her. But give her credit, she'd taken on a pet she didn't want to save it from being discarded, shot. If that was true. Megan was not a bad person. Just—not someone he could carry. And she wanted to be carried.

Dan wanted—to be saved?

Dan didn't want to believe he was drowning?

You needed to reach out a hand, though. And do your damnedest to kick your own feet to help stay afloat, if there was someone who would take it. Right?

>Best wishes, L.

That was pretty formal as the conclusion to something left in public on someone's FB. And distancing. Which was the point.

So … okay. Posted it.

Should change his name. Well, add Neill to it, anyway. While he was here. Thomas was reaching around him now, so he surrendered the phone and watched his *in a relationship with* get changed.

Oh hell, there was something from Megan.

>Thanks, I'm fine.

Direct message, then.

>Marcie's in a flap about nothing. I'm fine. I broke up with Logan. He was being a jerk. She shouldn't have called you. The last thing I need is you being all condescending.

"Whoa," said Thomas. "Right. Here. Phone's all yours."

"Was I condescending?"

"Not that I noticed."

>Ok. Sorry. Glad you're alright. Bye.

Sent that and logged off. And now she could remain hidden from his timeline indefinitely, thanks.

"At least you won't be stewing, thinking you're supposed to be responsible for her," Raleigh said.

"I'm not."

"I know you're not. But you would."

Yeah. Maybe. He sighed and leaned back against Thomas, eyes shut. "Did I tell you you were amazing?" he said. "Gorgeous. Glorious. All of you."

"Yeah, but you can tell me again—"

"Guys," said Anicky. "Save it till you get home." Something bounced off Neill's chest. Blueberry muffin.

Food fight? Seriously?

One airborne muffin did not a food fight make. Thomas poked him till he sat up straight again. Peeled the battered muffin out of its paper, gave him half.

And the trailer thumped and rocked, Kevin flinging himself up the step. "Tank! Anicky—Ivan, where the hell's Frankie, find Frankie, find Laura, we need to talk."

"What, God, is our truck on fire?"

"Don't be an idiot, Tank. Romeo."

"Romeo's on fire ... ?"

"Krown Imperial. US tour."

"Not ... on fire?"

"Shove his head under a pillow, Neill."

"What?" said Anicky. "Kevin, breathe. What?"

"He said they'd been talking. Romeo said, he and Kai Juneau and to their management and that was the CDs, that was before he heard Ivan."

"Oh God, was I bad?"

"Ivan, no, but I mean, that was before and now they're, he just, he phoned her, Kai, during the show, so she could listen, she heard, now they're like, even more yes."

"They're like even more yes? From the calm quiet coherent one who's supposed to speak four languages? Okay, I second Anicky, Kev. Breathe."

But Thomas was tense, fingers digging into his hip.

"Kevin?"

"Krown Imperial. They want us. Supporting them. Their US tour. Spring. Next summer. Their people need to talk to our people … "

"Oh God." Thomas flopped down on the bunk again. "I may have to start believing in God. No, sorry, I can't go that far. It was the sacrifice. The great ceremonial burning of the Icon of May. The guitar gods are pleased with—"

Ivan hit him with Frankie's lucky teddy.

Bear, not sleepwear. Bluebear. And nobody was ever, ever allowed to comment on the fact she wouldn't travel anywhere without him.

Anicky was texting Laura.

/Epilogue/

Mood:
Pet Shop Boys, "Here"
Willows flicker, silver in sunlight

>*D*ear *Professor Olivares Garcia,*
>*My name is Lindsey Frederick Quinlan, though I prefer to go by Neill rather than Lindsey. I was born September 3rd, 1988. My mother is Tricia Quinlan Kavanagh.*

>*I'm your son.*

>*This is a difficult email to write. I feel as though I should apologize to you for turning up like this. I only recently found out who my father was, when I discovered the program from the concert you gave with the Generalife Quartet at St. Mark's University in Canada back in December of 1987. My mother had decided it was best not to tell me, or you. She didn't intend any harm. She speaks well of you and has very happy memories of you. She felt her pregnancy was a complication that you didn't need in your life and career, and she always wanted me to look on my late stepfather as my father. He was a good man, and I did, but I've always wanted to know my real father as well.*

>*I really regret not having had an opportunity to have you in my life while I was growing up. I'm hoping that we might be able to get to know another.*

>*This may not be how you feel. If that's the case, I do understand. I*

can imagine what a shock it is to learn you have a grown son and the disruption it could be to your life, so please don't think I'm expecting or demanding anything. I just wanted you to know I exist, and that I hope we can perhaps meet, someday.

>I suppose I should tell you something about myself. I guess I hope you'd want to know. I look a lot like you, in the photographs in that old programme. I grew up with a younger sister, Carleen, and a brother, Raleigh; my brother died in 2008. I studied biology at university, botany to be specific, and have an MSc. I'm about to begin studying landscape design and gardening and have started a small gardening business called Quinlan Landscapes. At the end of October my boyfriend Thomas Gorev and I are marrying. He's a guitarist, too, which he thinks is very amusing. He's lead guitar in Strange Pilgrim Road, and does a lot of songwriting. His band is touring in Germany later this autumn, and they'll be in Berlin in early December. There's a chance I might be able to join them for a week, so if you would like to meet, that seems like a good opportunity.

>Best regards,
>Neill Quinlan

The brook had dried to puddles on the sheets of limestone where it ran through the donkey pasture, but higher up its course in the maple woods it still held water in deeper pools, cool and shaded. If you walked far enough upstream, just before you came to Dodger's back fenceline, there was a small waterfall, and there the water still poured, white and frothing, over the shelf of stone. There was a place between waterfall and pasture where in the dry summer the brook seemed to disappear into a pit of broken stone, which meant, Neill supposed, that some small channel of it actually ran underground year-round, even in the three seasons when it was a steadily-flowing brook for its full length, and that beneath the donkey pasture, beneath the stony course of the stream, there was some embryonic cave system forming. Over the road, where Dodger's neighbour's Herefords grazed, the water appeared again, grey limestone sheets giving way to an ankle-turning course of broken grey stone, overgrown with wild mint and purple loosestrife right now, and then suddenly there was a deep brown pool where black and white dragonflies—widow skimmers—swooped and Joe-Pye weed was going to fluffy seed among the blades of the blueflags, and then black willows leaned over the brook running onwards, seeking the little river and eventually, the lake that was like a sea, and the St. Lawrence, and the restless Atlantic.

This place by the waterfall, where there was a huge old black willow with branches stretching right across the brook, broad enough and horizontal enough to lie on—carefully— was his. Had been his since the moment he found it, following the brook back on the morning of his birthday, Bunny on her long rope. Too many rabbits for her beagle-ish instincts. He'd not gone for a run, waking early and happy, and everything fresh and cool and smelling of dew and green. Kissed Thomas and crept out without disturbing him, gone walking in the woods. Now he came here almost every evening. He and Bunny had their morning run along the road, over the bridge and along pastures, past a brick farmhouse, more maple woods, down a ridge and past a swamp, but the evenings were for the woods, and wading, and sitting by the water. Sometimes Thomas came along, if he was home when they set out. Sometimes he came to find them. The band was keeping late hours. They wanted the new album out before spring—*Time*, was going to be the title—before they left for the tour with Krown Imperial, and that meant a lot of intense work that was only just beginning, and was going to be mad, utterly mad, Thomas said, switching on his Dodger-and-Old-Folks accent, what with the European tour and all, and Kevin planning to fly back for a few weeks when the Critter arrived so they needed to line up an emergency bass player in France.

Not to mention a wedding. But it wasn't going to be a complicated wedding. Not mere paperwork, but not complicated. There'd definitely be cake, Isabel and the kitchen of the SandWitch and Brew were seeing to that, but not a lot of fuss and bother.

Thomas, it was turning out, was capable of a lot of fuss and bother in the search for the perfect rings, but Neill thought that was mostly under control now. Soothed away that frantic, *but it has to be unique, it has to be, to be good enough for you* state he'd gotten himself into.

"Warned you," Isabel had said. "Sometimes you just have to sit on him till he calms down."

They didn't need elaborate designs, they didn't need patterns in different hues of gold, or whatever. And they couldn't afford it anyway, there were serious things that needed their money, like their debts, their futures … Wedding rings are symbols, not things themselves, he'd said. Simple, was best for them. Classic. Just *Neill & Thomas* and the date, engraved, inside. That was perfect. That was enough.

Mom was coming up. Carleen would still be in Bolivia, and he'd told Mom the big celebration was going to be next summer, all the relatives from the UK and stuff then, but she was coming anyway.

That was going to be … oh well.

She could stay in the Gorevs' spare room. Unless it was an

out and out emergency, Mom on his living room couch was one of those background stresses he didn't need. Though if she was driving, she could throw a few extra woolly cushions in the car, he'd said. Their pair of church pews could use them.

Three of them in his apartment, and a dog. It's too much. Ivan's looking for his own place but hasn't found anything yet. Ivan's a nice guy but he's too close, living on the couch. There's no privacy, no space. There's a spare bedroom at the Parks but Kevin's not mentioning it as a solution, no, because Kevin's so protective of his father's peace and moving a stranger in—if it was a real emergency he would, but it's not a real emergency until Neill kicks Ivan out, which he won't.

And he and Thomas need a bigger place anyway. Thomas would really like to be able to bring his books from his parents' house, and right now the few clothes he owns are in a heap of grocery bags. He doesn't even have a suitcase for Europe, another casualty of the fire. Not even a backpack. There's not room for another dresser. It's the low eaves. There's floorspace, but no wall height to stand things against.

Ivan might be able to find a place in a shared house, as students quarrel and reshuffle themselves, these first few weeks of September.

Neill and Thomas look at a few places, and Neill looks at some more on his own, preliminary scouting. Too dark. Too dreary. No parking for the truck. No pets. No window-space for plants. A horrible shabby bungalow west of Odessa, with black mould in the bathroom ceiling and a suspiciously squashy feel to the linoleum by the toilet, as of plywood floor-ing in decay. And a landlord who asks him twice where he's from. Fredericton. Yes, but before that ... Dartmouth wasn't the answer the man was probing after. Kingston's full of people whose ancestors came from Spain, Portugal, Greece, Turkey, India … For God's sake … And he's not having Thomas live someplace full of mould, to make him ill and ruin his voice.

He doesn't want to get discouraged, feels to do so would be some sort of betrayal of this thing he's got, he's holding on to. That he's Thomas's. The hunting falls mostly to him; he's through at Dodger's long before the band crawls out of the studio.

He's seen the doctor. And she's okay, she doesn't make assumptions or try to shove him into boxes, she's willing to listen, to say, these are options …

He's okay for now. He's promised Thomas. If he starts to slide into not okay, he'll make another appointment, he'll be honest, he'll get the help he needs …

His courses have started. It's meant to be a part-time thing, so it's just two, right now. Interesting. Challenging, sometimes—not hard, challenging, it's not bloody biochem and stats—but challenging because it's a different way of thinking. He's enjoying it.

Challenging just fitting it in, sometimes, with Dodger's garden and other handymanning for her, and four people's yards to look after now, not just Mrs. Steinberg, and apartment-hunting, and this turning into one of the phases in the ebb and flow of their lives and work where it's him doing most of the cooking, which is more boring than when it's Thomas, but he's getting better at it and Thomas and Ivan are appreciative.

And then there's a Monday morning at Dodger's and he's hunting in the garage for the bow rake. Tries the storeroom at the back, where the stairs go up to …

Riiight. That's not Raleigh, but Michael Kitchen's *Foyle* voice.

The back half of the big hip-roofed garage serves as the woodshed, and this here is a storeroom, now, and there's the rake he wants, but—hot water heater. Washer and dryer hookup. Electric baseboard heater to keep the pipes from freezing and yes, these walls, this room, is wall-boarded, insulated, and there's a circuit breaker panel labelled in Dodger's neat schoolteacher script in black permanent marker over a faded ballpoint illegible scrawl from an earlier time, bath, bedroom 1, bedroom 2, stove …

Neill heads up the stairs. The door isn't even locked.

If it were a bear it would have bit you, Dad would say, when he and Raleigh were tearing around looking for something and Dad would just point, right there where they left it …

Boxes. Boxes stacked. Boxes heaped. Empty boxes. Shipping labels, on some. They've come from the UK. Long, long ago, by the look of them. Practically antique, empty boxes. Roll of chicken wire. Pieces of wallboard, not whole sheets, just edges and oddments. Cans of paint. A quarter-filled box of ceramic floor tile, Dodger's kitchen, and bathroom wall tile, too. This and that, generally.

Baseboard heaters. No appliances, of course. The floor is laminate, a pale imitation wood; the walls, a bit scarred from all the junk that's been moved around over the years, are painted pale greens and blues. Nice high ceiling. Not as many windows as he'd like but it's not dark.

Kitchen and dining—nook, he thinks a plan would call it, not a dining room. Big living room. Two bedrooms, bathroom—with a bathtub, even, in which more empty boxes are piled. Broom cupboard, with a paint-spattered shop vac squatting in it like a forlorn and abandoned droid. Someone has even painted cartoon eyes on it. Isabel, he suspects. Linen closet, dusty and empty but still smelling of fresh sheets, somehow, mixed with sawdust. Good grief, they'd talked about Dodger's flat over the garage and he'd pictured her camping out, a loft sort of space with insulation and electric heat, sure, but pretty much just a loft, bare boards, bare bulbs ... his Kavanagh cousin Jack and his girlfriend just got a house last year, and sent everyone they'd ever known pictures in their excitement. A Kent prefab, very popular down east, nice little bungalows, well-made as that sort of thing went, you saw them everywhere, and this is surely just as much floorspace, a thousand feet or so. No basement, of course, but the laundry's down below and that makes a big difference and—

Yeah, but if Dodger wanted to rent it she would be renting it, right?

Strangers were one thing. Thomas might be another?

Where could all the junk go?

They'd have to buy appliances. Stove, fridge, washer and dryer. Would he trust a used fridge? No.

Did she even need all those little pieces of wallboard?

Were those church pews?

Dodger's in her vegetable garden picking pole-beans, the donkeys at the fence, being social, keeping an eye on things. Bunny, off-leash for a little and so far not heading away for solo adventures, trots over to gossip, nose to nose.

"Dodger," Neill says.

"Hello, yes? That sounded—portentous. Found a body in the rhubarb?"

"Dodger—would you want to rent your apartment?"

"Rent my flat?" she repeats, and then, "Ah."

Well, yes, it is kind of right in her backyard, on the other side of the yard but still, maybe that's too close to have people moving in on you, when you've made a home that lets you have space and solitude and—everything he wants and can understand her wanting, and he shouldn't have asked, put that feeling of obligation on her—

"Why didn't I think of that?" she says. Tips her hat back to scratch her head. "Good grief, yes. Of course. If you think he'd want to live way out here—"

"I mean, only if you were thinking of renting it anyway—not, I mean, I don't want to mean that we thought you—"

"Neill, love, the pair of you could move in tomorrow and welcome. And rent, you don't need to bother about that. It's not like I have any other use for the space. I've thought sometimes about cleaning it up, listing in on one of those holiday home-rental sites, but then I think about having to deal with all that, strangers wandering around outside my church, and it's just too much hassle."

"Dodger, we do have to pay rent. We can't—we can't just live off you. We're not, it's not that bad for us, we're not desperate." On the edge of it. Maybe. Sometimes. This thing with Krown Imperial … maybe not forever.

They've found their magic now, Strange Pilgrim Road. He believes in their magic. But they still need a place to live for the next few years.

She seems to be studying him. Nods.

"All right," she says. "You're probably right. Keep it all official. But we'll go low and you don't need to discuss it with anyone else, it's between us, the three of us, what our arrangements are."

And what she suggests is—well, it's less than he's paying in town, and way less than he expected to be able to find for a place big enough for two plus plants and rowing machine, if Thomas buys another with his insurance, and dog and worms and all.

"It's on its own well," she says. "I had a new one drilled when I started working on the church and mine's deeper, so if the pair of you take too many showers and run yours dry, I'll still have water and you'll be trudging off to use the hand-pump in the barnyard."

"Right."

"That was a joke, Neill."

"I know."

"And the barn and henhouse are on your hydro entrance, not the church's. But it's just the one bulb on a timer so the hens get their twelve hours, and a bit of light in the barn when I need it, which is practically never, so it won't make much difference to your bill."

"We're not worried, Dodger. Bitter and Lager can sit up reading till midnight if they want."

"I don't think Lager's much of a reader. Bitter, though. She's probably into the Russians, Dostoyevsky and the like. It would explain a lot."

And then he has to go retrieve Bunny, who has squirmed under the fence and is heading off across the pasture with the donkeys, the three of them trotting as if they're on a mission. Conspiracy afoot. When they see him the donkeys break into a canter and Bunny's away with them, three tails whisking cheerfully.

When he finally gets back, dog in tow, Dodger has tea on the patio.

"You and Thomas," she says. Waves him to a chair. There

are muffins, too. He moves them further from the edge of the cast-aluminum table, out of Bunny's reach. She got her legs from her father, whatever he was.

"No," he tells Raleigh, who hasn't said anything but is thinking it, "it's fair to say that about dogs."

"Thomas," Dodger says. "He's had some bad times. I don't mean just the cancer. Later on, trying to find his way. He makes jokes, but I think it wasn't so easy as he pretends, even to himself."

Neill's not sure what to say. Nods and drinks his tea.

"You make him very happy," she says. "You're good for him."

"I—he makes me happy," he says. "He's—the best thing that's ever happened in my life."

"Yes, I get that impression. For both of you, mind. Both of you. Well. So. He's—" She shakes her head. "I don't say these things. I don't, my generation doesn't, my family doesn't? I don't know. But I'm it, the last of the Smiths. So I guess I can be sentimental if I like. He's a son to me. Well, a grandson, I suppose. Age-wise. No, a son. That place in me. It's not just, him being ill, getting close to him, then, bonding with a child that way, as if he were my own. I was always fond of his mother, as a cousin and a student, but him … It's, I see—so much of myself in him. In so many ways. Don't repeat this. I wouldn't—I'm very fond of them all, Elizabeth's pack of Gorevs. But—"

"I know," he says, because she's stalled, scowling at her tea as if someone's dropped beetles in it. "I—you sort of said something like that, once before."

"Oh," she says. "Yes. I suppose I did." Laughs. At herself? "I just wanted you to know. I haven't told him. I—it's time

I did. Talked about these things. Getting older. All that. It's him I've left things to, mostly. The church and all. A few odds and ends, investments. A bit to the others, something they can put aside for a rainy day, but mostly to him. Donkeys and all. One worries, doing that. Causing bad feelings. Seeming to favour one. But they'll understand, I hope. Understand all the reasons, I think. Everyone else having a good certain future—even young Isabel seems to have found her road now, Critter and Kevin and all. Law school. Who'd have thought? And she'll get in, whatever she's headed for, she'll do it. None of them are lacking in either brains or gumption. I've helped all of them, here and there over the years, not that anyone needs to know what or who or how. So my point is, Thomas works so hard and is every bit as good as he thinks he is. Possibly better. He'll get there in the end. But in the meantime, it's not easy and you've got your difficulties too, I do know it, not that he tells me, only I do pick up, hints, I suppose, and a lifetime of watching young people and from that—I see you fighting hard—"

Suddenly and fiercely, he wishes he'd had a teacher like her. To actually be *seen*. To say, not even in words, *Can I help?*

"—and the pair of you don't need to be fearing the future entirely, having to give up on *now* to worry about *then*, on top of everything else, is what I'm saying, anyway—"

"Dodger, you're not ill, are you?"

"Ill? Me? Good lord, no. But one thinks about these things as one gets older, you know. And the thing is, the thing is, I know if ever I do get ill, if I fall down the stairs and break my hip the way old ladies do—Thomas'll be here. Wherever he is, he'll be here. Three winters ago, I had pneumonia, and he was all for flying back from—France, I think they were in—to look after me. I made Elizabeth swear to him I was fine, it was just a cold after all, and he stuck it out and then David slipped and mentioned something in an email about my being out of the hospital—they had a chance at a few extra gigs and he sent the rest of them on without him, came home anyway, moved in to sleep on my couch and cook me chicken soup. And he was so angry at his parents for not telling him earlier, when I was worse. Lord knows he can't afford to lose any work and he did that. If, God prevent, my mind starts to go—it's him who gets to make the hard decisions. That much, he does know about, obviously I had to ask him. Poor boy. He gets so upset thinking about that kind of thing but one must face up to it. But ... here you are, the two of you, where I never had the chance or the courage to be, or the courage to find the chance, or—" She's ... flushed. Embarrassed, suddenly. Awkward. Scowling again. "Oh, never mind. Just, come live in my garage, yes. Be happy together. Hold on to one another. Pay me some token rent and we'll all say, yes, they're renting my flat. Plus, then you'll be here to look after me and the donkeys and the girls in the henhouse if I do suddenly tumble down into codgerdom."

"That's a Thomas-word."

"I'm sure he pinched it from me."

"Dodger ... "

"Tell young Tank I want to have a talk with him, one of these days. He might as well know what he's in for. Donkeys and all that. You don't need to say what about."

"No. Yes, okay. Dodger ... "

"You've very dear to me. The both of you. It'll be good to have you here."

Bunny, moved by some sudden impulse, bounces up, tail

wagging, paws on Dodger's lap. Sudden impulse to get her snout closer to the muffins.

"Yes, yes, and you too, you wicked, cake-coveting houndkin."

Bunny's ears lifted and she sat up from where she'd been lying, flopped on a bare ledge of stone, where water dripping off ancient elms and willows long gone had worn round craters big enough to hold a golf ball.

"Is that Thomas?" he asked.

Bunny stood up, tail wagging, looking away down the brook. A bounce and her *whoo-whoo-whoo* greeting howl and Thomas emerged from around the bend, walking along the edge of the water, the flat cracked sheets of limestone that would be the brook's shallows once the fall rains came. He was wearing jeans, a T-shirt and a collared shirt over it, blue, the sleeves rolled to the elbows. One of Neill's. He needed to be dragged out for more shopping. The sunlight had gone golden and mellow, slanting through the willows and the maples beyond, and though the leaves weren't turning yet there was that autumn feel in the air. Asters in the patches of sun, and wild grapes on the edge of the woods starting to show purple. The swallows were long gone and the grackles were flocking. And the sun was bright on Thomas's pale hair.

Neill let Bunny off her rope and she ran to Thomas, bounced off him, galloped back to Neill—ricocheted between them a few more times before taking off after a flicker. He whistled her back and for once she came promptly. He leashed her once more, put an arm around Thomas, leaning against him, welcome.

"I ate the quiche."

"That's what it was there for. How was the session?"

"We've got it. 'Passing Bells' is going to be one of the ones, you know. It is. The ones people say, Strange Pilgrim Road and that's one of the songs they think of."

"That and 'Runaway'." And "Black Mirror," and …

"And Ivan's just—he's got it."

He had Neill's bed, too, along with taking over the lease of the attic on William. We're buying a double bed, Thomas said, and they had, or Thomas's parents had, wedding gift, they said, bed and mattress and sheets to fit it, proper queen-size, a captain's bed with drawers for storage underneath, but it hadn't been delivered from the factory yet so they were still sleeping on air mattresses on the floor. This week, maybe.

Probably they'd end up sleeping crammed together on the edge of it, not to lose one another, so used to sharing a twin-size for so long.

"How was your day?" Thomas asked.

"I've finished putting the bulbs in along the path through the lilacs. It's going to be beautiful. Waves of them from April into June. If the rabbits don't eat all the crocuses, anyway."

"Bunny, anti-rabbit specialist."

"The irony. Thomas, I sent the email to Professor Olivares."

That was what ended up feeling most comfortable. Professor. He was used to professors.

"The same one you showed me?"

"Pretty much."

They sat down on the stone, still sun-warm, the spray from the drought-diminished waterfall just a faint coolness on the skin when the breeze gusted.

"I hope he answers, Neill. I hope—"

"He did."

"Already? Good?"

"Good. Very good."

That was why he was back here, just sitting, not walking. Too restless. Here, the sound of water, of leaves in the wind ... he could be still.

"His wife's name is Ingrid. She's a chemist. I have two sisters, Alba and Anke. They're younger than Isabel even. Still in secondary school."

"You have three sisters." And was that, hurt?

"Yes, I do. Raleigh, even if I had brothers in Germany too, you'd still be my best and first and dearest brother. Always."

And he needed to send Carleen an email tonight and he thought—he hoped—what she was going to say was, "Cool, I always wanted little sisters, and are they coming to the big summer belated wedding party next year?"

"It was just a short answer. Kind of awkward. Like what I'd write, probably. I'd guess he just, I don't know, called his wife, all stirred up, you know how it'd be, maybe. And then answered maybe twenty minutes later, just time enough to talk to her, because he didn't want to think I was sitting waiting for an answer and not getting one. I don't know. That's how I'd be, anyway."

"It's a good thing you never took up smoking," Thomas said. "You'd have been a chain-smoker for certain."

Took his hands, which were restless, fingers running over one another, over the stone, tracing the circles of ancient rain. Kissed them. Twigs, dripping, those great Gothic arches of American elm that must once have lined this brook, before disease wiped them out in the seventies. There were still a few crumbling stumps, a lightning-blasted log in the pasture, dead white skeleton, bark shed long before it was ever struck and years after that before it tipped over, Thomas said. Possibly helped by a small boy and his older brother and sister on the theory that if they didn't push it over, it was going to fall on someone.

Vast things. A time when this brook ran through that: ancient, virgin forest, giants, grey pillars holding up the sky, a vaulting of green. Singing over the stones the same way.

Thomas pulled him down. He squirmed around, made himself comfortable on the rock, seabed, before ever there were elms. Head on Thomas's lap. Thomas's hand interlaced with his on his chest, other hand combing through his hair. Clouds, small and white and churning into new shapes, through the narrow leaves overhead.

Long, deep breath. Bunny came back from wading in the water, flopped down, head on his crossed ankles.

Felt like home. Family. This.

Here.

"My father says, he's looking forward to meeting me and my husband in December."

/ACKNOWLEDGEMENTS/

Thanks are owed to many on this one! Tristanne Connolly and Ken Robinson, Romeo Kennedy, Tommy Mayberry, Tom Lloyd, Jonathan Harpur, Yahya Farooqi, Dave Hutchinson, and K.D. Edwards for reading and for caring about Neill and Thomas; Karla and Mike Henderson and Christine Fader for being feet on the ground in Kingston; Romeo and Ken for guitar thoughts; Glenn Barrington and Romeo for helping with the band and touring life (and Romeo for letting me steal his name as well); Jonathan the Lighting Guy, for much sarcasm on the subject of bands, advice on festivals, and practical help with other music-related and techy stuff. Also the nephews, for advising on the family colourblindness for Thomas; Myrtle, my own aunt with a chainsaw, who is not Dodger, but is always there when I need a tree cut down; Ian McKinley on South America and NGOs; Beth German and her son for first-hand accounts of The Tragically Hip's last concert and the report on Market Square on August 20th, 2016; Stev George of Olivea and John Henderson likewise; David Fancy for advice on Drama Studies; Ria Bridges and Dale Estey for answering questions about the NB school system in the nineties and fire aftermaths respectively; Lindsay Murray for the worms. Last but certainly far from least, Tommy Mayberry needs a second mention, for so much encouragement, enthusiasm, and advice, and for keeping Neill and Thomas honest. And fictional character or not, I want to thank Thomas Smith Gorev for getting me back into playing guitar again.

–KJ, August 2020